THE CHO

DAVID WURTZEL was born in Hollywood to a family that had worked in the movies since 1917. His great-uncle Sol made a star of Shirley Temple and discovered Rita Hayworth; as a special effects man his cousin operated the wind machine under Marilyn Monroe's skirt in *The Seven Year Itch*. After studying Law at Cambridge, he practised at the English Bar. He was elected a Bencher of Middle Temple in 2001 and for several years was consultant editor of the Bar's magazine, *Counsel*. His first novel, *Thomas Lyster: A Cambridge Novel* was published by Brilliance Books.

THE CHOSEN CITY

HOLLYWOOD IN THE 1930s

·⑃⑃·

DAVID WURTZEL

David Wurtzel

Discript

First published in the United Kingdom by
Discript Limited
67 Fishbourne Road West
Chichester, West Sussex
PO19 3JJ

www.discript.com

A catalogue record for this book is available from
the British Library.

The Chosen City is a work of fiction. All incidents
and dialogue, and all characters, are products of the
author's imagination and are not to be construed as real.
Any resemblance to actual persons, living or dead, events, or
locales is entirely coincidental.

ISBN 978-1-9163613-6-2

Designed and typeset in Monterchi
Printed in Scotland by Bell & Bain Ltd

This product is made of materials from well-managed forests,
recycling, and other controlled sources.

To Robert Wilson

CHAPTER 1

HOLLYWOOD, SPRING 1931

'WHAT I WANT more than anything in the world,' my cousin Elaine said, 'is not to go to Europe with my mother.'

'That's ridiculous,' I replied, 'everyone wants to go to Europe.'

Sitting in my parents' living-room in Los Angeles, the curtains were half drawn against the blazing sunshine but the room still felt hot. I had rolled up my shirtsleeves and Elaine squirmed uncomfortably in the large armchair.

'I didn't say that I didn't want to go to Europe,' she corrected me. 'Just not with my mother.'

They were due to leave in early June, just after Elaine had graduated from high school – for that matter, just after each of us ad graduated from our respective high schools. I tried to reason with her.

'You don't have to be with her all the time. You could just go and look at all the museums and cathedrals and...'

'She'll want to see that too,' Elaine said. 'I don't mind that. It's being with her when she is doing all the shopping.'

Elaine's father, my Uncle Stanley, was building a big new house; the purpose of the trip to Europe was to buy things to go into it.

'I can imagine all these antique dealers swarming around us, trying to sell us things. Probably fakes,' she added sourly. 'They'll think we're dumb Americans and sell us fakes.'

I knew nothing about economics, but I could see what was happening around me. It had been eighteen months since the stock market had crashed. You could tell the downcast or defiant attitude of the kids in my school whose fathers had just lost their jobs. The Steingroves however had managed to triumph, a feat due entirely to Uncle Stanley, who had 'merely' been head

1

of production. The man who owned the studio had ridiculously overextended his finances at exactly the wrong time. Just when the studio was threatened with closure, Uncle Stanley stepped up. Or rather he rushed to New York and convinced enough usually cold-hearted bankers that if it became his studio, it could flourish again. Everyone would get their money back, and more. That's about all I was told. So far, it was working. This grand new house in Bel-Air was going to be the signal to the movie world that he had succeeded and would continue to succeed. He and his talented brothers. The other brothers.

'I bet it's a buyer's market over there,' I said. 'And your Mom isn't the kind of person who lets herself be cheated. So I am not going to feel sorry for you,' I said. 'You could've gone to college. You could've found a job.'

She rolled her eyes at the prospect. 'Do you really want to hear why not?'

'I have. Remember?' I looked down at the tray that was on the coffee table. My mother had earlier brought in a pot of coffee, cups, and a huge, freshly baked coffee cake. 'We should eat some of the cake,' I said. 'Before my Mom comes back and asks whether we liked it.'

'I shouldn't,' Elaine said. She had inherited her father's physique, the stocky build of the Steingroves. 'My goal is to lose weight before our trip.' What she meant was that she did not want people in Europe to notice the difference between her and her thin mother. My Aunt Estelle believed that as the wife of a motion picture producer, she was obliged to dress well and to look good in her clothes. She had certainly succeeded in both.

'I'll eat a piece big enough for both of us,' I volunteered.

'You just burn it off,' she said. 'You're lucky.'

I shrugged. 'We had a swimming workout this morning, that's why.' I didn't want to rub in the fact that I had not inherited the Steingrove physique.

While I was eating, Elaine asked, 'Did you win? In your swimming.'

'Sort of.'

'You should've applied for a swimming scholarship,' she said, 'Yale would definitely accept you then.'

'I'm not that good,' I said. I was not being overly modest. I loved swimming. I loved the sensation of hitting the water and immediately having to start competing. Me, on my own, against the others. But our high school coach had told me that I would never be a great swimmer. He had his reasons – my arms weren't long enough, I wasn't strong enough, something like that – I only remember that I would never be a Varsity swimmer. No college would pay for me to go there and lose races. 'Anyway, do you know how many Jews the Ivy League colleges take? It's easy to count. There's less than you've got fingers and thumbs.'

'Maybe . . .'

'Yeah, maybe. I find out next week.'

'In time for the Seder.'

'Yale doesn't know about Passover.'

We would soon be celebrating the Jewish Passover, which in my house was referred to as Pesach, to emphasise that my father alone of his brothers had sufficient education to use the Hebrew term as a matter of course. It was one of the two events of the year when the entire Steingrove family sat down together, and always at Elaine's house. Pesach was actually a celebration of the Exodus and our deliverance from slavery in Egypt, but it was also about having a large meal.

'I mean,' she emphasised, 'if you get in, it can also be a family celebration.'

'If I get into Yale, the others will not be celebrating,' I said. 'That would require them to be glad for me. I don't remember the rest of the family being glad for anything I have done well.'

'Bobby!' It was the scolding look of hers.

'It's true. Do you remember my Bar Mitzvah?'

'That was nearly five years ago.'

'No one said how well I did.'

'My father did.'

'Uncle Stanley's different,' I said. 'You know, he's said he'll pay for college, no matter where I go.' In fact Uncle Stanley paid for everything for us. It wasn't my father's fault; he had a bad heart and couldn't work. Everything - this house, the furniture, our clothes, the food on our table which included the coffee that was going cold and the cake that was largely uneaten. All that came from him because my father was his elder brother.

'You'll be the first Steingrove to go to college and you'll be going to college anyway, won't you?'

'Your Dad said he'll always give me a job at the studio. Start to teach me the business. Maybe I don't need to go to college.'

'You, not with your head in a book? If I didn't know you better, Bobby . . .'

'All right.' By now I was leaning against the back of the sofa, with my arm across my chest and staring at the ceiling. Of course I wanted to go to college. I wanted to go Yale more than anything in the world. If possible, even more than anything in the world. But I was afraid it was bad luck to say so.

'I know, why don't you come out to the studio with me next week? My Mom will want me out of the house while she's preparing for the Seder. Daddy's going to be looking at a new movie. We can all have lunch and watch the movie.'

I sat up. 'All right.' It seemed churlish not to accept Uncle Stanley's hospitality even if the invitation was Elaine's idea. Was it also a school day? I didn't care about that any longer. 'What's the movie?'

'It's called *The Countess and the Cowboy*.' I laughed. 'Don't. It stars Sonya, that Russian actress he brought over. She's been making movies in Berlin.'

'I thought all the foreign actors lost their jobs with the silents.'

'I guess they've been giving her English lessons. We'll find out.'

I looked up and saw my mother standing at the doorway.

'Hello, Aunt Rose,' Elaine said.

'Elaine, darling, I just wanted to make sure that Bobby is feeding you.'

My mother had been an attractive young woman and never stopped reminding me that I looked like her side of the family - taller, leaner, better looking than the stocky, round-faced Steingroves. But as she put it herself, she liked her own cooking. She had grown larger. And she could not afford to dress as well as her sisters-in-law.

'The cake is delicious, Aunt Rose,' Elaine said.

My mother looked down and saw perfectly well that there was only one plate that had crumbs on it. She decided to take Elaine's compliment at face value.

'Let me cut you another piece,' she said.

She cut off a huge piece and put it on the plate with the crumbs. She handed it to Elaine and waited for her to start eating it.

'You must be looking forward to the trip to Europe,' she said.

Elaine made a gesture as if to show that she could not talk while eating, but nodded. 'That house is going to be beautiful when it's finished. And you'll bring back such wonderful things from Europe.'

'Mother wants to do a lot of shopping.'

'Of course. Things are bad there. The Depression is even worse for them. What bargains! You'll come home with treasures.'

'I guess so.'

'Let me tell you, your other aunts are already wondering what kind of presents they'll get.' She looked around the living-room. Apart from the mirror over the fireplace that we never used, there was nothing hanging on the walls. Was she imagining that Aunt Estelle would be bestowing her leftovers on us? When Elaine did not respond, she said, 'And it's so good of your mother to make Seder for the whole family, every year. She makes everything so beautiful.'

Elaine said, 'That's the day I'm going to the studio, to have lunch with Daddy and to see a new movie. I've invited Bobby to come too.'

'Isn't that nice of you,' she said, 'and what a wonderful thing for Bobby. Wonderful. To spend a day at the studio.'

'I have been there before,' I pointed out. 'You take me there to get my hair cut.'

'Why shouldn't you get your hair cut there? There's a barber shop on the lot. You're a Steingrove. Why shouldn't you have your hair cut where every other Steingrove has his hair cut?'

Because my father doesn't work there, I wanted to say. I am not equal to all the male Steingroves. They work at the studio and, like the other employees, plus their sons, take advantage of the barber shop Uncle Stanley had set up to make sure his staff did not leave the lot in the middle of the day. Taking me there was her way of saying to her sisters-in-law, 'Look, my son's no different from yours.' It also involved a very long car ride since the studio was nowhere near our small house in West Hollywood.

She carried on, 'But don't you want to be there, to prepare for Seder with your mother?' she asked Elaine. 'Not that I am criticising Estelle, God forbid I should, but when I prayed to God a thousand times for a daughter, I promised that I would teach her everything that a Jewish mother should teach her daughter.'

'Don't worry, Aunt Rose, she says I don't need to be there to set the table. Things like that. I'll be home in time.'

'Well, whatever she does, it will be beautiful. Of course, this year, something will be different.' She smiled at me as she said this. Elaine looked at her. 'Now that your grandpa has died, who do you think is the eldest male in the family?'

'Uncle Isaac,' Elaine replied correctly. My father, the eldest of the five brothers.

'Exactly. So he will lead the Seder. It is his right. It's written down.' She frowned. 'Unless his brothers make trouble.'

'Rules are rules, Mom,' I said. I wished she had not brought this up. I had heard of little else for weeks.

'Only if he stands up for himself,' she told me. 'You know what they're like. Not your father,' she assured Elaine. 'God only knows how good Stanley has been to us. He knows what's right. But the others...' She shook her head. 'They'll say, "Oh, Stanley, it's your house, you must lead the Seder."' She looked at me. 'And your father, he'll just sit there and take it.'

There was a silence. Elaine loyally said, 'I am sure Daddy wants Uncle Isaac to lead the Seder.'

'Of course he does.' Again there was a silence. 'Now I must look after them.' Uncle Stanley was at this very moment in our house, talking to my father in my father's study. He visited him, from time to time, though I had no idea what they discussed in private. 'I bet they're hungry,' my mother said, smiling, 'and they'll need more coffee. Your father loves my coffee cake,' she said to Elaine.

'It's very good, Aunt Rose,' Elaine repeated. She had now polished off the big piece given to her.

'Mom, please don't say anything to Uncle Stanley about the Seder,' I begged her.

'And why not?' she demanded.

'I mean, what can he say?' The last thing I wanted was for her to annoy Uncle Stanley. Not when he said he would pay for my college education.

'If he won't stand up for himself, someone has to,' she said. 'You were not at the luncheon I went to last week, which your Aunt Estelle gave for me and your other aunts. You were not there when the others were saying, "Oh, Estelle, at the Seder, now that Papa is gone, Stanley will lead the Seder, won't he?" Then they turned to me and said, "Rose, Isaac won't mind, will he? It's Stanley's house and he's the head of the family."'

'You've told me this,' I reminded her.

'You don't understand. How could you?' she said. She went over and stood by the sofa, and stroked my head. Then she felt my forehead. 'You're warm. No, you're not sick.'

'It's just the hot weather,' I said.

She turned to Elaine. 'Don't I have a smart son? Straight A's. Yale is begging to take him.'

'Mom, please don't say that. Everybody who applies to Yale has good grades.'

'I bet those Vanderbilts and Astors don't. Of course, Yale has to accept them. But they need smart boys too, boys with straight A's. Boys who will make Yale proud.' She had thought this all out. 'But what will I do if you're 3,000 miles away?' She kissed the top of my head. I knew she had conflicting feelings about this. If I got in, she would of course be able to brag about this to my aunts. She would point out that not only was I the first Steingrove to go to college, but it was Yale. That would set a standard that my younger cousins – in her estimation – could never reach. On the other hand, what kind of boy wants to put 3,000 miles between himself and his mother? Going away to college was bad enough; going all the way to the East Coast was to my mother incomprehensible. Unable to resolve this, she went towards my father's study.

I sprang up. I walked over to the front window and looked out. I jammed my hands into my pockets. Uncle Stanley's chauffeur was standing there, beside the Cadillac limousine. Our 1928 Model A Ford was in the driveway. I had learned how to drive but I didn't use it very much. When I had gone out on dates, they had been double dates, with a friend who drove the car his father was able to afford to buy before the Depression. I remember sitting in the back, with my arm around a girl in my class and having no idea what to do. I thought about asking Elaine about that, about what girls want you to do, but I could never bring myself to do it. My mind went back to the family and the Seder.

'And?' I asked.

'I didn't say anything,' Elaine said.

'I hate it. All week long about my dad leading the Seder and what everyone else is going to do to stop it.'

'It does seem unfair. I'm sure your dad would do it very well.'

'Of course he would. He's the only scholar. Why do they have to treat him like some kind of joke? The bookworm. And the bookworm's son.'

'Daddy loves your father,' Elaine said. 'That's why he's here. So he can talk to him. He told me. He said Isaac is the only one I can trust.'

'I can believe that.' I turned back. 'The rest of them are only interested in themselves. Our aunts even worse. Patronising my mother because she can't dress like they do. Patronising my father because we live on what your dad gives us. The others would have left us to starve.'

'Bobby, you can't dislike your whole family.'

'They dislike me even more,' I sniggered.

'Well, if you're in this mood, I'll go. I am going to leave you to be miserable on your own.' She got up.

'Please don't, Elaine. I'm sorry. I shouldn't.'

'You have to put up with them. You don't like being called the bookworm's son. I don't like them calling me a princess. I know it isn't the same, but I can't stand it either. You're not going to change them. Just put up with it.'

'I'll try. Princess,' I joked.

'Princesses inherit kingdoms,' Elaine pointed out. 'Girls don't inherit studios.'

I went and stood over her. 'You know, I wish you weren't going to Europe either. I don't mean for ever, I mean just until the fall, when I go to college. Just so we can talk.'

'You have friends you can talk to,' she said.

'Not really. There are guys at school. But I can't talk to them. They don't really care.'

I could hear voices in the hall. It was our respective fathers, coming out of the study. Uncle Stanley's commanding voice was unmistakable. We went out to meet them. Uncle Stanley was wearing one of his tweed, three-piece suits. My father, who looked much older than his forty-five years, was wearing one of his cardigans and carpet slippers.

'Elaine, honey, it's time to go,' he told his daughter. 'Well,' he said, addressing me. We didn't really have a conversation. He addressed me and I stood there, while he sized me up. Like the day of my Bar Mitzvah, when he clapped me on my shoulder and said to my father, 'Isaac, he has made you very proud today; no one in the family has ever spoken Hebrew so beautifully.' Then he had looked at my other uncles as if to say *That settles that*. They in turn of course had said nothing at all.

'Yes, Uncle Stanley.' I waited for him to speak.

'Look how tall he's got,' he said to my father. 'Tall and strong. We were never like that.'

'A football player. A swimmer,' my father said incredulously as if he still did not believe that he had produced a son who could play sports.

'It's not much of a football team,' I said, trying to sound modest. It wasn't. Most of my high school was Jewish, and Jewish football teams were notoriously unsuccessful. It was widely believed that we didn't like getting hurt. I didn't enjoy teams anyway. I could run fast and I could catch any ball that was thrown at me, but I couldn't think myself as part of a team. Diving into a pool and trying to come first - that was better.

'It's California,' my father said, proudly. 'All this sunshine. Warm weather. Swimming pools. What did we know about swimming pools on the Lower East Side?'

'Your father says you'll be hearing soon about colleges,' Uncle Stanley said, encouragingly.

'Yes. This week. I hope so.'

'Yale?'

'That's a remote possibility, Uncle Stanley. I can't count on that.'

'But you really want to go there?'

'More than anything.' I did not want to tempt fate but I wanted him to know how determined I felt.

He nodded. 'That's good. It's good to want things badly. If

you want it badly enough, you might just get it. I wanted to make movies, and look what happened.'

Yes, I thought, you have your own studio. You stepped in, and somehow, I didn't really understand about these things, it had become Steingrove Films.

We all moved towards the front door and said our goodbyes. My parents and I stepped onto the narrow porch and watched as Uncle Stanley and Elaine walked to the limousine and got in. We waved.

'I hope you didn't mention the Seder, Mom,' I said, as we walked back into the house.

'I did,' she said proudly. 'And he said everything would be all right.'

My father sighed. 'It's okay, Rose.'

'I had to,' she defended herself. 'If you don't stand up for yourself, then I have to. Your brothers would just have humiliated you. And I never would have heard the end of it.'

'It's my family,' he said.

He walked into his study. I followed him and closed the door behind us.

My father's study would have been the third bedroom of the house. It was lined with shelves - sturdily put up by carpenters sent over from Steingrove Films - and each shelf was filled with books. No point in Aunt Estelle bringing back a gift from Europe for my father; there was no room to put it. There was a small window that was always kept shut. The room perpetually felt hot and rather musty. I was used to the smell. My real rite of passage after my Bar Mitzvah was not my entry into Jewish manhood but the fact that my father started to give me books to read at the same time that he read them. That's what we did here. We read, together, and then we discussed what we had read. And plays, I really liked acting out the plays. The two of us, alone.

I sat down on the hard chair; my father settled into the old, well-cushioned chair opposite.

'So, did you have a nice visit with Elaine?'

'Yes. Of course. She's just about my favourite person.'

'She's a nice girl. A good girl.' He nodded. 'And she cares about you. She wants you to make the best of yourself. Only people who really care about you want that.'

'Did you have a nice visit with Uncle Stanley?'

My father shrugged. 'He talks. I listen. What do I know about motion pictures? He needs a sounding board.'

'Someone he can trust,' I suggested. 'Someone who doesn't want anything from him.'

'No one is completely unselfish, Bobby,' he said.

'What I mean is...'

'I know what you mean. The others all have big plans and big ambitions. I sit here quietly, reading books, nursing my heart, calming down your mother,' he smiled. 'When you grow up in a family crowded into a cold water tenement apartment, you can never have enough peace and quiet for the rest of your life. So when your Uncle Stanley comes and tells me about how difficult everything is at the studio, and how the New York bankers are breathing down his neck, and even what our younger brothers are getting up to... well, I am a little flattered. Isn't that wanting something from him?'

'Isn't it paying him back?' I asked. 'For helping us?'

'You mean for putting the food on our table? He does that because he's my brother. Because it's a mitzvah to help your family.' He looked at me. 'It's a man's job to support his wife and children. I can't do that.'

'You've given me an education,' I pointed out, and looked at all the books in the room. 'And I don't mean the stuff they kind of taught me at high school.'

'Thank you, Bobby. Now...' He reached down for a copy of Zola's *Money*.

'I wish I could pay Uncle Stanley back somehow,' I said. 'He's supported us and he's told me that he'll pay for my college education, no matter where I get in. But what can I do?'

'Just study hard and make everyone proud of you,' he said. 'That's all anyone could ask.'

I picked up my copy of the book. 'I love this book,' I said, 'but I wish all the financiers weren't obviously Jewish. It's such a cliché.'

My father thought about it. 'It's different now. All the movie-makers are Jewish and all the bankers who support them are Gentile. According to your Uncle Stanley. But they still resent the Jews.' He shrugged. I started to leaf through the book, try-ing to find a particular passage I had wanted to read out. 'By the way,' he added, 'never forget how difficult things are for your mother.'

'So I shouldn't have told her not to say anything to Uncle Stanley?'

'No,' he said. 'And she worries about losing you, if you go away to college.'

'Do you mean I shouldn't go?'

'How would you feel about staying here?' he asked.

I thought about it. 'I'd resent it for ever. And if I went away, I'd feel guilty. But I wouldn't feel guilty for ever.'

He nodded. 'It is a wise father who knows his own child,' he quoted.

'That's from *The Merchant of Venice.*'

'Correct,' he said, delighted. 'Now, back to Zola. He had quite a lot of say about the relationship between brothers in this book. Let's talk about it.'

◈

The next Tuesday I came home from school to find a letter from Yale, accepting me for the fall freshman class.

CHAPTER 2

THE CHAUFFEURED CAR came all the way out to our bunga-
low to pick me up. We had neighbours who had not had a
job in a year and I imagined they were staring at me through
their living-room windows, as I walked down our front path
while the chauffeur opened the back door for me. He had been
instructed to collect Elaine from their house in Beverly Hills
on the way to the studio. This subjected me to being the only
person in the back seat. This made it look as if it were our car,
although everyone would have known by now whose it was.
They had seen Uncle Stanley get in and out of it often enough.
I don't think the neighbours clearly understood the family hier-
archy. My mother would have been the last to explain that we
were the pensioners of her husband's younger brother, and that
although she took me all the way to the studio to have my hair
cut, I really was not entitled.

I got out when we got to Uncle Stanley's. Elaine emerged
from the house wearing a white dress, white gloves and white
hat, trimmed in blue. She gave me a hug.

'I'm so proud of you, Bobby. Yale! What you wanted more
than anything.'

'I know,' I grinned.

'Well, you deserved it.'

'You look really nice,' I said.

'My mother told me to wear it,' she said. 'It's nearly Easter, so
we can wear white gloves.'

'Does anyone in LA care about that?' I asked.

'She does.'

I was wearing my one suit, bought at Desmond's the year
before, in a sale. I had begun to fill out and it no longer fitted me
very well. Elaine did not compliment me on it. She knew better.

Then we set off for the studio for lunch and a viewing of
The Countess and the Cowboy.

'I think this is the first screening I've been to,' I said.

'I go when Mother wants me out of the house. Daddy parks me in a corner and forgets about me until it is over. It's business, they all wait for him to say something at the end, and then they talk about what they're going to do with the movie. Reshooting scenes or something. It's all very technical, about shots and whether it is been cut the right way or something. Transitions. Are you interested?'

'If I'm going, I guess I should be.'

'Daddy shows lots of movies at home, of course. Well, you know, Mother invites people to dinner and then they watch the latest Steingrove movie. I get to watch too, even if I am not at the dinner table.'

'And then do they have a discussion about whether or not to reshoot it?'

'Oh, no. You never criticise your host's movie. That's the etiquette,' she explained.

Now that I was going back East to school all this now seemed academic.

'So when you opened the envelope with your acceptance letter, what happened?' Elaine asked.

'It was hard for my folks. They were home when it arrived in the mail. They were dying, all day, to know what was inside but of course they had to wait for me to come home from school. My dad looked really pleased, like he had done something for me. Well, he had, with all the books we've read. That's why I did so well on the Scholastic Aptitude Test. I really learned so much from him.'

'And your mom?'

'She burst into tears.'

'Of course.'

'She kept grabbing me, saying how proud she was, and then saying "My baby's going to be 3,000 miles away, the house will be empty without him."' It was scenes like that that I wanted to escape from.

◈

The car paused at the gate to the studio, scarcely long enough for the guard to see whose car it was, let alone who the passengers were. He smiled and waved at us. Elaine smiled and nodded back. The guard at the gate tended not to remember my mother when she drove me there for one of my haircuts. She usually had to explain who we were and why we were there, while I sat there wishing we were not there in the first place.

Uncle Stanley's office was in a long, white building. There was nothing pretentious about the outside, there were no columns or a grand entrance. It was a place where people worked, that was how he liked it. It probably was what he wanted the New York bankers who had put up the money to understand. Elaine and I went into the outer office. It was lined with brown leather chairs for the many people who might have to wait to see him. This was the domain of Kay, Uncle Stanley's secretary, a short, neat woman whose hair was tied severely back in a bun. Kay might have been anywhere between thirty and fifty. She had always been Uncle Stanley's secretary. Kay remembered who everyone was.

'Elaine and Bobby,' she said, getting up from her desk chair. 'Now Elaine, don't you look beautiful. That's such a pretty dress. And Bobby, you've grown so much since I saw you. And even handsomer.'

'Hello, Kay.'

'But the big news, I know, is Yale.' She smiled broadly. 'Your Uncle Stanley told me all about it. He is so proud of you.'

I had called their house within minutes of opening the letter. Elaine and Aunt Estelle were there. Uncle Stanley wasn't home yet but he called me as soon as he was. He was pleased, and he was proud, no doubt about it. My mother wanted me to call my other uncles, but I refused. We argued but then she decided I was right; she would wait for the news to travel, and then she would mention it casually when she next saw her sisters-in-law.

I guess the news had travelled by now. None of my uncles had called to congratulate me.

'It's exciting,' I said. 'Thank you.'

She held out her hands. 'Now, I am sorry, Elaine, but your dad is so busy before the showing, he can't take you into the commissary for lunch after all. But he's asked your Uncle Al to take you. Now here he is,' she said.

I turned and saw my Uncle Al come in. He was an art director and the head of the art department, an important job.

'How's the princess?' he cried, giving Elaine a hug.

He extended his hand to me. 'Bobby,' he said, simply.

Uncle Al was wearing a well-cut tweed suit. He was a bit thinner than Uncle Stanley and looked good in his clothes. He saw himself as the dapper member of the family. But he was unmistakably a Steingrove. There were two Steingrove faces: the broad, flat face of my grandfather, which had been inherited by my father and Uncle Stanley, and the narrower face and larger nose of my grandmother, which had been inherited by her three younger sons. One or other of these genes had been imprinted, not only on their sons, but on each of their grandchildren except for me. I wondered if that was one reason why they had such contempt for my father – not only did he not work, he had not been enough of a man to stamp his visage on his only son.

'Hello, Uncle Al,' I said.

'Bobby got into Yale,' Elaine prompted him.

'Sure, sure, I heard that. That's great,' Al said quickly. 'But don't come back and think you can score points off us, just because we didn't go to college.'

'I would never think of doing that,' I said.

He gave me a slap on the back of my head, a gesture I hated. 'Hey, don't be a smart aleck, okay? You can be an arrogant kid sometimes. You've got to watch that.'

'All right.'

'You know my Iris has decided that she wants to go to college. We keep telling her "What for, you don't need a diploma

to make a diaper?", but you know Iris, that kid has a mind of
her own. But I've put my foot down, it's UCLA or USC. She's not
going somewhere back East where we don't know what will
happen to her. I bet there are a lot of anti-Semites at Yale.'

'I hope not.'

'You really think you can fit in there?'

'Well, they accepted me.'

He shook his head. I knew what he meant. Even me, in my
exalted state, realised that there was a difference between
'acceptance', as in being given a place in the freshman class,
and *acceptance*, as in being treated by the other guys as one of
them. I didn't really care about the latter. The idea of graduat-
ing from an Ivy League college, preferably magna cum laude,
was glory enough. Once there I could figure out how to get on
with the others. I was a passable sportsman. And I could study,
study hard, the way I always had. I had learned a long time ago
that the best way to avoid my mother's emotional clinging was
to sit at my desk and open a schoolbook. She knew better than
to interrupt that. And it had worked. My grades had got me
into Yale and she had something to brag about.

As we walked to the commissary, Uncle Al kept up a stream
of talk with Elaine. When we passed the barber shop, Henry,
the shoe shine man, was standing there waiting for his next
customer. He recognised me. 'How's my lawyer?' he cried. I must
have once, as a little boy, said that I thought of becoming a lawyer because whenever Henry saw me, he shouted out, 'How's
my lawyer?' I waved back. It was nice of him but I still thought
it was ridiculous, coming out here for my haircut.

In the commissary we sat at a prominent table. Everyone
knew who Uncle Al was and who Elaine was. They just looked
at me. The tables were full of men on their lunch break, talking
loudly about the movies they were working on. The walls of the
big room were lined with prominent paintings of scenes from
Steingrove Films' greatest hits. There was some scaffolding up
in a corner.

'That's for *Young King Hal*,' Al explained. Steingrove Films had started to make a series of movies about famous people in their youth. Europeans of the past were a good excuse for lavish costumes and sets designed by Uncle Al, and scripts full of bogus Elizabethan language written by my Uncle Jake. *Young Queen Bess* and *Young Columbus* had done well but *Hal* was the biggest success. 'I loved creating Tudor England right here on the back lot,' Uncle Al boasted. He looked to see if the painters were being faithful to his designs.

'Don't you think those movies should be a little more realistic, Uncle Al?' I could not resist asking.

'The public loved them.'

'Yes but I don't think Columbus had been Queen Isabella's boyfriend when they were kids. She didn't let him discover the New World as a pay-off for her marrying someone else. And those scenes in *Hal*. I think those kinds of buildings got built later. Maybe they were left over from *Young Queen Bess*.'

I was rewarded with another slap on the back on the head. 'Hey, I told you not to be such a smart aleck,' he joked, and then he went back to talking to Elaine. She looked at me as if she wanted me to stop making remarks. I could not help myself. Soon I would be in New Haven, where I would not care what they said about me.

◆

We got back to Uncle Stanley's office at two. It was a huge room, with a thick white carpet and white sofas and chairs. His massive desk stood at the end of the room. People who came to see him would have to walk quite a distance to get there.

'I've brought the little princess,' Uncle Al announced. 'We had a swell lunch. Everyone kept looking at Elaine, thinking she was your new star.'

Uncle Stanley went over and kissed Elaine and then shook my hand, very strongly.

'So you got into Yale,' he said.

'Yes.'

'You get straight A's, do you hear? Make your folks proud of you.'

'I'll try, Uncle Stanley. I'll make you proud of me too.'

'Well come on,' he said and led the way to the projection room.

Kay was there already, fussing and making sure that there were plenty of refreshments and lots of pens and pads of paper. There were four rows of deep leather chairs. I had no idea who most of these people were, apart from the Steingrove family: Uncle Stanley exuding as usual a sense of authority; Uncle Al, who had been the art director; Uncle Jake who was in charge of the script department, one of whose staff had written the script; and Uncle Morrie, the agent. Kay ushered Elaine and me over to a short, slim, dark-haired woman who was seated. She was smoking, using a pearl cigarette holder. She was not beautiful but she was one of those people you can't take your eyes off. Starting with her own eyes, which burned out at us.

'Sonya,' Kay said, 'may I introduce Mr Steingrove's daughter, Elaine, and his nephew, Bobby?' Sonya, the Russian-born actress from Berlin, who was presumably playing the part of the countess in the title of the movie.

Sonya extended her hand. Elaine shook it. I bowed. 'But I have heard of Elaine. She is the one who is going to Europe. It is a place for a young woman to grow up and to discover life.'

'I hope so,' Elaine said.

'Then you will. I know it.' That clearly settled that.

'My mother and I are leaving early in June,' Elaine said. 'We're going to London first, and then Paris. And a lot of other places.'

'Ah, to be in Paris in June. To see Paris for the first time and in one's youth. If only you could see my Russia.'

'I don't think we're going there.'

'How could you? The daughter of an American capitalist? Impossible.'

'I am sorry.'

'Yes, we should all be sorry. My soul is there.' She took Elaine's hand and pressed it to her breast. 'There is my Russia still.' She held up a glass, which was full of dark liquid. 'You see, Russian tea. Almost real Russian tea. Here in Hollywood. Your father has been very kind to me. I even have a dressing-room that I call my *dacha*. It is not like Berlin,' she said definitely. We nodded. 'What can I say?' she sighed, 'I am a seagull.'

'I beg your pardon.'

Sonya laughed. 'I was Nina. Stanislavski directed me as Nina. He told me that I was Nina.'

I stepped in. 'But you couldn't be Nina really,' I said, trying to sound gallant. 'Nina didn't have the talent.'

'Ah, a young man who knows his Chekhov. And such a handsome young man.'

'I've only read it. There isn't much live theatre in LA.'

'No, no time for theatre. No time for rehearsal. But an actor must prepare. Stanislavski taught me that. In Russia we prepared for six months. By the end, I was Nina. You are right, she probably was not an actress. But only a real actress could portray that.'

'That's what I was trying to say,' I said. I was surprised at how easily I found that I could talk like this.

'Handsome and charming,' Sonya replied. 'Here in Hollywood, Victor tells me, just put on your costume as a barmaid and act as if you're happy. Happy!'

'Come on, Sonya,' said a tall, thin man with large glasses. I soon learned that this was Victor Hill, who directed the movie. 'You can turn your emotions around like a car turning on a dime.' He had an English accent. 'I think that's the expression over here.'

I noted the leading man make his entrance. If Donald Marshall wasn't the best looking man in Hollywood, he was certainly the best looking man working for Steingrove Films. He was usually seen on screen in white tie and tails, waiting patiently for a debutante to fall into his arms. He had also been the love interest in *Young Queen Bess* and was the dashing Christopher Columbus. He now wanted to break into musicals. Donald could actually dance, as certified by Elaine. She and then I had been given lessons by the studio choreographer at Uncle Stanley's house. I had been dragged in so that Elaine and I could practice together. Donald dutifully danced with the boss's daughter at the annual New Year's Eve party when Elaine said he was the best dancer she was ever going to partner. The idea of him playing a cowboy in this picture seemed perverse.

As Elaine predicted, we were parked in a corner. My uncles sat in front, making a whole row of Steingroves, led by Uncle Stanley, who tapped his pen on the pad of paper and made notes.

I did not know at first what to make of the movie. Donald Marshall played an East Coast rich boy who somehow inherits a ranch in Montana. When he goes out to see it, he encounters Sonya as the rather unlikely saloon owner. We are supposed to believe that his life on the East Coast was effete and that the old West would make a man out of him. Or rather it was Sonya who makes a man out of him. It was about the most risqué movie I had seen. Although they are never seen in bed together, he is half dressed in the same room while Sonya remains in bed. Movie-goers had not previously seen the upper half of Donald Marshall's body when unclothed. He had a fine physique but the camera was more interested in the expression on his face in what was presumably the morning after.

If they had left things there, it could have been a romantic comedy. Instead, it was a mess. It was as if everyone was in a different movie. Sonya had clearly decided to dominate the movie, and she was such a good actress, she overwhelmed every scene she was in. Maybe it was her idea that she would make a man of Donald Marshall. I did not know what Donald Marshall felt about it. He was used to playing the dominant half in every relationship on screen. Maybe he thought that it was the Old

West, which should make a man out of him. Maybe the director was so busy dealing with Sonya, he had no time to direct the male lead. Whatever, Donald Marshall did not seem to know how to cope with the role.

There were ridiculous subplots, when some evil person from Europe turned up to claim back Sonya for reasons that I could not follow. There was no chemistry between the stars. Sonya was frankly too old. And whatever voice lessons she had been given had not got rid of a very thick accent. It was hard to imagine any of her cowboy customers in the saloon taking her seriously, unless they were also Russian aristocrats who had wound up for some reason in Montana. But the cowboys in this picture were tough Americans. Donald Marshall was the last man to conquer the old West. He could no more hold his own against Sonya than he could against the bad guys who suddenly appeared and wanted to take the ranch away from him. Long before the end, I lost interest. I assumed that Sonya had been brought to Hollywood to make her a star. I doubted she would become one. Uncle Stanley must be feeling very disappointed.

Elaine hated it too.

'I can't stand it,' she whispered.

'It's awful,' I agreed.

She shook her head.

When it was over, the lights came on in the projection room. There was an uncomfortable silence. Everyone waited for Uncle Stanley. Sonya looked at him, expectantly. Victor Hill, the director, smirked, as if to say, I got it right, didn't I? Slowly, Uncle Stanley got up.

'Time to go back to work,' he declared.

'Well, Mr Steingrove?' Victor prompted him.

I sat back and waited for it. Uncle Stanley paused. His face had an expression that I had never seen before. It looked like a combination of anger and betrayal. Suddenly he looked directly at me. 'Ask the kid,' he said.

'I beg your pardon?' Victor gasped.

'I said, Ask the kid.'

Everyone turned around and looked at me. For a moment I just stared back. What was going on? Did he really expect me to say something about the movie? I turned to Elaine but she too was looking at me, having, like everyone else, realised to whom the remark had been addressed. I saw the look of incredulity on the faces of my other uncles, as if to say 'What does this have to do with the bookworm's son?' That gave me courage.

I looked again at Uncle Stanley. He was furious, that was obvious. He hated the movie as much as I had. It was his job though to pronounce the verdict. What was Uncle Stanley doing? Then I realised that if he had liked the picture, he would have said so. If he had disliked it, he would have said so. If it could be fixed somehow, the way Elaine said happened, then he would have said so. What Uncle Stanley wanted now was some kind of vengeance. And I had been made the tool of that vengeance.

I had just said to my father that I would love somehow to thank Uncle Stanley, not just for supporting us, but for paying for my education. For Yale. This was the chance to do it. If I said the right thing. And if I didn't, if I made a fool of myself and of Uncle Stanley, what would it mean? More humiliation for my parents? Spending four years washing dishes in New Haven to pay for my own education?

There was no escape. I paused and then said what I thought, and what Uncle Stanley must have thought: 'It stinks.'

'What?' Victor cried.

'It stinks,' I repeated. There, I thought, now they could go and fix it, do whatever happened next. But something far more momentous was about to happen.

Uncle Stanley snorted. 'You heard the kid,' he said to his English director. 'You're through.'

'Now wait a minute.'

'I said you're through. Go back to England.' He turned to Sonya. 'Sorry, honey. I'll pay off your contract. You'll be better off back in Berlin.'

I was unable to move. He had not just canned the movie. He had just canned two careers. Just like that.

Uncle Morrie, the agent, thought of his clients and alone had the courage to speak.

'Stanley, Stanley, think about it. Okay, maybe there are problems with the picture. You can fix them. It's going to be okay.'

'I said . . .'

'Sonya's a great actress, she . . .'

'I can make any dame in this town a star if I want to,' he shouted. He waited for someone to disagree with that. No one did. 'Watch me. Kay?'

'Yes, Mr Steingrove?'

'Where can I find the most girls in one place on this lot?'

'I guess in the typing pool.'

'We're going there.'

In a moment, they were all rushing towards the door – my uncles, Kay, some of the other men who were there. I looked and saw that Sonya had walked out instantly. I was sorry for her. I had no concept of what she must have gone through in the last decade, with the Bolsheviks taking her Russia away from her, and trying to make it in Germany, and then her big Hollywood break. And I, the charming, handsome boy who knew who Nina was, had killed it off. No, Uncle Stanley had killed it off. I had acted without thinking of the consequences.

Donald Marshall held back, as if he did not know what was next in his career. Elaine quickly got up and followed. I was so stunned, I moved slowly. When I reached the door, Victor, the director, was standing in my path.

'Who the hell are you?' he demanded. I said nothing. 'I asked who the hell you are.'

'I'm Bobby Steingrove.'

'Steingrove? Stanley's son?'

'Nephew.'

'Neat little conspiracy between the two of you. He didn't have the guts to come out and say what he thought of the movie, he

had to humiliate me through his nephew.' He said *nephew* like
a dirty word. 'Are you happy now?'

'I swear, I didn't know he would say that.' I was afraid he was
going to hit me. Although he did not look very strong, I knew
better than to get involved in a fight at the studio.

'Shall I tell you what a total shit your uncle is? I don't just
mean dragging me all the way from bloody England with some
bloody promise about directing quality movies, or dragging
Sonya all the way from bloody Berlin, and then just dumping
us in it. I mean the way that he cut my balls off all through this
film.'

'I don't know...'

'Then let me tell you. Every time Sonya and I had a little dis-
agreement about what to do, she would go over and screw him.
You know that about your uncle, don't you? The way he needs
to screw a starlet a day? But he always had the energy for Sonya
as well. She'd go over to that bloody white building and when
she came back, it was to tell me that the producer had decided
that the scene should be shot her way.'

I was staggered. I was an innocent sexually and the last
thing I had thought of was that my uncle was having sex with
women who weren't Aunt Estelle. If my father knew, he certainly did not think that I ought to.

'Have you been to his office?' Victor sneered.

'Yes.'

'Do you know what's behind his desk?'

'No.'

'It's a little room which everyone on this lot calls the starlet
room. That's where young women go who want to break into
the movies. And if they pass the Stanley Steingrove sexual test,
they get a proper screen test. And if they don't pass the sexual
test, they get on a bus and go home to whatever hell-hole they
came from. Well if that's how they do things in Hollywood,
good luck to them. But don't drag me here to make quality films
and then hand the movie over to some over-the-hill Russian

who's screwing the boss. And give the blame to me.' He stood back. 'So is your Uncle Stanley still your hero?'

'You don't understand.'

'Whose son are you then? Al? Jake? Morrie?'

'My father doesn't work at the studio.'

'Jesus, some schoolboy who doesn't know motion pictures from his ass.'

We stood looking at one another. Then I managed to push past him. In the street, there were some men walking around. And Elaine was standing there. I went up and took her arm and quickly started to walk away with her.

'What happened?' she asked. 'What did he say?'

'I don't want to talk about it.'

'Bobby, how did you know to say that?'

'I thought it was what your father wanted me to say. I don't even know what I'm doing. Where are we going?'

'Everyone has gone to the typing pool.'

'Where's that?'

'I think I know the way. At least I saw the direction they were walking in.'

Around the corner was a one-storey building. I could see two of the men from the projection room in the doorway. As we walked up they stood aside, as if Elaine and I had some right to go in and see what my verdict had led to.

Even I could tell that there was a terrible atmosphere in the room. There were rows of women who were standing up next to their typewriters. Their desks were piled with work. Behind them was a middle-aged woman with a severe bun whom I guessed was in charge. Uncle Stanley was looking around at them. No one was saying anything. I had no idea what a future star would look like, but it was clear that he had not spotted one. His round face had grown dark, as if he was terrified that he was making a fool of himself. And I was responsible for the situation. If he could not find someone, he could well turn on me next.

Then, miraculously, he noticed one woman, who had been standing at a filing cabinet. She had remained motionless, with her back to him.

'You,' he called out. 'Would you turn around?'

In the dead silence, she slowly turned. She was blonde and very pretty but badly dressed. As she turned, she flicked back her hair.

'Yes, Mr Steingrove?' she asked. It was a good voice, clear and strong: beautiful, and possessing that voice.

'Morrie,' he called to his brother, 'go and introduce yourself. Arrange a screen test. No, send her to the Max Reinhardt School for as long as it takes before she's ready to take a screen test. And to teach her how to act.'

'Sure, Stanley. Come on, sweetheart,' he beckoned to her.

She did not move. 'Excuse me,' she began.

'What's the matter? What do you think you're doing in Hollywood?'

'I am sorry, but do you want me to be an actress now?'

'You can stay in the typing pool until you're fifty, if that's why you're here, or you can go with my brother and do what every other broad has come to Hollywood to do.'

'Don't you even want to know my name?'

'Who cares? Okay, what is it?'

'I'm Laura Svensson.'

'Svensson? Change it,' Uncle Stanley said, and walked out.

The rest of us followed. Elaine and I let everyone else go into the white building. The car was parked outside.

'I have to go home,' she said. I noticed that Uncle Stanley had not said anything to her. He had marched back into the building. Maybe he assumed that she could look after herself. Maybe he had forgotten she was even there.

'I'll see you tonight,' I said.

'Aren't you coming too, Bobby?'

'There's no point in my going home. By the time I get there, it will be time to leave. And I'm already in my suit.'

'Come with me, you can just sit and wait at our house. Kay will call your parents.'

'I don't think so.'

'Bobby, I want to talk to you. You aren't staying here, are you?'

'I think I should,' I said. 'After all of this, I've just got to see your father. I'll wait and get a ride from him. I can't just see him at the Seder as if nothing has happened this afternoon. For all I know, he'll never talk to me again after what I did.'

'He did say, "Ask the kid."'

'Yeah, but I've got to find out if I did the right thing. Don't you see, what if he suddenly won't pay for college?' I still said college rather than Yale. I had not got used to the idea that I was actually going to Yale.

'I'm sure he wouldn't do that.'

'I need to be sure too.'

Reluctantly, she got into the car and left. I walked back into Kay's office.

'Oh hi, Bobby,' she said. 'I thought you were leaving with Elaine.'

'No. I think I need to talk to my Uncle Stanley. After what's happened.'

'Well, he's really busy right now.'

'Yes but eventually he's got to leave. Fairly early. Tonight is Passover. It's the Seder. At his house.'

'I know,' she said. 'Why don't you sit outside for a while? It's such a beautiful day. Real southern California spring weather.'

It was the start of April but already the roses were out.

'All right.'

'I'll call your folks and let them know.'

I left and went out. I realised that I had no idea where to go. I knew my way to the barber shop but I had only been there two weeks before. I did not feel I could walk into the commissary and order a coffee. I walked around the white building a couple of times but felt that people were staring at me, wondering who this teenager in a suit was who clearly was not here on studio business. After thirty minutes I went back into Kay's office.

'Can't I just sit here and wait?' I asked.

'Well, okay,' she agreed. 'I'm leaving early today. It's Good Friday tomorrow and your uncle said I could leave early.'

'I don't mind waiting,' I said.

Kay eventually did put on her coat and hat and bid me a good Passover and weekend. It was very quiet in her office. The telephone rang a few times but no one came in or went out. Finally about 5 o'clock I began to worry. What if Uncle Stanley had left by some other door and had no idea that I was here? When no one answered my knocks, I just walked into his office.

There was no one there. I walked further in, and stood in the middle of the vast white carpet. There were a few side tables with photographs of Steingrove Films stars and one of Estelle and Elaine, taken a few years before. I was trying to figure out what to do, when a door opened. I knew there was a door behind the desk but I had always assumed it was just a private bathroom. Two people came out: Uncle Stanley and Laura Svensson.

So Victor the director had been right. There was a starlet's room and daily, or maybe not daily, young women who wanted to break into Hollywood would wind up there. If the sex was good, whatever that meant, then they got a screen test, and if the sex was not good, whatever that meant, then they went home.

From the expression on their faces, I guessed that Laura Svensson had passed the first test. How? She looked about twenty. She seemed, close up, even more beautiful than before. Was she married, and if she wasn't, how did she know how to please my uncle? All I knew was that women should be virgins when they married and that men somehow should have experience. It was obvious now why Kay had asked me to go out, so Laura Svensson could arrive without my seeing her. But why was she here at all? She had already been promised an acting course.

Uncle Stanley was dressed, maybe showered, maybe not, but

could he really go home to Aunt Estelle wearing the scent of
Laura Svensson, to sit down at the Passover table, and thank
God for leading us out of slavery and into the promised land?

'Bobby, what the hell are you doing here?' he demanded.

'I . . . I waited behind. To get a ride from you.'

'You should've gone back with Elaine.'

'Yes, but . . .'

Laura stepped in. 'Are you Mr Steingrove's nephew, Bobby?'

'Yes.'

'Your Uncle Morrie told me what happened today. I think he
wanted me to understand that it was a kind of fluke. Nobody
knows if I can act or not. But if you hadn't said what you said,
no one would have found out.'

'I don't deserve any credit,' I stammered. 'I just said what
I thought and . . .' Where did I go from there? 'You're Laura
Svensson.'

'Hampshire,' she corrected me. 'I was told to change my name.
And so I will. Your Uncle Morrie liked Hampshire. Are you going
into the movie business?'

'I'm going to Yale in the fall.'

'Yale? That's impressive.'

'It was my dream. That's another thing, Uncle Stanley, I wanted to thank you, on my own, for paying for my education.'

He growled. This was clearly not the time and place for that.
'Just get straight A's.'

Laura smiled at us both and then left.

'She's beautiful, isn't she?' I said. 'She's the most beautiful
woman in the world.'

'Bobby, what a woman looks like in the flesh only matters
if you want to lay her. What matters in the movies is what
she looks like on screen. If she's beautiful on screen, then she's
beautiful.'

We looked at one another. He had never spoken to me like
that. I guessed there was no point in him pretending about what
had happened. Laura Svensson or Hampshire had come here

- or maybe Uncle Morrie told her to come here - to say thank you, and to make sure that Stanley Steingrove would not forget her. Which meant that Victor the director was right about Uncle Stanley and Sonya. That she had used sex to get what she wanted in the making of the movie. Except that the movie was a disaster. That is why he felt betrayed, and why he wanted his revenge on the two of them. And I, the most unimportant person in that projection room had been the tool of that revenge.

It was not just the revelation of how things worked at the studio, though. My own parents, I was sure, were completely faithful to one another. They were probably the only people they had ever had sex with. The idea of adultery was laughable. But it was equally laughable to Uncle Stanley. He couldn't behave like this if he felt he was betraying Aunt Estelle. Betrayal brings guilt and right now guilt was probably the last thing he felt. Which meant that sex did not have to have any connection to morality. It was just sex - he did it because it gave him pleasure, and the young women did it because he wanted them to and there might be a reward at the end.

For once, Uncle Stanley waited for me to speak. I thought of the various possibilities. I wanted to do the worldly thing. I wanted him to know that he could trust me, the way he trusted my dad, and that I deserved to get a college education. I decided to say nothing.

'You're a helluva kid,' he said at last.

'Yes, Uncle Stanley.'

'What did you really think about *The Countess and the Cowboy?*'

'Just what I said.'

'It's a shame about that picture. So are you going to come back and work in this crazy business?' he asked.

'Of course,' I said. It wasn't true, but I felt that I had to say it.

'I don't know why,' he said. 'It's the craziest business in the world. Especially now. Do you know how many movie theatres are closing down all over this country? Hundreds. The whole thing could go broke any day.'

'There are so many kids at my high school whose fathers are out of a job now,' I agreed.

'It'll be 50% out of a job before this Depression is over,' he predicted. 'And they won't have a quarter to go to a movie.'

'But don't things have to get better, eventually?'

'I don't know. Look at me. I'm building a Renaissance palace in Bel-Air and sending my wife and daughter to Europe for months to buy things and to play the queen of Hollywood.' He shook his head. 'I don't know what's around the corner. But I know you've got to make people think that you'll succeed. The second they think you're failing, or that you're even afraid that you might fail, then you're finished. If you want something, you go for it. If you don't get it, then find something else and get that. You hear?'

'I wanted Yale more than anything. And I got that,' I said. 'I can't always expect to get what I want more than anything but...'

'Never say that, Bobby,' he told me. 'Just get it. Come on, let's go.'

CHAPTER 3

THE ENTIRE FAMILY sat down together at the same table twice during a year: Thanksgiving and Pesach. This Passover was also the last family gathering to take place at Uncle Stanley's house in Beverly Hills. It had been built a decade before in the American colonial style, with columns and a big *porte-cochère*. Aunt Estelle had filled it with mahogany furniture and simple fabrics. The table was set with heavy English silver and with her huge set of Wedgwood cream ware. Tonight there were twenty of us: five brothers, five wives and ten children.

Uncle Stanley and I were the last to arrive. As he walked through the entrance hall and into the living-room, which faced the big back yard, his brothers and their wives instinctively came towards him. They ignored me. I stood there, and then felt my mother tugging at my arm.

'Bobby, come here,' she said. We went into the hall. She seemed to have tears in her eyes. 'What have you done?'

'What do you mean, Mom?'

'I said to your aunts, and I am not even going to mention their names, they don't deserve to be in this family, I said to them, my Bobby has been accepted at Yale. Because not one of them had congratulated me, not one had wished me mazel. And do you know what they said? They said, "Bobby doesn't need to go to college, he already thinks that he's taken over the studio." And another said, "That movie wasn't so bad, Stanley just gave Bobby a chance and he went and embarrassed everyone in the room. Poor Stanley didn't have a choice." What did you do?'

'Mom, it's a long story. I can't start telling you the whole thing now. But it's going to be fine. Uncle Stanley wasn't upset. He agreed with me.'

There wasn't time to discuss it further. We all moved into the dining-room, standing around the extended table with cries of praise for the setting. There was then an agonising pause.

Uncle Stanley had promised that my father would preside over the Seder, as the eldest Jewish male present. There should be no argument about it now. Or had my behaviour at the studio changed the rules? Would the bookworm really be allowed to preside, in Stanley's own house?

Uncle Stanley gestured, and my father, in an old suit he had nearly worn out, shambled up to the big armchair that had been placed at the centre of one side of the table: his father's old chair. He sat down and held out his arms. The rest of the family took their places, without comment. Their silence told me quite enough. No one seemed to want to sit next to my dad, so my mother and I took the chairs on either side.

From his jacket pocket, my father took his white satin yarmulke, discoloured after thirty years of use, and put it on his head.

'Come,' he said, 'let us praise the Lord for letting us go forth from Egypt.' He stood, filled his glass with wine, which, because of Prohibition, was not the wine of his childhood but instead Welch's Grape Juice that had been made under the supervision of rabbis. Everyone else filled their glasses. Then he pronounced the blessing, in Hebrew. Everyone put their cups down. He sat and began to read in Hebrew, 'Blessed art Thou, Eternal Our God Ruler of the universe, who chose us from all peoples and exalted us among all nations, by making us holy with His commandments.'

When he finished, he leaned to his left, and drank from his cup. He then ceremoniously washed his hands in water in a silver bowl, which had been put by his place. Everyone ate the parsley, the vegetable of spring. It was all being done exactly as it should be. Everything my father did demonstrated how right it was that he should preside. He broke the middle piece of matzo, half to be replaced and half to be hidden as the Afikoman for the small children to find at the end of the meal.

Then he lifted the plate of matzo and said, 'Behold the bread of affliction, which our forefathers ate in Egypt. Let all who are hungry come and partake. Let all who are in need come and celebrate our freedom and the Passover.'

He put down the dish and poured the second glass of 'wine'. It was now time for the Four Questions, to be asked by the youngest person there. He looked at my youngest cousin, and asked, 'Can you recite the Ma Nishtana?'

The little girl leaped up. 'Yes, Uncle Isaac.'

'Wait,' cried the wife of Jacob, the head of the script department. 'It isn't the youngest person, it's the youngest boy.'

'Don't be silly,' said the little girl's mother, 'in my book it says "the youngest of those present".'

'But my son has always asked the Four Questions,' the boy's mother insisted. 'And he can say them in Hebrew.'

My father considered the problem. 'Two questions to each child,' he said. 'Ladies first.'

This did not get very far. There was quickly an argument between the two mothers as to how many questions counted. 'In my book it is not a question, it does not say, "Why is this night different from all other nights?" It says, "How different is this night from all other nights." That is a declaration, not a question. And it's only a short question and if it's a full question then there are five questions and everybody knows that there are only four.'

'Well, Isaac?' someone asked.

He looked at my girl cousin, who was fighting back the tears. 'It was not polite to interrupt.'

'She hadn't started yet. Anyway, she can't really read yet, can she? Someone must have made her memorise it.'

'Stop arguing,' Uncle Stanley growled. 'Let's have a Seder.'

So the two little ones shared the Four Questions, the girl in halting English and the boy in loud Hebrew. Not entirely accurate, I noted, but loud, so everyone knew he had done it. Then he stood and smiled, waiting for praise. His mother gave him a big kiss. My father continued, 'Slaves we were to Pharaoh in Egypt,' before starting to read in Hebrew. That was his mistake.

'Can't we have it in English?' Uncle Al asked.

'There is a translation in the Haggadah,' my father told him.

'But you're the only one who understands Hebrew.'

'Is that Isaac's fault?' my mother suddenly asked. 'I understand that when you had your Bar Mitzvah, you had to do it on a Thursday, when they open the Torah, they couldn't embarrass the family by having your Bar Mitzvah on a Saturday, when everyone in the congregation would have been there and seen how badly you did.'

I thought Uncle Al would explode. 'Rose, you weren't there. You know nothing about it. And you're a woman, you wouldn't know Hebrew anyway. Isaac is only saying it in Hebrew because he knows the rest of us won't understand. Who benefits from that?'

My father tried to defend himself. 'The story of Pesach began in Hebrew. As we've just seen, all the problems have arisen because of problems of translation. There are no problems in Hebrew.'

'Let him say it in Hebrew,' Uncle Stanley said. 'We can follow in English.'

'Great, like Catholics with the Latin Mass.'

Aunt Estelle chose this moment to address the other mothers. 'Could the children please not lean back on their chairs? They're by Duncan Phyfe. You can't buy those in May Company.'

'Look, Isaac,' Al suggested, 'you've made your point. Why don't we take turns reading? That's what we did with Papa.'

'Papa got tired,' my father reminded them. 'He didn't want to do all the reading.'

'I can't stand this,' my mother said loudly.

My father stood up. I tensed myself. I was ready to stand up too, and leave. Apart from Uncle Stanley and Aunt Estelle and Elaine, all these people hated us. I did a quick calculation. I did not think my vacations at Yale were long enough for me to come out here for Pesach. That meant that this was the last Steingrove Seder I would ever sit through. Fine by me.

But my father had no intention of leaving. He simply wished to assert himself. 'On the evening of Passover,' he said, 'it is essential that each person present realise that the Exodus is not something which happened long ago, but a celebration of what the Lord did for each of us, when we went forth from Egypt. When each of us ceased to be slaves. Therefore, each of us will read a passage from the Haggadah, read until you feel that you, too have helped to tell the story of the Passover.' He sat down. 'Bobby, you will begin.'

'Dad, I've lost my place.' I had closed my Haggadah in preparation for leaving.

'There,' he opened the book and jabbed his finger at the right passage.

I took a deep breath. 'Therefore,' I read, 'were we all wise men, men of deep understanding, and all well versed in the Torah and the Laws, yet we would be bound to tell the story of the exodus from Egypt; and the more one dwells on the story of the Exodus, the greater his merit.' I stopped. Duty done.

And so the task of reading from the Haggadah passed from one to the other, from parent to child. Together we told the story of the Exodus, of the bitterness of slavery and the sweetness of freedom, dipping our finger in the wine glass as we counted the plagues of Egypt, and saying that if God had only granted some of them, it would have been enough. We did not simply list the plagues, we exulted in what had been done by God to the Egyptians. The Egyptians got everything they deserved.

Finally the meal was served, the matzo ball soup and the gefilte fish and the chicken and turkey and mounds of vegetables and then cakes and sweet things. My father went out of the room to hide the Afikoman, the piece of matzo that the children had to find. It was the moment when the formal part of the meal ended. The only thing left was opening the door for Elijah. The children started running round the house. Elaine and I went out into the back garden and sat on a stone seat.

I put my head in my hands. 'I am so glad to be out of there. I should have known it would turn out like this. All my mother cared about was that my dad led the Seder. They still humiliated him. And her. I can't stand it, Elaine.'

'I know. There was only so much Daddy could do.'

'My mother told me what they've been saying about me. The official story is that the movie was okay, your father asked me out of some kind of politeness, like I was one of those guests you told me about, who don't criticise their host's picture. And because I think I run the studio, I said something that forced your father to can the movie. As if he'd pay any attention to me.'

'I can't believe anyone would say that,' she said. 'I was there. I know.'

'It's true.'

'What did the director say to you?'

I couldn't tell her the whole truth. 'That Sonya persuaded your father to let her do her scenes the way she wanted to. That's why he reacted the way he did, because he knows he shouldn't have, and look at the result.'

'But Daddy isn't angry with you?'

'No. I did exactly what he would have wanted me to do.' I smiled. 'My two seconds of glory at Steingrove Films.'

'But you'll want to come back and work in the business,' she urged me.

'Who wants me to do that?' I asked. 'Okay, maybe your father does.'

'You see.'

'Do you believe what's in the Haggadah?' I suddenly asked. 'That God chose us and exalted us above all nations? That we are the chosen people?'

'Well, yes.'

'So when your Dad and Louis B. Mayer and the rest of them came out here, they chose to make this the place where they would make movies that the whole world would want to watch. The chosen people in their chosen city.'

'I guess so.'

'Do you know what your father said to me earlier? That a woman is beautiful only if she is beautiful on screen. It's as if he can create beauty. People watch his movies and they think, "So that's what beautiful is, so that's what love is really like, so that's what truth is." Do you know what that means?'

'It's entertainment.'

'No, it's more than that.'

'You really ought to go into the business.'

'I don't think so.'

'Look what you did today,' she reminded me.

'Your father wanted to humiliate his leading lady and the director. Humiliate them in front of everyone. He used me to do it. I did it because it was what he wanted me to do, and it was all I could do to thank him for everything he's done for my folks and for me. Especially for me. Do you want me to come back here some day and treat people like that?'

'You'll come back,' she said, confidently.

'Oh, Elaine, why should you care?'

She took my hand. 'I've already told you why.'

'Remind me.'

'Remember when I said that princesses inherit kingdoms but women don't inherit studios?'

'I think so.'

'I've been thinking. When we come back from Europe, if I ask Daddy for a job, he'll give me one. I guess maybe something in the script department. But women are film editors too. I've seen it on the screen credits. So I could learn about the business.'

'That's great,' I agreed. 'Do it.'

'But you're a boy. You can be a writer or director or producer or anything. And Daddy likes you. He doesn't care what the others think.'

'What are you saying, that the two of us should take over Steingrove Films?'

'Not yet,' she rocked back and forth. 'Maybe in twenty years.'

'You're crazy,' I said.

'No, I am not,' she said definitely. 'All right, tell me what you want.'

I suddenly stood up and faced her. 'Do you know what I want? I want someone someday to say, "There's Bobby Steingrove." Just like that. "There's Bobby Steingrove." And everyone will know that that means something.'

There was a sound of laughter in the garden.

'Who's there?' Elaine asked.

Two of our cousins emerged. One of them, a fourteen-year old, came forward, laughing. 'There's Bobby Steingrove,' he said. 'The bookworm's son, the bookworm's son.' Then he started to run across the lawn.

I ran straight after him. I quickly caught up and held on to his shoulder.

'Say that again.'

He was still laughing. 'Boy, am I glad that wasn't my Dad tonight. It stinks! It stinks!' he shouted and burst out laughing.

Without giving it another thought I punched him in the stomach as hard as I could. He gasped, doubled over, and threw up in Aunt Estelle's flower-beds.

'Stay there until you're okay,' I ordered. 'And if you say one word about this to anyone, I swear to God you'll pay for it.'

'Bobby!' Elaine cried. She started to go to our cousin's aid, but he had moved further down the garden, where he carried on being sick.

'He insulted my father,' I said. 'And I'm fed up being patron-ised by everyone in this family. You are crazy if you think I'm coming back.'

'Would your father be proud of you right now?' she asked, gently.

'I don't know. No,' I finally admitted. 'God, why did you have to say that?' I looked at her, stricken with guilt. 'I'm going back in,' I said.

CHAPTER 4

YALE, AUTUMN 1931

IN MY FRESHMAN YEAR I lived in a boarding house, a few blocks from the campus. It was the first time in my life that I had to share a bedroom. My roommate came from Philadelphia and was a brilliant scientist, in the Sheffield Scientific School. We had absolutely nothing in common. He was pleasant enough and we quickly agreed the times for lights out. The others in the boarding house liked going out in the good weather and throwing a football around. I joined in. Being able to catch a ball was the only team sport skill I had. Sometimes others came along and there was an impromptu game of touch football. I liked telling the joke of the hopelessness of a football team in a Jewish high school. Very few had ever met a Jew. I did meet the handful of Jews who got in under the quota. They were all from the East Coast and utterly brilliant. They seemed surprised that I was there.

Basically I was not sure what to do with myself. I did what I knew I could do well - swim and study. Everything was so different - the weather, the architecture, the campus, finding myself in classes where there were no girls. I amused myself by relating the people around me to the people I had seen in movies.

Elaine, in her letters, seemed to be discovering that abroad, no one seemed to care who she was at home. She was a well-off American but beyond that, the people she met had no interest in the details. She wrote about making friends in London with an heiress from Chicago who was there to be presented at Court, something which some American girls could do, and an opportunity which my otherwise assiduous Aunt Estelle had missed for her daughter. Elaine and her friend met some Englishmen who took them to nightclubs where they ran into all kinds of people and where the dancing lessons we'd had from the choreographer of Steingrove Films at last paid off. This life continued in Paris. The Chicago girl had decided that she would marry a Frenchman. 'She says that sex in a foreign language might be more interesting,' Elaine wrote. With several exclamation marks following.

I bided my time. I tried to strike up conversations in and out of lectures. There seemed to be a lot of guys who knew one another already. I considered trying out for a swimming team but I remembered my high school coach's verdict that I was good but not that good. Still, I went to the Carnegie Pool almost every day, to keep in shape. The huge gothic tower of the Payne Whitney Gymnasium was being finished off. Even better facilities to look forward to next year.

One morning, late in September, I quietly took a seat in my first lecture. It was a big room, with a tall, coved ceiling and hanging overheard lights. I always sat in a chair at the end of a row, a few rows back. Just before the professor started, a tall, lean, fair haired youth rushed in. He squeezed past and sat by me. I had seen him before. I had imagined him in a movie part as a guest in an upper-class Manhattan party scene, or maybe the heroine's boyfriend who went big game hunting but came back to find that his girlfriend had fallen in love with someone more interesting.

As usual, I took swift and careful notes. The blond guy only scribbled. After a while I glanced over and saw that he had dozed off, more than once. He remained upright, so you would need to be close to him to see that he had slept through most of the lecture.

When the lecture was over, I shook his arm. 'Hey,' I said, 'the show's over.'

He blinked and then looked up and smiled. 'I think I missed quite a bit of that.'

'I think you did.'

'Are you in a hurry?' he asked.

'Not particularly.'

'If I bought you a coffee, would you tell me what the professor said?'

'I could try.'

'I need some food as well.' He stuck out his hand. 'Peter Van Haessler.'

'Bobby Steingrove.'

We walked off the campus and to a café that seemed to be patronised largely by what to me looked like professors' wives. Peter ordered scrambled eggs and toast. I had had breakfast, so I drank coffee and watched him eat. Finally I took out my notebook and started to summarise what the professor had said. Peter nodded.

'You take brilliant notes,' Peter said. 'I don't just mean today.'

'How would you know that?'

'Don't you realise how serious you look in class?'

'Have you been watching me?'

He shrugged. 'I didn't just sit in that chair at random.'

'I noticed you as well.'

'Really? Why?'

'This is going to sound really stupid. I didn't know anyone when I arrived. I haven't got to know anyone very well yet. So I play a kind of game with myself. I try to think what kind of role they might play in a movie.'

Peter laughed. 'So what role do I get?'

'Forget it. I got you wrong.'

'I'd give up that game. So what else do you do all day? Apart from attending every lecture and taking perfect notes.'

'I take a swim. To keep in shape. Yeah, I study a lot. I promised someone I would get straight A's.'

He laughed again. 'Sounds as if I have rescued Bobby Steingrove just in time.' He looked at his watch. 'We have been together an hour. Everyone in the library must be thinking, "Where's Bobby? Don't tell me he's just sitting in a café, getting to know Peter Van Haessler. He'll never make Phi Beta Kappa that way."'

'All right. I get your point.' I watched him finish eating. 'Are
we getting to know one another?' I asked.

'Sounds to me like a good idea. Okay, so where are you
from?'

'California. Los Angeles.'

'Not many of you here.'

'There are some. I met a guy from San Francisco. I think his
family went west during the Gold Rush.'

'Gosh. Did they find any gold?'

'I think they found something golden.' He'd been snooty, one
of those guys who manage to let you know how rich they are.

'Did your family make it in a covered wagon?' he grinned.

'Someone had invented the transcontinental railroad by
then. You?'

'New York. Been there?'

'I was born there,' I said. He looked as if he expected me to
tell him where. I doubted that a Van Haessler would even know
where the street was. 'Not in your part of town,' I said.

'How do you know where we live?'

'Just guessing.'

'Good. Keep guessing.'

I looked at his fresh face and the quality of his tweed jacket.
'Not the first Van Haessler to come to Yale.'

'Every man in my family has been here since...' he
shrugged.

'1701?'

'What happened then?'

'Yale was founded.'

'It's possible. And you?'

'Steingroves have been coming here since September 1931. I
can count the number of days.'

He leaned back and smiled and lit a cigarette. 'I can guess
about you too.'

'Go ahead.'

'You don't really want to spend your time getting straight A's.

You'll do fine anyway. You're smart. You're here because you are smart. You want to feel part of Yale. You want to feel part of something that you can't have anywhere else. Which you can do because you made it through the door and the door has slammed shut. We're here. Now we can enjoy ourselves. How am I doing?'

'Is that guessing or are you just telling me?'

He held up his hands. 'If I'm wrong, just say so.'

'No, I don't think you're wrong.' I was about to ask *How did you know?*, but maybe he was telling me, telling me what he had decided he wanted me to be.

'I'm here because I'm a legacy. So you must be a lot smarter. We've all been legacies since, when was it?'

'1701.'

'What the hell.' He leaned back. 'Steingrove. California.'

'My uncle makes movies. But like you said, that's on the other side of the door that's slammed shut. What about the Van Haesslers?'

'My grandfather made a family tree. I'd show it to you but it's boring. We're really bad at breeding males. I have three younger sisters. Not very clever of Dad at the time.' He lit another cigarette. He offered me one but I shook my head.

'I don't think you can will your child to be male,' I pointed out. 'That's not modern biology.'

'You're being clever.'

'Sorry, I can't help . . .'

'I enjoy it. Carry on.' He looked at me, as if finally deciding to make up his mind. 'I wondered what you were like. I didn't mean to fall asleep but here we are.'

'True.'

'So what you doing this afternoon?' Peter asked.

'I've got another lecture. Not until later.'

Peter sat back. 'I feel better now, with some food in me. Come back to my room.' He added, 'I can offer you a drink.'

'A drink?'

'It's not illegal to drink. Only to buy or sell or transport intox-
icating liquor. Read the Eighteenth Amendment.'

'I have. I wish they'd repeal it. We should've elected Al Smith.'

'We can talk politics later.'

'What does your roommate say?'

'About the bootleg? He's law-abiding, I think.'

'You think?'

'He got sick. Or there was some family crisis. I can't remember. Anyway, they've let him take off most of this term. I have
the room to myself. So I can do what I want.'

'Sounds good. Where are we going?'

'Vanderbilt. I know, it's for guys from my part of town. Who
cares?'

As we walked back to Peter's room I began to feel a strange
excitement. This was not the kind of conversation I had had
with anyone else.

In his room, Peter produced a bottle of Scotch from a locked
cupboard. 'It's safer to keep it under lock and key. I assume
Scotch is all right.'

'I've never drunk it. I haven't drunk anything, I guess,
except...'

'What?'

'Religious wine.' I should have said kosher Welch's Grape
Juice at Pesach, but I guess that wasn't wine at all.

'You're not a Catholic.'

'Hardly.'

'That's what I thought.'

Peter held up his glass. 'To friendship.'

'To friendship.' I took a gulp and choked.

Peter took my glass, put it down on his desk, next to his own.
Then he put his hand on my shoulder. 'Drink it slower. It's just
a relaxer.'

I had long imagined that my sexual initiation would be the
culmination of a long seduction with a girl, though I had almost
no idea how such things happened. Or indeed what Peter had

had in mind from the start, except that he had been trying to draw me out and so far I had given all the right answers. There was the bed. And no roommate around. And a bottle of Scotch, as a relaxer. I couldn't help but think of that moment when I stood in my Uncle Stanley's office and seen him emerge from the starlet's room with Laura Hampshire. If the sex is good, the director told me, you get the screen test, and if the sex is bad, you go home, but the sex itself was without guilt.

'I know what's illegal in the state of Connecticut,' Peter announced.

'Like transporting liquor,' I replied.

'Two bad laws.'

'Look, I want to be friends with you,' I said, trying to buy time, while I came to terms with what I knew I would agree to.

'Actually what I was doing in the café was figuring out whether I wanted to be friends with you,' Peter replied. 'We've both answered those questions.'

'So if I say I'd really don't want to . . .'

'Is that what you feel, that you don't really want to?' Peter stepped back.

'I didn't say that.'

'You said in the café that you'd got me wrong.'

'That was something different.'

Again, I thought of Uncle Stanley and Laura Hampshire making love within an hour of meeting. Of Uncle Stanley and Sonya. Of all the starlets who the director told me about. And what about my other uncles? What did they do? It was a town full of women trying to get into the movies.

'It may help,' Peter said, 'if I explain that I don't really believe in sexual morality. It's not just me; it's what my friends believe too, I mean my real friends, the ones I pal around with. I think you should just do what you want. Then there is nothing to worry about except enjoying yourself. This isn't about being queer. I mean, I'm not and using my guessing powers, I'd say you're not either. Which is ideal. It's much more fun this way. Because it's only about pleasure. We're not having an affair or some kind of label. We're just two friends, enjoying themselves.'

I drank some more. I did not choke this time. The Scotch began to have its effect. 'I think I agree with every word you said, Peter.'

Peter came up and kissed me. 'Just what I guessed.'

Peter had a narrow bed but he was experienced in getting over the challenge. In the circumstances he took the lead but I felt that he would not always want to. Which was fine. Everything about this was fine, the feel, the smell, the lust.

I waited to feel some kind of reaction: a sense of self-disgust for what we had just done, or terror that I might in fact be queer. I felt nothing like that. Only that my body felt different and I liked it. This was one kind of pleasure, and in due course I would experience another – my adolescent fantasies had been about women and I was sure that the reality would happen at some moment in the future. Meanwhile everything Peter had said seemed right. It would just be part of our friendship. And it sounded as if his 'real' friends would only shrug if they found out. As for everyone on the other side of the shut door, like my family, that was why the door was shut.

Afterwards, he said, 'Since I presume no one has been in a position before to tell you, not only do you have a good body, you have a sexy body.'

'Thank you.'

'What were you thinking about?'

'Well, what we were doing. Should I have been thinking about something else?'

'You should definitely not have been thinking about something else. Were you?'

'No,' which wasn't quite true.

'Good. I've never seen it circumcised before,' he suddenly said. 'Does it feel different?'

'How would I know? I'd need two to test the difference.'

Peter laughed. 'I like your cleverness.'

'I was kind of a show-off in high school. And I used to try to impress my family but that was a waste of time.'

'Families are.' He reached towards my middle. 'The rumour is that it's more sensitive. And larger.'

'We've both something to learn. Sorry, have learned.' I had worried so much about being a Jew at Yale, it had not occurred to me that in one respect, it was a positive advantage.

'Lie here just a bit longer,' he asked. 'Just get used to what happened, and think about whether you want to do it again.'

'I think you know the answer to that, Peter.'

'Excellent.' He sat up. 'I guess I should let you go to your lecture.' I nodded. He got up and found a cigarette and lit it. 'Don't you want one, even now?'

'All right,' I accepted it. 'I'm trying to keep in shape.'

'Good.' He lit it for me and looked at me. 'Let's have dinner tonight. I'm having dinner with a couple of pals. Join us.'

'Like a screen test,' I joked.

'What's that?'

'You know, like an audition. An actor or actress is filmed, doing some of the dialogue. And then the director has to decide whether or not they get the part.'

'We're not playing parts any longer,' he said.

The pals stood in contrast to Peter. Alan Pearson was tall and very well built, as aggressive in life as on the sports field. George Hudson was much thinner and never raised his voice. He peered at me through round spectacles, as if amused by what Peter had been up to. We ate in a restaurant frequented by students. I recognised a couple of guys I had met. They looked over and nodded and looked a little impressed at my companions.

'Do you know them?' Alan asked.

'We just talk after a lecture.'

'I was at prep school with them. They're nice guys.' He continued to look around.

George noted this. He explained, 'Alan is deciding whether this English tavern or whatever it thinks it is, is the real thing. He spent his childhood in England, and he defines civilisation accordingly. Unfortunately getting drunk over dinner is not on the menu in this uncivilised country.'

'It wasn't my childhood,' Alan pointed out. 'After my Dad died my Mom had an affair with a Brit so we spent a couple of years there, before she learned not to make a bad mistake worse. They sent me to Harrow. Taught me how to play rugby, for which I am eternally grateful. Have you heard of it?'

'Harrow? Trollope went there.'

'Who?'

'Anthony Trollope. English writer of Victorian novels. No one reads them any more.' I had slipped into clever mode but just as quickly retreated.

'I meant rugby.'

'Sure I have. I thought only the British played it.'

'Yale has had a rugby team since 1875.'

'And Alan is going to be the star,' George announced. 'Of that we have no doubt.'

Alan looked at me. 'You should think about it. You look in good shape.'

'He is,' Peter said. No one sniggered.

'Strong? Fast?'

'I'm a swimmer. I don't know about trying out for any teams.'

'So what were your plans for this semester?' George asked. Were, I noted. I made a gesture as if to say, I don't remember any more. 'Did Peter give you the morality speech?'

'If you're saying what I think you're saying, yes. Sure. I agree completely.'

'Hear, hear,' Alan said as he tucked into his steak.

'The removal of guilt is the removal of inhibition,' George said. 'But only about sex.'

I grinned. 'No Nietzschean supermen?'

'We're not Leopold and Loeb,' George said.

'Good, I like to draw the line at murder,' I joked.

'And rape,' George replied. 'Certainly not rape. The idea is to end hypocrisy. We're aware that our parents preached one thing and did something totally different.'

'My father died in a Paris brothel,' Alan suddenly declared. 'It's no secret to George and Peter. Obviously the rest of the world doesn't know. An uncle told me. My Mom doesn't even know I know. Isn't that stupid?'

What was stupid, I wondered. To die like that, or to bury the truth? I could think of a lot of silly replies, but instead I just nodded. I was feeling very worldly.

'At least he died quickly,' Peter said. 'Mine is soaking himself to death, very slowly.'

I wondered how one could be an alcoholic during Prohibition. But if Peter had access to the real stuff, presumably his father did too. The father over-indulged; the son just used it as a relax-er. Or so I assumed.

'My father keeps telling me that I'm a waste,' George complained to me. 'I've actually spent most of my life trying to avoid my parents. Sending me away to a prep school was the most merciful thing they ever did.'

They had all thrown their cards on the table for me. Here we are, that's why we think the way we do. It was my turn. 'My Dad has a bad heart so he can't work,' I said. 'But he's the one who really educated me.' There was nothing about my father's carnal habits that was worth citing in this company.

'Gosh,' George said, 'I can't imagine that. Respecting your own father. So who makes the movies in your family? You are those Steingroves?'

'My uncles. Especially my Uncle Stanley.'

'Hollywood must be knee deep in women,' Alan observed. 'Lucky you.'

'They weren't standing outside the gates of my high school,' I told him.

'That's tough.'

'Hollywood must seem a long way away,' Peter suggested.

'Today it seems a million miles away.'

'The point of us,' George explained when they got to coffee, which Alan insisted was not served until after dessert, 'is that we've known each other all our lives.'

'Before then,' Peter said. 'Alan's grandmother entered society the day my grandmother called on her.' Alan rolled his eyes. It was clearly an old tease.

'For that matter,' George said, 'my grandfather was Alan's grandfather's lawyer. When the workers wanted a pay rise, he's the one who said, don't negotiate. He called out the Pinkerton men instead.' He raised his arms to simulate holding a rifle. 'Strike over. Those were the days.'

'Don't believe any of this, Bobby,' Alan said.

'What it means,' George said, 'is that we've been friends longer than either of us can remember. That papers over a lot of cracks.'

'I think that's great. So you're not joining a fraternity?' I asked.

'Bunch of them asked me,' Alan said. 'They wanted a rugby player. But I told them to get lost.'

'It's all that brotherhood stuff,' George said. 'At least you don't live in the houses here but you still have to sit around and pretend that you're bound to each other for ever because you all know the same secret word and handshake. Talk about conventional.'

'We have plenty of other friends here,' Peter said. 'A lot of guys we knew at school, guys we've always known. Like the ones you said hello to. You'll meet them soon enough.'

'There's a game this Saturday,' Alan invited me. 'You'll come along.'

'Football and rugby,' George reminded me. 'We don't want to miss a second of Alan on the rugby field.'

'Sounds like a lot of fun,' I agreed. The whole thing sounded like a done deal.

After dinner, I walked back alone with Peter.

'I knew you'd like each other,' Peter said.

'How?'

'Guessed. You and I are good at that. Remember?'

'Sure. I did like them. A lot. I'm just taking it all in.'

'That's excellent.'

'Peter, can I ask you something?'

'Yes.'

'It's just looking around at the rest of you. I kind of felt that I was dressed as if I just off the train from LA.'

'That's where you're from.'

'From.'

'So you want to go shopping. Easy. Just go down to York, that's where all the stores are. Langrock. J. Press. Do you want any advice?'

'Would you come along?'

Peter stopped. 'Sure. New clothes for the new circumstances. I mean, being here, rather than there.'

'Look, I want to say something, Peter, but I don't know how to put it.'

'Don't bother. Just carry on being Bobby.' He held out his hand. 'Pals?'

'Pals.'

❧

I dutifully wrote once a week to my parents, and once every other week to Uncle Stanley. He did not mind paying for the new clothes, he understood people who dressed for the part. And I told him about the people I was with. There were now so many distractions – parties, trips down to the city, football games. Like they said, we went to all the games, in a crowd, with our friends. Everybody seemed to like each other so much, but it was just accepted that those three were pals and always had been. I sat with them in the stadium, with the collar of my new, heavy tweed overcoat turned up and my scarf tied the way the others did, and when the crowd turned up Peter would say, 'You know Bobby Steingrove, don't you?' and we'd shake hands. Very soon, everybody knew Bobby Steingrove. Then it was just 'Hi, Bobby,' and everyone accepted that the three had become four.

CHAPTER 5

PETER JUST ASSUMED that I would spend Thanksgiving with the Van Haesslers in New York City.

The Van Haesslers lived on a cross street between Madison and Park, in a huge, neo-Georgian house that had been built early in the century. I tried to compare it to Aunt Estelle's colonial style house in Beverly Hills, but it was not the same at all. For one thing, Aunt Estelle's house always smelled of the flowers of southern California. Here, there was the smell of age. The Van Haesslers had been collecting Chinese export porcelain since American ships first went to China after the Revolutionary War. I reckoned that the furniture had been theirs since then as well.

It was the first time I had been shoehorned into a family other than my own. I was told to expect various relations and friends to be around, but for Thanksgiving itself it was only the immediate family. Mrs Van Haessler came from Boston; her father was a Congressman in a staunchly Republican area of Massachusetts but her parents spent the holidays 'at home' with their other children and grandchildren. Mrs Van Haessler had been allowed to debut in New York where she met Peter's father when he still looked like the blond hero he had actually been on the Yale football field.

The Van Haesslers, Peter explained, had always lived in Manhattan. George told me that the Van Haesslers had lived there ever since they bought, or, if you looked at it another way, stole a chunk of the island real estate from the unsuspecting Indians.

'I can't save you from my parents completely,' Peter warned me. 'You'll have to think of some clever way to get out of the room if you find yourself alone with them. My Dad is only allowed in the house if he promises to keep sober. That's my Mom's rules. She makes all the rules. He can't keep sober for very long, so his visits are always pretty short.'

'Where is he the rest of the time?'

'He goes to Europe a lot.'

'Gosh, does he know people like Hemingway and Fitzgerald?'

'Don't ask. In fact, don't get him to talk about himself ever. You'll never get out of the room if you do.'

'Okay.' I thought of the calm of my father's study while the two of us read books and acted out plays.

'The only good thing is that he'll be sleeping in the guest room. And we have to make room for my grandparents. They'll stop over on the way back to Washington. Which means that the only place left is to share my room.'

'Sounds good,' I said.

'I thought you'd say that.'

◆

It was of course impossible to avoid his parents. It soon became apparent what Peter had told his mother about me.

'And how does your family celebrate Thanksgiving?' she asked, when I suddenly found myself alone with her after breakfast.

'Pretty much like everyone else, Mrs Van Haessler. Turkey with all the trimmings. We usually go to my uncle and aunt's, they invite the whole family. It's only a couple of times a year that every one of us is together around the same table.'

'But not Christmas. Or do you celebrate Christmas?'

'No, we don't. Well, my folks don't. My uncle has a Christmas party at the studio but I've never been to that.' It was a great big party with lots of treats and clowns and dancers for the children. I could have gone but I had always refused. My obnoxious younger cousins went because their fathers actually worked at the studio. Mine didn't. If I had turned up they would have demanded to know why I thought I was entitled to be there.

'So when is the other time you all get together?'

I was about to say Pesach but then remembered to anglicise

it. 'Passover,' I replied. 'It's in the spring,' in case she did not know. She did.

'Don't you find that whole story of the Exodus to be fascinating? What I've always wondered is, why God did it.'

'How do you mean, Mrs Van Haessler?'

'The Exodus. Why did God do it?'

'Because the Jews were slaves in Egypt.'

'Yes but slavery has existed throughout time. The Greeks, the Romans, the coloureds in this country. Eventually they were freed. But it wasn't God who led them into the promised land. God apparently only did it once. Why?'

The reason, I wanted to say, is because we are the chosen people, exalted above all nations. Now the chosen people were in their chosen city. Except for me. I was sitting at the breakfast table in the heart of old New York, trying to think of an answer that would allow me to make a quick exit.

'Maybe it's nothing to do with God,' I suggested. 'Maybe the Bible is just setting an example. Like handing down the Ten Commandments and then leaving it to the Founding Fathers to write the Bill of Rights.'

To my surprise, she burst out laughing.

'I'm glad you're as much of an atheist as I am. When Peter said he was bringing home a Jew, I didn't know what to expect. Does Peter go to church at Yale?'

'No.'

'Is he any kind of Christian?'

I thought about this. 'He's really nice to his friends.'

Mrs Van Haessler laughed again.

◈

The afternoon of Thanksgiving Day was trickier, when I went into the little room which displayed the export porcelain and some leather-bound books. There was Mr Van Haessler sitting on his own. He was a big man and he probably once looked impressive, back in the days when he was the hero of the Yale football team. Now his face was red and he had put on a lot of weight. He had probably been to a good tailor but even a good tailor could not hide the reality of a ruined body.

'Bobby, take a seat,' he said, before I could beat a retreat.

Accepting the inevitable, I tried to think of something bland to say. 'I am looking forward to tonight,' I said.

Mr Van Haessler nodded. Arrangements for the feast had had nothing to do with him. Nothing in this house had anything to do with him any longer, even though I guess it was technically his house, and paid for by his family's money. 'So you're from California.'

'Los Angeles.'

'What does your Dad do?'

I trotted out the usual formula. 'He has a really bad heart. He can't work. But he's the best-read person I know.'

'What do you talk to him about?'

I was not expecting the question but the answer was easy. 'Books. We read them at the same time. And we read plays aloud. Plays are meant to be performed, not just read.'

'So you have a good relationship with him?'

'I respect him a lot.'

'I hoped that we'd have the chance to talk. I'd like your advice on what to talk about with Peter.' I was flabbergasted. 'It's important to have a good relationship with him.'

It was done in such an amiable, man-to-man kind of way, that I almost wished I could help. This surely was my cue to say that Peter wanted to have a good relationship with his father. But he didn't. He did not want to have any relationship with him.

Mr Van Haessler went on.

'I used to take Peter to the Yale games. When I was your age, football was my life. I was on the Varsity team.'

'I know. You won the national championships that year.'

'Peter told you that?'

'Yes.' It wasn't Peter, it was George, filling me in as usual about the history of Yale football.

'I enjoyed taking Peter to those games. I want him to feel the same way about football as I do. Dads with sons. We should be able to talk about that.' He paused, thinking of the painful memory. 'Peter never seemed interested, and he's not good at hiding his feelings.'

Peter told me that he hated those outings. He had no interest in discussing football with his father and he had no interest in going to games with him.

'We go to all the games now,' I said.

'Really?' Mr Van Haessler sounded pleased if surprised.

'Bull dog! Bull dog! Bow wow wow, Eli Yale!' I recited, grinning. It felt silly to say it here, in this room, but it reminded me how much I liked singing it, how much I liked going to the games, of how happy I was there with my pals and our friends.

Fortunately he realised that I was not being sarcastic. 'You still sing that?'

'We go with the same bunch of guys all the time. Of course we made sure we were at Harvard Stadium last Saturday.' It was the game we had all looked forward to. Alan had a car and we had all driven there, and back. Peter had supplied the bootleg. I loved that day. 'We wouldn't have missed that. You bet. Bull dog won.'

'Not even a touch down,' Mr Van Haessler pointed out critically. 'Three to zero.' Of course he had followed the game. 'I wish Peter played. He's tall like me but he inherited his physique from his mother's side of the family.' Peter had a perfectly respectable body but he was never going to develop the bulk of his father.

Time to stop talking about how disappointing his son was. 'Our friend, Alan Pearson, is a rugby player. So we go to all his games too.'

'I remember his father. He would have been proud of Alan.'

I tried to think quickly of something Mr Van Haessler should be proud of as a father. All I could think of was what a good friend Peter had been to me. And of the sex.

'Well,' he said, having not forgotten after all the purpose of this conversation, 'what do you and Peter talk about?'

I threw out my hands. 'You know. What do students talk about? We're in some of the same lectures.'

'Sports? That's all I ever talked about.'

'After the game, you know, we talk about it, you know, the way guys do, about who made a good play and who didn't and what they should have done. Usual stuff. I can't really remember.'

'What does Peter say?'

I couldn't think of anything to quote. 'I seem to be the one who does a lot of the talking. Not as much as Alan. Alan always has opinions about the way a game should have been played. And George Hudson. You wouldn't think it, looking at George, but he's a real sports fan.'

'Did you play football?' Mr Van Haessler asked hopefully.

'Yes, in high school. It wasn't the best team in the world. The only thing I am good at is swimming. I go to the pool, to keep in shape. Peter does too. But we're not in training for anything. We just mess about in the pool.' In fact we had developed a certain horseplay that wouldn't look out of place to the other men in the pool but which was as erotic as we could get in public.

'*Mess about?*'

He picked up on this phrase, which was obviously the wrong thing to say. I should have been listing all the things Peter did excellently.

'Politics?' he tried. 'Is Peter interested in politics?'

'Kind of. My own folks are Democrats but everyone I've met at Yale is a Republican so I just avoid the issue.'

'Hoover is doing a good job. People don't appreciate how good,' he said. 'No one even understands what families like the Van Haesslers have given to this country.'

I still thought that if only they had elected Al Smith in 1928 maybe the Depression would not have happened. At least they would have repealed Prohibition, which would have made

Mr Van Haessler's slow suicide through alcohol a lot easier. I just said, 'Things need to get better.'

'What do you think of Governor Roosevelt?'

'He seems to be doing a good job.'

'Democrats are Socialists in disguise,' he said. 'They say he wants to be president, like his cousin. He can't be president. You can't have a cripple as president.'

I had to escape. I got up. 'Sorry, Mr Van Haessler, but I guess I better...' I couldn't think of anything I had better do. I just wanted to leave.

'Well, thank you, Bobby,' Mr Van Haessler said. He stretched out his hand as if reaching for the glass that wasn't there. 'Any friend of Peter's... We'll talk again.'

◆

Peter's room had twin beds, which were normally placed together. We didn't bother to pull them apart. That night, after the feast, we lay awake.

'Bull-dog! Bull-dog! Bow wow wow, he must have loved that.'

'I had to say something. I'm sorry, I really wanted to get out of there.'

'Did you like him?'

'He's your father.'

'So?'

'Not much.'

'At least you've seen him when he's sober. You definitely do not want to be there when he's drunk. That's when I get the "What kind of son are you?" stuff. And how the Van Haesslers built America and none of the Bolsheviks and immigrants understand that.'

'You didn't build America,' I corrected him.

'What do you mean, Bobby?'

'You bought some farm land from the Indians for a couple of bucks and now it's called downtown Manhattan.'

'Who told you that?'

'George.'

Peter laughed. 'George knows too goddamn much.'

'I like these stories. Like the one about your grandmother letting Alan's grandmother into society.'

'That one is true.'

'Maybe you did cheat the Indians.'

'That was 300 years ago. Who cares?'

'It's too bad about your father.'

'I can't stand my father,' Peter said.

'He knows that. That's why he drinks.'

'No, he drinks and that's one good reason why I can't stand him,' Peter corrected me.

'Maybe he drinks because he knows you can't stand him. So he carries on doing what makes you despise him.'

'What is that, Freud? All that psychoanalytical crap. Give me a break, Bobby. At least I can hold my liquor.'

'That's right, it's only a relaxer,' I teased him.

'Are you complaining?'

'You know the answer to that one.'

'Did you enjoy tonight?'

'Seeing your Mom and Dad together wasn't much fun. Every time he reached for his water glass I could tell she was thinking, "It isn't a wine glass." But I like your sisters a lot.'

'And they adore you. It never occurred to me that I was bringing home someone who could dance with them.'

They had told me about their dancing class and I suggested putting on records. It had been a huge success. We had started with the dances they had been taught, the waltz and the foxtrot and the two-step. I expanded their repertory to the Charleston. I had heard of the lindy-hop, which was really a Negro dance, and I tried to improvise, but all I knew was twirling your partner around and swivelling your hips. We had to make sure that Mrs Van Haessler was nowhere around then.

'Why talk about dancing at Yale?' I pointed out. 'There are no girls to dance with. My cousin, Elaine, is even better.'

'Did she teach you?'

'No, we were both taught by this guy at the studio. He choreographs the musicals at Steingrove Films.'

'Hollywood!' he said, as if it were somewhere on another planet. Which is how it felt to me right now.

We lay there for a while in the dark. 'Are you ashamed of your parents?' I asked.

'Probably. Maybe not my Mom but she's always making rules. Trying to make up for my not having a father really. You?'

'Probably,' I agreed, 'but not in the same way.' It seemed a terrible thing to admit to, but in the dark, I could say it. 'I meant what I said about my Dad being the best read person I know and I really respect him.' I didn't want to start explaining how the rest of the Steingroves treated him, and me. 'My Mom's difficult too. In a different way.'

'Who cares?' Peter said.

'You're right. Who cares?' I replied.

'My sisters are all in love with you.'

'You've said that.'

'You can dance. You're a much better swimmer. You take the best notes in class.'

'Yeah, yeah, don't go on.'

I was about to drift off when he said, 'Bobby?'

'What?'

'I'm not queer.'

I turned over in the dark. I could see the outline of his body. I reached out and took his hand. 'Neither am I. We said that, right at the start. We're just enjoying ourselves. Just take it easy. Girls are going to be crawling all over you. There is no sexual morality,' I quoted at him. 'If there were, we'd feel guilty. And we don't.'

'Guilt? Is that Freud too?'

'Go to sleep.'

'Bobby?'

'Yes?'

'Happy?'
'What do you think?'
'Pals?'
'Pals.'

CHAPTER 6

ON THE SATURDAY we escaped by going to see Alan Pearson. The Pearsons still lived in their house on Fifth Avenue. It was not the biggest, but the façade was arguably the most ostentatious. We stood in the cavernous hallway and watched as Alan came ambling down a pseudo-Renaissance carved staircase with a stone balustrade.

'Come on upstairs,' he said. 'George is here already.'

The bedroom floor was above the drawing-room. Alan's room was very big. After my tiny bedroom at home and the little space I had to myself in the boarding house, it looked like luxury to have room for a double bed, a desk and a sofa. There were photographs of him on sports teams, including one of his house rugby team at Harrow.

We sat around smoking. The others complained about how much they hated family Thanksgivings.

'They're hell,' I agreed. 'But I could always escape with my cousin Elaine. She's the only one in my family I really like.'

'My grandmother just stared at us all,' Alan complained, 'with that "Who am I going to leave my money to?" expression on her face.'

After an hour there was a quick knock at the door. Before Alan could answer, a dark-haired teenage girl came in. She looked so unlike Alan that I could not at first figure out who she might be.

'Oh, hello,' she said. She was trying hard to sound world-weary.

'What do you want, Diana?' Alan demanded.

'Just wondering who was here.' She looked around the room. 'I should have guessed, the usual crowd.' I had been sitting on the floor but scrambled to my feet. 'Who's he?' she asked, looking at me.

'Christ, Diana, didn't anyone teach you manners?

May I present to my awful sister Diana my friend Bobby Steingrove.'

'I didn't know Alan had any new friends. Where are you from?'

'Los Angeles.'

'Bobby's family makes motion pictures,' George told her, 'but Bobby isn't interested in that.'

'That's all right, I'm not interested in becoming an actress,' Diana said. 'I saw you and Peter run upstairs. Alan complains about my manners, but I didn't see him offer to show you the house.'

'Bobby isn't a tourist,' Alan said.

'I only offered.'

'Oh, let her, Alan,' George said. 'It's not going to last much longer.'

'I'd like that, Diana.' I said. I turned to the others. Alan rolled his eyes. Peter took another drag from his cigarette.

When we got outside to the landing, Diana said, 'That was brave of you.'

'What did George mean, it's not going to last much longer?'

'Nobody lives in a house like this any more,' she explained. 'Almost nobody.'

'You do.'

'True. It's a long story. Well, would you like a tour?'

I held up my hands. 'You're in charge.' The longer I looked at Diana, the more attractive I found her. Alan was broad and strong; Diana was slender. There was a sensuality about her, or at least the start of a sensuality which would bloom in a few years' time. She took me through the big, high-ceilinged, darkened rooms of the mansion. Each one seemed to have a different motif. The dining-room was gothic, the study was Renaissance and the drawing-room, which is where we wound up, was French. Appearing to be exhausted by her efforts, Diana collapsed on a sofa covered in tapestry.

'Do you like it?' she asked.

'It's amazing,' I said. 'Is that true, that no one lives in houses like this any more?'

'Most of them are coming down. This one will, when Grannie dies. She and my grandfather built it and she's declared that we're not touching one thing until she's dead and buried.'

'Don't you want to keep it?'

'Well it's nothing to do with me, but if you ask me, the answer is No. The art is terrible. Did you see that painting on the stairs, with the horses? Do you know who did that?'

'No.'

'Rosa Bonheur. My grandfather paid a fortune for that. No one wants pictures like that any more.'

'Are you interested in art?'

'Certainly. But not this dead stuff. I want to meet living artists. People who create it right now.'

'Being creative isn't necessarily romantic. My uncles make movies. That's creative. But it's a lot of hard work.'

'Artists work hard. But there is so much going on their heads.' I was still standing there. She indicated for me to sit down in the chair next to her. 'I'm going to find out all about that.'

'How?'

'Obviously Alan didn't tell you. I'm going to Europe next spring. With my mother. She's depositing me in a finishing school so I can, I don't know, whatever it is she wants for me, I know that it will be so passé. But I insisted that it's in Paris. That's where I want to be. Have you ever been there?'

'I've never been to Europe. My favourite cousin, Elaine, is there right now.'

'What does she say about it?' she asked eagerly.

'She writes about all the museums and things she's seen. People she's met. Also about the nightclubs. She goes to a lot of nightclubs.'

'Where artists go?' she sounded interested. 'You must tell me.'

'I'd be surprised if artists went to those places.' I doubted if they could afford them. I imagined that artists went to dives where the bad wine would kill you sooner rather than later, like the places in Greenwich Village that I knew nothing about. 'Basically, she's there because my aunt is buying things. My uncle is building a new house, and they're on a shopping spree.'

'She could buy all of our awful stuff and save time,' Diana said.

'That means waiting for your grandmother to die. And maybe Alan will want all of this. He hasn't said anything to me, but he seems pretty aware of his family.'

'He's only interested in money,' she said. 'Which is depressing. You know, he's still nineteen years old.' She waved her hands about. 'The business,' she said sarcastically. By 'the business', I presume she meant the coal mines and steel mills and quite a lot else which George had explained to me made up Pearson Industries. 'He's a total Philistine.'

'I've noticed.'

She laughed. 'Don't you mind my calling him that?'

'Why not, he's your brother.'

'You're his friend.'

'Yes, but you get priority.'

I could feel myself getting into the sparring mode once more. This was different from Peter, though. Here I was trying to impress a very pretty girl.

'I like saying what I think,' Diana said defiantly.

'That certainly runs in the family.'

She smiled.

'You're good at that.'

'What?'

'Matching Wits. It's a game my friends play. You say something and then someone tries to say something clever in reply and you carry on until one person can't think of a rejoinder.'

'I wasn't playing a game,' I said.

'Are you good at other things?' she asked.

'I study hard.' I got into Yale, I wanted to say, which was more of an achievement than it was for your brother.

'I don't mean reading books,' she said.

'I can swim. I can dance.'

'Is that why you're here?'

'There's no pool. And I only dance with girls.'

'You know what I mean.'

She meant, the others are here because of who they are, so what exactly does Alan think you can add. I was not going to answer that. 'I'm here because I'm Alan's friend. We pal around together.'

She took that in. 'But then you'll go back to Hollywood.'

'I don't think so. I like it here. I'm only a freshman so I don't have to worry about it yet.'

'Do you think wanting to meet artists, maybe even live with artists, is an ambition?' she asked. 'Because that's the only thing I can think of right now. I'm bored here.'

I stood up and looked down indulgently. 'You'll figure it all out once you're in Paris.'

'How would you know? It's easy for Alan, he'll just take over all that stuff that our grandfather owned.'

'The thing is, Diana, if you really want to be someone else, you start off by asking yourself what you don't want to be.'

'I know I don't want to come out as a debutante and marry someone like Alan.'

'Marrying your brother went out with the Pharoahs.'

'What didn't you want to be?' she asked.

'That's a lot of information for a first date,' I said. This was such fun, trying to impress a girl because I wanted to see her again. Simple. Maybe one day I might even meet this grand-mother, who had queened it in this house while my own grand-mother lived in a cold water walk-up, in the same city, trying to shield five children from the brutality of their father. I smiled at the thought.

'This isn't a first date,' Diana asserted.

'A first meeting then. Unfortunately we live in different cities. But Peter and I aren't going back until tomorrow night. What are you doing tomorrow?'

'Going to a matinee with my mother. Katharine Cornell in *The Barretts of Wimpole Street*. God.'

'It's about a girl who defies her family, marries the man she loves, and then goes and lives in Florence and writes poetry. Sounds right up your street.'

'Have you seen it?'

'No, but I know who Elizabeth Barrett Browning was.'

'You're not a Philistine.'

'No.'

'I like your plot summary.'

'Why don't you ask your mother to let me take you instead?'

'I could.' She got up.

I leaned over and kissed her. It seemed the easiest thing in the world. It felt nice.

'Why did you do that?'

'Because I thought you wanted me to.'

'And you didn't?' she asked back.

'I would have liked to kiss you like this,' I said. I took hold of her and kissed her for longer. That felt nicer. 'I'll come here, in a cab, an hour before the matinee starts.' I wanted her so much to say yes.

'All right.'

I grinned. 'I better go back upstairs.'

When I rejoined the others they looked at me. 'Diana and I are going to *The Barretts of Wimpole Street* tomorrow,' I announced.

'Diana's a pain,' Alan said.

Peter shrugged. George looked very amused.

❖

Just after Thanksgiving, and back in New Haven, I woke up very early one morning. I had breakfast first thing, and then sat in my room, studying before my first lecture. My roommate as usual had long disappeared off into the depths of the Sheffield Scientific Institute. I was glad I was dressed and shaved, because just as I settled down, Alan turned up. He was wearing a suit and tie.

'I've got to go down to the city for a meeting,' he said. 'Come and keep me company.'

'I've got lectures.'

'Cut them. And don't bother to change your clothes, you don't have to go to a meeting.'

There was never much point in arguing with Alan. You either went along with him or you said No. I tended to say Yes. 'All right.'

On the train, Alan explained.

'You know I have to take over one day,' he said. 'I mean the business.'

'Diana mentioned it.'

'Diana doesn't know anything about it.'

'I don't either. So tell me. I know there are steel mills and coal mines but somebody must be running things right now.'

'Yes, my uncles and cousins and some anonymous people who probably know even less than my uncles and cousins do. I mean, you can go out and buy shares in us, but basically it's Pearsons who give the orders at Pearson's.'

'Okay.'

'George's grandfather did a funny job of drafting my grandfather's will. To cut a long story short, I'm going to inherit when I'm twenty-one.'

'That's sounds like quite a job. Do you know anything about steel?'

'That's why they think I should start coming to board meetings. Things are as bad as they can be right now, as you can imagine.'

'Mr Van Haessler said that Hoover is doing a good job.'

'Give me a break, Bobby. Politicians don't do anything. They're all bluster. Even Mussolini is bluster. Who cares, as long as they leave business alone? Business has to do it itself. The way my grandfather did.'

'Shooting the strikers?' I reminded him.

'I told you not to listen to George's stories. All right, maybe somebody did get shot. Nobody wants that kind of thing now.'

'So what's your plan?' I asked.

'I don't have one yet. I am happy to start learning, even if I just sit there and listen to a bunch of old guys. An uncle introduced me to someone a couple of months ago. "This is my nephew, Alan, a chip off the old man's block." He didn't mean my father, he meant my grandfather. Which is fine. He was a buccaneer, a man who didn't care what anybody else had done before him.'

'You're a bit young, aren't you?' I suggested.

'You can be King of England when you're eighteen.'

'True.' I looked out of the window. 'So I really am here to keep you company on the train.'

'What else?'

'I thought you might have invited me because you wanted to have a man-to-man talk with me.'

'About what?'

'Well, I went to the theatre with your sister a week ago.'

'Diana's a pain, I told you.'

'Not when you get to know her.'

'Bobby, do you want to go out with her?' He sounded astonished.

'It's a bit hard, with her in New York and me in New Haven. But yes, I'd like to see her.'

'Suit yourself.' He seemed completely indifferent.

'Thanks. I wasn't asking for your permission but I just thought...'

'What did you expect me to say? That if you lay a hand on my sister I'd cut your balls off?'

'That's a little extreme. But thanks for the warning.'

When we got into Grand Central Station Alan got a cab to

the meeting. It was in the Chrysler Building, which was almost across the street, but he thought he ought to arrive in a cab. I strolled down to the Morgan Library, which had opened a few years before. I looked at the display of prints and drawings, and marvelled at the grand library room itself. My father would love to have some of these books. Being on my own, I didn't care where I had lunch, so I just found a coffee shop. I thought about Diana. It was frustrating, being in the city and not being able to see her. Finally I met Alan in the lobby of the Chrysler Building.

'Where are we going to now?' I asked.

'I need a drink,' Alan announced.

'I'm in your hands when it comes to that.'

We started to walk up Lexington. As we did, a woman came up to Alan. I was looking the other way at the time, so it took a moment for me to realise that Alan was talking to her and another moment to realise that he didn't know her and that whatever they were discussing did not include me.

'Wait here, Bobby,' he said.

They went off. I stood there but it was cold, even in my coat and hat and gloves. I wondered what was going on, so I walked down the side street and then saw there was an alley. No one was around. The woman was up against a wall, with her dress hitched up, and Alan was pressing against her. I retreated back to Lexington.

When he rejoined me, I asked, 'What was that about?'

'There's a Depression, if you haven't noticed,' he said shortly.

'I have.'

'Girls get hungry.'

'You could've just given her some money,' I suggested.

'It's a different kind of charity,' Alan sniggered.

'You mean, she offered herself to you, on the street, just like that?' I was astonished.

'"Offered herself to you." Sounds like a phrase from a novel. Come on, Bobby, you can't be that naïve.'

'How much?'

He paused. 'She asked for a quarter.'

'A quarter?'

'I gave her a buck.'

'What if a policeman or someone came along?'

'I wasn't going back to her place, if she has a place. Why do you think it was so quick?'

'Right.' There was no point in arguing further.

He stopped and looked at me. 'You really don't know, do you? Have you ever got laid, Bobby? I mean properly.'

'No.' There was no point in pretending.

Alan looked at his watch. 'I like your honesty. And this is the least I can do for you. Change of plan. Come on.'

'I thought we were going for a drink.'

'We can kill two birds with one stone.'

'Where are we going?'

'A place I know. Call it a café.'

The street door was somewhere down a side street in mid-town. Alan talked himself in fairly quickly. He was clearly known there. We were taken to a back room, behind a locked door. It was dark inside. There were various tables and chairs. Alan ordered coffee. Two coffee cups with brandy in them were served. Very soon a couple of women came up and asked to join us.

'Be our guests,' Alan said.

The preliminaries were not long. There was a hotel around the corner which seemed to serve the café. Alan took two rooms. He gave me the key to one of them. Events were moving so quickly and Alan was so definitely in charge that it wasn't until I was in the room alone with the prostitute that I fully realised that this was in fact my much-anticipated first sexual experience with a woman. And the first time I had seen a woman naked. She was not beautiful but she knew how to use her body. I smiled when I realised that the moment I looked at her, I began to think about how differently Diana would look naked.

'I think I should tell you,' I said, 'that I don't know anything.'

'You could have fooled me,' she laughed.

'But I'd like to learn something.'

'That's funny. Some college boys say they want to learn everything. As if they could. If you've got enough time and money, that's fine, but things are really busy at the moment.'

'"Something" is okay,' I said.

'I know, we'll do what's important,' she said, 'and call it a day.'

It did not take that long to learn what was important. Fortunately the woman clearly had experience with virgin college boys, complete with her own stock of rubbers. The whole thing was over in 15 minutes. I felt that even that was stretched out in order to flatter my ego.

'You'll be fine,' she said to me, giving me a pat. 'Excuse me for saying it, but lots of college boys in your situation worry about things. You're the type you don't have to worry about.' She looked down. 'I can see that "something" isn't enough for you, but I'm sorry, I'm having a busy day.'

Alan had not told me how much to pay her so I paid whatever she asked. She got dressed and left.

I sat up in bed. I thought of the pleasure I had just had. The feel, the smell, the lust. That's what struck me the first time with Peter, but now everything was different. Everything. And I already knew that this was not restricted to friends or within marriage or an affair. I could not see where the limits were.

I wondered what was going on in the next room. Finally there was a knock. I put a towel around my middle and opened it. Alan was standing there, in a singlet and his boxer shorts. He walked straight in, holding his room key.

'Hell,' he said, 'I went into the bathroom for a shower and when I came out she had gone.'

'Mine just left,' I said, closing the door behind him. 'Was I supposed to stop her? You didn't tell me how much so I gave her whatever she asked for.' I told Alan. 'Was that too much? Was I supposed to ask for seconds?'

'As a matter of fact, yes. Well, so how was it?'

'Great. She gave me a certificate of commendation. You?'

'Better than the earlier incident.'

'I bet. Well, thanks for arranging all of this.'

Alan didn't move. He lit a cigarette. 'We have the rooms for the rest of the afternoon,' he said. He seemed incredibly restless.

'Maybe the café can provide another coffee,' I suggested.

'I'm so goddamn angry,' he blurted out.

'Why?'

He had stopped thinking about the woman. 'That meeting. I sat there, saying nothing, like I am supposed to. The rest of them are all living in the last century. Two uncles, three cousins, a bunch of lawyers and who knows who else. Bluster, like the politicians.'

'When you're twenty-one, you can change things.'

'Goddamn right I'll change things.'

'You've had a stiff brandy and two orgasms. How much does it take to calm you down?' I asked.

He laughed. 'Do you know why I like playing rugby so much? It's not just the game and everything that can happen in it. It's because for one moment, at the start, I feel as if I am part of one, powerful whole. And then you realise how strong you really are.'

'What about that as a plan for the business?' I suggested. 'Everybody goes about their little job while feeling part of one powerful whole known as Pearson Industries? Too busy and too loyal to go on strike.'

'What's wrong with that?' he asked.

'Nothing. I think my Uncle Stanley wants to run his studio like that.'

He looked hard at me. 'Have I told you about dorm games?' he asked. He had again moved on.

'You mean like pillow fights?'

'It's only an expression. When I was at Harrow, most of the guys had older brothers or cousins who'd fought in the war. Who told them everything they used to get up to, in the army. Mess games. Incredible. Dorm games are really mess games. Wrestling. Fighting based on piggy-backing. Lots of stuff. It can get rough. So there's no point in being sober. Have you done any wrestling?'

Before I could answer, he suddenly lunged at me on the bed. I knew almost nothing about wrestling but I struggled as best I could. Alan so much had the advantage in terms of weight and strength that I could only fight back by being as aggressive as I could. We rolled around on the bed and then fell on the floor where he finally managed to pin me down for a moment before just as suddenly sitting back. He was grinning. To my surprise, my first reaction, once I got my breath back, was that I had actually enjoyed that.

'You're in pretty good shape,' he said. 'Swimming's good for the shoulders. But you should build yourself up more. Try hitting a punching bag, or lift some weights. Ask one of the coaches at the gym, they'll help.' He stood up. He reached out with his right hand to help me up. Then he slapped me on the shoulder. 'That was good.'

'I wouldn't call it an even contest,' I said.

'I know that. It was the way you fought. The way you wanted to fight. It's good. You can treat this as an invitation to join in. I'll tell you the next time I organise it. Like I say, it can get rowdy and you need someone who has some bootleg so it isn't easy to arrange. The important thing is just to enjoy it.'

I had no idea what I was letting myself in for. I just knew that another door had opened for me. 'Will I know anyone else there?'

'You've met several of the guys already. Not Peter. Not the right attitude. George'll be there. George is the referee.'

I had come so far from home in such a short time, that the

prospect of dorm games just seemed another thing that had come my way. Peter, my pals, their social network, Diana. And Alan Pearson looking at me with respect. We were not however finished yet.

'I told you that my father died in a brothel.'

'I would hardly forget that.'

'Well, when my uncle went to get the body in Paris, he went to the brothel to find out exactly how it all happened. He told me all about it on my eighteenth birthday. That was his birthday present.'

'Great present.'

'I told him that I intended to try it all out.' He smiled. 'Let's just say he can point me in the right direction. Some of it is just me and a girl. But some of it needs others. Easy stuff, like doing it side by side. And less easy stuff. That's when the imagination gets going. That's how I think it's going to be.'

'You're not suggesting...'

'You said you've got a certificate of commendation. And that first night, when George talked about the morality speech, I got the impression that you were the kind of guy who was just waiting to hear something like that. Peter had already broken you in. And now... I don't think I need to persuade you.' He waited for me to protest, to back out.

'Well I guess I shouldn't disappoint you,' I said. I had no idea what I was letting myself in for but by now I was used to going along regardless. 'Except I haven't the slightest idea what you have in mind.'

'Leave everything to me,' Alan said. Then he grinned. 'I like to get guys right,' he nodded. As far as he was concerned he had got me right.

'I've always wanted to know what goes on in a Paris brothel,' I joked.

'You know Bobby, I don't normally like clever guys, they're so busy talking, you don't know what they really think. But I'm glad Peter brought you in.'

❖

I had one more trip down to New York just before the December exams started. I took Diana to a Sunday matinee of *Grand Hotel* at the National Theatre. We were both more relaxed this time. Her mother was used to Alan's friends being nicer to Diana than Alan was and did not think more about it. She offered the use of their car but I declined. I preferred a taxi. Diana and I spent the journey back from the theatre kissing. She agreed with me that that was better than sitting politely side by side in the back seat while her mother's chauffeur checked up on us through the rear view window. She said I could see her again in January.

I did take her out in January. Alan had spent the night at their house. When I took Diana indoors, Alan was waiting for me, in the vast hall, with a small case, ready to join me in the journey back to New Haven. We hailed a cab and set off in the direction of Grand Central but we didn't go there. We gave an address in the East 40s, of an apartment recommended by Alan's uncle. There were two women there, who proved to be far more accommodating than the pair who had joined our table in the speakeasy café-cum-brothel.

'Bobby and I are kind of inseparable when we do things we enjoy,' he said, which I presume was his way of suggesting that we each pick a woman and have sex next to one another.

As accommodating as they were, they did not immediately agree to that. 'I know,' one of them said, 'we have two bedrooms, so let's use both. You can swap, if you really want to, and then you'll find out which of us you like the best.'

But Alan didn't see why we couldn't combine his idea with theirs. Yes we could swap, but in the same room. I had no idea how much his uncle had paid for this evening but it turned out to be enough. So our adventures began.

❖

One other event happened, just before I set off for Los Angeles and the Christmas break. It was just after our finals for the semester. One of my professors invited several of his students to lunch. Also present was one of the Deans, who introduced himself.

'I'm Bobby Steingrove,' I said.

'Steingrove. Now that's a name I know,' he replied. I was about to launch into my usual thing about the movies but that was not what he meant. 'Is Stanley Steingrove your father?'

'Uncle.'

'We owe him a great deal.'

'I beg your pardon?'

'Oh dear, I trust I haven't said the wrong thing. He insisted on anonymity.'

'I'm sorry, sir, but I am afraid I don't know what this is about.'

He sighed. 'Your uncle, Stanley Steingrove, made an extremely generous contribution to the college. About a year ago – was it? Yes, it was a year ago. Apparently it was at the recommendation of one of our alumni, whom he knows. We asked if it could be used towards building the colleges. He said we could spend it in any way we thought best. But it was to remain anonymous. I am so sorry, I assumed that...'

'I guess he didn't want me to get big-headed about his donation,' I made this up on the spot. 'I'm the first person in the family to go to college. He wouldn't have known how to make a donation. That's why he must have asked the alumnus.'

My embarrassment was so obvious that he patted me on the shoulder. 'We're very glad you're here, Bobby.' He turned to our host. 'And your professors?'

'Brilliant. I'm getting the best education in America.'

'We like to think so,' he smiled. 'But we don't want the young men working all the time.'

'I've made some really good friends. We go to all the games together. We were right there at Harvard when we won. I'm extremely happy,' I said.

Until now, I thought. Now that I discovered that I had not

been admitted because of my grades or my Scholastic Aptitude Test or because I had some qualities of mind or body which would justify slipping me in as part of the Jewish quota. I was at Yale because Uncle Stanley had bought me a place. Bought it and didn't even tell me.

CHAPTER 7

WINTER 1931

IT WAS A SHOCK, seeing my parents at Union Station. It had been over three months since we had parted. I had especially worn my new overcoat and trilby, though I reckoned it would be too warm in Los Angeles to need them there. I had just been again to the barber Peter had recommended and who had started to train my hair, to brush it in a neat parting and to allow a lock to fall over my forehead. I was looking more and more like my pals.

My parents on the other hand were completely themselves. My mother was wearing a hat she had bought earlier that year, and the coat I knew she had brought from New York when we moved out to California. My father was just in one of his old sports jackets. It probably had once belonged to Uncle Stanley but was given to him when Aunt Estelle had one of her spring cleans through her husband's wardrobe. Their faces lit up though when they saw me. As I went over to hug them, my mother began to cry.

'My baby,' she said, and murmured something in Yiddish which I didn't understand. My father patted me on the shoulder. 'You look even handsomer,' she said. 'And those clothes.'

'Well, it's colder back East,' I said.

I carried my case to the 1928 Model T, which was parked outside. As we drove home, Los Angeles seemed so spread out, the temperature so mild. I had forgotten that. My father parked the car in the driveway.

Indoors, I took off my hat and coat, revealing the J. Press jacket and the cashmere Fair Isle sweater I had been wearing on the train. They noticed it. I knew they would notice it, but there was nothing I could do about it. I decided to take the initiative.

'Uncle Stanley's been really generous, in letting me buy some clothes,' I said.

'Of course,' my mother said, 'you want to dress like the other boys.'

But she was already aware I had changed. Back in New Haven and in the city, there had been a growing sense of the impending Christmas. Not here. Hanukkah had come early this year and was finished on the 12th. The nine-candle menorah was still sitting on the mantelpiece. When I was younger, Hanukkah was one of my favourite holidays. It was a wonderful story, how the Maccabeans had thrown the Greeks out of Jerusalem and then there was this miracle when a day's worth of oil burned for eight days and eight nights in the holy lamp. Every night, for eight nights, my father would take my hand and together we would light a candle, while my mother beamed at us. On Friday nights, on the Sabbath, I would watch her light candles, but that was a woman's task; I could only watch. These rituals made us a family.

'Were you able to celebrate Hanukkah?' she asked.

'Not really. It wasn't really possible,' I said. Actually I could quite easily have gone to join in the candle lighting at Beth Israel synagogue on Orchard Street, which had been founded a few years before and had the good manners to be built in a colonial revival style that conformed to the town. The truth was that I had forgotten all about it.

◈

All during the train journey, as I travelled across the continental United States, I thought of what I had to say to my father, once we were alone. Fortunately, when my mother went into the kitchen to make dinner, it was all right for the two of us to go into his study and to close the door.

'Well!' he said, as we sat down opposite one another. 'It seems a long time since we've done this. May I say, Bobby, college appears to agree with you. We've enjoyed your letters but I'd like to hear even more about your classes. Do you think you did all right on your examinations?'

'I think so. I worked hard.' He nodded. He expected nothing less from me. It wasn't, actually, quite true. I had started out by working hard. I had indeed written brilliant lecture notes, which I cross-referenced with the textbooks. I carried on with that as best I could, in part because Peter simply borrowed my notes instead of taking his own. I told myself that by going over everything with him, I was reinforcing my own knowledge. It also provided a perfect excuse for the number of times I was in his room. But the time I spent with him and the others was also a distraction. And I spent hours writing letters to Diana. They were short but it took a long time to achieve the light, clever tone I was aiming at.

'I know we only get the best from you,' my father said.

I decided to plunge in. 'Dad, there is something I have to ask you, and I'd like to ask it right now.'

He looked slightly worried. 'Of course.'

Then I explained what the Dean told me about Uncle Stanley's donation. 'It's true, isn't it? That he gave a big donation to Yale, a year ago, just when I was applying? So when the admissions office got to my application, they knew I was the nephew of the man who had given them a lot of money?'

'I'm not going to lie to you about it.'

'Hell.'

My father sat back and shook his head. 'Your pride is hurt.'

'Of course it is. Quite apart from the fact that when he told me I had no idea what he was talking about. It means that I didn't get in on merit. I mean, when I met the other Jewish boys I knew I wasn't as smart as they were, but I thought at least they accepted me on my record. All my friends assume that's how I got in, that I must be brilliant. But I'm not. I was bought a place. I probably shouldn't even be there.'

'Bobby, don't say that.'

'Why not, Dad? It's true.'

'But when you do well on your examinations...'

'Yeah, Uncle Stanley told me to get straight A's. Well, Yale isn't high school. I can't imagine I'm going to get anything close to perfect grades. So if that's why he did it, he didn't need to bother.'

'If it upsets you so much, then blame me.'

'It isn't your fault.'

'I asked your Uncle Stanley to do it.'

'You?'

He leaned forward and took my hands. 'Bobby, you are all I have. All your mother and I have. We would do anything for you. But there is almost nothing we can do for you. You wanted Yale so badly. It's a great school, one of the greatest, I know that, but I still don't know where this desire came from. But I couldn't bring myself to talk you out of it, to make you see that you probably wouldn't get in. That you could get a good education somewhere else. So I suggested to your Uncle Stanley that maybe he could help. And he did it for you, and for me.'

'I didn't know.'

He shook his head at my naïveté. 'He told Yale that it had to be anonymous. You were never supposed to know. I was so afraid that somehow you would find out and then you'd do something stupid like refuse the place. I couldn't let that happen.'

'I still don't understand. They said he knew some alumnus.'

'That's right. We had no idea how to go about this. Did one just write a letter? No, it needed to be done in a way so that everyone understood why it was being done. I suggested that he contacted one of the bankers.'

'Who?'

'You know that when he took over the studio, he needed the resources to buy it. It was just after the crash. The man who had owned the studio had been ruined. Your uncle stepped in. He was the only one who could save it. He'd been running the production side for years, your other uncles were there as well. He just needed the money. The money came from the bankers.'

'I just remember hearing him curse them.'

'Yes, well, they don't like one another. Stanley doesn't like being held on a leash, and they don't understand anything about making movies. It's a battle. As long as the movies make money, it's all right. They get along because they have to get along.' He paused. 'One of them went to Yale. So he told him that his nephew was applying and how could he make a contribution to the college. I know how difficult it was for my brother to have to ask that man for a favour. But I told him, the banker wasn't doing him a favour, he was doing Yale a favour. And if Yale did you a favour, that was their business.'

'What did the banker think?'

'If you ask me, I think he was pleased for the wrong reason.'

'Which is?'

'To humiliate your family. To let you get in, and to watch you fail. To teach the Jews that they should know their own place.'

'That makes it even worse.'

'Doesn't it make you even more determined to succeed?' he asked. 'Your Uncle Stanley is intrigued by your letters. He gets the impression that you are being accepted by exactly the people that the banker thought would reject you.'

I could not disagree with that.

'I am not worried about your examinations,' my father went on. 'You will never disappoint me. Of course you don't want to spend all your time studying. It sounds as if you're having a good time. Going to New York, seeing theatre, going to football games. You have made friends?'

'Yes, Dad.'

'And they're good friends to you? Real friends? They accept you?'

'They know I'm Jewish and that I come from here, if that's what you're wondering about.' There was so much I could never tell him, or my mother, things they wouldn't understand, things they'd disapprove of. 'We're pals,' I told him.

'If you don't mind, I won't tell your Uncle Stanley that you know.'

I felt better after that. After all, Peter was only there because he was a legacy. George was so smart, any college would have taken him. Alan's father went to Harvard which is why Alan decided to go to Yale. You didn't say no to a Pearson. My pride had been hurt but it remained my secret.

◈

Christmas Day came and went in our house as it always had. It was just another day of the year. My mother succeeded in inviting Uncle Stanley to dinner. While the mock-Italian palazzo went up rapidly in the Bel-Air hills, he continued to live in the colonial style house in Beverly Hills. Aunt Estelle had made sure that the servants would look after him. Nevertheless my mother fussed that he could not possibly be eating properly when he was living on his own. He had resisted her invitations for months, it seemed, but as even the studio was closed on Christmas Day, he was out of excuses.

'Here's the college kid,' he greeted me when he arrived. 'Are you studying hard?'

'Yes, Uncle Stanley.'

'Good. Your folks expect great things from you.'

'You know how grateful I am. I hope I'm not buying too many clothes,' I tried to joke.

'You need to look good. Those East Coast guys...' He didn't finish the sentence. He then added, 'Your allowance is okay?'

'Yes, thank you.'

'I don't want you to be embarrassed in front of your friends.'

'I'm fine, Uncle Stanley.'

There was no further discussion of life at Yale. I now knew how important it was to him that I succeeded, and not just academically. I was the best friend of Peter Van Haessler and the partner in crime of Alan Pearson while George Hudson applauded. It was my Uncle Stanley who first taught me that there was no sexual morality and that if you want something, you go for it. As far as I was concerned, I was doing him proud.

◈

I met up one night with a couple of high school friends. We had spent years going to each other's house to study, and I had double dated with each of them. I remembered sitting in the back seat with a girl, not really knowing what to do or what she wanted me to do. I had got over that much. One guy was now at UCLA. The other had gone into his father's clothing business. They still saw each other all the time. They were nice guys and they told me about their nice girlfriends. The Depression seemed to be getting worse, if possible, but they didn't talk about it. They were the kind of young men you knew would always be all right.

I didn't know what to say to them. I made the mistake of wearing that cashmere Fair Isle sweater. We all came from families that weren't very well off. Suddenly I was wearing cashmere. They noticed. I wanted to tell them what had been happening to me, but as I drove over there, I realised that every story of my life back East ended with something that would sound pretentious. I had friends but they were Gentile and rich. I had a girlfriend but it wouldn't last because she was going to finishing school in Paris. I was in every way no longer a virgin but what could I tell them - the incident of the speak-easy that doubled as a brothel sounded like I was some kind of gangster. Yes I would be back in Los Angeles in the summer, but I wouldn't be there all summer because I was already invited to stay with the Van Haesslers in Maine. At the end of the evening we shook hands. I promised to keep in touch but I wasn't sure that any of us wanted that.

◈

When semester started, my pals and I went out to dinner to celebrate being back. It was the same faux-English pub where we had had the first dinner. The three of them said what 'hell' Christmas had been with their families.

'Do you celebrate Christmas?' George asked.

'It's just another day in our house,' I explained.

'You seem to have all the luck, Bobby,' he said.

By now it seemed like a big reunion. Guys kept coming up and saying hello and talked about the game coming up the next Saturday.

As we walked back towards the campus, Alan said to me, 'I've finally got a place organised for the next dorm games. We couldn't go back to the place we used last time, so I've rented an apartment in some god awful part of New Haven, where no one minds some noise.'

'Why couldn't you go back?' I grinned at him.

'You'll find out. Okay?'

'Sure. By the way, I went to see the boxing coach. I told him I am definitely not entering the ring but he gave me a lesson in how to punch a bag and showed me how to lift some weights.'

'Good man.'

'He also told me to do push-ups but at an angle. I've figured out how to rest my feet on my bed and do them at 45 degrees. That's what I spent Christmas doing, working up that routine.'

'Excellent. I know exactly who to pair you with.'

The apartment was indeed in a poor area, but there was a big living-room. When I arrived, the furniture had been pushed back against the wall. That, it was explained to me, was for Circumnavigation, where you had to make your way round the room by using the walls and the furniture and without touching the floor. I did indeed know the other guys. There were ten of us plus George who was acting as bartender before he took up his role as referee.

'Bootlegger's best,' he told me. 'The real bonded stuff. Don't ask, Bobby.'

'I never do.'

'That's Bourbon and that's scotch and that's beer, and don't mix them.'

'I know that much, George.'

Most of them were drinking beer. I decided to try Bourbon. I poured a large glass and put some ice and water in it. I liked the taste. We all stood around for a while the alcohol took its effect. Some of them were talking about USC having won the Rose Bowl. They had all read about it; I was blamed for not having been there since I was the only Californian in the room.

George said, 'The only things that matter right now are that the Japanese are taking over Manchuria and Hitler's going to run for president of Germany.'

'It doesn't matter,' someone contradicted him, 'my Dad said that as long as Hitler loses but gets more votes than the Communists, things will be all right.'

When Alan started the games, everyone stripped down to their shirts or under shirts and boxer shorts. He had paired me off with a tough looking sophomore who was about my size and shape. We were in the first race, which involved getting from one end of the room to another through an obstacle course – two tables which we had to crawl through without rattling the dozen glasses which had been placed on top. George awarded me the win. While the others took their turns, Alan suggested that my opponent take me into the bedroom and show me a few wrestling moves.

He was experienced but I fought back, as before, with as much aggression as I could muster. After a long tussle in which he just failed to pin me down, we sat back. I noticed that we had both become excited.

'Shit,' he said, 'the only thing wrong with Yale is no women.'

I leaned over and said, 'It doesn't matter, it's just enjoying ourselves. And you don't want it happening out there.'

When we finished and cleaned ourselves up we joined the others.

'Good,' Alan said, when he saw us. 'We're just about to start mess rugby.'

◆

I continued to go down to New York to see Diana. Her mother had now realised that I was not just one of Alan's friends being nice to his kid sister. When I arrived one day early in March I found her waiting for me.

'Oh, it's you, Bobby,' she said.

'Good afternoon, Mrs Pearson. I am glad to see you. Diana and I have arranged . . .'

'It's kind of you to keep taking her to the theatre,' she announced. I could tell her tone of voice. I was determined not to be intimidated.

'I really enjoy it. I think we both do,' I said, sweetly.

'You do realise that I am taking her to France shortly,' she warned me.

'Yes. It will be a great opportunity for her,' I agreed.

'She'll be gone for at least a year.'

'You'll miss her,' I said.

She smiled a thin smile. 'I've arranged for the car to be here in a few minutes,' she said. 'You should take it.'

'Thank you, but that won't be necessary,' I said. 'I thought we'd go and see the American murals exhibition at the Museum of Modern Art. It's the last show at the Heckscher Building. It's only on 57th Street. We can walk there. It's a fine day outside. And then I thought we'd go and see the modern architecture show at the old Rockefeller mansion. It seemed a good combination, the last in the old building and the first in the new. Have you seen them?'

'I'm not interested in modern architecture,' she declared.

'I'm not sure that I am either, but it will be fun to find out. I think Diana will be interested. If she isn't, we can always go to the movies.'

Diana came downstairs at that point.

'Bobby wants to walk to the Museum of Modern Art,' Mrs Pearson told her. She expected a different reaction to the one she got.

'That's all right, Mother,' she said. 'Is it cold outside?' She already had her hat and coat on.

'Not particularly,' I said.

When we set off, I told her about the conversation. She laughed and put her arm through mine.

'She deserves that, for interfering,' she said. 'I like the way you stood up to her. She needs defying, sometimes.'

'I did it for you,' I said. 'And us. I don't want to be chauffeured around. I just want to be with you.'

'Bobby, will you promise me something?'

'If I can.'

'Will you promise always, always to do what I ask you to do?'

'That's a little open-ended.'

'Promise.'

I stopped and looked at her. 'I promise. But I reserve the right to say No if I have to.'

'That's not much of a promise.'

'It's as much of a promise as you're going to get,' I smiled at her. 'Come on,' I took her hand and resumed our walk. 'Don't worry about your mother, you only have to put up with her until she leaves you in Paris.'

'That seems for ever. There's my party, first.' Diana was turning eighteen, and she was leaving The Brearley School. Two days before she sailed for Europe, her mother had planned a huge party, which, from Diana's description, seemed to be more about her mother than it was about her.

'I was going to ask you about that,' I said. 'My cousin Elaine and Aunt Estelle are coming back from Europe the day before your party. Please can Elaine come? I'll ask Peter to be her escort.'

'All right. Is she the one who's been to all the Paris nightclubs?'

'The same. By the way, her Chicago friend succeeded in marrying a Frenchman. It's a real dollar princess story. He's got a crumbling château and a title that goes back a very long way.'

'The last thing I'd want to do is to bury myself in a château,' Diana said.

'Ah yes, it's all art and artists and Paris for you,' I said. I stopped again. 'I'll miss you, Diana.'

'And I'll always think of you, Bobby.'

'That's not the same.'

'It's better. I don't think we miss people for very long. I don't. I can't even remember my father now. But you can think about people forever.'

'Okay, think about me forever then,' I said.

'Now I'm going to ask you to do something,' she said. 'I don't feel like the Museum of Modern Art. But I'd love to go to the movies.'

'Fine. Do I get to choose?'

'Yes.'

I had already noted that a Steingrove Films release had just opened in the city. I hailed a cab and we got to the movie theatre just as the opening credits were finishing. We settled into our seats and I took Diana's hand. She leaned against my shoulder.

The movie began on a farm. The younger sister of the family had a chance to go to the big city, where her boyfriend had gone to find work. His family farm had been hit by the Depression and by the drought, his parents had died, and he felt that he could not carry on alone. The elder sister of the family was the practical one. Their parents had died too. She would have liked to give up the struggle as well, but she felt that she owed it to their memory to carry on. She knew that she was the one who was most likely to make a go of the farm. She would never be well off, she would doubtless age before her time, but she would make the sacrifice to let her younger sister go off and to have the opportunity for the good life that would be denied to her.

It was a powerful beginning. The younger sister was played

by one of Steingrove Film's established stars, so I assumed that the rest of the movie would be about her and her life in the city.

The older sister dressed severely and the gingham dress hid her figure. But you could tell that she had some beauty that was being heavily disguised. It took me a moment to realise that she was being played by Laura Svensson, no, Laura Hampshire, she said she would be called. I stopped listening to the movie, I conjured up in my head the day in Uncle Stanley's office. If I hadn't taken the moral lesson from him, I might not be in this movie theatre today; if I hadn't said 'It stinks', Laura Hampshire wouldn't be in this movie. I liked the symmetry.

She had obviously been to the Max Reinhardt School and had been found to be sufficiently talented to be given a small but important part. Talent, she certainly had, at least in my opinion. There was a moment when the younger sister promised that she would come back, though you sensed that she never would, at least not to come back and stay. The two women embraced. The younger turned aside and faced the camera, showed her sadness at leaving, and walked out of the room. Laura Hampshire watched her go. Then she glanced briefly at a mirror on the wall. Hesitantly, she put her hand up to her face and slowly brought it down, as if she realised that her fate was to grow old and plain, alone. It was all the more brilliant because in that moment – was it because of the lighting? – one had a flash of how beautiful Laura Hampshire was.

When it was over, I pointed the scene out to Diana.

'I'm not sure I noticed all of that,' she said. 'I guess I was too busy thinking how lucky the younger sister was to get out.'

'It was really good,' I said.

'You notice things like that,' she said. 'You notice all that stuff in plays that I don't pay attention to. You ought to be a critic.'

'Hah hah.'

'You still don't want to go back to Hollywood?'

'I don't think so. I thought I might stay out here. In case you ever come back to New York. We could meet up and talk about old times.'

She put her hand up to my face. 'No one's ever liked me so much,' she said.

'Well then I suggest you take advantage of it for as long as you can.'

CHAPTER 8

LATE SPRING 1932

ON THE DAY Aunt Estelle and Elaine arrived, I waited for them in the lobby of the Plaza. I had especially worn my new J. Press suit and had just had a haircut from Peter's barber. My clothes, my hair - they were different, and I wanted them to see the change. I had volunteered to come down to the docks to meet them, but they cabled that it was easier to meet them at the hotel.

I was amazed when I saw them. Elaine was thinner and I wondered if the outfit she was wearing was something made for her in Paris. Aunt Estelle looked as elegant as ever, even more so; she had clearly picked up on something in Europe.

'Now there's a classy lady,' I said to Elaine. 'And a great lady. Welcome home, Aunt Estelle,' and kissed her first. I took her hand. Her mother, who had stayed on living in New York, had died a month earlier. My mother had written to tell me. 'I'm so sorry about your mother,' I said.

'Thank you, Bobby.'

'You look different,' Elaine said. 'Very East-Coast.'

She did not sound or look impressed or pleased.

'I am, I guess.'

'You look very handsome,' Estelle said and patted me on the shoulder. She looked at me. 'You've filled out. It suits you.'

'You welcomed us home. We're not really home yet,' Elaine pointed out.

'Elaine, don't be pedantic,' her mother said, 'we're back in America, that's what counts. I hope you're not hurrying back to New Haven.'

'No, I'm in the city for a couple of days.'

'Don't you have classes?'

'They can wait.'

'Elaine tells me you made a lot of new friends this year.'

'I have. They're great. In fact, there's a party tomorrow night. Quite a big one, for young people, I'm afraid. I was hoping you'd let Elaine come. I've asked and they said they'd be happy if she did.'

'Elaine makes her own arrangements now. Ever since London, I've just given up trying to organise her social life.'

'What kind of party?' Elaine asked.

'It's a big eighteenth birthday party for Diana Pearson. She's the sister of a friend of mine. I've been kind of going out with her. It's at their house. You'll never see anything like it again.'

'All right. Thank you.' She sounded less than enthusiastic.

'I bet you brought something fabulous from Paris that you could wear.'

'As a matter of fact, I have,' she said.

'And if you're going to the cemetery, Aunt Estelle, I'd be happy to go with you.' That seemed right for me to do. I was the only male Steingrove around.

'Thank you Bobby. That's very nice of you.'

I followed them up to their suite. After the porters had left the trunks and cases, Aunt Estelle took a box out of her bag. 'Since you are the first to meet us, Bobby, I think you should have the first coming-home present.'

I opened it. It was a set of Cartier onyx and diamond cuff-links and shirt studs. They were magnificent. I could scarcely believe that they were mine.

'You're always writing about the parties you go to,' Elaine said, 'so we thought you'd get a lot of use out of them.'

'They're the most beautiful thing I've ever been given,' I said, and hugged them both. 'I'll wear them tomorrow night. Your timing could not have been better.'

❖

We set off, after lunch, for the cemetery, cocooned in a limousine.

The cemetery was in Brooklyn, a part of New York I had never explored. It was like being in an alien city.

'Everyone looks so poor,' Aunt Estelle complained. 'I don't remember poverty like that in Europe. Maybe the peasants in the countryside.'

'You weren't looking,' Elaine said, crossly. 'There were cold and hungry men huddling around fires on street corners in every city we visited. Germany is falling apart. You must have seen it.'

'I don't know. We didn't meet anyone like that.'

'No, we didn't meet anyone like that.'

'Elaine, please don't scold me.'

'Do your friends care about what's happening in our country?' Elaine asked me.

'Everybody knows there is a Depression going on,' I replied. 'And they're glad that Hitler lost in Germany. We're all just hoping that things will get better.'

'Who told you that they will?'

'I said we hope.'

'I understand there's a Hooverville. In Central Park.'

'Yes. It's there,' I said. What was all this? Of course there was poverty in New York. I knew that. I thought of the woman who had come up to Alan and offered herself. She had not been the last woman I saw do that.

'Men living in cardboard boxes or something. In the cold,' she said.

'I think so.'

The limousine stopped at a red light. While we waited, in silence, a young woman who was holding a listless baby in her arms, stepped off the kerb and stood by the car. 'Please,' she said.

Elaine rolled the window down. 'What is it?' she asked.

'Please.'

'Elaine, what are you doing?' Aunt Estelle demanded. 'You don't know anything about her.'

The woman had a dead white face, and lank, unwashed hair. She could have been any age between eighteen and forty. 'What can I do for you?' Elaine asked.

She looked straight ahead. 'A dime,' she finally said. 'Can you give me a dime?'

'What does she want?' Aunt Estelle asked. 'Is this what America is like now? Panhandlers coming up to your car?'

'She wants a dime.' Elaine opened her handbag and rummaged through it for some coins but she couldn't find any American money.

'The lights are green, ma'am,' the chauffeur said.

'Stay here!' Elaine cried. 'Don't move. I don't have a dime.' Finally she found a dollar bill. She handed it to the woman. 'Here, please,' she said.

The woman took it and turned it over in her hand. It was as if she hadn't seen a dollar bill in a long time.

'Bobby, give her something too,' Elaine ordered. I put my hand in my trouser pocket but it was difficult, getting the coins out. 'Give her something,' she repeated.

'Here,' I said, at last, and handed over a fist-full of coins. Elaine cupped them in her hands and then handed them to the woman but they spilled out into the road. The woman leaned down to pick them up but it was difficult, with the baby in her arms. There were other people who were on the sidewalk. A couple of them came over and picked up some nickels and dimes and put them in their own pockets.

'All right,' Elaine said finally. The chauffeur drove off.

◈

It took a while at the cemetery to find the information about where the burial site was. There were rows of marble monuments and stones but having been recently buried, there was no marker for Aunt Estelle's mother, just a little tag stuck in the ground.

Elaine and I stood back and let her mother walk forward. She had brought some flowers, which she put on the grave. It felt strange to be out here, paying respects to a woman whom I did not recall ever having met. For that matter, I had no memory of my Steingrove grandmother, who had died while the family was still in New York. I had been to our grandfather's funeral in Los Angeles back in '30 but it had been an uncomfortable, cold event. He had been gruff and distant even to his grandchildren. His own sons hated him for the brutality of their upbringing. They had all attended the funeral, of course, but no one cried. That was mentioned over and over when we had all gathered back at Uncle Stanley's house; a funeral where none of the deceased's descendants had shed a tear.

Then Elaine put a bunch of roses on the grave. 'Goodbye, Grandma,' she said aloud. 'Thank you for loving me.'

She stood between her mother and me. They both looked hesitant. Each of us realised that one ought to say the memorial prayer, the Kaddish, but they had not brought a text with the transliteration with them and of course neither had ever been taught Hebrew.

'*Yis-gad-dal, v'yis-kad-dash, s'meh rab-bo,*' Aunt Estelle began and then stopped.

I did know the words. They had been taught to me and memorised, the way I had been taught to memorise certain prayers and even the Torah portion for my Bar Mitzvah. My father had insisted that I learn the Kaddish by heart, so that when the time came for me to say it for him, I would not be stumbling through a book, but could recite standing upright and facing forward, like a proper Jewish man who was stepping into his father's place in the community, when I would become the senior male Steingrove. I had stood by my father's side and recited it with him for his father. Although I had failed to practice my religion ever since that last Seder, which concluded with my punching my cousin, I recited it now on behalf of all three of us.

'…*b'olmo, d-v-ro, kr-seh,*' I picked it up. '*V'yam-lich mal-chu'she',*' I continued. The others followed after me as best they could. Together we remembered the departed who had entered the peace of the life eternal.

'Mrs Steingrove?' It was a man's voice. 'My name is Sam Gold, of Gold & Gold. We conducted your mother's funeral arrangements. My condolences to you and yours. I can assure you that everything possible was done and everyone sympathised with your grief. You can see that your mother is resting in a very special place.'

'Thank you. Excuse me, we have to go back to our hotel.'

'I understand. At a time like this. But may I please ask you something?'

'What is it?'

'I don't need to tell you that under our religious laws, we can only unveil a memorial stone after a year. I have spoken to your brother but... your husband has already said very generously that the bills should be sent to him.'

'Yes, my husband will look after everything.'

'It was the finest funeral we have ever had here. It is a tribute to you as a daughter. But the stone. I know the name and dates. But the inscription... Should it be, "Beloved wife, mother, grandmother"? And maybe a passage in Hebrew? Something that sums up your beloved mother's life. Many people prefer the holy words that a woman's price is above rubies.'

'Yes. Yes. The biggest and most expensive stone and everything in gold.' Aunt Estelle's impatience mounted. It was as if all the unexpressed grief and the tensions of having been an absent daughter were coming to a head.

'Mrs Steingrove? I apologise for intruding on your grief.' He gestured towards a small building. Aunt Estelle followed him in, presumably to sign some kind of document.

Elaine and I waited outside. 'That was beautiful of you, Bobby,' she said.

'I'm glad I was here,' I said. 'But that man, butting in like that, to sell your Mom some expensive headstone. It's people like that who create anti-Semitism.'

'You don't know what you're talking about.'

'Fine, I don't know what I'm talking about,' I muttered.

'How much of a Jew have you been this last year?'

'I don't really know what that question means, but if you're asking if I've been to services, no, I haven't. I've met a couple of Jewish guys at Yale. You can count us on the fingers of one hand. They didn't seem interested in becoming friends with me. I don't care. I have my own friends.'

'We were in Berlin on Yom Kippur,' she said. 'We went to the great synagogue, in the centre, it's huge, with a golden dome. I don't think I understood a word of it, but I didn't care. I had such a sense of belonging. And so many of them looked frightened. They sat there, telling God about their sins, and outside, millions of their fellow Germans think they're responsible for the Depression, and the Nazis are just whipping it up. That's anti-Semitism, not selling headstones.'

'Hitler lost,' I reminded her.

'He got 13 million votes last month,' she said. 'A lot more than the Communists.'

We drove back to the hotel largely in silence. Aunt Estelle excused herself and went up to the suite.

'Let's sit down,' I said to Elaine. 'We can order tea, here, in the lobby, maybe like they do in London.'

'All right,' as if she had decided to give me the benefit of the doubt.

Tea arrived, with sandwiches and a huge piece of cake. We sat in the big armchairs and looked at one another. I decided to start again.

'I'm so glad to see you,' I said. 'You look so well. There's so much to catch up on.'

'What you did at the cemetery, that was beautiful, Bobby. I have to thank you again.'

'Remember when you said that you wanted more than anything not to go to Europe? How wrong was that?'

'You were right.'

Then I decided to plunge in. 'Why are you so angry, Elaine?'

'I'm not angry, Bobby.' She sat back and looked at me.

'You've been cross since you arrived. Bickering with your mother, and with me.'

'Well Mother was so silly, pretending that we hadn't seen poor people and suffering in Europe. It's terrible there. I am so frightened at what could happen. It's bad here too, but it was bad when we left. Maybe it's worse, I don't know. She should be angry that there are women like the one who came up to the car, women who have to beg for pennies for food for their children.' She smiled wryly. 'Maybe we never saw that in Los Angeles.'

'It didn't stop you going to nightclubs in all the big cities you visited,' I pointed out.

'But at least I was aware. She would've just driven on this afternoon.' She took my hand. 'I can't tell you how I felt when I saw you, Bobby. You looked so different. That smart suit and your hair like a movie star's and I thought, Oh God, Bobby has completely changed. You looked... I don't know, dazzling. I wanted so much to see you and to talk and talk with you, but then I thought, "It isn't Bobby any longer."'

'That's absurd.' I laughed.

'You have changed.'

'All right, a lot has happened to me too,' I conceded. 'And I wore this suit to signal that. I think I have grown up, a lot, in the last eight months. And I'm in the city, so I want to look nice. And I want to dress like my friends. But please don't go overboard. You've had quite a lot of experiences too.'

'Who are these friends?'

'My friends. My pals. We do things together.'

She sighed. 'Don't fob me off, Bobby. They're not like the boys you knew in high school.'

'No, they're not. You know, I'm getting the impression that actually, you're not glad to see me.'

'It's not that.'

'You'll meet them all at the party. Try to like them. They'll like you.'

'And what will you look like at this party?'

'I'll be in my white tie and tails and wearing the most beautiful set of studs and cufflinks. Now, you've been in Europe all this time. You must have learned something.'

'Oh, yes. I can tell you all the periods of decoration.' She looked around. 'Would you like to know about Louis Quinze as filtered through Allard et fils? Or maybe . . .'

'What about those nightclubs in London you wrote about? And who was that guy you went with?'

'Philip. That was a long time ago.'

'And that French aristocratic wedding?'

'That was Charlotte, marrying the Frenchman of her dreams. I was with her in Paris for a couple of weeks. When her trousseau was being made.'

'You see?'

'Have you told your Yale friends about your past?'

'My past?'

'Or that you're Jewish?'

'They know I'm Jewish. Nobody cares about that.'

'Are they dazzled by Hollywood?'

'Look, I'm just Bobby to them. That's all.'

'I don't understand.'

'Look at me, Elaine. I'm not different. Not to you.'

She did not look entirely convinced but at least she dropped the subject. 'Tell me about your friends, and stop avoiding the question.'

'You'll meet them all tomorrow night. You're actually going with Peter, Peter Van Haessler. That's who I'm staying with.'

'The people you spent Thanksgiving with?'

'Yes. And this August. They have a place in Maine. It's supposed to be beautiful there. Swimming every day.'

'So you won't be spending much time in LA. Is this where you think you belong?' she asked.

'It looks that way.'

'When we were in Europe people just saw us as Americans. Hollywood, when they figured it out, but they didn't ask beyond American. But back here, isn't it different? I mean, what makes you different?'

'I'm their friend,' I said.

'Do you ever talk politics with them?'

'They're all Republicans, so I avoid the subject.'

'Did you know there are men living in shacks in Central Park? I read about it. Have you gone and seen it?'

'I haven't been to see it. What's the point?'

'I don't think you understand what's going on. In Germany, the choice isn't between democracy and not democracy any longer. It's between the Communists and those Nazis. There are Blackshirts everywhere in Italy, swaggering around while people say how nice it is that the trains run on time. That woman who came up to the car, that was real suffering.'

'I know.'

'Charles-Xavier, that's the man Charlotte married. He's charming but his family are monarchists, if you can believe that. They think that history stopped in 1789. Like your friends.'

'My friends are Americans. They think 1789 was a great year, George Washington became President.'

She smiled. 'You, coming up with a fact like that. Is that what your friends like about you?'

'Among other things.'

'So who is this birthday party for?'

'Diana Pearson.'

'Is she your girlfriend?'

'She's going to finishing school in Paris. As of next week. So there's not much point in thinking of her as my girlfriend.'

CHAPTER 9

With no one else staying, I was given the main guest room at the Van Haesslers'. I took particular pleasure in getting dressed for Diana's birthday party. I looked in the mirror after putting in my new Cartier studs and tying my tie. It was going to be fine. I went into Peter's room. He was sitting there in his dressing-gown. Worse, there was a half empty bottle of Scotch on the side table.

'For God's sake Peter, what if your Mom saw that?'

'She doesn't come in here.'

'You know she does. Come on, we're going to be late.'

'Do I really have to go?'

'What is this? I made a point of asking if we could bring Elaine. You can't disappoint her.'

The three of us had had lunch that day.

'She's nice,' Peter said.

'She's my favourite relative. We grew up together. So you're going to give her a great time. Now come on.'

'What will she expect me to do?'

'To be her date. If you want to kiss her, do. I advise you to take her upstairs and find a dark corner and start making out.' I threw out my arms. 'It's easy.'

'It's so goddamn easy for you, Bobby.'

'Just stop worrying about it,' I said. 'It'll happen.'

'You and Alan come down here to the city. I don't know what you both do, but it's obviously something you have no problem doing. Do you enjoy it? What does it feel like?'

'That's our business. You're the one who first told me there's no sexual morality.'

'Of course there isn't.' He said it as if he were clinging to a life raft.

'How drunk are you?' I demanded.

'I can hold my liquor.'

I put my hand on his shoulder. He put his hand on mine.

'Are you in love with Diana?' Peter suddenly asked.

'Diana is going to Europe next week with her mother.'

'That doesn't answer the question.'

'I'm very happy when I'm with her. It's hard to describe and as of next week, when she gets on that ship, it won't matter any longer. Except missing her.'

'Is that all? How do you feel, physically, when you're with her?'

'If you really want to know, I feel that I want to do things which are not acceptable and are never going to happen.'

He nodded. 'Alan has taught you how.'

'He wasn't the teacher. And we're leaving that subject right there.'

'She's eighteen now. It's legal, I think.'

I put the lid back on the Scotch bottle. 'Peter, just get dressed.'

'Don't do that,' Peter said.

'You've drunk too much already.'

'I told you ...'

'I'm your friend. As far as I'm concerned, I'm your best friend. At least, you're my best friend. I happen to care what happens to you.'

'For God's sake Bobby, don't start on that.'

'Why not, it's true.'

He looked up at me. He looked utterly miserable.

'I got a letter from my father this week. He does this sometimes. He wrote, "I remember that friend of yours from Thanksgiving. Try to be more like him. He's going to be twice the man that you are. Even if he is a Jewboy." And he's right.'

Without pausing to think I leaped on him. Peter's unmade tie was lying on the bed where he was sitting. I grabbed it, pushed Peter down and pressed the tie against his neck. 'Don't ever say that word again,' I shouted.

'Stop it, Bobby,' he gasped.

'Don't ever think of me that way.'

'Please.'

'Swear.'

'I swear.'

I stood up and threw the tie on the bed. 'You father is a drunk. He wants to destroy you so you'll be like him. Another drunk.'

'I don't think of you like that. You know that.' I kept staring at him. 'You haven't walked out,' he said.

'Do you want me to?' I asked.

He shook his head.

'Then what was that about?'

'For God's sake, don't make me say it.' He looked close to tears.

I thought of the cool, assured way he had talked me into his room and into his bed, to do something which probably would have got us thrown out of Yale if not straight into jail if anyone had caught us. If he could do that with me, audacious as it was, how difficult could he find doing it with a woman? My adventures with Alan, which Alan organised, gave me physical pleasure but no emotional ties. They ended with a sort of affectionate detachment with women who rightly treated us as over-eager boys. With Peter there really was a friendship. He was the bedrock of my life here. It could not end, I would not walk out, but it could not carry on unless he saw me for myself alone. If I could, I would do anything to make his life easier.

'You're fine,' I said.

He laughed. 'Do I look fine? Bobby, I want to apologise...'

'Forget it.'

He shook his head. 'You don't think I'm going to turn into my father, do you? He said that word and meant it.'

'He's sick, forget him. Forget families. We're not queer, we're just enjoying ourselves. We don't need ever to discuss that again. You know what? In ten years' time we'll both be married. We'll go out together, the two couples, and some time, in the

middle of the evening, you and I will look at one another and
we'll burst out laughing. And our wives will ask what the joke
is about but we won't be able to tell them. And then we'll go
home, to the beds we share with our wives, and we won't even
remember any of this. That's how I see it.'

I sat down next to him on the bed.

'Are you all right?'

He turned his neck. 'Just about.' He put his arm around my
shoulder. 'August in Maine, and then next year.' He already
looked less miserable.

'Sounds good,' I said.

Peter nodded. 'I'm thinking of August. Surrounded by my
mother and my sisters. And the whole summer crowd. You
haven't met them yet.'

'We'll manage,' I said. 'We're good at that.'

'Pals?' Peter asked.

'Pals. Now get dressed.'

◆

We went to the Plaza to pick up Elaine. She had borrowed her
mother's cloak and had found the dress she wanted to wear, a
long black dress with very little back from Worth.

'You look wonderful,' I said. 'Paris?'

'Yes, well, Paris. I like your shirt studs.'

'Yes, well, Paris.'

'Hello, Peter,' she said.

'Bobby always talks about you,' he said, 'but he forgot to say
how beautiful you are.'

'Why thank you. Bobby also doesn't say how handsome his
friends are.'

'I'm glad we've got that settled,' I said. 'Shall we go to the
party?'

We were being driven in Mrs Van Haessler's car. On the way
to the Pearsons, Peter said, 'There should be lots of dancing
tonight.'

'Elaine has danced in every nightclub in Europe,' I said, 'including with the Prince of Wales.'

'I did not.'

'Close?'

'He was there. A friend of mine danced with the ex-King of Spain. She didn't like him.'

At the house the butler knew us.

'Good evening, Mr Van Haessler. Good evening, Mr Steingrove.'

'And this is my cousin, Elaine Steingrove.'

We were announced as we made our way up the gothic staircase to the drawing-room. Every reception room in the house was now lit and decorated. I had never seen it like this before. I had begun to think of it as a mausoleum, waiting for old Mrs Pearson to die so that it could be torn down. Now it was back to its full glory, at least for one night.

At the top of the stairs, Diana stood with her mother. Her short hair was tightly waved, framing her fresh face. She was wearing a white sequined dress which, like Elaine's, was cut very low at the back. She looked wonderful. Sure I was in love with her, how could Peter even have asked?

'My cousin Elaine,' I introduced her. 'Really nice of you to let her come too.'

'I love your dress,' Diana said. 'Where does it come from?'

'Worth.'

'I must go there when I get to Paris. Bobby said you've just been, you must tell me everything.'

'Okay.'

'You look like a dream,' I said to Diana, 'even better, a dream come true.'

We entered the drawing-room, I felt Alan's strong hand on my shoulder.

'Intending to look after my little sister tonight?' he joked.

'I had it in mind.'

'There will be a lot of competition for that.'

'I look forward to it.'

'Peter looks drunk.'

'Just some Dutch courage.'

'What for? Is he after your cousin?'

'Ask him.'

It was one of those occasions which people dub 'the end of an era', though arguably that era had already ended, some time around 1913. Everything was brought out, the French porcelain, the English silver, the furniture, which aped the treasures of Europe but had to be made specially and specially large for this house because real Chippendale would have looked dwarfed. All in aid of Diana's birthday, Diana, who didn't even like this stuff, and who dreamed of going to artists' garrets and inspiring their great works. In a Worth dress, apparently.

Elaine stood with Peter. They were an incongruous couple. Peter, lean and fair-haired, looked flushed. Typical Alan to notice that he'd been drinking too much. Elaine had lost weight but she looked every inch a round-faced Steingrove, there was no getting away from that. Various young people came up to them. There were a lot of girls whom I guessed had been at The Brearley with Diana or maybe they were cousins or family friends; I had never actually met any of her friends. I had only ever wanted to be with her and she had never introduced me to anyone.

There were only a few of the Yale crowd, those who had been at prep school with Alan and had known the family for ever. They were polite, well groomed, good looking and agreeable to Elaine. 'Oh you're Bobby's cousin,' they all said. 'Bobby is so much fun.' Those who had been there talked about Europe with her. A band which had been culled from a fashionable night-club got set up. The guests drifted in from the other rooms. I kept looking around, beaming. I did not care that I knew so few people. There was only one person in the room I cared about.

At last it was time for a speech. In the circle which was going to be the dance floor, Mrs Pearson stood with Diana.

Elaine and Peter were nearby. I could overhear what they were saying.

'I haven't really met her yet, Mrs Pearson,' Elaine whispered to Peter. 'Is she nice?'

George was just behind them. He answered the question. 'Mrs Pearson? None of the Pearsons are nice. They're a lot of things, but nice isn't the point of being a Pearson.'

'What is the point of being a Pearson?' she asked him.

'Going through life knowing that whatever you want, you'll get.'

'Aren't they your friends?' she asked.

'They are all our friends. And the one we like best is Bobby.' He held out his hand. 'I'm George Hudson. And you must be Bobby's long-awaited cousin Elaine.'

'Long-awaited?'

'Well you are the only relation he talks about. You and his Uncle Stanley.'

'That's my father.'

'I know. Are you going to give him a full report on tonight?'

Mrs Pearson called for attention. She said how sorry she was to be doing this speech; that Diana's late father had looked forward to such a moment. As she said this, George and Peter exchanged glances across Elaine. He had found other priorities in his life rather than keeping himself fit to live to see his daughter's eighteenth birthday. She was sure that everyone wished Diana a happy birthday. Everyone duly sang happy birthday. Diana smiled and I could see her mouthing, *Thank you, Mother*, but she did not speak herself.

The band began to play the tune for the first dance. It was a waltz, an amalgam of several tunes that I could identify. Waltzes were not the specialty of this dance band. I guess they were asked to start with one so that the older guests could join in and then retire to the Louis-style sofas, having done their duty.

I had moved away from the others when Mrs Pearson began her speech and found myself standing next to Alan. Everyone watched Diana, waiting for her to fetch her brother, to be her partner for the first dance. But Diana did not choose Alan. In a moment that I thought I would live on for the rest of my life, she held out her arm to me. There had been no warning that this would happen, but without hesitation, I took a few steps forward, took her hand, and led her to the centre of the floor. We began to dance, with the whole party looking at us. And most of them wondering who in the world I was. I knew I could waltz and I wanted to waltz in a way that made Diana look glamorous.

I smiled down at her. 'Of course Alan can't really dance,' I said generously.

'Really? That never occurred to me.'

Others took the floor, but I did not notice them. After a second dance, I graciously gave way and let the other men take their turns.

It was shortly after this that I danced with Elaine.

'We've come a long way since the choreographer at Steingrove Films,' I said, leading her through a foxtrot. 'Are you sure you didn't dance with the Prince of Wales?'

'Positive. You have no idea how impressed everyone was that I've danced with Donald Marshall.'

'You bet. I told Peter's sisters you did, and they went crazy.'

'Bobby, who is that woman over there who looks as if she doesn't like us?'

'Who? Oh, that's old Mrs Pearson. The grandmother. She's about one hundred and fifty. Fifty years ago or so she entered society only, I repeat only, because Peter's grandmother agreed to call on her. It's a great story, ask Peter, he loves telling it. He thinks it puts Alan in his place.'

'Do you find that amusing?'

'It's kind of funny, that anyone cares. I think our grandmother was still in the shtetl then.'

'Or trying to get away from the Cossacks.'

'Cossacks are Russians. We're Austrian, remember?'

'Bobby, what are we doing here?'

'I think you'll find that we're at Diana's eighteenth birthday party. Aren't you having a good time?'

'Yes. Lots of nice young men have asked me to dance. They're all your friends, they all like you. They think you're great.'

'Told you so.'

'And Peter kissed me upstairs.'

'He has good taste. How did it go?'

'I'm afraid I didn't encourage him.'

I shrugged.

'What are we doing here?' she repeated.

'Elaine, don't spoil it. I'm so happy tonight. Did you see, did you see Diana ask me for that first dance?'

'Yes. You looked as if you'd gone to heaven. She is beautiful, and you danced beautifully and you looked as if you could devour her, there and then.'

'Please don't tell your father that I'm wasting his money. I'm not, I promise. And I'll pull all nighters to make sure I get straight A's.'

'It's not that. I mean I was standing there and your friend George said that the Pearsons are not nice and Peter didn't disagree.'

'They like teasing Alan. They've all known each other for ever.'

'All right. I give up.'

'I belong here, Elaine. I know it doesn't look like that to you, but it's true. I've got three more years at Yale. Life can only get better.'

The party went on and on. Peter came up and said that he was going to take Elaine back to the Plaza. As far as I was concerned, the party was not over yet. 'I don't think I'll come back. You've got a key?'

'Sure. Sleep well.'

'You're staying? To the bitter end?'

'You bet.'

Elaine kissed me. 'Thank you for getting me invited,' she said.

'Thank you for coming. I'm so happy, Elaine, I can't tell you.'

'I thought Diana's going to France next week.'

'But not until this party is over. That's why I'm going to drink every last drop of it.'

I stayed until the band finally stopped at four and everyone else had left.

'It's time to go to bed,' Mrs Pearson told Diana. 'Goodnight, Bobby.'

'Wonderful party, Mrs Pearson, thank you very much.'

But I did not leave. We watched as her mother went upstairs. Alan had long ago disappeared.

'Let's get some fresh air,' I said.

'Just what I was thinking.'

We found our coats and my hat and together we stepped into Fifth Avenue. It was actually rather warm. When we were outside, I kissed her.

'I've wanted to do that all night,' I said.

'Alan said you looked as if you wanted to undress me.'

'I won't apologise for that.'

She put her arm through mine. 'I want to walk.' We headed north. 'I never got the chance to talk to your cousin.'

'You don't need her advice; you'll have your own experiences in Paris.'

'I can't wait.' Then she said, 'How did Mother look when I asked you to dance with me?'

'I wasn't interested in what she thought.'

'You looked pleased.'

'I was the luckiest man in America.' I let go of her and suddenly turned around and around on the pavement. 'Some day, very soon, you'll meet some artist. And twenty or thirty years from now, when someone is studying that artist, they'll say, he wasn't much good, but then, you know, around 1933, he met this muse, and he started painting those nudes of her and that's

what we'll always remember, those brilliant, genius nudes of his
mistress, oh what was her name? Diana Pearson? I thought she
was someone else's muse, I guess she knew everybody. If you
want to understand art and Paris in the 30s, you have to understand Diana Pearson.'

She laughed. 'I love the way you talk. I said I'll think about
you. And I will.'

'All part of the service.'

'Let's go into the park,' she suddenly said.

'Now? It's about 5 o'clock in the morning.'

'I've never been in the park in the dark.'

'Dressed like this?'

'You'll protect me,' she said.

'I mean, what for?'

'Because I'm leaving New York in a couple of days and I want
to do something I haven't done before. And you promised to do
whatever I asked you to do.'

'With the right to say No.'

'That time hasn't come yet, has it?'

It was silly and probably dangerous but I could not deny her
anything.

'Isn't there a Hooverville somewhere?' she asked.

'My cousin Elaine was talking about it. She couldn't believe
I'd never seen it. She thought I didn't care that men are living
there in shacks.'

'Well now you can kill two birds with one stone.'

'It's hardly a happy end to the evening,' I pointed out as she
started to cross Fifth Avenue.

'Don't you think I should know about things like that? When
I'm in Europe and they say, "Oh you rich Americans, you think
poverty doesn't exist." I don't know anything about New York,
except where my mother allows me to go.'

'Don't blame me if it gets ugly.'

'You'll get us out of it,' Diana said. 'You can talk your way
out of anything.'

We entered the park and then walked without a very clear idea of where we wanted to go. It was only chance that we reached the camp, with shacks and a few fires burning against the chill of the early morning. There were men sitting around. I held her arm, to stop her getting closer. I could see how shabby and probably unshaven they looked. It seemed incredible that in the midst of this rich city, with its massive apartment buildings and great houses and skyscrapers, that there were people who were allowed to live like this, with nothing. And that they would see me as one of the rich. Me, in my white tie and tails and top hat and cloak and Cartier studs and cufflinks. I thought bitterly of Mr Van Haessler telling me that President Hoover was doing a good job.

I turned to see what Diana was doing. She had lost interest in it already. She was looking up, at the faraway buildings. Like me, she had never seen New York from this perspective. Standing in this vast, dark space, with the flickers of light in the distance, as if this were really our own private garden in the midst of the city. Then she looked down, and saw a grassy area at our feet.

'Here,' she said.

'Here what?' I asked.

'Here. I want to make love with you here.'

'Honestly, Diana, let me take you home.'

'No.'

She was entirely calm about it, which is more than I was. She could not be serious. I would have given my soul to make love to her, but not here, not like this. This had to be a bad joke.

'I thought you wanted to see the Hooverville so you could tell your French artist friends that you knew all about the real America.'

'And I have. But it was really just an excuse to get you here. I thought you were playing along too.'

'If I thought for one second ... I could've found somewhere - anywhere - else. I mean be serious, Diana.'

'Where? One of our unused bedrooms, listening for foot-
steps in the corridor? Trying to sneak past Mrs Van Haessler at
Peter's? Checking into a hotel as Mr and Mrs Smith? It's too late
for that now. It's our last night, Bobby.'

'Stop joking, Diana.'

She looked at me. 'Don't you want to make love to me?'

'You know I do. I dreamed of it, but I never thought for a
second . . .'

'Bobby and Diana, a story of unfulfilled passion.'

I kissed her. 'Isn't that enough?' I asked.

'No. Is it enough for you?'

I had stopped arguing. But I couldn't think of how we could
manage it.

'I'm not a virgin,' she said, 'so you don't have to worry about
all of that.'

I was shocked at the news.

'And you do know what to do.'

'Yes.'

This was not the moment to bring out my credentials, which
consisted of whoring with her brother.

'I mean, I'm not getting pregnant.'

I had only ever been where there was an ample supply of
rubbers. I knew perfectly well that I would therefore have to
calculate when to withdraw, something I had not had to do
before. 'Don't worry about that,' I said.

She smiled. 'You see, I knew I could trust you.' She touched
my face.

I kissed her hand and then let go of it. I took off my hat and
coat, and spread the coat on the ground. It was uneven, but not
too hard. I took Diana's cloak off her and laid it over my coat.
At least we wouldn't be on the damp grass. Then I took off my
tailcoat and folded it, carefully. This was such an absurd outfit
for the occasion. It was nakedness which had always excited
me; and the sooner one was naked the better. I untied my tie
and loosened my collar. It was too much to undo all the shirt

studs, much as I wanted to strip down. Finally came my waist-coat and suspenders. It all seemed to take a long time. Diana sat on the cloak, looking at me, until finally I took off my shoes and trousers.

'I was right,' she said, 'about your body. I've been told that story about men falling in love with women's bodies and women falling in love with men's minds, but that's silly. It should be both.'

She lay back. I kneeled over her and started to kiss her. She drew her dress up and pulled her underwear down. Then she reached my cock. I carried on. There was no question of stopping. I kissed and caressed her as best I could.

'Pause, I have got to take this dress off,' she said. I sat up, excited as I was, to help her take it off. Then with some help from her, I did what she wanted, what we both wanted, what I thought could never happen. Despite what she said, I could tell she wasn't completely sure what to do but she seemed reassured that I did. The only question was withdrawing in time but I managed that and came on her stomach. I reached into my trouser pocket for a handkerchief. Then I lay down next to her and covered her body with mine. As happy as one could be in a situation that seemed utterly unreal, I was happy.

'You're so beautiful,' I said, 'I can't tell you how beautiful.' And then, 'I'm in love with you. I can't help it.'

She smiled at me. 'Perfect,' she said. 'Now you can go back to your friends.'

'What?' I sat up.

'That afternoon, after Thanksgiving, when I went into Alan's room to see who was there, and you just came after me. The expression on Alan's face! Expecting you to come back, bored to death. To tell him that I was as much of a pain as he thinks I am. And ever since, he's been waiting for you to agree with him. But you kept asking me out again and again. And you were so sweet to me. And I got you to fall in love with me. Perfect,' she said again.

'Is that what this has been all about? Getting back at your brother?'

'You're so nice, Bobby. The way you beam down on me as if I'm the best thing that ever happened to you. And what we just did, we both liked it. You deserved it. I'm sorry if you don't like the way I planned it. All through the party I kept hoping that you'd stay and stay, and you looked so ridiculously happy there. I knew you would stay until someone threw you out. I'm glad I did what I did. So don't feel as if I cheated you.'

'But it was a game for you?' I could feel myself getting angry. 'Has this all been a game, from the start? Were you only acting?'

'I wasn't acting,' she said fiercely. 'I'm not one of the women you and Alan throw your money at. Or probably his money.' I stared at her. 'I know what you and Alan do. Don't worry. I don't know the gory details. But when I found out I thought, "Good!" You're very attractive, Bobby, but if you'd only been some virgin freshman, we wouldn't be here.'

'What are you going to do now, wake up Alan and tell him you've won the game?'

'Maybe some day, probably never. At least I know that you aren't going to. That was something else I had to think about. Not to choose someone who would get drunk and tell stories. Not our charming Bobby. You'll go back to the Van Haesslers' and snuggle up and think of me. You know, maybe the next time you and Alan do whatever it is you do, it won't be so easy, because you'll be thinking of me. Maybe the next woman that Alan pays for won't be as exciting as she should be.'

I put my head in my hands. 'You didn't want me, not for myself.'

'Have I hurt your ego? It will heal.' She sat up. 'We can go,' she said.

I looked at her. 'Not yet.'

'I'm cold. Like I said, you can go back to your friends and feel pleased with yourself. Sometimes I wonder if you're really more of a plaything for them. They're so possessive of you. Especially Peter.'

'We're not leaving,' I said, coldly. If it was a game, I was not going to let her win it.

'Bobby, it's enough.' She looked at me, every inch a Pearson, as if I would not dare to do anything that displeased her. It was her will against mine.

'Just lie there,' I told her.

'What are you talking about?' This was not supposed to happen.

'Turn over,' I said, 'we could try it that way, if you're interested.'

'No.'

'All right. I don't mind.' We looked at one another.

'Bobby, it's enough, I'm going home now.'

I took her arm, gently. I knew what was going on her mind. She was willing me to stop. That's what this was, a conflict of wills. She had used me, thrown out a few compliments, but very definitely put me in my place. A plaything for his friends, Alan's paid companion for things that couldn't be mentioned, and unable to get her out of my mind. For Diana the game was over, we could go back. I was determined that it would have to go on. 'I wanted you so much, it could have been wonderful. Why can't we make love for its own sake?'

She had lain down again and shook her head from side to side. I couldn't think further than the fact that she had won the first game but that I would win the second. Without her help this time, I managed to enter her. I knew she wanted me to fail and to feel duly humiliated. I kept on until, once more, I pulled back just in time.

'Bastard,' she said.

I sat up. 'There, you've had your experience.'

As I stood up, I turned around. There were three, shabbily dressed men standing there. 'It's all right,' I said. 'She's my girlfriend.'

The men kept staring at us, at one and then the other. They were unshaven, in old clothes. They had had the life beaten out of them, and now they were watching two rich kids enacting something. As quickly as I could, I threw on my clothes. I didn't care how I might look. I dug into my pocket and found five dollars. I held it out to one of the men to say nothing and just go away.

Diana got up, and started to put on her dress. I went over to help her, which she tolerated. Then she pulled away from me. She put on her cloak and her shoes and began to walk away. She had clearly lost her sense of direction because she moved towards the shacks. The ground was more uneven, and she stumbled as she walked past. Finally she saw that she had been going in the wrong direction. There was no choice but to turn back and to walk past the men and the shacks all over again, until she reached me. The men stared but said nothing. There was this beautiful young woman in her evening clothes, as vulnerable as she would ever be, and they just stared. She looked up at me, and I saw the look of fear, regret and disgust on her face.

'Are you satisfied?' she asked.

'As much as you,' I replied.

Then the anger seeped away, and I felt overwhelmed by a sense of shame. It seemed the worst thing I had ever done. I had ruined absolutely everything. She looked ahead and I sensed that there was nothing I could say to her that would make the slightest difference.

We both started walking back towards Fifth Avenue. She couldn't stop me keeping up with her. I wanted to get her out of the park safely.

I was horrified but I had no idea how I could ever put it right. She would not listen to anything I might say.

When we reached the Pearsons' house, I asked, 'Are you all right?'

'What are you suggesting?'

'I just asked if you were all right.'

'You'll find out,' she said.

She turned and walked up the steps of the house. She took her keys from a small bag and let herself in. It was the last sight I had of her.

CHAPTER 10

I STOOD AND WATCHED FOR A WHILE. I put my hand in my pocket. It was empty. Where was the key to the Van Haesslers? Had I dropped it in the park when I found the $5? I couldn't go to Peter's and wake up the household to get in. And I had to talk to someone. I realised that I was not far from the apartment where George's family lived, on Park Avenue. It was a risk, but I went there.

'I'm Bobby Steingrove,' I said to the doorman who looked askance at me. I had no idea how dishevelled I actually looked. 'I'm a friend of George Hudson. I've come to see him.'

The doorman pointed out how early it was.

'Would you call anyway?' I begged.

'Mr and Mrs Hudson are out of town. The only one there is George.'

'Please.'

With great reluctance, he called up. Miraculously George was awake.

The doorman took me up in the elevator. George stood at the open front door in his pyjamas and bathrobe. 'You're lucky, I couldn't sleep. What are you doing here? Do you have any idea how awful you look, Bobby? What in the world has happened?'

'Can we just talk, George?'

'Weird time of day, but come on in.' I followed him into the huge, quiet hallway. 'I suppose I could offer you breakfast. There's no one here. I think you better go into the bathroom first. Take a look at yourself in the mirror and don't come out until you do something about it.'

My face and hands were dirty, my tie was hanging around my neck, my collar was undone, my hair was a mess. I looked stricken. My hands were shaking. It took several attempts to put my collar back and to tie my tie. I washed my hands and face. I needed a shower, badly, but that would wait. Luckily there was a hairbrush. By the time I finished, I bore at least some resemblance to how I had looked at the start of the evening. I found George in the kitchen.

'Better,' George said. 'You should sit down, though.' He was going round the kitchen trying to find things. 'There's some bread, so I can make toast. There are eggs, I only know how to scramble them. The cook left some Danish pastries. And coffee. You look as if you need coffee.'

'Thanks.'

'Good party,' he said cheerfully. 'I liked your cousin. I was a little flippant about the Pearsons. I don't think she liked it. I guess she's not used to the way we talk to each other. About each other.'

'Look, I've just got to talk to someone.'

'That's obvious.'

'It's about after the party.' And then, in fits and starts, scared to tell him everything but feeling that I could not go on without making a clean breast to someone, I told George exactly what had happened. I ended with, 'George, I'm so ashamed. I don't know what to do. I just ruined everything.'

'Anything else? Anything in addition to shame?'

'I wish I could explain, to apologise, but she'll never let me. I'm terrified. I am so scared, I don't know what to do. It's the end.'

'You did rape Diana.'

I looked up, horrified. 'I did not rape her.'

'Sorry, I only have your side of the story.'

'It wasn't like that. That's what I'm trying to explain. She wanted me to make love to her, she'd planned the whole thing from the start, about going into the park, and then it was obvious that she was using me. Somehow in my mind I was thinking, if we dropped the bit about using me, if we just made love, it would be different.'

'With you giving the orders.'

'She's always been using me. I was angry and I just felt...'

'Yes, you've said that already.'

'You weren't there.'

'I think that's the usual excuse.'

'I know I shouldn't have done it. I should have dragged her out of the park and back home and never touched her.'

'True. But you didn't.'

'I didn't rape her,' I insisted.

'Bobby, she didn't want you to, but you went right ahead and had sex with her. You're the one who talks about becoming a lawyer.'

'I never wanted to go into the park. I never wanted to do something like that, I mean, on the grass in the park. But I was so happy with her, I couldn't refuse her, I couldn't refuse her anything. She made me promise always to do whatever she asked me.'

'I'm not going to argue with you, Bobby. I made it absolutely plain, when you were given the morality speech, that rape is not part of it. You said yourself...'

'What's going to happen to me?' I cried. 'She's all right, I think, but, my God, anything could happen now.' I put my face in my hands. 'What's going to happen to me, George? The way she said, "You'll find out".'

George sat there. For a while he closed his eyes. I thought he had fallen asleep. Then he opened them and looked at me. 'Nothing,' he said.

'Nothing?'

'I'll explain. Option 1, Diana has gone home and cried rape. In which case the police may already be downstairs. But I don't think so. Since you are feeling guiltless, you will plead not guilty. Which means a trial. Which means the papers full of stories of how Diana Pearson lured a college student into Central Park in the middle of the night and then cried rape.'

'Would they say that?'

'Your uncle must have a publicity department at his studio.

They'll feed that story. It sounds good. Nice boy from California goes to Yale, and look what happens. Rich girl having a good time before she goes off to a snooty Paris finishing school, and gets more than she bargains for. Yeah, I can see that.'

The idea of Uncle Stanley getting involved was horrific. He might help but this would humiliate him. The New York banker who helped him make the donation would be proved right: Jews did not know how to fit in. And it would kill my parents.

'They'll be on her side,' I said.

'Not necessarily. Your sick old father sits there and reads books while his innocent son falls into the clutches of the Pearson heiress. Whose grandfather used to get my grandfather to arrange to shoot the workers rather than pay them an extra nickel an hour.' He shook his head. 'It cost them a fortune to keep the truth about how Alan's father died out of the papers. They won't back her up. And I can't see Diana playing the victim, can you?'

'Depends.'

'Option 2, she goes to Alan and tells him what his shitty friend did to her.'

I sniggered. 'He once said that if I touched her, he'd cut my balls off.'

'It's a shame you didn't believe him. On the other hand, would she do it? This is where options 1 and 2 come together. The Pearsons are basically games players. You said yourself she was playing a game with you. Dorm games, sex in the park games, whatever it is, they play and they win. Would Diana go to her brother and admit that she lost, that it was you who took command? You know Alan, whose side would he really be on? Frankly, I am not sure of the answer to that one. But neither would she.'

'She's his sister.'

'Those two never got on, not since their father died. That's when she decided to play the rebel. As you know, Alan is a chip off the old block, and I mean old. Everyone says he is the reincarnation of his grandfather, which means he's going to be a very rich and successful man, and as hard as a rock. If you ask me, it's a waste of time, throwing yourself on Alan's mercy, even if you are his sister.'

'Is there an option 3?'

'Option 3 is she says nothing, goes to France, and forgets all about it. That last thing she said, that was just a bit of bravado. I don't think she'll waste time asking herself what she was doing last night in the first place. She'll feel sorry for herself and she may hate you for the rest of your life, but that's fair enough. I could be wrong, but I think it is likely to be option 3. Quite apart from the question of not upsetting her grandmother.'

'What does she have to do with it?'

'Money. You're thinking about justice and blood ties. It's charming, but we're living in a more practical world. Diana's dreams of *la vie bohème* in Paris are not based on her earning capacity. If the old lady hears anything which might even hint at Diana behaving disgracefully she'll cut her out of her will. And she holds a lot of the purse strings. Diana took a risk last night, dancing with you, of course.'

'The old lady was looking at me.'

'She kept asking, "Who is that young man who Diana is dancing with?" Alan told her a story that you were a friend of his, from California. She assumed you were a visitor, so nothing to worry about. Anyway, she's never met a Jew in her life so it was best to keep the explanation neutral.'

George got up. 'I'm hungry at least and I'm going to make us both breakfast.' He set about breaking eggs in a bowl. 'I guess it means that you'll go through the rest of your life and never get punished or forgiven. Diana will go and do whatever she feels like doing, that's Diana. And meanwhile you can go back to being Alan's buddy, not to mention Peter's best friend. As if nothing has happened. You have to behave as if nothing has happened. How is that going to make you feel?'

'Lousy.'

'You'll get over it,' George said. 'You're not going to spend the rest of our time at Yale wearing sackcloth and ashes. You're just going to carry on, enjoying yourself.'

'You make me sound like a shit,' I said.

'You're not,' George said. 'You're much more interesting than that. And nicer. Yeah, deep down, I always thought you were a nice guy.'

'Thanks.'

'Anyway, we like you. You're part of us now. We don't have to pal around with you. We didn't go to prep school with you. Our families don't know one another. You're the best friend Peter will ever have and in his dim way, he knows that. Alan seems to have found a kindred spirit. Or at least someone with a sexual appetite as big as his own. It's too bad he didn't tell Diana that before tonight but, like I said, those two don't get on.'

I looked at George and almost asked "And you?" Thankfully, I didn't. The fact that I was here and we had had this conversation was all the answer I needed. At what I felt was the worst moment of my life, he was there. Whatever might happen later on, the memory of this morning bound us together.

I needed George's cold, cynical rationalism, neatly divorced from the moral judgments he was capable of making but which he didn't. Except for his belief that I had raped Diana. I nodded, and said nothing.

'How did you feel after dorm games, by the way?' he asked.

I shrugged. 'It was a lot of fun. But afterwards, as if nothing has happened. Just like Alan predicted.'

'We're heartless bastards, aren't we? At the moment we're still kids, we can pass it off as the arrogance of youth or whatever it's called. But basically, those guys you like to hang around with, they're heartless. You'll be too if you stick around.'

'No,' I said. 'I'll live with last night for the rest of my life.'

'That's what you say now.'

'It was just unreal from the start. I couldn't believe it when

Diana said I wasn't the first. I'm sorry, I probably shouldn't have told you that.'

'Some girls at her school warned her against the kind of man who takes your virginity and then thinks he owns you for ever. She decided to get that over with. She didn't think the French artists she intends to seduce would be attracted to an American virgin, and she certainly didn't want to seduce the kind who were. She's a bit young to be that worldly, but that's Diana. I guess it narrows the range of men who will want to marry her one day, but she doesn't seem interested in marriage either. At least that's her story.'

'How do you know?'

'It was me.'

'I beg your pardon?'

'Don't say it like that, Bobby. I've known Diana all her life. I think I had a crush on her when I was 16, or something. She knew exactly what she was doing. She wanted someone who was willing, guiltless, and a little eager to do the job. I say guilt-less because my parents would disown me if they knew I had taken the virginity of a girl I had no intention of marrying. Especially Diana. But it wasn't the kind of offer you refuse.' He dished out the eggs and toast. 'It wasn't passion, but that wasn't the purpose. It could have been a lot worse. Anyway, I was the convenience. Not you. You were the one she lusted after.'

'She used me.'

'You asked for it,' George said calmly.

I sprang up.

'Bobby, your breakfast is getting cold.'

I sat.

'Diana is spoiled and wilful. For reasons of her own she want-ed to tell herself that she could make one of Alan's friends like her a lot more than they like him. She hit the jackpot with you. You've spent the last months going around like a cat who ate all the cream. And then you fell in love with her. It's rather sweet and sentimental that you never saw any of this until this morning. But don't change. As I said,' he concluded, his mouth full of food, 'I'd hate to see you become heartless.'

Slowly I began to eat. I hadn't realised how hungry I really was and how much I needed the coffee. 'She seemed to know about Alan and me, coming down to the city and . . .'

'Bobby, she offered herself to me. She had some prurient interest in Alan's sex life. I couldn't not answer a few questions.'

'Some friend.'

'She already knew he goes down to the city and does something so that he only comes home at 3 a.m. Looking back, maybe she just wanted to make sure you would know exactly what to do. Which naturally you did.'

'Can we talk about something else?' I asked.

'Like what? What are you doing this summer?' George asked.

He said it sarcastically but I ignored his tone. 'I'm going to spend August in Maine, with the Van Haesslers.'

'Fun. Like I said, carry on as if nothing has happened. What about your family?'

'Oh, I'll go out to the Coast. See my folks. Then head back.'

'You never talk about them. Your parents.'

'Yes, I did.'

'Your father can't work, so he reads books.' He shrugged.

'All right. He was a mailman. Happy? He had no ambition. That all went to my uncles. My Uncle Stanley respects him, but the others, they just despise him. The bookworm, they call him. My Mom complains about it all the time. I can't even sit with him for a while without her coming in with coffee and cake that doesn't taste of anything, just to remind us that she's still there. And getting in the way of whatever relationship I could have with my own father.'

'And you're ashamed of them.'

'I didn't say that.'

'Peter said you did.'

'Peter also said you know too goddamn much.'

'I'm curious. Peter was complaining again about his father, et cetera, and then, as if to justify himself, he said that you were ashamed of your parents. As if that made it all right for him to be ashamed of his father. Except that Mr Van Haessler is a drunk and your dad sounds poor but honourable. And well-read.'

I suddenly noticed some papers sitting on the table. 'What are these?'

George grabbed them. 'Nothing. I was trying to write a short story.'

'Really? About what?'

'A prep school boy who goes to an Ivy League college. It's crap.'

'Try something else.'

'I can't write. You might as well know, I am going to start a literary magazine next year. I have to do something while I'm at Yale. Some people said they'd get me elected to the Elizabethan Club so I ought to do something literary. I'm sure I can edit. My father said he'd give me some money. I'm so bored with my classes.'

'Isn't there a literary magazine already?'

'Not like this one.' He suddenly became animated. 'I want to surprise everyone. I want short stories from athletes and sports columns from aesthetes.'

'It's a great idea.' I cheered him along. 'Can I be the theatre critic? I did enjoy all those theatre outings. And there are student productions on campus. And I go to the movies every week. Of course, I should write under a pseudonym.'

'Are you that afraid of your uncle?'

'It would look a bit funny, having film reviews from a Steingrove.'

'Okay, you can do films and plays, and call yourself whatever you like. Can you write?'

'My professors think so,' I grinned.

'Fine. You're hired.'

It was not until seven that I excused myself.

'I think a maid will be on duty by now,' I guessed. 'I ought to go back to the Van Haesslers.'

'What will you tell Peter?'

'Nothing. I can't tell anyone. Ever.'

'Quite right,' George agreed.

'I don't even know what to say to you right now. Except thank you.'

He looked hard at me. 'Go to bed, Bobby,' he said.

⊕

I approached the Van Haesslers' house with a sense of dread. The police wouldn't know I was at George's but Diana could tell them about staying at Peter's. The faux-Federal redbrick looked solid and respectable. By luck, the cook was arriving at the lower door that led to the service rooms. I told her that I had forgotten my key and made up a story about why I was out at this hour. It didn't matter to her, I was overdoing it, but I was still overwrought.

I bounded quietly upstairs. Fortunately everyone was still asleep. I had a long, hot, much-needed shower, put on my pyjamas and went to bed. When I slept, I had a nightmare. I was naked and there was a knife somewhere. I was woken at noon by Peter. The only word I could hear was 'downstairs'. I sat up with a start.

'Don't look so panic-stricken,' he grinned. In the sunlight he looked blond, sleek and sober.

'You said . . .' It was the moment between dreaming and reality, when I had to remind myself that the dream had not actually happened. Was it the police? Or a vengeful Alan?

'I said, your cousin Elaine is downstairs.'

'Elaine? What is she doing here?'

Peter shrugged. 'She said she'd gone for a walk and it was all very Jane Austen of her or something but she decided to call on us. I think she wants to see where you spend so much time.'

'How is your Mom coping with her?'

'Everyone's out, doing something. I've been waiting for you to wake up.'

I lay back on the soft, white pillow. 'I don't know what to say.' I felt so relieved to see him there, looking exactly the same. Looking at me exactly the same. Thank God he doesn't know anything about what happened, I thought.

Peter sat on the bed. 'I can entertain her until you get dressed. You look a little peculiar, Bobby.'

'I feel a bit peculiar.'

'Too good a party. I could see how much you were enjoying yourself. Diana just winds you around her little finger.'

'Yeah,' I agreed. I told myself, act as if nothing happened, and that I was glad it's finished. The important thing was to go back to the way things had been, until last night. 'She'll be in Paris in no time.'

'So that's all over,' he said.

'It sure is.'

He said, 'You know, when I woke up this morning, I suddenly thought that I said a lot of stupid stuff last night...'

'Forget it.'

'That's right. Lesson one, don't get drunk.'

'Only get drunk to enjoy yourself,' I said. 'With any luck, the Democrats will win in November and we can get rid of Prohibition.'

'I look forward to it.'

'Pals, remember?' I said.

He nodded, and got up. 'You were right about Elaine. She's great. I'm glad you arranged all that, for me to take her. In fact,' he paused a moment, 'I lured her upstairs to kiss her.' He held up his hand. 'Don't worry, she wasn't interested. Nothing personal, she just wasn't interested.' He had done what any red-blooded young man would do in the circumstances. He stopped at the door. 'What are you doing today?'

'I need to go to the Plaza. To say goodbye. They're going to

Los Angeles tomorrow. Aren't we going back to New Haven
this afternoon?'

'Of course. Everything back to normal.'

I sat up. 'That sounds good to me.'

I shaved, had another shower and dressed as quickly as I
could. I had bought a tweed jacket at J. Press, which I wore
with a silk tie. I felt a little unsteady as I walked downstairs. At
least I had had that breakfast at George's. I was not hungry but
I was desperately in need of coffee.

I found Peter and Elaine in the little library. Someone had
in fact produced a tray with coffee. Elaine was wearing a hat
with a small brim and a dark blue dress. Like Peter she looked
like someone who had had a good night's sleep. I went over and
kissed her.

'This is a nice surprise,' I said.

'Peter's been a very good host. I was ashamed to find out that
my cousin was asleep when everyone else in New York was having lunch.'

'I've shown her around,' Peter announced. 'Now if you'll
excuse me.'

I sat on the Chippendale armchair and poured myself some
coffee.

'It's a beautiful house,' she said. She looked around at the
books in the library. 'I still prefer your father's study.'

'I don't think much reading happens in this room,' I admitted. 'But it's a serious book collection. Peter's grandfather was
some kind of bibliophile.'

'Didn't anyone inherit his tastes?' she asked.

'All the Van Haesslers have the same taste,' I declared. 'And it
is good taste, even if they don't read all the books.'

'You obviously know them very well,' Elaine observed.

'I have spent Thanksgiving and Easter here and I know that
the point is that they've had all of this for a long time and everyone just accepts that this is what you have and what you live
with.'

'And you feel comfortable with that.' It sounded like an accusation.

I sighed. We were back to *You've changed, Bobby.*

'Yes. I feel comfortable here.' I took some more coffee.

'You looked comfortable last night,' she observed. 'More than comfortable.'

I took a breath. 'I have been to that house before. And those were my friends there. I wanted you to meet them, so you'd understand a little of what my life has been like the last six months. And you did meet them.' I tried hard not to sound as if I was attacking her. I wanted her approval. Soon she would be 3,000 miles away, but she was Elaine, my favourite relation.

'They were very nice to me,' Elaine said. 'Especially Peter. We danced and he introduced me to everyone and he made sure we sat at the best table at supper, and . . .' She took a sip of coffee.

'And?' I cocked my head and smiled at her.

'What did he tell you?'

'That he wanted to kiss you but you didn't want to kiss him. Exactly what you told me last night.'

She put her cup down. 'I felt that he wanted to kiss his date, who happened to be me.'

'That's a bit hard.'

'There is a difference and I happen to know it.'

'Has my cousin become a woman of the world over in corrupt old Europe?' I teased her. 'What about that English guy you wrote to me about? The one who took you to all the nightclubs and kept you out dancing until dawn? And that romantic meeting.'

She could not resist the temptation to put the record straight. 'We met at this old house that his grandparents own. Some awful dealer took Mother and me there. The idea was to sell us something to keep the whole place going so Philip could inherit it one day. I just couldn't stand it, going into a house where people still live to find things to buy. I wandered off from where Mother and the dealer were haggling over something and just found Philip in the library. Then he turned up at the Ritz, where we were staying, and we started going out.'

'Nightclubs. Swims in the river at midnight,' I recalled her letters. 'And then you stopped mentioning him. Did you dump him?'

'He asked me to marry him.'

'Smart guy.'

'But I said no.'

'You could've been engaged and you didn't think that was worth telling me?'

'No,' Elaine said. 'I considered it something private. It wasn't just that he wanted to marry me . . . he said that he wanted me.'

Elaine had spent her life comparing herself to her mother. It was a recipe for self-loathing. Then this Englishman came along and made her feel attractive. Because he had desired her. I knew all about that by now.

'Like I said, smart guy.'

'I couldn't put that in a letter,' she said.

'Sorry, I shouldn't have teased you,' I said. 'Any man would want to marry you. The question is whether he is good enough for you.'

She said firmly, 'Philip is good enough for any woman. I just wasn't in love with him. And I've spent the last months try-ing not to think about it. You're not exactly very forthcoming about yourself,' she added.

I threw up my hands. We had spent our lives telling each other things. Now, I couldn't tell her anything. Peter? My sex-ual adventures with Alan? Diana? Impossible. I could start to explain but where would it end?

'What's there to say?' I joked.

'You looked so happy when Diana held out her hand to you.'

I closed my eyes. I did not want to be reminded of that. 'It was just a party,' I said. 'She'll be in Paris in no time. I don't think I'll ever see her again.' Neutral. Draw a line under the whole thing.

'You said she was your girlfriend. Surely you want to keep in touch.'

'Nope. So what are you going to do when you get back?' I asked suddenly.

'I'm going to ask Daddy to give me a job. In the script department.'

'That's great.'

'I can read scripts and scenarios and comment. I still wonder about editing. But I've got to start somewhere. I don't want to sit at home.'

'That's wonderful.'

I was pleased for her. But Elaine working at the studio? Would that drive another wedge between us? Instinctively I pushed my hair back. It reminded me again that it was cut the way Peter's barber cut it, not the way it had ever been cut at Steingrove Films.

'When are you next coming to Los Angeles?' she asked.

'The summer,' I hastened to tell her. 'For a while. I'm heading back here for August. Like I said, the Van Haesslers have a place in Maine and I'm going to stay with them. There are a bunch of other guys I've met who'll be around there too. I've promised to teach Peter's sisters how to dive. He has three sisters. It's funny, being a kind of surrogate older brother to those girls. Do you ever wonder what our lives would have been like, if my parents had more kids? Or if your little brother had lived?'

'But it didn't happen.'

'No, it didn't happen. But it means that we've always had each other. Not just as cousins, but friends. That's why I don't want you to worry about me. Or to wonder what kind of people I'm going around with. I'm still the same Bobby.'

'I hope so.'

'You only hope so?'

'I'm afraid for you, Bobby. Where is it going to end?'

'I thought of becoming a lawyer. Here.'

'You mean you're not coming back to Los Angeles. You're not going to work in the business.'

I shook my head. 'I know what you're thinking. Why is my Uncle Stanley spending all this money to give me an education? So I can be a Wall Street lawyer, like all the anti-Semites who look down on us? But in fact I'm doing exactly what he wants me to do.'

'How do you know that?'

'Can I tell you a secret?'

'Of course.'

'I didn't get into Yale on my grades.'

'Oh, Bobby.'

'It's true. I mean, the moment I met the other Jewish freshmen, and there are scarcely any of us, I thought to myself, I'm not half as smart as they are. And then, last December, I found out. A Dean told me how grateful they were for my uncle's donation and they would always respect his request for anonymity.'

'What donation?'

'Exactly. At Christmas I forced Dad to tell me the truth. It turns out that he persuaded your father, for my sake, to make a donation to the college. So that my dream would come true. Of course Uncle Stanley didn't know how. He had to go to the New York bankers he's always cursing, the ones who keep the studio afloat.'

'Them.'

'The same. They told him exactly what to do and how much and who to contact. One of them went to Yale, so he was all in favour. That's as much as Dad told me. Sure they wanted the money for Yale, and he wanted to buy me a place. Only they were really trying to show him up. They couldn't believe that his nephew could be a success at Yale, that anyone would accept him. Only I haven't failed, Elaine. And I'm not going back to LA. What counts is what you do when you get here. What you make of yourself.' I paused. 'I've shown those bankers that a Steingrove is as good as they are. I think your Dad is proud of me.'

'And you?' She looked at me intently.

Me? Right now I had no idea whether the next person to knock on the front door would be a rampaging Alan Pearson or the police. Everything could come crashing down. Unless George was right.

'It's great,' I told her.

I let go of her hand and stood up. 'Come on, it's a lovely day. We'll walk back to the Plaza and I'll stay goodbye to your Mom. Have you told her how good those studs and cufflinks looked on me last night?'

CHAPTER 11

AUTUMN 1932

At the start of our sophomore year, George duly launched his literary magazine, which he managed to bring out every six weeks or so. When I think about those two great middle years, as a sophomore and a junior, I think a lot about that magazine. It started my career as a writer.

George duly pursued his goal of subverting expectations. The short stories and poems were notable largely because of the authors. He got the Varsity quarterback to write a story about a young man who goes sailing with his father. The cynics dismissed it as little improvement on 'What I did on my summer vacation', but it created a stir because no one had expected the Varsity quarterback, who was there on a huge scholarship, to know how to string a sentence together. The write-up of football and basketball games by what George called the 'aesthetes' divided opinion. Some thought it was a satire on sports, while the rest considered it a satire on the aesthetes. Everyone had to admit though that the depictions of the games were totally correct. George, the editor and ultimate sports fan, made sure of that. But whatever anyone felt about the articles, everyone read the magazine. To George, the highest compliment was that guys didn't know whether to take it all seriously or not.

My brief was to write waspish reviews and to treat the student productions with the same critical eye that I cast on Broadway shows. Nothing was supposed to be quite good enough. Highest praise tended to go to shows that had already closed. That was supposed to create exclusiveness. People began to stop me on campus to ask me what I had tickets for, just to be sure they didn't miss it.

This approach made me a number of enemies amongst the student actors and directors. I loyally wrote good reviews of

Steingrove Films productions, trying to hide behind my pseudonym, although my anonymity didn't last long. I saw every
Steingrove release during those years, which meant that I saw
every film that featured Laura Hampshire. By the end of my
junior year, she was a big star.

Uncle Stanley had decided that she should play romantic screwball comedy, as Steingrove Films' answer to Carole
Lombard and Claudette Colbert. But Laura managed to instil
more than that into her performances. She was usually paired
with Donald Marshall who had put *The Countess and the
Cowboy* far behind him. As often as not she was the sassy girl
from a distinctly lower social class who catches the eye of the
handsome, eligible rich boy. At the end he asserts his authority as the man, but you know that sooner rather than later she
is going to be calling all the shots. He was an old style patri-
cian who tried to give orders because his family always had; she
was the practical and resourceful one from America's heartland
who got things done.

I particularly enjoyed *Neighbourhood*. Donald Marshall
plays a sad widower who finds that someone is doing nice things
for him, like preparing his breakfast so it's waiting for him when
he comes downstairs in the morning, or fixing his boiler when it
breaks down. But he doesn't know who. He thinks it's the awful
woman across the street who is only interested in his money.
But it's Laura, the maid from next door who is secretly in love
with him, who sneaks in and then sneaks out again because she
is afraid that he couldn't possibly fall in love with the maid. But
he does. At the end we see them happily together at the breakfast table, as she is pouring coffee for her new husband.

It was a wonderful time to be a critic. *King Kong, Duck
Soup, Queen Christina, It Happened One Night, The Scarlet
Empress* and *The Barretts of Wimpole Street* comparing the ver-
sion on screen with the one Diana and I had seen on stage.
I started to note dialogue, camera angles, pace, characterisa-
tion - the elements as much as the whole. Peter and Alan, my

usual companions, just wanted to sit back and enjoy the movie without worrying about why. Alan was transfixed by Laura Hampshire. Not by her ability to make breakfast or fix the boiler, but by her radiant beauty. The camera couldn't take its eyes off her and neither could he. He sat there staring at the screen and afterwards could remember nothing of the plot of the picture. I did not tell him that my Uncle Stanley had bedded her within an hour of their meeting and for all I knew, still had sex with her.

I knew what was going through Alan's mind when he looked at the beautiful actress on screen. He was thinking that he ached to do with her what he did with the women we met on our outings to New York. Steadily, we expanded the repertory of techniques. He never actually sat down and told me everything his uncle had related about what was done in the Paris brothel. Whether the list really was as long as this or whether we were now in the realm of Alan's erotic imagination in full flood, I never knew or cared. Correspondingly, dorm games became rougher and, when Prohibition was finally abolished, drunker. There was a pleasure in that sweaty, competitive, alcohol-fuelled camaraderie that was not explicitly sexual but was the next best thing.

I came back one Sunday from a matinee in New York and found George in the little office off-campus that he had rented. His father had indeed bankrolled this venture, apparently on the basis that his son was at last *doing* something.

'How was the play?' he asked me.

'Awful. I swear, George, I could do better than that.'

'Why don't you?' He looked eager. 'Yes, that's what you must do. You should write a play, and we'll publish it in the magazine. And you can get it produced here, at Yale. Are any actors here still talking to you after your reviews?'

'A couple. The good ones.'

'Fine. I hereby commission you,' he said.

I spent the next two weeks cutting lectures and writing the

play. About what? The only things I knew were living in Los Angeles and being at Yale. So I started a play about a boy from somewhere else who goes to an Ivy League college. Along the way he meets the wrong girl. I knew that when I started Act 2 it would have to be about Diana. I had met plenty of girls in those summers in Maine, girls whose families knew the Van Haesslers. It was easy to have a summer romance with lots of kisses and cuddling on the strict condition that we would never go *too far*. I had not come close to falling in love again. The dramatic potential of that was zero.

I recognised that the 'wrong girl' either had to ruin the boy or the boy would have to ruin her or possibly himself over her. I wrote a dialogue for them that I felt was the conversation I should have had with Diana standing on Fifth Avenue and which would not have led us going into Central Park. This provided the play with an ambiguous ending.

I slipped the completed play under George's door late one night and the next morning wished that I hadn't. I had written myself back to that night of Diana's party. It was the last thing I wanted to do. The task was to bury those memories, not revive them. I decided that the whole thing was a mistake.

'It's good,' George said, the next time I went into the office. 'Would you like me to tell you why?'

'No. It's crap, George.'

'You can write, Bobby, you know that.'

'I think I'll go back to reviews,' I said. I picked up the manuscript that was sitting on his desk and dumped it in the wastepaper basket. 'I'm going for a swim,' I said. The pool on the third floor of the new Harkness Gym, 25 yards long, was the best pool I had ever swum in. 'Swimming is what I'm good at.'

CHAPTER 12

AUTUMN 1934

By THE START OF OUR SENIOR YEAR, it was only Peter who appeared not to have changed at all. He was good company; he joined in everything we did; he liked being at Yale; he liked his friends; he liked me as his best friend. As far as I was aware, he had no interest in finding someone else to have sex with. This was the way he wanted to live, and that was the way he wanted things to continue. The problem was that it would end, by definition, at graduation.

In the end, he could not keep it up. When drunk he took on that stricken look I had seen in his bedroom the night of Diana's party, as if he wanted to escape but could not bring himself to say what he wanted to escape from or where he wanted to be instead. Three or four times he went down to New York. When I asked what he was doing he hesitated, as if trying to think of something that sounded plausible even though it wasn't true. He said, 'My Mom wants to talk about my future.'

We were all thinking about our futures, I guess. I was busy applying to law schools, and imagining the place in a Wall Street firm that that would lead to. It forced me to think about my grades. I had let them slip. I had perfected a technique of pouring a semester's worth of work into a couple of weeks of studying for exams. The results were mixed. I called my grades 'good enough for law school' though, to be honest, I had no idea whether they were or not. I was determined to put everything right in the fall semester. If I could produce outstanding results I could say that once I concentrated, I could do really well. Surely no law school wanted to take a boring man who had done nothing but study for four years.

I assumed that George would go into publishing of some kind. Or start another new magazine, maybe in New York. He was a good editor. He brought to it the same cool, amoral logic he brought to everything else. He was rarely in his office now though. People were lining up to write for the magazine but he seemed to have much less interest in it. No one knew where he was hiding himself. He still expected to receive everyone's copy on time.

Alan's future had been ordained by his grandfather's will. I could feel his impatience, like a superbly trained racing horse at the starting gate. He turned twenty-one early in December but he reluctantly accepted the advice of the Board, which he was now entitled to chair, that he should finish his education first. Meanwhile, he was incensed about the New Deal. For him, the road to recovery was paved with a paternalistic capitalism, where Pearson Industries created jobs and produced the steel that would help to rebuild America. Everything that was coming out of Washington was getting in the way. A lot of our friends agreed. I knew I was still a Democrat and didn't argue with him.

George and I instead teased him endlessly. George did it because he had never taken anything Alan said seriously. I did it because I had actually seen the look of despair on the faces of the men in the Hoovertown, who were so beaten down that they had not even had the energy to do anything when two spoiled kids played their sexual games in front of them. I knew that the Hoovertown was gone. If Roosevelt was responsible for that, that was fine by me. I was proud of Uncle Stanley who had joined with the Warner brothers in campaigning for Roosevelt in '32 and did his best to fill the Memorial Coliseum with movie people for their big pre-election rally.

Mrs Pearson threw a massive coming of age party. George of course understood my hesitation about accepting the invitation.

'Diana won't be there,' he told me. 'She's already made it clear that there are far more interesting things happening in Paris.'

'Has she got what she wanted there?' I asked. I knew that George was in touch with her.

'I think it's turning out the way she wanted. Oh by the way, Bobby, she asked me to tell you something.'

'What's that?'

'She said, "Tell Bobby that I am not thinking about him". You know that doesn't make any sense.'

'I get it, George, don't worry.'

◈

Peter was the only man I knew who only spoke about the future in passive terms. Everyone else talked about what they were doing about jobs or graduate school. Peter only said, 'They'll think of something for me.' By which he meant that one of his relations would create a job for him, maybe in a bank, to keep him occupied during the day, until some suitable girl came along and made a man out of him. He was Peter Van Haessler, and there weren't many better catches than him.

◈

Then in the winter of 1934-5 the roof fell in. It started over Christmas. I was due to go back East a few days early, to stay with the Van Haesslers, as I had every Christmas vacation. Before leaving Los Angeles I received a telegram from Mrs Van Haessler that simply said:

PLEASE DONT COME STOP PETER ILL STOP

When I got back to New Haven I dumped my things in my dorm room and was about to set off to find Alan and George, to see if they knew more of what was going on. I didn't have to do that because they arrived together while I was still trying to put on my coat.

'I hate this,' Alan said, when he came in.

'It's lousy,' George agreed.

It was clear from the start that what they had to say had been carefully rehearsed.

I sat down on my desk chair. They sat on the narrow bed, side by side. It emphasised their physical differences. Alan had become taller, broader, and more powerful. No one would call him handsome but he had a strong and determined face. The face of a man you didn't argue with. George looked exhausted. He peered at me through his round glasses and sat up straight.

'What's going on?' I asked. 'What's wrong with Peter? I got this cryptic telegram from his mom. Have you seen him?'

'Yes, we saw him in New York yesterday.' It was Alan's job to deliver the bad news. 'Peter's had a breakdown. He cracked up over Christmas. He's at home. He's been seeing a psychoanalyst for a couple of months now…'

'Are you kidding? He didn't say anything about that. He thinks all the Freud stuff is crap.'

'He didn't want to tell you. For obvious reasons.'

'I'm his best friend.'

'It's about you, Bobby,' George said. 'Peter has reached the belated if firm conclusion that he's queer.'

I shook my head. 'No, no. We've discussed this dozens of times.'

'Maybe he believed it,' George said, 'and maybe he's got so mixed up with that older brother, younger brother, mutual admiration society relationship the two of you have – I mean, has he had sex with anyone else but you since you met him?'

I shrugged.

'Well what if he is queer?' I said. 'We don't care. We don't have any morality about that.'

'Of course we don't. We're talking about society, though. And his mother. Van Haesslers are not queer. They get married and produce children. Drunk yes, queer never.'

'So what's going to happen?' I asked. 'The poor guy. If I'd known, I would have gone straight there the second I got into the city.'

'You can't go there,' Alan said. 'The psychoanalyst has come to the conclusion that he can cure Peter.'

I guffawed.

'He can cure him because you are the problem.'

I stared at him.

'I know, it's crazy. I tried, but you can't talk to his mother right now about this. She's convinced that it's all your fault. If you ask me, the shrink is only saying this to please her. She's writing the cheques, after all. Doctors,' he sniggered. 'He's said and she's said that Peter must never speak to or see you again. That's an absolute. Otherwise, he can't cure him.'

I sat back, flabbergasted. I felt as if my life over the last three years had just disappeared. 'So what's going to happen?' I asked again.

'We don't know when he'll be well enough to come back here,' George said.

'But if he can't see me, how I can see you, if he's around?' I was about to add, 'Or you him?', but I knew right away that the ring was going to close in. The four pals would go back to being three.

'I'll think of something,' Alan said, but he did not sound convinced. He went on, 'Of course this makes it very awkward when you next come to New York. You don't realise how many people Mrs Van Haessler knows.' I had met quite a number of her friends already, what with the summers in Maine and then the coming out party she had organised for Peter's eldest sister. In my head I could hear the sound of doors slamming shut.

'You've got to be realistic,' George said. 'What did you expect, when you graduated?'

'To see you all, to carry on as we always did,' I said.

'Sure,' Alan said. 'We'll run into each other. New York's not that big of a place.' This sounded like the way he would treat someone he barely knew. 'Of course it isn't possible to ask you to join the Knickerbocker or the Metropolitan clubs. And there's a lot of other stuff.'

'Where did you want to practise, after law school?' George asked.

'New York, of course. Some Wall Street...'

'Bobby, the firms you're probably thinking of don't take Jews.

I mean, I thought you understood all of that. We told you the first night how much we despise the hypocrisy of the outside world. We still do. But we can't change the outside world. Be realistic,' he used the word again, 'there are lots of good Jewish firms.'

'I have no intention of practising in a ghetto,' I said coldly. 'Being patronised by my opponent because I'm with a Jewish firm.'

'Then don't be a lawyer. You probably shouldn't be anyway.'

We sat there silently for a while.

'Hollywood,' George said. 'You know it, it's wide open, so no one cares who you are. You can write, believe me, you can write.'

'It's what families are all about,' Alan said. 'They'll look after you. You'll be knee deep in women out there.' He almost sounded jealous.

They both got up. Was this it?

'Peter's nuts,' Alan said. 'You were the best friend he'll ever have. If I were you, I wouldn't be sorry for a single thing.' He shook my hand. 'You'll get through the next few months.'

'I'm shutting down the magazine,' George said. 'It's had its day. This will be the last issue. Don't forget to get your copy in on time. You were the star writer, remember that.'

'I'm playing rugby on Saturday,' Alan said.

'I'll be there,' I promised.

'You always are,' he grinned, and slapped me on the arm. 'You and I have had amazing times. There's no one on earth who knows that better than you.'

'Carry on as if nothing has happened,' George said. 'You're very good at that.'

When the door closed behind them I sat down on the edge of the bed and put my head in my hands. For a long time I couldn't think straight. Then gradually, the thoughts came together. They were right. I had to go back. There was no choice. I would write to Uncle Stanley and ask for a job. I would explain how

I had changed my mind. I could make it sound convincing. It would have to wait, though, for a couple of weeks. I had just seen him, in Los Angeles, over the holidays. Maybe I could say that coming back East after that great time in California made me realise ... or something like that.

I haven't failed, Uncle Stanley, is what I wanted to say to him. These were my friends. What happened with Alan and with Peter could only have happened in terms of friendship and total trust. It's the damned East Coast anti-Semitic world out there that's to blame. I was accepted here, I really was.

And then the emotional and physical ache came through. I must have been alone in that room for a long time. By the time I finally got up from the bed, I had missed dinner. I went out and started walking. Finally I found a diner where I was the only student. I had no one but myself now.

❧

Two weeks later, I sat down and wrote a long letter to Uncle Stanley. I said that I had been having second thoughts about law school, all the time I had been in Los Angeles over Christmas, but I hadn't wanted to say anything. When I got back to New Haven my thoughts became clearer, and I had reached the decision that I did not, after all, want to be a lawyer. I wanted to come home and to go into the business, if he would be willing to give me a job. I didn't ask for a specific job because I had no idea what was available or what I wanted to do. Elaine was already in the script department, as was our cousin Iris, who called herself a Communist, so there were enough Steingroves there already. I had no talent as a budding art director. I could learn one of the manual skills – painting, plastering, electrician, grip, carpenter – but that isn't why I went to college. Was there some way a youngster could begin to learn directing? Producing? I was completely ignorant of the industry I had decided to enter. I finished by assuring him that my time at Yale had been invaluable, and that I had not wasted any of my time here - or, by definition, his money. I knew that I could have written the same letter four years before, but I didn't say so.

His reply was formal. He had no views about my becoming a lawyer. It had been my idea and as a young man I was entitled to change my mind. If I wanted to learn the studio business I should put what I learned at college to one side. It would not do me any good. The best thing was a start at the bottom, and to get a sense of how things worked. I should spend some months in the construction department. I had told him that I had worked hard at building up my muscles and since I had clearly succeeded, that would stand me in good stead.

He offered me a job as a labourer, as soon as I returned to Los Angeles. I accepted. I felt that I was being punished but that it was pointless to complain. I probably deserved it, but it was pointless to think about that either. I told none of my friends what my job was going to be. I just said that I was going back to Hollywood and would find out the details once I got there.

The decision actually made my last months easier than I thought they would be. The men who had treated me as some-one they would know for the rest of their lives, the kind of man they would run into with a smiling, hearty, 'Bobby, how have you *been?*' now saw me as some guy they knew at college. Some guy who had moved thousands of miles away and with whom they had immediately and forever lost touch. Mentally I began to decouple myself from the place. I was not writing reviews because there was no longer a magazine. I spent a lot of time studying in my room. The assumption that I would see my pals all the time slipped into a habit of not seeing them.

Peter finally came back after Easter. I caught a glimpse of him a couple of times. He looked thin and distracted. His moth-er had arranged for someone to tutor him through the lectures he had missed. She apparently thought that if he got a degree and graduated, as opposed to dropping out with a nervous breakdown, there would be fewer questions in the future. I kept away. A lot of other guys did too, perhaps the reaction of the healthy to avoid the sick. No one seemed to know what the cause had been.

Finally I decided not to attend my graduation ceremony. There had been considerable discussion over Christmas about my parents making the trip at last to New Haven, to be there to see their only son graduate from college. My parents expected me to tell them about trains, to confirm the dates and to make the hotel reservation. My mother had even made me write out the names of my closest friends so she would get them right when she was introduced to them and their families. More and more though I was feeling that there was no point to it. I was immensely proud of having been at Yale but I reminded myself that I was not here on merit and that I had achieved a respectable but not memorable academic record. People thought of me now as the guy who wrote the reviews for a literary magazine that would soon be forgotten. My pals had gone their own way. After four years I was going back to a job I could have had after high school. Wrong, a labourer; I could have done that without a high school diploma. The triumphalism and self-congratulation of a graduation ceremony seemed inappropriate.

I wrote to my parents of this decision. There was no point in their coming East. I would take the train westwards the moment my finals were over. It was only when I got their reply that I took into account what this meant to them. My father made no comment about my decision. My mother added a note to his letter.

Dear Bobby,

You've broken my heart.

I love you,

Mom.

CHAPTER 13

LOS ANGELES, SUMMER 1935

I HOPED THAT my parents would get over it. The moment I saw them in Union Station I realised that I had indeed made a terrible mistake. We drove home in near silence. I piled my luggage into my little bedroom. I found an old shirt and some jeans in a drawer. That is how I went to work at Steingrove Films, as a labourer, the next day.

The following weekend, Elaine turned up. I was in my room when she arrived. I spent a lot of time there, lying on the bed and trying not to think about things. When I heard the bell I opened my door. I could hear the conversation in the hall.

'Elaine, darling,' my mother was saying to her, 'I only hope that when you're a mother, you shouldn't know such grief.'

'Where's Uncle Isaac?'

'In his study, where do you think? I brought him coffee and cake an hour ago. Do you want something?'

'Not yet, thank you, Aunt Rose. Where's Bobby?'

'In his room. If you can get in, with all those trunks. He must be hungry but I'm not going in there to ask.'

I stepped into the hallway and gave her a hug.

'Thank you for coming,' I said. 'Come in,' I invited her into my little bedroom. I had a suitcase and a trunk open, and a stack of shirts on the bed. 'I'm trying to summon up the energy to unpack,' I said. 'Please don't think I'm a coward for not having rushed over to your place. So much happened at once. What am I going to do with all these clothes? I don't need heavy sweaters and tweed jackets out here. They're too good to get rid of. And my white tie and tails.' I shook my head.

'I'm so glad to see you,' she said.

'You look great. How's life in the script department?'

'Fine. I'm still trying to persuade Daddy to let me learn how to edit. He does actually employ women in that department. The only drawback is that our cousin Iris is working down the hall.'

'Iris? Is she still a Communist? What's Uncle Jacob giving her a job for?'

'You'll see. We can have lunch.'

'Lunch? Didn't your Dad tell you? I don't think labourers are supposed to eat in the commissary.'

'You won't stay as a labourer.'

'I know that. The question is, what will I become?'

'What does Daddy say?'

'We haven't discussed it. He wants me to learn the business from the bottom up. Well, I am learning quite a lot, about how things get made. The head of the construction department is so nice. He thinks it's a joke, my working there. Everyone is nice, really. I've just got to be patient and wait for your father to forgive me.'

'Why? Do you think you're being punished?'

'Oh, Elaine, it wasn't supposed to happen like this. Coming home and ... the way I went on and on about going to law school and staying out East for good.'

'Bobby, what are you doing here?' she asked.

I laughed. 'Do you remember the last time you asked me that? I was in white tie and tails and you were in a dress by Worth and we were dancing in the Pearson mansion on Fifth Avenue, and I thought, *Is she crazy? Life doesn't get better than this*. So here I am, back in LA, living with my Mom and Dad, being a good kid, starting my life in Steingrove Films. And you still ask me that question?'

'You know what I mean. Your Mom is upset.'

'Yeah, well, when I said that I'm not staying for graduation so please don't even think of coming back East, I didn't realise what that would mean.'

'It would have meant everything to them to see their son graduate from Yale.'

'But what was the point? I'm not Phi Beta Kappa or some-thing special, I didn't get the straight A's your Dad told me to, I did all right, but I'll just be standing there with a bunch of other guys, so don't bother, you can mail me my diploma. To be honest, I just wanted to get out of there. And then I saw them standing there at Union Station and it was like someone had died. I felt guilty when I saw them, I felt guilty when we got back here, and I've felt guilty every second of every day since then. I kept telling them that I wanted to go to law school. She was probably telling everyone already about her Wall Street lawyer son. Now she can't. That's what's killing her.'

'Maybe she's just upset now.'

'You think she'll get used to it? Never. Brave face, sure, but she will never forgive me. But it's your Dad who's entitled to feel cheated.'

'You wanted a Yale education. He gave it to you.'

'I was a lousy investment.'

'You know you don't mean that.' She sat on a trunk and looked at me. 'Are you going to tell me what happened, or aren't you?'

I held up my hands. 'Let's say it was brought home to me that outside Yale, being Jewish was more significant than I realised.'

'You told me that your friends knew and didn't care.'

'That's true. But in the big wide world of Wall Street law firms and society and ...'

And Mrs Van Haessler. I suddenly had a vision of her coming up to my parents at the graduation and telling them what kind of person their son was.

'Let's not talk about that, okay? I'm back here. That's all that matters. You'll see me at the studio on Monday. I'm the guy pushing a broom.'

She considered whether or not to press me. Then she gave up. 'You need to stop brooding.'

'That's true.'

'You can write. You sent all those reviews to me. They were brilliant.'

'Thanks.'

'Write a screenplay this time.'

'Uncle Jake will make sure it never sees the light of day.' Stop brooding, she had told me. 'If I try to write a screenplay, will you read it?'

'Of course, if you don't mind my feedback.'

'Yours is the only feedback I'd listen to.'

'That's a deal then.'

'I am learning things,' I said. 'I was taking some lumber to a set a couple of days ago, and on the way back to the mill, I passed a sound stage where they were filming. I suddenly thought, "Why not go in for five minutes? No one will miss me." It's fascinating, the way they set the whole thing up.'

'I know.'

'But I heard someone say that the writers are the lowest of the low. Just factory workers, churning out pages.'

'They're not the director or the producer,' she admitted. 'But Daddy does respect them.'

'So how's life at home?' I asked.

'All right. No responsibilities. No one bothers me. I can do what I like.'

'Why don't you get a place of your own?'

'That won't answer the question.'

'And the question is?' I asked.

'Wondering when my life is going to start.'

'Join the club.'

'Don't you know anyone you can go out with?' she asked.

'Not really. I've lost touch with all the guys I knew in high school. I don't really feel like calling them up and saying I'm back. You and I could go to the movies.'

'I'd like that, Bobby.'

'Come on, my Mom is dying to feed you.'

'All right.'

'I'm being really nice to my mother, by the way,' I said.

'She loves you. She wants the best for you.'

'I know.'

We went into the kitchen where my mother was just making a pot of coffee. A freshly baked cake was on the counter.

'That looks delicious, Mom,' I said.

'Of course,' she said, turning to Elaine, 'he had to come home to get decent cooking.'

◈

I worked five and half days a week. Saturday afternoon was the only time I could do anything. One such afternoon in September I drove downtown, and browsed in bookstores. There were enough books in our house already but I was bored. I had to get out. And then I saw it.

There was a small pile, on the novels table, of a new novel: *And Some By Virtue Fall*, by George Hudson. I grabbed it. I looked at the photograph in the dust cover. It was George. So this is what he'd been doing our senior year, the reason no one saw much of him. And he had never told a soul.

The salesman saw me.

'I'm returning those on Monday,' he said. 'It's all about students at some Ivy League school who behave badly. No one is interested out here. Do you want it?'

'Yes, please.'

I rushed home, closed the door of my bedroom and started to read.

It was about me. The main character was called Joe. He was the son of an Italian grocer. Joe got into college on a baseball scholarship. I guess that sounded more plausible than getting a rich uncle to make a donation. Laced through the descriptions were all the things that George had casually picked up about me - the comment to Peter that I was ashamed of my parents, about my mother offering coffee and tasteless cake and spoiling whatever good moments I had with my father. Joe had made friends, but they weren't really friends. He was a kind of play-thing, this working-class sap who looked up to them. Joe was so naïve that he actually thought he belonged. There was one boy who maybe was a real friend, who went a little crazy when Joe started to spend his time with other students. That was as far as the relationship with the Peter character went. No one asserted that there was no sexual morality. I guess publishers had rules about that.

Everything and everyone else was there, only far more exaggerated than in reality. The parties, the arrogance, the snobbery, the obsession with clothes and sports and the drinking. Prohibition didn't matter to these young men.

'Two bad laws', the Peter character liked to say when he was getting drunk with Joe, only he never refers to what the other bad law is.

It was as if George had sensed what the outraged middle-class reader wanted to see: rich, insensitive young men from families who had probably caused the Depression in the first place, been uncaring during it and who now opposed every effort to end it. For anyone who imagined that Ivy League colleges were the habitat of spoiled brats, here was the evidence. There was a massive party to celebrate the end of Prohibition, where everyone jeers at those stupid people who never had their pet bootlegger and who had actually obeyed the law since 1919.

Alan was too easy a target to miss. There were descriptions of dorm games, which were run by this powerfully built son of an industrialist for a select group of the super-elite, the prep school boys who had spent their lives playing football and base-ball, crew and sailing, not on some inner city sand lot like the rest of the impoverished nation, but in the most expensive and well kept schools in America. When they'd finished with their ruthless competitiveness and drinking, and in an atmosphere of manliness and beer, they would talk politics. They hated FDR and everything he stood for. They thought their fathers had been suckers to fight for democracy in Europe when Europe wasn't interested in democracy. They looked forward to the day when Hitler and Stalin had a war with one another, so long as Stalin and his reds got obliterated and so long as the young English aristocrats they imagined they were emulating were safe. So long as America was untouched, the Fascists could do what they liked. And there was Joe, with his athletic prowess and capacity for drink, thinking that here at least he was their equal. After all, the boy who organised these had chosen him to go on a few adventures in New York. With Joe's good looks and the rich boy's wad of money, they could have whatever women they wanted.

A lot of the dialogue sounded familiar; too familiar. I realised that George had taken my play out of the waste paper basket and plagiarised it.

And then a woman entered the story, Denise, a sister of the industrialist. Joe was stupid enough to fall in love with her, but she used him too. It all led to a scene in Central Park where he forced himself on her. The description was frighteningly similar to what I had told George happened that morning. After that the boy carried on with his friends, as if nothing had happened, the way I had.

This from George, who told me never to tell anyone what had happened and to carry on as if nothing had happened.

Finally the book changed gear. It was Denise's story that then took over. None of this had anything to do with Diana. This was where George began to use his imagination. It was what he would have liked to think Diana would do had she indeed been the girl of his dreams. She grew up, she turned against the false values of her family and her brother's friends. It became a story of redemption, in which at least one person of her class showed that she could be a good person. Someone who dedicated her life to helping others. There was a great scene when Joe finally repents of what he did and the two of them tried to see if they could get back together but as better people. They even stood on Fifth Avenue, near an entrance to the park, as if they could bring themselves to believe that they had never gone into the park that night. In the end, it doesn't work. She has achieved something that is beyond Joe. Contrite and now abandoned by his false friends, he goes home to his father's grocery shop, wiser and sadder.

I emerged from my room long enough to have dinner with my folks and then went back. I finished it at five in the morning. I had never felt so exposed in my life.

◈

I wrote and tore up a dozen letters, and then finally sent a note to George at his parents' apartment. 'What the hell are you doing?' I asked.

He did not reply. I waited to hear from Alan as the outraged brother, but again there was silence. I was alone here, hoping that no one I knew had even heard of this book. After a while I concluded that no one had.

When I walked across the studio lot, I sometimes ran across one of my uncles. It was difficult not to see a Steingrove. They treated me with the cool politeness they would show to any labourer. I supposed they felt that I had got my comeuppance, and that I could now be left to wallow in my own failure. When I lay in bed at night I thought of my father asking Uncle Stanley to get me into Yale. For nothing. Then there was my mother who had been clinging to the story that I would be a rich Wall Street lawyer. So much for that.

I felt that at least I could remain loyal to them. When my parents went to synagogue, I went with them. During the long day of Yom Kippur I stood by my father. There were lots of reasons why God should not write me in the Book of Life for the New Year, so I confessed all of them to Him, silently, in the desperate hope that I really could put them behind me.

◈

In October, I was moved to the mailroom. Surely there was

something else I could do in order to learn the business – but as what? I was too young to know how to manage men. I had heard all about second assistant directors, whose task was to make sure that when the same scene was shot over a number of days, the actors always appeared in the same clothes and with their hair parted in the same way. While doing my mail rounds I did what I had started as a labourer. I sneaked on to the sound stage and stood at the back whenever possible, just to get a feel of the atmosphere, to see how movies got made. I was fascinated. I hadn't realised how fascinated I would become.

At least I could now dress in a jacket and tie and meet Elaine for lunch in the commissary. We were usually joined by our Communist cousin, Iris, who had dropped out of UCLA to take this job.

'Nothing very political happening here,' I once pointed out to Iris.

'Bobby, you are so blind. Hollywood is one of the most politically active places in the United States. If you heard what was said at some of the meetings I have been to . . .'

'So tell me.'

'You wouldn't understand.'

Sometimes, Elaine and I got to the commissary first. Iris never let us alone.

'Hey, what are you two plotting?' she would ask.

'Just because two people are talking together at the studio, does not mean that they are plotting anything,' I pointed out. 'But come and join us. We're all one big happy family at Steingrove Films. That's company policy.'

Iris was indifferent to sarcasm. 'I've been stuck in the most ridiculous meeting, they're trying to figure out an ending to their latest screwball comedy.' It irked me that she had already reached a stage where she went to such meetings. 'Can I have some of your pecan pie?' she asked Elaine, who had not finished hers.

'Sure.'

'I don't think I can wait until a waitress gets here, I'm starving. By the way, Hitler has beheaded another Communist. And we're worrying about how to end a screwball comedy.'

Elaine looked at me. She had warned me about what could happen and what was happening in Germany. She had been right, it was happening now. All I could think about that day was Diana Pearson's party.

'I thought beheading was for French aristocrats,' I said.

'My friend Charlotte is married to a French aristocrat,' Elaine said. 'He seemed to think it was a matter of pride that some of his ancestors were beheaded.'

'You're both hopeless,' Iris said.

I did try to write a screenplay. I talked it through with Elaine during lunch, before Iris arrived, and when we did go out to the movies together, which went some way to persuade my parents that I had not become a hermit. I was desperate not to write anything which remotely resembled anything I had done at Yale or anyone I had ever met before I entered the employment of Steingrove Films. The screenplay was based on the letters Elaine had written to me from Europe. An American girl goes to England, marries a Lord, who then gets killed in the World War; she then turns the stately home into a hotel, teaching the English about the American virtues of equality and openness. One of her American ex-boyfriends tracks her down and wants to marry her and take her home, but she won't go because the whole village had adopted her way of life and needs her to keep the place in business.

'I think it's the kind of movie you could take your girlfriend to,' I said. 'But it isn't very good. I just want to know how to write a screenplay.'

'You're learning,' Elaine said, as she took out a red pen and started scribbling comments on my typescript.

I got along with the other young man in the mailroom. Together we would add up the fan mail, and kept a chart as to who was doing best. When the envelopes were loose I read the contents. I was curious as to which the fans loved most, the person or the movie. They loved Donald Marshall, who still managed to be the heart-throb. But that was as nothing compared to Laura Hampshire. I reckoned that half the men in America went to bed dreaming about Laura Hampshire. There was also a director, Sam Price, who got letters in pink envelopes from some place in Malibu. When I picked up letters from Sam's office there was always one that was addressed to that place.

CHAPTER 14

WINTER 1936

THINGS WERE SLOW ONE AFTERNOON at the very end of December. I was idly reading the latest fan letter to Donald Marshall. I handed it to my colleague. 'Read this, it's juicy.'

The telephone rang.

'Mailroom,' I answered.

'Is that Bobby? It's Kay here. Your Uncle Stanley would like to see you, right away.'

'Is something wrong?' I was alarmed.

'No, nothing is wrong like that. I mean, nothing has happened to anyone in the family. But he wants to see you now.'

'What's happening?' my colleague asked.

'I don't know. Uncle Stanley wants to see me right away.'

'Jesus, are things that bad in this studio?' he grinned at me.

I found my jacket and retied my tie. Looking in the mirror, I ran my fingers through my hair in an attempt to make it look neat. I had decided that labourers and mailroom boys did not use the studio barber shop. I had my hair cut at a shop near my folks' house. It wasn't very good, but I was beyond caring.

'Hi, Bobby,' Kay greeted me. I had scarcely seen her since my return from Yale. 'You are a young man now,' she said. 'You've got so husky.' She opened the door and showed me in.

I was startled by what I found.

It had been a long time since I had been in Uncle Stanley's office. Labourers and mailroom boys do not get instructions from the head of the studio and even when I was in Los Angeles on my college vacations I did not go to the lot. I had forgotten that his desk was raised on a small platform so that everyone else was seated just below him. Later I was told that this was the arrangement when he wished to assert his authority on an issue. He was capable of going round and sitting next to someone when the occasion arose. It did not arise very often. Today he was seated behind his desk. Seated just below him was Laura Hampshire. I had not seen her in the flesh since the day the three of us were in this room. Laura Svensson had been transformed into an elegant, sophisticated woman who wore a smart suit and sat with her legs crossed as a permanent reminder of how good her legs were. There was also my Uncle Jake, the head of the script department, with his narrow Steingrove face and thick, round glasses and his trademark tweed suit. And Uncle Morrie, who was Laura's agent, looking like his brother Jake. It felt like a convention of the people in my family who most disliked me. The final person was a florid, overweight man whom I recognised as Sam Price, the man who conducted some kind of secret correspondence through the mailroom.

'Bobby,' Uncle Stanley ordered. 'Take a seat.' There were no empty chairs. He indicated with his hand to where there were more against the wall. I took one and carried it over, placing myself between Laura Hampshire and Sam Price and away from my uncles. 'You know everyone,' he said.

I turned. 'Miss Hampshire,' I said.

'You're Bobby. The one who went to Yale,' she remembered.

'That's right.'

'And did you get straight A's, like you promised your Uncle Stanley?'

She said it in a way that made me regret that I had ever done anything at Yale except study. 'Not exactly,' I confessed. 'But a friend of mine started a literary magazine. I wrote movie reviews. I saw every one of your movies. I gave them swell reviews.'

'Thank you,' she awarded me with a radiant smile.

'Uncle Jake,' I said. He looked as if he wanted to hit me for some reason.

'You were always such a smart aleck, Bobby,' he said. 'I hope you're satisfied now.'

'You think it's clever,' Uncle Morrie said. 'But I didn't think you had it in you.'

I looked desperately at Uncle Stanley but he did not look any more pleased than they did.

'I wasn't going to keep you in the mailroom for ever,' he said. 'You didn't need to force the issue.'

I sat there, stunned, and then the large florid man held out his hand. 'Sam Price,' he said. I shook it. It was very fleshy. 'So tell me what your experience is in the motion picture industry, Bobby.'

I swallowed. 'I've worked as a labourer for about four months. Now I'm in the mailroom. But...'

'Jesus H. Christ,' Sam said, 'am I the only person in this room who hasn't gone crazy?'

'Bobby, what the hell is going on?' Uncle Stanley started. I stared back. Surely I wasn't being fired already. Not for reading Donald Marshall's fan mail. 'You must know what this is all about.'

'I am sorry Uncle Stanley but I have no idea what anything is about right now.'

And then Laura Hampshire held up a copy of that book, *And Some by Virtue Fall.* I felt a cold fear. 'Have you read this?' she asked, kindly.

'Um, yes.'

'You never told me that,' Uncle Stanley said.

I was about to point out that I had never discussed any book I had read with him. Neither did I imagine he would be interested. This was not however the moment for that. 'It's not very good,' I said.

'Why not?' he snapped but he did not seem annoyed with my reaction.

'Well, it's highly exaggerated. I felt that it was being written for a political purpose, to stir up... class hatred,' was the phrase that came to me. 'If you were a Socialist or something...'

I noticed that the smile was gone from Laura Hampshire's beautiful face.

'Didn't the dialogue impress you?' she suggested.

That was awkward. I had written quite a lot of it. 'In a way,' I agreed.

'But the story of Denise,' she persisted. 'Forget the awful boys. Maybe forget for a moment how she's raped in Central Park.'

'Raped!' Uncle Jacob cried. I presumed he had not in fact read the book himself. 'No one told me there was a rape in this book. Has no one heard of the Hays Code? Shall I remind everyone . . .' Uncle Stanley waved his hand to make him stop.

'It wasn't rape,' I said automatically. 'I mean, I'm not sure it can be read that way.'

'But afterwards,' Laura said, 'the story of Denise. It's a story of redemption, isn't it? The story of how one young woman could redeem not just herself but her family and her whole social class. It shows that her social class isn't an enemy or a figure of fun.'

My God, I thought, she wants to play Denise. I stood up. 'I guess you have a point there, Miss Hampshire, but this discussion is getting out of my depth.'

'Sit down,' Uncle Stanley ordered. 'What's so goddamn important in the mailroom?'

'Nothing, Uncle Stanley.' I sat back down.

'Stop playing naïve,' Uncle Jake told me.

'What is going on between you and George Hudson?' He jeered at me.

'George? Nothing. I haven't seen or spoken to him since Yale.'

'So you do know him.'

'Yes.'

'And you had no idea that he was writing this book?' The cross-examination continued.

'None. He kept it a complete secret. I was browsing in a bookstore one day. I bought the book but they were sending the rest back to the publisher. The clerk said that no one wanted to buy a book like that out here.'

'I came across it in New York,' Laura explained.

Finally, Uncle Stanley got down to business.

'Your friend, George Hudson . . .' he began.

'George is no friend of mine,' I snapped.

'Why not?' Uncle Jake shot back.

I had no intention of telling him or anyone else how George had betrayed every confidence bestowed on him and had caricatured everybody who had meant anything to me over those four years, not to mention plagiarising my play and using a version of me as his main character, all for the sake of launching himself as a writer to the applause of people who didn't care that they were not being told the truth.

'He thinks highly of you,' Uncle Stanley said. 'I've just been on the telephone to him. As you will have guessed by now, Laura would like this studio to make a film adaptation of the novel, as a vehicle for her. Approaches were made to Hudson's agent and then, out of the blue, while we were having a conference this afternoon, he called me. He told me that he would sell the rights to Steingrove Films, and he isn't asking for much money. But there is one provision. You are to write the screenplay.'

I burst out laughing.

'You see,' Uncle Jake said, 'it's a joke, between the two of them.'

Sam added, 'Can you ask Bobby to go back to the mailroom and continue with this meeting?'

'It's not a joke,' Uncle Stanley said. 'The guy meant it.'

'Look, Stanley, it's all right,' Uncle Jake said. 'There are plenty of good people in the script department. We'll put together a swell treatment, which makes Laura the star. If we have to put Bobby's name on the credits somewhere, don't worry, I'll square the other guys.'

'No, Uncle Jake,' I said.

I could see it now. It was not just George saying *Sorry* for the novel. 'You can write, believe me, you can write!' That's what he'd told me. He believed it. Maybe he was correct.

I had no wish to write a screenplay about what had happened between me and Diana. I had no wish for anyone to see that movie. On the other hand, if it was going to happen and there was nothing I could do to stop it, I could at least make sure that nothing in the novel which connected Joe with Bobby Steingrove would ever be seen on screen. I was afraid that I would hate every minute of this, but I could not refuse.

'If you do that, Uncle Jake, I will tell George and he'll sue.'

'I think we should give Bobby a chance,' Laura said. 'Sam, you don't mind giving Bobby a little help, do you?'

'I'm a director, not a teacher, Laura.'

Uncle Jacob declared, 'Bobby knows nothing about writing screenplays.'

'I have been writing one.'

'You didn't tell me.'

'Elaine's been helping me with it. I didn't think you'd be interested.'

'So the answer is Yes,' Stanley said.

'Yes, I'll write the screenplay.' I announced.

'Now, I am going to tell you what to do,' Sam said, 'and you'll do it. Do you understand?'

'Yes, of course, Mr Price.'

'I'll pay you $100 a week,' Uncle Stanley said. From the expressions on the faces of the others, I reckoned that I was coming cheap but not that cheap. 'Jake, give him an office.'

'Maybe I should write from home.' I suggested, thinking that if I had to put up with Uncle Jacob and Iris looking over my shoulder, I would never write it.

'You don't have a home,' Uncle Jake said. 'I thought you just had a room. That you couldn't move for the books in that house.'

'We'll talk more after New Year's,' Uncle Stanley said.

'Thank you, Uncle Stanley. Thank you, Miss Hampshire and Mr Price.'

'How long do you need?' Uncle Stanley asked.

'I don't know. How long does it take to adapt a novel?'

'Jesus H. Christ,' Sam groaned.

'Two months,' Uncle Stanley said. The others began to protest. 'I am going to give you two months. You and Sam.'

I staggered out of the room and paused in the outer office. Kay as always was seated at her desk, ready to take in what might have just happened.

'Bobby,' she said, sounding concerned, 'you look as if a truck just hit you, but that you couldn't be more pleased. Which is it?'

'Both,' I said.

◈

Back at the mailroom, my colleague refused to believe the story of what had just happened.

'Bobby, do you know what it means to start out like this? Laura Hampshire is the biggest star on this lot. If you screw this up, you're through.'

'I know. Right now it's so unreal, I almost think I could do it.'

Just as I was getting ready to leave for home, Sam Price suddenly appeared.

'Kid,' he said. 'Okay?'

'Okay what, Mr Price?'

'Okay, you're coming to my office and we'll talk about this.'

'All right.'

'We just finished our meeting. I didn't think I'd find you here.'

'Why not?'

'You don't work in the mailroom any more.'

Sam's office was at the top of the white administration building but you reached it by an external staircase at the rear. He was wheezing by the time we got there. It was a small office, just room for his desk and some chairs and piles of scripts. He went to a cabinet and produced a bottle of Bourbon and two glasses.

'I have some water,' he said. 'Is that okay?'

'Sure.' I had barely drunk anything since I got back. My parents never touched a drop. I hadn't had a social life apart from going to the movies with Elaine and having dinner and a beer with her.

'I don't normally drink when I'm making a movie,' Sam said.

'Of course not.'

'Don't get self-righteous,' he said.

I held up my glass, expecting us to toast the success of the project but Sam had already started to drink it.

'So what is your plan?' he asked. 'What was that story about having a room and not being able to move for all the books?'

'I'm living at home with my folks. I think...' By now anything was coming into my head. 'I think I'll find somewhere to rent. Somewhere I can bury myself and not be bothered by anyone. Except you,' I hastened to add.

'Right, so hermit produces masterpiece, is that it?'

'I want to make Uncle Stanley proud of me. He's stuck his neck out. Miss Hampshire too.'

'Save that for the Academy Awards speech.'

'I've got a lot to learn,' I said. 'Which is why I'm grateful for your help.'

'Don't butter me up,' he snapped.

It was clearly going to be difficult, trying to find the right thing to say to him. 'I just thought that I shouldn't have distractions. I couldn't be at my folks', and I'd rather not sit in an office here, on the lot.'

'You obviously don't get on with your uncles. I don't mean Stanley. The others.'

'It's a long story.'

'There's plenty of gossip in this place. You know that joke about the starlet who went to bed with the wrong Steingrove?' I smiled, politely. I had not heard that one. 'That wasn't your dad, was it?' he grinned.

'My father's never worked in the business,' I said. 'He has a bad heart. He spends his time at home. He's the best-read person I know. Hence that joke about how many books there are at the house.'

'Okay. By the way, keep that perennial sophomore pecker of yours buttoned up until you figure out how things work here.'

'Don't worry. I am definitely the wrong Steingrove.'

'You are a kind of smart aleck, aren't you, Bobby? But I like the way you stood up for yourself in that meeting. So what do you really know about writing?'

'Like I said, I've been working on a screenplay. My cousin Elaine has been helping me. She's in the script department. And I've seen hundreds of movies. Including every one with Laura Hampshire in it. Being a critic made me think of how they all get put together.'

'Critic for . . . ?'

'There was a literary magazine at Yale. I wrote the reviews.'

'So you said. Friend of yours?'

'Ex-friend. George Hudson. I don't like the way he portrayed Ivy League life. It wasn't like that. It's a potboiler.'

'I only leafed through that book but it sounded as if you college boys all had a great time.'

'That isn't a picture of me,' I said. I knew I was lying but I also knew that if I said that Joe was me, I would never hear the end of it.

'Sounds as if you missed out on a lot of fun then. I assumed the two of you wrote it. You know, let's write a bestseller. George stays East, and becomes a writer. You go west and he makes sure you become a screenwriter. It was clever, and it worked.'

I shook my head. 'No. I was completely taken by surprise today. Either you believe me or we can't work together.'

'I don't care how this happened,' he said. 'We work together anyway. Start with a scenario, write out a treatment. Remember, a movie isn't a book. Things don't happen A, B, and C. There is no description. Sometimes dialogue gets in the way. You let the camera and the actors tell the story.'

'I figured that much out already,' I asserted.

'So maybe you won't need two months.' He poured some more Bourbon in my glass and his. 'But don't rush it. Every

Friday afternoon, come here and we'll go over what you've done. Expect to stay late. And expect to hold your liquor.'

'I thought you said you didn't drink when you were working.'

'You're the one who is going to be working on this, Bobby. Right now you're a kid who doesn't know shit. You need to loosen up. And when I get my blue pencil out, you'll sober up fast.'

'Fine.'

'And don't worry if this movie never happens,' he warned me.

'Why shouldn't it?' I demanded.

'Couldn't you tell? Your Uncle Stanley doesn't want it to happen.'

'But he just hired me. I assume he's going to pay George for the rights.'

'Don't worry, your friend will get his money and you've already got a job.' I started to protest but he went on. 'It's not the kind of movie for Laura. It's a movie Laura wants to do.'

'So?' I asked.

'Jesus, you have a lot to learn about this place. Things are not that easy. You just take your time with that script and maybe by the time you finish, she'll have something else in mind. You will have earned your points, and everyone is happy.'

I was surprised but it sounded like a reasonable outcome. I was out of the mailroom for good, *And Some By Virtue Fall* would never see the light of day.

'Like you said, I have a lot to learn. Thanks, Sam.' The Bourbon was working through me and I was feeling relaxed at last.

'I said, don't butter me up. It's your ass on the line, Bobby. If you screw this up, your uncle will just pension you off like any other family member needing a job in this business, some crap thing on the back lot so no one will even know you're there.'

'That won't happen to me, I promise.'

'Laura said you promised to get straight A's, so I know what your promises are worth.' He put the bottle away. 'So what did you do at Yale?'

'I watched every movie Laura Hampshire has ever made.'

He shook his head. 'You are a smart aleck bastard. But I think this could work. Come on, I've got to go home.'

I looked down at his desk and saw a letter in his out-tray. It had the address in Malibu that I had noted already.

He looked at me. 'You don't work in the mailroom any more.'

CHAPTER 15

A FEW NIGHTS LATER was Uncle Stanley's annual New Year's Eve party. It now happened at the Renaissance palace in Bel-Air, which was splendidly furnished with the treasures of Europe that Aunt Estelle had brought back. It was the first of the New Year's Eve parties which I positively looked forward to. I was happy to see the end of 1935. As far as I could tell, 1936 was very promising.

In the previous few days I had bought, with the help of a loan from my father, my first car, the cheapest model Chevrolet for $475. I had found a tiny house for myself near the beach in Santa Monica at $30 a month, which I would move into on the second of January.

I chose Santa Monica because it was the other side of Los Angeles from my parents and not that close to the studio. There was a bedroom, an area I could use for storage, a bathroom, a kitchen and a living-room that had room for a big sofa and a huge table where I could work and eat. I had no intention of entertaining anyone. The house was five blocks from the beach. I planned on starting each morning with a run and a swim in the sea, after warming up with my daily 50 push-ups done at a 45 degree angle. I decided that a healthy body would produce a clear head. I was also acutely conscious of the fact that it had been months since I had had sex with anyone. I needed to do something about that.

The New Year's Eve party was a white-tie affair. I was pleased to be able to wear my tails once more and the Cartier studs and cufflinks that Aunt Estelle and Elaine had given to me. As I dressed that night, I felt a sense of satisfaction. I tried to remember the last time I had felt like that. Of course, it was the night of Diana's party, when I had then come into Peter's room and found him drunk. That seemed a long time ago.

My father wore the tuxedo he had worn at his wedding. My

mother had felt that she could not afford a new dress but she knew a seamstress who could alter an old one to make it look different. They were waiting for me when I emerged from my room.

'Isn't he handsome?' my mother said. 'The writer.'

'Thanks, Mom, but wait until I starting putting pen to paper. Or paper in typewriter.'

My father's mind had been on other things. 'A house needs books,' he suddenly said. 'You must take whatever you want with you to Santa Monica.'

It was a long drive to Bel-Air, along Sunset Boulevard. We always arrived very late. My parents felt that they had to put in an appearance, having been invited as family, but it was not a very social occasion for them. They did not know the people who worked at the studio and although the other Steingroves said hello at one stage or another, they kept it short. I did not like hanging around either. I knew the house already: the vast drawing-room with the faked beams painted with grotesques and the huge velvet-covered sofas; the dining-room with the Venetian chandelier and the huge buffet. None of it had anything to do with me or with what I had planned for my life.

Until tonight. As we arrived at the house, and someone took the car to park, I had a sense that maybe I did belong. I was a real employee of Steingrove Films, with a specific job on a specific movie project. The rest of the family would have to come to terms with that. I was not going to pander to them, not after the way Uncle Jake and Uncle Morrie had treated me in that meeting.

The party was in full swing when we arrived, and the dancing had begun. Fortunately Elaine was near the front door.

'Elaine, that is such a beautiful dress,' my mother said. 'You look like a real princess.'

'Thank you, Aunt Rose.' She looked around, for someone to introduce them to. Luckily, there was another couple who

seemed at a loose end. The husband turned out to be a composer who had come over recently from Austria, and had been
given a job to write film music. They didn't know anyone else
at the party. They spoke a little English and my parents, as they
later told me, managed to have a long conversation in a combination of broken English, German and Yiddish.

I was glad to find myself alone with Elaine.

'Great dress,' I said. 'Paris?'

'Yes, but a while ago. I love your shirt studs.'

'Paris. A while ago.'

'My mother was furious that I didn't bother to get a new
dress for the party. I told her I couldn't be bothered.'

'You look fine,' I told her.

'That's because you don't remember what I wore three years
ago. Which was this.'

I went into what Aunt Estelle called the morning-room and
got a glass of champagne and helped myself to some caviar. It
was late and I was hungry. I looked around at the crowd of
people. Some I knew, some I recognised, and others I guessed I
would now have to get to know. I wandered around and then
stood in the hall, at the edge of the drawing-room. The dancing happened there. Donald Marshall was doing a foxtrot with
Elaine, his annual dance with her. I stood and admired them
and then realised someone was next to me.

It was Laura Hampshire. A moment before she had been in a
group, surrounded by men. How had she extricated herself so
quickly? She wore a shimmering white dress with a halter neck
that showed a good deal of her back. She looked even more
beautiful than in Uncle Stanley's office.

'Miss Hampshire,' I said.

'I think you should call me Laura, Bobby. We are going to be
working on the same movie.'

'I hope so.'

'Hope so?' she smiled. 'I thought you were hired?'

'Oh, I mean, I haven't even started on a screenplay yet.

Anything could happen. I could do a lousy job. You might not want to play Denise once you saw it.'

I must have sounded stupid because she looked at me as if I was talking complete nonsense. 'On the other hand,' she said with the authority with which she dealt with Donald Marshall on screen, 'George Hudson might know exactly what he's doing. I'm putting my money on the fact that he does.' She looked out at the floor. 'They dance well together.'

'Yes, Elaine is really good. We were both taught by Adrian, the choreographer.' For a second I wondered if I should ask her to dance but I quickly decided that would not be right. 'There's a story to this,' I said.

'Tell me the story,' she urged me. It was that voice, that low, seductive voice, which was even more effective in person.

'When Elaine was in London, she met a girl from Chicago who was completely overwhelmed when she found out that she dances with Donald Marshall. They became great friends. Went to nightclubs.'

I stopped. On second thought, that maybe wasn't such a notable story. The rest of the world was star struck; so what, to a star herself? She had been in endless movies with Donald Marshall. She wasn't Peter's sisters, who were overwhelmed with the fact that my cousin danced with him on New Year's Eve. For a moment I remembered being at the Van Haesslers.

'You're looking rather wistful, Bobby. That's not a party face.'

I smiled. 'You're right.'

I looked again at the dancers. When I looked back, Laura was gone.

As the band changed tunes, I saw Elaine coming towards me.

'Let's get some supper and talk,' she suggested.

'First a dance,' I said. 'We are the only Steingroves not to have two left feet. And if I stand here any longer, Uncle Jake will find a way to put poison in my champagne.'

'Then put your glass down,' she suggested.

The band was playing *Cheek to Cheek* and I began to sing along. 'Heaven, I'm in heaven . . .'

'I think you think you are,' she said, as I lead her around the floor.

'Don't tell me, you're going to spoil my fun. Again,' I joked.

When we finished we went into the morning-room and loaded our plates with food from the buffet.

'Let's go outside,' she said. 'Mother has put up so many braziers, it's like a hothouse out there.'

We went and sat in the loggia, overlooking the pool.

We ate for a few minutes in silence. Then I said, 'Well, it's New Year's Eve. Time for resolutions.'

'I've made mine,' she declared.

'What's that?' I asked.

'I'm moving to New York.'

'What?'

'Daddy has an agent there. She's a literary agent in her own right, but he hires her to scout for novels and plays and talented actors. He said she has good judgment. And they respect each other a lot. She told me that this afternoon, when I asked her for a job.'

'Elaine, you can't do that! I need you here.'

'What for?'

'The screenplay. You were such a help with the one I've been working on. I need to bounce ideas off you.'

'Daddy said that Sam Price is going to help you.'

'Have you ever met him?'

She shook her head.

'I've had one session with him already. It's going to be a battle between us. He doesn't want to teach some kid how to do his job. He'll eat me alive, if he can get away with it.'

'You'll stand up to him,' she predicted.

'Even if I do, I don't want to feel alone in this. You're my friend. When we were growing up you were the only one to believe in me. I don't know how many awful family occasions I only survived because you were there too.'

She ignored this. 'I've read the book,' she said calmly. 'Daddy brought it home after that meeting. He wasn't interested but he told me that I could read it. You should have told me about it first.' Her voice had gone much colder.

'No one knew George was writing it,' I said. That wasn't much of an excuse, but it was all I could think of.

'When did you read it?' she asked.

'I found it in a bookstore. Months ago. They were sending all the copies back to the warehouse. No one was interested. I couldn't believe that Laura just stumbled into it in New York.'

'Bobby, I was at that birthday party. You're Joe. And you took Diana into Central Park.'

I couldn't let this rest. 'No, she took me into Central Park. For stupid reasons of her own.' I paused. 'And then I did something that I am ashamed of. I felt that she'd been using me. We did have sex. But I swear it wasn't rape.'

'I saw you the next morning,' she reminded me. 'You did not act like someone who had just done something very wrong. You were so cool and collected.'

'I was anything but. When Peter woke me, and said someone was downstairs, I was terrified that it was the police or Alan. I was frightened for days.'

'Why? Diana was leaving the country,' she said wryly.

'That's right. And according to George she's had exactly the life she wanted all along.'

'So that makes it all right.'

'No it doesn't,' I said. 'I'm ashamed. I will be for the rest of my life. But there's nothing I can do about it. If I could get on my knees to her...'

'But knowing what had happened you still told me that you belonged,' she said. 'You carried on at Yale for three more years. George describes it all.'

'It was not like it is in the book,' I begged.

'You keep saying things like that,' she said. 'So what is the truth?'

I looked at her. 'If I tell you, will you stay here in Hollywood and not run away to New York?'

'First, I am not running away. I told you that I sat here wondering when my life is going to begin. It isn't going to begin here, so I am going there. And second, I'm not making any promises about what I'll do. I'll listen to you first.'

'All right. Peter was the first one I met. Because he wanted me.' I waited to see if she was shocked, but she just looked ahead, towards the pool. 'They told me, Peter and George and Alan, that what they believed was that there was no sexual morality. And when I had sex with Peter, I thought, "That's right, there can't be any because I don't see what's wrong with this." Do you want me to go on?'

'Yes.'

'We told each other anyway that we weren't queer, we were just enjoying ourselves. In my case, it's true. I think Peter must have always been afraid that he was, but I kept telling him not to worry, girls would flock to him. And then Alan wanted a partner in his escapades. With women. That was me. Dorm games aren't about sex, but that's just too hard to explain. I enjoyed all of it. I freely admit that. I assumed that after graduation we'd put all that behind us and everything would be normal. Only Peter cracked up over Christmas and his mother blames me for everything. Which is another reason I couldn't face living in New York, with her on the rampage.'

'No sexual morality. How could you possibly have believed that? That's not your parents.'

I hesitated but then went on. 'Do you remember after the screening of *The Countess and the Cowboy*? The director cornered me. He hated me so much for what I did and he told me what the problem was: whenever he had a fight with Sonya, she'd go and have sex with your father, and then your father would say that things had to be done Sonya's way. There. I couldn't tell you that at the time. Maybe I shouldn't have told you that now.'

She stared ahead. 'When we were in Europe, Mother finally sat down and told me that, so long as she was Mrs Stanley Steingrove, she didn't care what Daddy did. That's the point of this house and the things she bought, and her beautiful clothes. So everyone would say how lucky he was, that she wasn't like the other wives who still looked or acted as if they had just left the Lower East Side. So he would never divorce her.'

I nodded.

'When Philip asked me to marry him in London, I knew how much he wanted me.'

'You told me that.'

'But I thought, when that wears off, what will happen. I don't want a marriage like my parents', Bobby.'

'Of course not. You're absolutely right,' I told her.

She turned to me. 'You just said there is no sexual morality. Why should you care about adultery?'

'No one should be hurt,' I said.

'Well, that's a nice distinction,' she said. 'Is that going to be the theme of your screenplay? So long as Diana or Denise hasn't been hurt.'

'Stop it, Elaine. You said you read the book. George exaggerated everything in order to show how awful young upper-class men can be. But he believes in redemption. That's the whole point of what happens to Denise. That never happened to Diana. That's the story I have to write.'

'With Joe not in it.'

'Joe has to be in it.' I sighed. 'Look, your father doesn't want this movie. He only bought the rights to please Laura. Sam told me that by the time I finish the screenplay, she will probably have forgotten all about it.'

'What about your career then?'

'I will have shown your father that I can do something.'

'I don't think you need me here for that,' she declared.

'Hey, what you two plotting over there?' It was the voice of cousin Iris.

'No one is plotting anything.'

'You two look very serious,' she said as Iris came up and sat next to Elaine with her plate of food.

'It's New Year's Eve, we're thinking about resolutions and the future,' I said.

'You mean how you're going to write the script of the next Laura Hampshire prestige project.'

'It kind of looks that way.'

'You'll never do it, Bobby.'

'Come on, Iris, do me a favour and get off my back.'

'I'm only being realistic. It's a big project. I'd be scared to take it on. If you weren't so nasty to me all the time, I'd offer you some help.'

'I don't need your help. Sam Price is going to make sure I get it right.'

'So you say. By the way, I notice that you don't attend family Seders any longer but since we are all here together tonight, I am going to ask you to leave my brother alone.'

'Gladly.'

'You don't remember how you punched him in the stomach so he threw up all the way home in the car.'

'Oh God, that. I was teaching him some manners. He was rude about my dad.'

'You must have said something terrible to him because he wouldn't say anything in the car. I got it out of him. You hit him for nothing. I thought you'd ruptured his spleen.'

'I didn't hit him that hard, and I'm a lot stronger now.'

'You see, you're not even sorry. Even after all this time. Is that what you do? You hit people? I hadn't thought of that before. That you might actually be violent. Have you done anything else violent since then?'

When she said that, I looked at Elaine. I could tell what was going through her mind. How it all fit, the punch, Central Park, dorm games. I wanted to say, 'It wasn't like that', but she was getting tired of hearing it.

'God, I hate this family,' I said.

Iris stood up, with her plate in hand. 'I can see that I'm not wanted. I was actually trying to be nice. You're impossible, Bobby. I know that Elaine is the only person who likes you. I hope you're grateful to her at least.'

'Elaine is leaving,' I said dully.

'Where?'

'I'm going to New York,' she said. 'I'm going to work for Peggy, Daddy's agent.'

'That sounds like so much fun! There's so much going on there. I could put you in touch with some people if you're at all interested in politics.'

'More Communists?' I asked.

'Bobby, if you had any idea what is going on in Europe right now you would realise that the Left are the only people who are standing up to Fascism. You probably have never even heard of Hitler or Mussolini.'

Elaine said, 'I'll think about it, Iris.'

I was left alone with Elaine.

'I see. So it's a political thing,' I said.

'It's a lot of things,' she said. 'And I'd feel better if you were a little more understanding about how I feel.'

'Try me,' I said.

'I'm going to New York,' she said. 'I think the conversation went downhill after I said that the first time.'

'Look, do you remember? You said yourself, after that Seder, you could go into the business. Become an editor, not just someone in the script department. I'm just starting out. If I make a success of this, and I swear to you that I will, we could be a team.'

'Bobby, I don't want to stay here any longer.'

'If you're running away from something, I can tell you, it doesn't work. We really are the chosen people and this really is our chosen city. I am going to succeed. That's my New Year's resolution. I want you here to see it.'

She got up. 'I don't want to see what's going to happen.'

I followed her back into the house. Uncle Stanley was standing on the stairs, making his traditional New Year's Eve speech about the glorious future of Steingrove Films, the upcoming movies in particular and the United States of America in general. Then it was midnight, the band played Auld Lang Syne, and everyone was kissing, hugging, shaking hands.

I looked around, but Elaine was no longer there.

CHAPTER 16

SETTING UP HOUSE FOR MYSELF was not difficult. I only wanted a place where I could sleep and write, and that's what I got: a place that was completely and totally mine. I refused everything my mother offered to loan me. I knew I wasn't coming back, so I might as well make a start on my own.

She kept saying, 'I apologise. I never taught you how to cook or look after yourself. Whenever you came back from Yale, I was so glad to see you, I just wanted to look after you. I don't know how you're going to survive out there.'

'I'll learn, Mom,' I promised her.

I discovered that boiling and grilling were not difficult and that in a house without much furniture, it was easy to sweep up. There was a Chinese laundry two blocks away. That took care of housekeeping.

I began each morning with exercise. It was wonderful being so near to the beach. I would go out and run or just walk and certainly have a swim regardless of how cold the ocean was. Then I came back, had a shower, and breakfast, and went to work.

When Elaine set off for New York, I loyally went to Union Station to see her off, along with Aunt Estelle. Uncle Stanley was busy at the studio. I waved goodbye and then got in my car and drove all the way back to Santa Monica. I closed the front door behind me and basked in the sense of being alone. It was good for me. I started by rereading the novel, twice. By the time I finished, I no longer had an emotional reaction to it. I was not Joe. Joe was a character. He could be anything I wanted him to be in the screenplay. Then I started to write the scenario that Sam had suggested, and to outline the scenes I thought should be in the movie.

I was due to see Sam every Friday afternoon but in addition once a week I went to the studio on my own. I resumed my habit of slipping into sound stages and standing in the darkness to watch what was going on. What struck me before was how many people were involved in the shooting - the electricians, the grips, the make-up woman, the script girl, the director... far more people than the number of actors. Now what I saw was how short the scenes were. When I went to the theatre in New York, I could watch the entirety of the performance in a couple of hours, and how the actors made that emotional arc from their entrance to the curtain. In the movies, it was much shorter. The joy or anguish they felt just before or after this scene might be filmed days or weeks before or later. It meant that what happened in this scene had to matter in itself but also had to connect. And as Sam warned me, sometimes they did not have to say anything at all.

I had gone into sexual hibernation after returning to Los Angeles but I had no intention of remaining celibate. If nothing else there had been logistical difficulties: I could hardly bring a woman back to my parents' house. Anyway I had no idea where to meet a woman in LA. Santa Monica was different. People had moved out here precisely to avoid the morals of established neighbourhoods, and the combination of sun and sea had opened everything up. It was cheap to live here, and so it attracted artists and writers. There was a bohemian disregard for what was left of bourgeois morality in the rest of the city.

It wasn't difficult to find the right bars or the right women. It was what Alan Pearson used to pay for, but one did not pay here. People did it because they wanted to, because they were artists and so free from all restraint. 'I'm Bobby, I'm a writer,' I would say. That's all they needed to know. A writer who lived in a crummy little house.

'Where did you learn all that?' one woman asked me after a sweaty session.

'Second hand from a Paris brothel,' I replied.

'You're so full of shit, Bobby.'

'Fine. Don't believe me,' I said. 'It's nice to think that I have that much imagination.'

✦

Once every two weeks I loyally went to my folks' for dinner.

'Your Aunt Leah' - she was the wife of Uncle Al, the art director - 'is killing herself over you writing that screenplay,' my mother told him. 'Killing herself. She keeps saying, "What about my Iris? Why didn't Stanley ask Iris to write the script? This is a woman's movie, what does Bobby know about women?"'

'I don't think Iris has that much writing experience,' I pointed out.

'I said, "My Bobby is a brilliant writer. He was the official critic at Yale. Everyone read every word he wrote."'

'I wrote reviews for some guy's literary magazine,' I said. 'It was probably only our friends who read them.'

'Iris writing a woman's picture! What does she know about being a woman? Nothing,' my mother pronounced. 'Look at her. She has the face of a Steingrove. Who is going to look at Iris? You have to feel sorry for her.'

'It's genetics,' my father pointed out gently.

'Ah,' my mother said, and stroked my cheek, 'my Bobby looks exactly like my father, let him rest in peace, and he was the handsomest man anyone had ever seen. People would tell my mother that.'

'And she would say, "Handsome faces don't pay the bills",' my father reminded her.

My mother waved this away. 'That was her joke. You know, when someone pays you a compliment, you can't just take it, they may be giving you the evil eye while they're doing it.'

'Grandma was warding off the evil eye?' I asked, incredulous.

'You don't think there is an evil eye? When you were a baby I never let you out of the house unless I'd tied a red ribbon around you. You don't remember that. But people would come up and say, "What a beautiful baby", and you could never be sure.'

I looked at my father, who was studying what was on his plate. 'Well, if they gave me the evil eye, it didn't do any harm,' I said.

'But you still have to be careful,' my mother warned. 'Do you have a girlfriend yet?'

'I wouldn't say that.'

'And you didn't have one at Yale?'

'Not really.'

'They know. Those women know that about a man.' She nodded. 'You've got a good job now and they'll look at your handsome face and they'll think, "Aha!". I only ask one thing, Bobby: don't bring me home a Gentile.'

'Mom, I've only just got a job. I'm not getting married.'

'It doesn't start with marriage. It starts with going out with them. They know what they're doing and you don't. They're all charm and smiles, and once you're married,' she shook her head. 'They're all anti-Semites.'

'Mom, I've got to get back,' I said.

'To what? This is still your home.'

'I've got to write, remember?'

I got up from the kitchen table where we ate. I could see the look of disappointment on my father's face.

'I just wanted to talk to you about something I've been reading,' he said.

'Next time, Dad, I promise.'

'I started the book, by the way.'

'What book?'

'*And Some By Virtue Fall.*'

It was the moment I was dreading. 'Oh yes?'

My father shook his head. 'I didn't like it. The first few chapters. That boy, Joe, he comes from a poor family but he has courage, he's made himself a really good ball player, without any help. Those boys he meets, they just look down on him. It's not nice. It's something about the author, I think.'

'Don't bother to finish it,' I said. 'Wait for the movie.'

'That's right,' my mother said. 'We'll wait for the movie. That's where the genius writer is.'

⬥

I worked away in happy solitude but every week Friday after-noon came around. I got in the car with a sheaf of papers and drove to the studio to meet Sam Price.

'Kid,' he said, when he saw me on the first Friday in January. He didn't ask me to sit down, I just found a chair while he got the Bourbon bottle, two glasses, and a jug of water. 'Let me see the treatment,' he said. I handed it over. I sat there sipping the drink and beginning to relax when he finished. 'This isn't a treatment,' he said. 'It's a plot summary.' He had clearly been expecting this. He reached for a stack of folders and handed them over. 'Read these, and start all over again.' He took my efforts and threw them in the waste-paper basket. Then he put the stopper on the Bourbon bottle. I got up, said goodbye, and left.

On the second Friday we began in the same way. This time though he greeted me with: 'What crap have you brought this time?'

I did not rise to the bait but handed over what I'd written. He read it, and then threw it on the desk. 'All right. Have you written any scenes?' I handed over a dozen typed pages. He read them quickly, while I sipped my drink.

'This is Joe?' he asked.

I nodded.

He threw the pages into the waste-paper basket but this time he poured me another drink. 'I remember the old man. Your grandfather,' he said.

'What about him?'

'You sound as if you didn't like him.'

'No one did. The one thing you learn as a Steingrove is that all his sons hated him. No one cried at his funeral,' I repeated the damning verdict. It was no secret. He was a grim, silent man who lived on his own because no one in the family wanted him living with them. I could barely remember exchanging many words with him. He only seemed to like his granddaughters. He even had a smile for Iris.

'I remember seeing him walking around the lot,' Sam said. 'I guess Stanley put him on the payroll. He always had his head down. That was because he was picking up loose nails that some labourer had dropped. I couldn't believe it. Finally I went up to him one day and asked what he was doing. Do you know what he told me?'

'No.'

'He said they shouldn't waste money at his son's studio.' He laughed. 'So why don't Al and Morrie and Jake like your father? They had the same terrible dad.'

I couldn't see the point of this conversation but I went along with it. 'Ask them.'

'I'm asking you,' he said.

'For one thing, they're big successes. My father lives on what Uncle Stanley gives him. They call him the bookworm. That's not a compliment.'

'Where's the charity? He's their brother, that should count for something.' Sam asked, 'There must be something more. Why did they hate their father so much?'

'I don't know,' I felt slightly irritated. 'He was a poor man living in a slum on the Lower East Side with five sons. I guess the only way he could discipline them was to beat them. Shout at them and beat them.'

'And your Dad helped him? As the eldest, did he have to impose discipline too?'

'No. Nothing like that. All my father wanted was some peace and quiet. Which you don't get in a slum with a new baby every year or two. Also he was a scholar. He was the one who wanted to finish high school,' I was dredging up family stories now. 'The others weren't interested in books. They just wanted to go out and do things. Get a job. Make money. Chase girls.'

'Tell me again. What did your dad do before the doctors said he was too sick to work?'

'He was a mailman,' I said.

'A mailman?' Sam cried. 'Stanley Steingrove runs a studio, his brother Morrie is one of the smartest agents in Hollywood, Al is a really fine art director, and Jake knows who to hire in the script department. And their brother was a mailman?'

I could feel myself getting angrier. 'It gave him time to read. It's all he wanted. He doesn't have their ambition. He doesn't have any ambition.'

'But you do, Bobby,' he bore down on me. 'You have ambition pouring out of you. You want to succeed so badly, you'd do anything, I bet. You'd put up with anything. You'll put up with anything your friends do to you. So long as you don't turn into your father. Anything is better than turning into your father.'

I stood up. I could feel my fists clenching. I didn't think I could take the humiliation any longer.

As I stood there, Sam poured another glass. 'Sit down, Bobby. I got you right. I knew I would.' I sat down, slowly. 'Now you're ready to write Joe.'

I am not sure how I got home that Friday evening. I was pretty drunk and still furious. I must have obeyed the traffic lights and what the other cars were doing because I did arrive safely. I parked the car in front of my house, went in, and starting to pound away at the typewriter. Just what Sam wanted me to do, damn him.

◆

The next Friday, Sam read what I had written. This time he threw it on the desk and started to make markings with a red pen. He did not throw anything more into the waste-paper basket.

At the end he said, 'By the way, stop being the ghost of Steingrove Films.'

'What are you talking about?'

'The way you sneak on to sound stages. Everyone thinks you're there to spy for your uncle on what the company is doing. They are going crazy.'

'I'm learning the business,' I said.

He pointed to the pages on his desk. 'This is your business. The actors and I will make the movie.'

◈

The next Friday he said, 'There was a scene in the book, where Joe goes home to talk to his father. He's scared about what is happening to him there. He doesn't know if he can trust his friends. Or Denise. His father is the only man he can trust. But just as he's about to talk, his mother walks in with a tray of coffee and cake and spoils the whole thing. So he goes back to college and makes all the mistakes he wanted to avoid. It's a crucial scene. Why haven't you written it in the screenplay?'

It was the last thing I wanted millions of Americans to watch, starting with my parents who were of course the people George was portraying.

'It's not needed,' I said.

'Of course it's needed. It's crucial. It's when he realises that he can't connect any longer with his family, and he's at the mercy of his so-called friends.'

'I'll think of something.'

'Damn it all, if you can't see why, you shouldn't be writing this screenplay,' Sam shouted.

'I said I would think of something.'

'Goddamn it, Bobby, why are you doing this? Your Uncle Jake made you a good offer, he'd get some real writers to do the script, you could put in a couple of scenes, your name would go on the screen credits and we could start shooting this.'

'George made a condition...'

'George can go to hell. He's sold the rights. It probably isn't even in the contract.'

'I've been hired to do this,' I pointed out as coldly as I could.

'I know all about the deal you and George made from the start.'

'I told you, Sam, that isn't true.'

'Yeah yeah yeah. You're a writer. You can write this. But you've got to finish it while Laura is still young enough to play an eighteen-year-old.'

I was about to stand up again but then I sat back. I knew I had to take this.

'Have another drink,' Sam said. He sat back. 'What about Central Park?' he asked.

'What about it? I guess they can't do more than kiss.'

Sam shook his head. 'There's kissing and there's kissing. Ask the Production Code Administration. Just get them into the park. The actors and I will figure the rest out.' He poured himself another drink.

'I can do this,' I insisted.

'Yeah, yeah, yeah,' he said again.

'Look, I know you don't want to make this movie,' I said.

'Who told you that? I'll do it. The more I think about it, the better it sounds. I'm busy with another picture now. That's why I'm not on your back to finish this goddamned screenplay by next week.'

I saw how the liquid left in the bottle kept going down.

'So what did you college boys get up to?'

Lecture time was over, and there was apparently nothing further to discuss about the progress of the screenplay. It was time to humiliate me again.

'In what way?' I asked.

'Bobby, what do you think I mean?'

Having emasculated me through my apparent inability to write the screenplay, it felt as if Sam was now turning his guns on my sexual prowess. Well, fine. 'I had a good friend who knew a lot of girls and he and I used to go down to the city and enjoy ourselves. Do you really want to know the details?' I dared him.

'You're a Steingrove,' Sam said. 'You'll be all right. And you're in Hollywood.' He leaned over his desk. 'Do you know how many parts there are in movies compared to the number of girls who want to get into the movies?'

'Is that why you became a director?' I asked.

'I'll take the Fifth on that one. I'll give you a piece of advice.' I saw how red Sam's face was now. 'A "Thank-you" lay is a helluva lot better than a "Can I have the part?" lay.' I nodded. 'She's much more relaxed, and she's got to know you. A woman needs to know what a man really wants, and in a thank-you lay, she gives it to you.'

'I'll remember that,' I said. 'Right now, I'm not much of a catch.'

Sam ignored me. 'Laura Hampshire was the best lay in Hollywood.' He waved his hand. 'It was years ago, it was basically her first picture. It was the best thank-you lay of my life. I wouldn't dare touch her now.' He looked at me.

I laughed. 'Like I said, I'm no catch for any woman.'

'I bet that's what you tell all the girls as you steer them towards your bedroom.'

'Maybe you ought to make a movie about that, about a woman who learns when to lay the director.'

Sam laughed. 'Yeah and get kicked out. I'm not ready to make porn movies yet.' He shook his head. 'Laura's a great woman and a great actress. And I've been dying to direct her again.'

'So you think she still wants to play Denise?'

'You bet. She just needs to persuade your uncle.'

'I get you, Sam.'

Sam got up. 'I gotta go.'

'You're not driving, are you?' I asked.

Sam looked at me as if I had suggested he was unable to get an erection. 'The best way to sober up is to look at the steering wheel of car,' he said. 'Go home, Bobby, and come back next week with something better.'

◈

By the end of January it felt like I was losing sense of time. The days stopped having the same disciplined timetable that I had made for myself at the start. Some days I would wake at 3 a.m., sit at the typewriter until 5, and then sleep until 11. Other days I would be at work by 8 in the morning and go straight through to 10 at night. I still managed to do my push-ups and to have a run and a swim. I was pleased to see that I was losing the extra weight I had put on while eating my mother's cooking. I would sometimes walk down to the ocean and just stare, trying to clear my mind. Or I would drive down to one of the local bars, have a few drinks and look at the others, in the hope that they might say or do something I could incorporate into a scene. I was afraid that I was losing the sense of how real people talked.

One night I went into a bar, sat on a stool and ordered a Scotch and water. I did it without thinking. The smell of Scotch reminded me of Peter Van Haessler and his bootleg liquor. As if on cue, a male voice said, 'Can I buy you a drink?' He was a slender, blond young man who came and sat next to me. 'I'm new to LA and I'm leaving tomorrow already,' he explained. 'Got to head north.'

'LA is that kind of town,' I observed.

I brought him back to the house and persuaded him without difficulty to do all the things that I used to do with Peter. He wanted to as much as I did. But I was also trying to remember what had bound Peter and me together, something more of course than the sex.

'Do you trust me?' I asked the man at one point.

'Sure,' he grinned. 'You're different. A lot of guys, once you get them into bed, they're so scared and screwed up, it's no fun for either of us. You're really enjoying this. Without any - what is it?'

'Inhibition,' I suggested. 'Without inhibition.'

'That's it. Where did you learn that?'

'It's all part of a college education.'

'Sorry, I didn't go to college. But yeah, I do trust you.'

When the man fell asleep, I sat up in bed, smoking a cigarette. Trust, that was it. Joe trusted his new friends with his loyalty to them, and they trusted him with their secrets and arrogance. That's what I had to convey in the screenplay. Without a hint of sex. Trust. And betrayal in Central Park. And then redemption, but not for Joe.

I wondered who could play Joe. I thought of the stable of Steingrove actors, but none of them seemed quite right. He ought to be handsome, that went without question, as well as big and strong. But how? He was a great baseball player but somehow he would not have the grace of a really practised athlete. I decided that he got strong by doing the chores in his father's grocery store. He was the only boy in a family of girls so he had to do all the lifting and carrying. But it was brainless work. That's when he started dreaming of going to an Ivy League college. Working in the grocery store gave him time to dream. And it made him strong. He would have the body of a transplanted peasant and the head of an Adonis. That would fit. Everything in the movie had to fit.

◆

One night I was working away at my desk. It was about nine o'clock. I had made a typical dinner for myself - I grilled a steak and boiled some potatoes. I ate at the same table where I worked. When I finished, I just put the plate to one side. I was not really aware of the fact that a car had pulled up outside the house. I kept the front door open, to air the place, with the screen door locked. It wasn't cold, at least not the cold I had got used to in New Haven. I never bothered to close the front curtains. I owned nothing that was worth stealing, apart from a pile of papers called the script. Finally I looked up and saw a woman wearing a long coat and a big hat walk up the path. She was halfway up the path when I realised that it was Laura Hampshire. Unannounced.

I met her at the door. 'Hi,' I said, 'this is a surprise.'

'Should I apologise?' It was that voice. 'I should've called first. But I don't know your number. And in the circumstances I didn't want to ask.'

'Come on in.' I opened the screen door for her. 'It's not much,' I said, 'but please sit down.' I moved some papers I had strewn on the couch.

Laura walked around the room. She stood in front of the large chart that I had pinned to the wall.

'I call it the action chart,' I explained. 'Sam told me to do it. You can follow all the scenes, see what's happening. To make sure things get resolved. So it doesn't just go from one thing to another. So it works like a movie is supposed to.'

'Good idea.'

She looked at my desk. She looked at the sheet that was in the typewriter. She read out:

> 'DENISE: You think I am using you? What do you
>   think they do?
> 'JOE: They don't. They're my friends.'

'Remind me, what is going on here?'

'They're in Central Park. He realises that she's just been play-ing him along all this time. So she taunts him with the fact that he's just the plaything of his friends, to amuse themselves with until they graduate. But he still believes that they are his friends, that they like him for himself.'

She shook her head as if she were considering whether or not she wanted to say that. 'Maybe you could think of something more subtle for her to say.'

'Frankly, this scene is driving me crazy. Sam says that I just have to get them to Central Park and he and the actors will fig-ure out what to do. But that's cheating. I've got to figure it out. Unless the audience believes in what Joe and Denise are doing, they won't believe them for the rest of the movie.'

'You'll find a way,' she said.

I was not sure that she believed that or whether she was just being polite.

She sat down on the couch and took her hat off. It made it easier to see how beautiful she was.

'I'm sorry again for not calling. But I was afraid that if I did, you'd worry about why I wanted to see you. And then I'd waste half my time reassuring you.'

'It's all right,' I said, 'I really was just working here, on my own. I don't see anybody when I'm here. I just write and think and then I go out and look to the ocean or maybe have a swim. And then go back to writing. I can't remember any longer. I hope that doesn't sound crazy.'

'Nothing is usual about this project,' she smiled.

'You can say that again. Look, can I get you something? Something to drink?'

'No, thank you.'

'So...'

'I wanted to know how you're getting on.'

'I'm making real progress now,' I said. 'I'll be honest, it was really difficult at first. And Sam is not the easiest teacher in the world.'

'No,' she said calmly. 'I knew that but I didn't want to scare you. He either makes you or he destroys you. I had to guess what would happen to you. What do you think?'

'I think he's made me. It's beginning to flow now. And he isn't throwing what I've written into his waste-paper basket any more.'

She nodded. 'What else has he told you?'

'That he wants to do the picture. He wants to direct you again.'

She nodded.

'What has Sam told you?' I asked back.

'The same. He's impatient. He has to finish another movie first. He doesn't cut corners. He wants to get that right. But when he's ready, he expects you to be ready. Will you be?' she asked.

'Yes,' I said definitely. What else could I say to Laura

Hampshire? 'And it's too late for Uncle Jake to find someone else, I think. I guess it all depends on you.'

'Did you think I was going to give up on this?' she looked a little offended.

'To be honest, I think Uncle Stanley wanted you to forget all about it.'

'That's probably true,' she said, 'but I haven't forgotten. Can I tell you a secret, Bobby?'

'Of course.'

'I've told him that if he won't let me do this, I'll go on suspension.'

'Gosh.'

'I grew up doing the cooking and mowing the lawn,' she smiled. 'So threatening to cut off my salary doesn't get very far with me.' She paused. 'So it all depends on you. You've got to produce a screenplay that's good enough. If it's good enough, then maybe he'll agree. Do you see?'

'Surely . . .' I began. Surely this couldn't depend on me. Whether or not it did, I could hardly let her down. 'I'll do it, Laura. I promise.'

She got up and stood in front of me. 'I want to do this movie. I want to play Denise.'

'Am I allowed to ask why?'

She thought about it. 'Yes. It's because Denise grows up. She's ghastly at the beginning, but then she grows up. She grows up in the most amazing way. If only you can bring that to life. That doesn't happen very often in the movies. Have you noticed? There are characters but they don't really change. Just . . .'

'"The good end happily and the bad end unhappily. That is what we mean by fiction",' I quoted.

'Did you write that?'

'No, Oscar Wilde.'

'Then you should understand. I am feisty or charming or funny or whatever your Uncle Jacob has written for me, but that's me, from beginning to end. I'm allowed to be a tough and independent woman sometimes. Donald Marshall grows up, he has to grow up because there has to come a time when he decides that he wants to marry me and he knows that he has to deserve me. So basically I have to carry on being feisty or charming or funny and patient until he gets there.'

'I noticed,' I said. 'I was thinking of writing about that in my review, but then I decided that would look like criticism. I only said nice things about Steingrove Films. I was pretty nasty to everything else. That's what the editor wanted me to do.'

'Who was?'

'George. George Hudson.'

'Of course. That's how George Hudson knew you could do this. I don't want this screenplay to come out of your Uncle Jacob's department. This isn't just a job for you, Bobby, is it? It isn't just a ticket out of the mailroom.'

'No. And don't worry, I think about you every time I am writing about Denise. I think of the way you move and talk.'

'No', she said, definitely. 'That was me doing charming pictures with Donald. This has to be different. I want to be someone I haven't been before. A moment ago I thought you understood that,' she said firmly. 'I'm not leaving here until you do.'

'I do understand. Thank you for telling me.'

She brushed her hand against my cheek. 'I remember you. You were the boy who started it all. The one who said, "It stinks." Do you remember?'

'Of course.'

'How did you know to say that?'

'Well the movie wasn't very good and I could tell Uncle Stanley wanted to get rid of it. I tried to say something that would let him do what he wanted to do. It just came to me. As if it were my destiny,' I added.

'All right,' she said, 'I want you to repeat that. Think of what other people want and you are going to let them get it. Think yourself into these characters, every one of them because every one of them is different and has to come over that way.

Everyone has to talk differently and act differently. Do you understand?'

'Yes.'

'Can you imagine how Joe feels?'

'Of course.'

'And Denise? Denise is on a journey. She has to get there.'

'I know.'

'Then get to work,' she said.

I took her hand and held it up to my lips. Then I remembered what Sam had said about Laura. I let go of her hand.

She smiled. 'Goodnight, Bobby. I'm looking forward to the result.'

I walked with her to her car and stood there until she drove away. Then I went back inside, and closed and locked the front door. I sat back down in front of the typewriter. For the first time, I felt inspired. I was sure that Uncle Stanley and Sam Price knew nothing about this visit. That was fine. I would write a great part for Laura Hampshire and no one would ever think that Bobby Steingrove was Joe.

CHAPTER 17

E LAINE WROTE:
    Dearest Bobby,

I love New York. It has nothing to do with your New York. Peggy (agent) lives in the Village, in a house she inherited from her grandparents. She was an orphan and they brought her up. It's very old, very thin, and very tall. You would never have seen this neighbourhood. Real people live here and the reality of the city isn't far away, I run into panhandlers every day. But inside the house, the place is buzzing with people and ideas. You can't move for all the books. I told her your father would feel right at home here. The house is full of young authors and actors. She calls them her orphans. I can't remember which of them is in work at any one time. Plays open and close so quickly here. They all shout and argue with one another.

One of my jobs is to feed them. Peggy can't cook but I am learning, fast, in this old kitchen in the basement with an ancient edition of Fanny Farmer as my teacher. The orphans are all hungry but some are too busy talking to eat. I've learned how to distribute the food, a little to those who won't eat it anyway and a lot to those who don't get a square meal anywhere else. They all say that I am learning the principles of socialism. Which they approve of. They talk about the Socialists and the Communists making an alliance. They call it the Popular Front. It's going to happen in Europe. Bobby, are you even aware of what's going on in the outside world?

You know, Iris can be irritating but she was right, what she said on New Year's Eve. I am becoming more and more aware. This was definitely the right decision, to come here. I am so sorry you didn't see that then and that we argued, but I pray that you've begun to understand. It's funny how we both want the approval of the other, but that's the way it's always been, hasn't it?

My real job is to go to every single play being performed on the island of Manhattan. I am scouting for playwrights and actors, but I still have so much to learn. One of the orphans usually comes with me and sometimes knows one of the younger members of the cast, so we go to the stage door afterwards and ask them to join us for a drink. It's such fun.

How is the screenplay going?

Love,

Elaine

✦

I replied:

Dearest Elaine,

I'm sorry we argued too. I hate that. So let me say right away that if you think you've done the right thing by going to New York, then I'm behind you 100 per cent. All right? I was being a bit selfish but you know - well, let's forget it.

In respect of the outside world, I read a newspaper every day but they are pretty lousy in this town. What do you expect from Hearst? I don't have a radio, it would distract me from my job. Which is to write that screenplay. It's going okay. It will be more than okay if Sam Price doesn't kill me off first. More and more I think this movie is actually going to happen. Wouldn't that be something! But it scares me for all kinds of reasons, one of which only you know.

I'll have time for the outside world when the movie is in the can. How's that for Hollywood talk?

Don't get too converted to Socialism and please leave Communism to Iris. I still think FDR is swell but lots of guys think he's gone too far and your orphans probably think he hasn't gone far enough. The guy can't win but he'll get the last laugh in November, just you wait and see.

Love,

Bobby.

◆

Much later, she wrote:

Dearest Bobby,

I finally got a glimpse of the kind of world you wanted to be part of. Remember my Chicago friend, Charlotte, who married the French aristocrat? They were in town for a couple of days, en route. Some people on their ship were having a huge coming home party and invited them and Charlotte insisted they invite me too. I adore Charlotte, we became friends at such a weird time of our lives, but I didn't really want to go. But Peggy said it was good for dialogue, I have to listen so often to actors talking like upper-class people on stage, that I should find out whether upper-class people really talk like that.

The reality is worse. The party was in some huge apartment and there was so much drink and food I was appalled, when I think of the panhandlers around my part of town. Some man said that if he were Italian he'd be a Fascist too. Charlotte dragged me away just after that. I don't know what I would have done.

But I did pick up some gossip. About your friend Alan Pearson. They think he's some kind of boy genius who's showing Roosevelt that private enterprise works better than the New Deal. Can you believe it?

Also he's been working his way around a lot of married women so they've banded together to find him a woman whom he can marry and who can keep him under control. I asked about George, very casually, and was quickly told that his was a name that should never be mentioned. If he meant to burn his boats, he has.

Love,

Elaine.

◈

That letter was only written in the spring. By then the screenplay was finished, but not without further fights with Sam. We went through the whole thing, all over again. Sam took his red pen and scribbled comments on every page. He drew arrows to show where things needed to be shifted, where scenes should be somewhere else or cut out altogether. It was too long and too wordy. But the main structure, the route of the plot, the role of the characters, I wasn't really asked to change those.

'That scene at the party where they first meet,' Sam pointed out. 'Too much talk. This is a Romeo and Juliet story, isn't it?'

'I don't think I'd put it that way,' I said.

'Come on, smart guy, Romeo goes to a party and who is he lusting after?'

'Rosaline.'

'Hey, they taught you something at Yale.'

'It was my Dad. We read Shakespeare together.'

'Meeting Juliet was the unexpected. Meeting Denise was the unexpected. That's where the electricity comes from. The electricity between them.'

'Joe has already met Denise.'

'Change it. She stalks him,' Sam said. 'She follows him around the party. You don't need dialogue for that. This is a motion picture, you can use images, don't forget that.'

'But they knew each other already. He couldn't afford to take her out on dates, but whenever he went to her brother's house, he slipped away and found her and that's how it started.'

Sam shook his head. 'Is that in the novel? Forget it. It works better if it all happens in one night. Make Denise a dame who plays the whore to get her man.'

'Would Laura like that? I think of Denise as playing with him all the time. But she never thinks that she is going to deliver. And she isn't going to deliver if she can help it.'

'No,' Sam said.

So I went over it, all over again. After a week there was a fresh draft I delivered it to the studio. Then there was silence for a couple of weeks.

In that strange waiting period I started to go through the books my father had loaned me, so that I would always have something to read. They were all written in the nineteenth century. *Great Expectations.* Hadn't anyone made a movie of that yet? And Zola. Sam Goldwyn had made a terrible *Nana* with the absurd Anna Sten a year or so ago. What about *Money*? A story of speculators ruining ordinary people sounded just right for 1936 but it would need careful handling particularly when some of the worst were Jews. I was on such a high, I couldn't stop thinking of writing and adapting.

Finally, Sam called me one afternoon.

'Kid. It's okay.'

'What's okay, Sam?'

'Stanley's given the movie the green light.'

'Really?'

'Yeah, it was touch and go. We had an amazing meeting. Laura insisted on doing this movie. Said she refused to do the next picture he had lined up for her. Threatened to go on suspension. Morrie didn't like that.'

'I bet. So how did you persuade him?'

'Laura has her ways. She said she could go back to the farm. Told us how she lived on a dollar a day and still had change left over. I don't think they've taken the farm out of that girl yet.'

Had I known that she came from a farm? Svensson: I imagined some sturdy Swedish farmer father struggling against the
elements and wondering why anyone thought that America
was the promised land. 'Laura has her ways.' I had seen that
at the start. Did that still happen? Would she, like the now-
forgotten Sonya, take Uncle Stanley into the starlet's room and
get him to tell the director to do what Laura wanted to do?

'Anyway, he agreed. That's fantastic. When do we start?' I
asked.

'Grow up, kid. There are lots of things that have to happen.
Like designing and building sets. Laura's tied up now so we'll
probably start with some location shots of the college.'

'All the way back East?' I asked.

'Too expensive,' he replied. 'We'll do it at UCLA.'

'But UCLA doesn't look like an Ivy League college,' I pointed
out.

'Jesus H. Christ, Bobby, nobody in the audience knows that.
Are you going to be a class-A pain on this shoot?'

'Of course not,' I assured him.

'By the way Laura said she likes your screenplay. She thinks
it's good.'

'It is,' I defended it.

'Don't let it go to your head. I swear that if you say once that
we can't change a word because you wrote it, I am throwing
you off the set for good.'

'You can trust me, Sam,' I promised.

◈

Weeks later, the location shoot began, very early one morning
at UCLA. It was chilly first thing although I knew it would
warm up quickly. I wore one of my Yale scarves for luck.

I had had nothing to do with the casting and the choice of
Paul Hill to play Joe. I had seen none of his movies. No one had.
He had been chosen to play the part of a footballer in a col-
lege football film that would not be released until the autumn.

Uncle Stanley had chosen him because he looked and walked like an athlete. A real all-American of the Nordic variety. I did not think that he looked in the least Italian.

That first day at UCLA was a revelation. I had never seen an exterior shoot before, and I stood well back to observe what was going on. I met Paul Hill that day. He seemed a nice, easy-going guy who was thrilled to find himself starring in a movie. He felt lucky that it was Laura Hampshire's name that was going above his own. I could imagine every cheerleader throwing herself at him. Denise was not a cheerleader. She was supposed to be attracted by something darker, something Joe did not even realise he possessed. Paul also walked with the grace of the natural young athlete. I could not imagine him spending his youth shifting crates in his father's grocery store.

I closely observed the members of the crew and what they were doing. I paid equal attention to what the actors were wearing. After a while I slipped up behind Sam and said, 'You know, I don't think those clothes are right.'

'What?'

'Paul's, I mean Joe's, clothes.'

The wardrobe woman looked alarmed. 'Why? I did quite a bit of research on this.'

'I'm sorry,' I said, 'but he's dressed like the other guys. Joe has come to college straight from his town in New Jersey. There's a scene where his new friends take him to a clothing store and buy him things that will make him look as if he fits in.'

'That scene looked stupid,' Sam said. 'It's fall, isn't it? It's cold. Put a goddamned coat on him, no one will know the difference.'

'Also his head looks too well-groomed. Joe has never been to a good barber in his life, until now.'

'Thanks, Bobby,' he said, and went back to what he was doing.

I retreated after that. There were several takes of Joe standing outside a building talking to his new friends, looking shy but eager to please. There was a late morning coffee-break. Caterers had emerged from somewhere with coffee and doughnuts. I sat on my own, with my copy of the script. Paul Hill came up to me.

'Hi,' he said, sitting down next to me.

'Hi, Paul. How's it going?'

'Okay. Nervous. The other guys are great. Sam really knows what he's doing.'

'Sure he does. If you want to concentrate on this scene, I won't talk to you.'

He grinned. 'It's not like that. Hey, I understand you said something about the clothes. What's wrong?'

'Well, it's only me saying it, but Joe's wardrobe kind of follows what is happening in the story. At first he turns up at college wearing the stuff he wore in New Jersey. When the others start making friends with him, they take him along to a store where they can dress him like the kind of guys they are. It's a big thing for Joe. He looks at himself in the mirror and he thinks, "I'm one of them now".'

'Yeah, I see. Is that in the script?'

'Sam doesn't like it. So he probably won't shoot it.'

'That's too bad.' Paul sipped his coffee. 'Did someone tell me that you know the author of the book?'

'Yeah, kind of.'

'And you were at Yale?'

'Yeah.' I brushed the scarf but in a way that said, 'So what?'

'Then you know all about these guys.'

'I knew guys like them. But you know, everyone is an individual.' I had decided that the less I gave away, the better.

Paul nodded. 'Can I ask something, Bobby?'

'Sure.'

He looked around to see if anyone was looking at us. 'Sam's the director, so he's the boss. But I was thinking, maybe sometimes I could talk to you. About Joe. Things I should be thinking about. But I don't want to show any disrespect to Sam.'

'Absolutely.' I should not have jumped at the opportunity.
I should have said Sam is the director, don't look at me. But I
could not resist.

'Awkward to do it on the lot,' he said.

'I have a place in Santa Monica. It isn't much to write home
about. All I need is a place to eat, sleep and write. If you don't
mind the surroundings, you could come round any time. I'm too
busy working to go out. We could open a few beers. Talk about
whatever you like.'

'That would be swell, Bobby. Help me build my confidence.'

Sam had the script, and now he was going to shoot it his way.
This was one way I could fight back. I was doing this because I
wanted to make sure this story came out the right way.

'You're going to be great,' I told Paul.

He smiled. That football hero's smile. 'I'd like to surprise Sam,
show him how good I am.'

'You are good, Paul. You'll get better all the time.'

◆

I did spend most of my nights at home. I started working on
those adaptations. It felt good, doing it on my own. I might be
making a mess of it but at least I didn't have to report to Sam
with them every Friday afternoon. In addition though I never
stopped working on *And Some By Virtue Fall*. On the set, Sam
would tell me to rewrite something.

One morning, he tore five pages out of the script, handed
them to me, and said, 'Take the crap out.' Nothing else, just that.
Like I should know better.

It was the scene where Joe goes back to his parents and tries
to explain to his father what is happening to him at college, but
he is quickly interrupted by his mother barging in with a tray of
coffee and cake. It terrified me that this was going to wind up
on screen. It had gone through several drafts, each one a miserable attempt to make sure that no one watching it would think
for a moment that these in fact were my folks.

Paul Hill did turn up, late one night.

'Hi, Bobby.' He stood at the door. 'Remember I said I'd come. Didn't I say tonight?'

'Sure, Paul, hey, come on in,' though I could not recall Paul actually giving me a date. Paul looked around the living-room. He did not look surprised at what he found. He sat down on the couch. 'I promised you a beer.' I went into the kitchen and found two bottles of Budweiser in the icebox.

'Thanks,' Paul said, when he was handed the glass. 'By the way, this is my limit.'

'There's more in the kitchen.'

'No, I promised myself that I wouldn't drink once the shoot started.' He shook his head. 'I'll never be able to drink like Sam.'

'Can anyone?' I joked, thinking of the sessions at the studio, after which Sam just drove home.

Paul laughed. 'You wouldn't believe it, even if you saw it. After I got the part, he invited me out to a bar. That stuff about you don't know a man until you've got drunk with him. Well, boy, did we get drunk. And at the end he just walked out, got in his car, and drove home. I don't know how he managed it. I was three sheets to the wind so the bar tender had to call me a cab. I felt like hell the next day.'

'Just between us, I've seen it. When we were working on the screenplay.'

'I can't believe it. I've heard incredible stories about his drinking.'

'So what happened during your drinking session?'

'I can't remember anything I said. Or Sam said. But I just felt, I don't know how to say no to this guy.'

'I know the feeling.' It was small comfort to discover that Sam bullied everyone who didn't have the status to tell him to go to hell. It was good to have an ally.

We sat there a moment while Paul drank his beer. Finally he spoke. 'This is hard to say, so I hope it's okay if I say it to you, because you've got to swear not to tell anyone, and I mean all your relations at the studio.'

'Don't worry. I don't tell them anything.'

'I don't know how I can get through this movie.'

As bad as that. 'It's only just started,' I tried to sound encouraging. 'You're nervous. It's a big break for you.'

He nodded. 'Those other movies haven't even been released yet. If I mess this up, it's all over.'

'Why do you think you'd mess it up, Paul?'

'You know what happened a couple of days ago.' Sam had decided that both the early and late scenes outside one of the campus buildings should be filmed at the same time, with suitable changes of clothes, since everyone was all out there. In the early scene, Joe has just met his new friends. He isn't sure what to do, but they stick their hands out, confidently, to show that they are now all friends. In the later scene he has seen through them. They expect him to offer them his hand, despite everything that has happened, but Joe won't do it. Finally, they turn away. There had been so many takes of the last scene that Joe had got confused. He kept offering them his hand when he wasn't supposed to. Sam had exploded. 'Did you hear what he called me?' Paul said.

'I think we all did.'

'"I asked for an actor and they sent me some footballer with too many head injuries who can't read!" On and on. I didn't argue back, I stood there and took it. That's the way I am, Bobby. My folks taught me that if you get a job, you turn up on time, you work your ass off, and you stay until the boss tells you it's time to go home. But I felt like a whipped dog. And then he told me to do the scene again.'

'Which you did. He must have realised that you were upset.'

'Damn right he did. This morning he called me in to look at the rushes. "Look, Paul, you look just like a whipped dog. Like a guy who just found out that his so-called friends aren't his friends". He knew what he wanted to get out of me and he got it.'

'That's his method. I went through the same thing, with the screenplay. You've just got to be strong enough to put up with it.'

'Everyone says you just have to put up with Sam. I tried to talk to Laura but she's so tough, she just looked at me as if to say, "So, the big football player doesn't even have a backbone." I can't talk about it to anybody. That's why I came here.'

'It's fine. It won't go any further.'

He kept playing with the empty bottle in his hands. 'I can put up with it sometimes, but I can't go on for a whole movie. He's going to destroy me, Bobby. Someone told me that's what he does. He wrings the performance of a lifetime out of you, and then he spits you out at the end. Great performance, and then I'm through.'

'Don't worry, he treated me the same way,' I repeated.

'Really? But you're Stanley Steingrove's nephew.'

'That doesn't mean anything. I got this job as a fluke. You may have been told already that my other uncles like taking pot shots at me. Uncle Stanley's different, but he's letting Sam whip me into shape. He doesn't know how many blows I've taken and I'm not about to tell him.' After a pause, I asked, 'How much does this mean to you, Paul?'

'What, acting? Everything. I had a football scholarship to go to college. I dropped out after my sophomore year to come to Los Angeles. I bummed around, took any job that needed a strong guy, took some acting classes, and then finally I got lucky. That screen test. Apparently I have a really good voice.'

'You do.'

'All I want to do is act. Sam is going to destroy me,' he repeated.

'He's not going to destroy you,' I said. 'You've got to relax.'

'Yeah.' Paul nodded. He put his glass and the bottle down on the floor and leaned back on the couch. 'I should head home. Early start tomorrow.'

'You don't have to,' I said.

'I'd like to stay a bit longer. You know, it feels, I don't know, safe here. You must be the only Steingrove who isn't living in some kind of mansion.'

'My folks don't. I don't care right now. Like I said, I just want to work.'

'That's all I want to do too. I mean, I'm not complaining, Bobby, I've been so lucky. Your uncle is paying me an amazing salary. Amazing to me. I have a nice place. But my family is far away, I haven't made that many friends yet here. It feels lonely. It's stupid, but here I am in LA and I feel so lonely.'

I wondered what this conversation might lead to. 'Sam told me that when you take the number of women who want to get into the movies and count up the number of roles there are, the odds are definitely in favour of the men. When your movies come out, you'll be fighting them off.'

'That's a funny idea.'

'This is Hollywood, Paul. All that clean cut, kiss the girl on her cheek stuff only happens on screen. Hays Code stuff. But you, you can have anything you want, any way you want it.'

'That isn't why I came here.'

Could this be true? Paul was an Adonis actor who had not come to Hollywood for the sex. Paul really was totally straight-forward. But surely not an innocent. I could imagine his back story - no long seductions, maybe not much foreplay either, because two beautiful bodies wanted it so much. No girl would ever lead Paul into a park in order to say no when they got there. 'No' was not a word that even registered with him. Perfect for Joe.

'What about you, Bobby?' he suddenly asked.

'Girls? I can't complain.'

'It's kind of cheap, sitting here and talking about girls.'

'It would be worse, sitting here and talking about boys,' I said, laughing.

Paul sniggered. 'Can you believe any guys do that kind of stuff?'

I just shrugged. 'We could talk more about Sam.'

'The last thing I want to talk any more about is Sam.' He paused. 'Tell me about the novel. Sam says I'm not allowed to read it. He thinks I'll get confused between that Joe and the movie Joe.'

'He's right.'

'What happened to you at Yale?'

'How do you mean?'

'How did it feel, to go there, not as an East Coast guy, but ...'

'It doesn't matter,' I said. 'You're playing the Joe that's in the movie.'

Paul sat up and looked at me, and gave me that languid smile. 'It's brilliant, by the way. The screenplay. It's brilliant. I don't know how you did it.'

'Thanks. It wasn't easy. And Sam really did help.'

'I wish I could just sit here and talk to you about it. Without being shouted at.'

'Any time.' I looked at my watch. 'You've got to go.'

'You're right,' he agreed. We both stood up. 'You know I never had an older brother. I really wanted one. I really need one. Right now, I really need one.'

'Come back any time. We'll talk about the movie.'

'That's a deal.'

I stood at the door and watched Paul Hill drive off. I closed and locked the door. I poured myself a Bourbon and water and drank it quickly. Then I collapsed into bed. I always fell asleep now as soon as my head hit the pillow.

The alarm woke me at 6 o'clock. I smiled to myself. It was good to know that someone hated Sam Price as much as I did.

◈

Paul came back four nights later.

'Don't tell me, only one beer,' I greeted him at the door.

'That's right.'

'Take a pew.'

'Sam wants to shoot the grocery store scene. The one when he goes to talk to his father.'

'I know.' The actors who were playing the parents were needed on some location, so Sam had switched things around. Most of the set could be borrowed from another movie they were shooting.

'Well what do you think he's doing, going back like that in the first place? I thought he was having a great time at college.'

'I guess he's scared,' I suggested. The scene had come out of George's imagination. 'It means the audience can see that he's in two minds. Then he makes up his mind. They can see him putting his past behind him.'

'Sam says he wants to put something back into the scene, something he said you took out.'

'What's that?'

'Joe actually walks into the shop while a customer is there. A really arrogant woman who treats his father like dirt. And his father just stands there and takes it, because she's a customer and he's scared of offending her. And Joe watches it, watches his father's humiliation. That's why he can barely talk to him.'

'No,' I said, 'that isn't how I wrote it. Joe comes in as the woman is leaving, he doesn't see the way his father is treated. That would be too cruel.'

'That's the way Sam wants it. We started to rehearse it. Joe sees it and he turns as if to go but then his father sees him in the shop, and they both know what Joe has seen. It sounds powerful but I don't know if I can do it.'

'The scene can't be played that way,' I said. I could feel myself becoming agitated. In my mind, I could not divorce Joe's father from mine. I could not bear to see him humiliated on screen, with this customer standing in for the Steingroves who had treated us like the contemptible poor relations for all of my life.

'That's lousy of Sam to play around like that with your script,'

Paul said, while drinking his beer. 'I guess there's nothing we can do about it. What do you think I should do when the mother comes in with the cake and coffee?'

I hesitated. If Sam wanted Joe to look like a monster, then there was one way to prove it. 'Don't eat the cake. That's the worst thing you can do.'

◈

Sam started the shooting early in the morning. He liked to take a lot of takes, from all the various angles. It also seemed to me that he wanted to exhaust the actors. The scene was taking place at the end of the working day. The actors did seem fresh in the morning. By the afternoon they all looked suitably beaten down.

The parents were played by very experienced character actors. They had little to say; they were the kind of performers who didn't need to say much. Their faces said everything. Paul looked lost between them, as if he had already taken leave of this family. My horror was increased by the recognition that the scene was in fact very good. I knew that I was not hiding my emotions, but I did not care any longer. On his own terms, Sam had been right. There was no basis for arguing that it should be cut. It was made all the worse by the fact that the actors, without realising it, were doing an extraordinarily good imitation of my parents.

When the day was finally done, I just wanted to go home. Paul came up to me, as he always did now at the end of the day's shooting. I patted him on the back, told him what a good job he'd done, and then left. I drove back to Santa Monica, stretched out on the couch and started to kill the rest of this bottle of Bourbon.

I had almost finished it when Sam Price appeared, holding a fresh bottle of Four Roses.

'Sam, what are you doing here?' I asked. The place felt violated just by him walking in.

'You ran away this afternoon,' Sam said.

'The working day was over,' I pointed out.

'Look, I've had to come all the way out here, Bobby. Just to talk to you.'

I held out my arms. 'I'm afraid the couch is the only place to sit. I think I can find a couple of clean glasses. Thanks for bringing your own, I'm just about out.'

'Jesus, Bobby, what are you doing in this place? Is this all Stanley is paying you?'

'It's all I feel like paying for rent.'

'Or for liquor,' he said, noting the label on the bottle. 'Always drink the good stuff. Everything else is a false economy.' He opened his bottle and poured out two glasses. 'I thought I'd find you here.'

'That was a good guess.'

'I asked myself, what does Bobby do when he's upset? He could go to a bar and forget about it all. Or he could go whoring and wake up in God knows whose bed the next morning without remembering how he got there. Or he could sit at home. A solitary drinker, that's interesting.'

'Not usually. It was a shitty day, Sam.'

'Are you sore because I messed around with your script? Forget it, it works better this way.'

I had no argument left except the one argument that meant anything to me: the personal one.

'I'm sore because you probably know that my other uncles treat my father with total disrespect. You shot that scene to show Joe's father being totally humiliated in front of his own son. You did it to humiliate my father and me.'

'Like I said, it works better that way.'

'And like I said . . .'

'Get off your high horse, Bobby. Okay, I've worked with Al and Jake for years. I know all about the bookworm. Sorry, mailman. I've never met your dad, he's probably a nice guy. Did George Hudson ever meet him?'

'Of course not.'

'Of course not. Of course he never met your parents. Then how did he know to put that in the book?'

'Look, George has quite an imagination.'

'Really? Then don't take things so personally.'

'It's my screenplay.'

'Jesus H. Christ. I told you that the moment you get high and mighty over that goddamned script, you're out. It's a starting point. I've thrown more pages of more screenplays down the toilet than you've used toilet paper.' I just looked at him. 'You're giving the creeps to everyone on the set.'

'What makes you say that?'

'You start off by telling the wardrobe girl that Joe is wearing the wrong clothes. Then you told me about the way Paul combs his hair. It goes on and on. Today you looked as if the scene was there to torment you. Every day is something else. Guys keep asking me what's going on.'

'I'm trying to help. It's part of my job.'

'You're fighting me, Bobby. I can't have that. You're the writer, I'm the director.'

'Fair enough.'

'What's going on between you and Paul?' he asked suddenly.

'What the hell do you mean by that?'

'The two of you are like twins.'

'I hope you're not suggesting what I think you're suggesting, Sam.'

Sam poured himself a large glass and lit another cigarette. 'Boy, you jump to conclusions fast. I wonder what's going on in your head.'

'It's the way you said it,' I shot back.

'Okay, you're the greatest of buddies. Is that better?'

'He's a young actor. You treat him like dirt. All right, I try to boost his confidence. Someone has to.'

'Nobody has to,' Sam declared. 'If he thinks he's good enough to be in a major motion picture, then he can stand up to anything. Jesus, they put anyone on a football field nowadays.'

'Sam, we've got a lot of this picture yet to shoot. You don't want to destroy the leading man before he even encounters Denise.'

'Destroy, shit. Have you looked at the rushes?

'Yes.'

'And?'

I paused. I knew they were good but I did not feel like giving him any compliments. 'That's not my job, remember?'

'Paul is also fighting me. I've been doing this job too long not to see what's going on. That's what I was referring to before you assumed that I would of course be talking about sex. Are you giving him direction on the side?'

'I'm allowed to talk to the actors.'

'You are not allowed,' Sam shouted. 'You can talk about football, if you have to. If you know anything about it.'

'I know about it. I used to play it in high school. I went to every college game. You can stop accusing me of being a pansy.'

'Jesus, Bobby, talking to you is like walking on hot bricks. Can you drop the sarcasm and the clever remarks?'

'I'm all ears, Sam.'

Sam rolled his eyes and then drained his glass. 'Look, I've never been in this situation before. I've always dealt with established writers. Suddenly, on a prestige project, I get the boss's nephew landing in my lap, a total novice, and I'm turned into a writing teacher. Try to see it from my point of view.'

'Sam, I'm grateful to you. It was Laura's idea that you should help me and I was pleased, really, I was. But you are a bastard to work with. There have been times when I wanted to give the whole thing up but I was going to show you I could do it. You probably did that deliberately; like the way you humiliate Paul the whole time.'

'I'm trying to teach him how to act. Someone has to. He's

going to be a good actor and he's going to be a star. In that order.'

'I'm here to stay too.'

'Don't tell me that. Once you and your friend George have had your fun with this movie, you'll be - what? Trying to crash into Broadway? His money and your so-called talent? The latest hit, a nasty little satire on Hollywood, I guess.'

'Do we really have to go through this again? I had no idea George was even writing that novel. I haven't spoken to him since we graduated. The idea that I write the screenplay came completely from him.'

Sam sniggered. 'It got you out of the mailroom.'

'It certainly did.' I picked up the bottle and poured another drink for Sam. 'Am I being banned from the set?'

'Not in so many words.'

'Just don't turn up.'

'Something like that,' he agreed.

'And you think no one will notice?' I asked.

'They'll think you've finished your job.'

I sat there, and then remembered. 'Been under a lot of pressure, Sam?'

'What about it?'

'I've never seen you without a cigarette in your hand. And you're drinking a lot, aren't you? Or maybe it's just the usual amount for you.'

'I'm sober when I need to be.'

'Is it the movie? Having to work with Laura without being able to touch her? Is it me? I'm kind of a special case. I'm a Steingrove but I'm the bookworm's son, so it's okay to kick me a around a bit. More than a bit. Paul's been a good whipping boy for you but maybe you need more than one.'

'Shut up, Bobby.'

'So,' I said, handing him back his bottle. I was alarmed to see him pour himself another glass. 'Where's your next stop? Not home. Malibu?'

'What are you talking about?'

'I was in the mailroom, remember? I guess she thought it was safer to write to the studio.'

'You don't know where to draw the line, do you?' Sam said.

'I want to work in this business, all right? I want to earn my salary. We want the same thing, a great movie. We have different ideas. We'll fight with one another. I don't mind. I am not going to stop doing everything I can to help you make the greatest movie Steingrove Films ever made.' I sat back. 'I'm a bit drunk too, so in vino veritas or something.'

'You're an arrogant little bastard.'

'I'm tired of being bullied by you, Sam.' I drained my own glass. 'But I'm glad you came. It's great Bourbon.'

Sam stood up.

'Come on, sit down,' I said. I'd got it out of my system. There was no point in parting as enemies. 'We've got to end this on good terms.'

Sam started to walk towards the door. God, I thought, he's going to get behind the wheel of his car. I had to stop it.

'Sam, look, I'm sorry if I've been an asshole, but take it easy. Don't go. Sit here and sober up. You can't drive now.'

'I told you that the best way to sober up is to get behind the wheel of a car.'

'That's bullshit. You're lucky you haven't killed yourself before now.' I stood in front of the door.

'You think I'm going to pass out on your couch and wake up in this dump, with that superior look on your face?'

'Sam, I'm begging you.'

'You couldn't care less. Don't worry, if anything happens, no one is going to blame you.'

He pushed me aside.

'Give me the keys, Sam,' I ordered him. 'You're right, I don't care what happens to you, but not yet. Now give me your car keys.'

'Stop the heroics.'

Desperately, I thrust my hands into Sam's trouser pockets, trying to find them.

'Jesus, you enjoy that. You really are screwing Paul. Or the other way around.'

I stepped back. Sam produced the car keys from his jacket pocket. He shook his head and left. I watched him go and then suddenly sprinted out of the house and tried to run in front of the car. Too late, he had started it up and screeched away.

I went and sat down. I thought of calling the police but then thought what that could lead to. I staggered into the bedroom and collapsed on the bed.

CHAPTER 18

I MUST HAVE PASSED OUT for hours. The next thing was the incessant ringing of the telephone. It took a while to get up and answer it.

'Is that Bobby?'

'Yes.'

'It's the call service at Steingrove Films.' There was an all-night switchboard. 'There's been an accident. Mr Steingrove wants you to come in, first thing in the morning. Can you be here at eight?'

'What's happened?'

'It's Mr Sam Price.'

'Is he . . . hurt? dead?'

'It's bad. It was along the Pacific Coast Highway, some hours ago.'

I put the phone down and threw myself back on the bed and took deep breaths. If only Sam hadn't come here, if only he hadn't drunk so much, if only I'd persuaded him to stay. Locked the door, wrestled with him until I got the keys, anything. If only, if only, if only. It's the goddamned movie. The goddamned novel. Suddenly I wanted desperately to be back at my parents' house, back in my tiny bedroom, before all of this happened. Spending the day reading aloud a play with my father or swapping favourite passages in a novel that no one else read any longer. Safe. I would even welcome my mother's arrival with a tray of coffee and cake. I would be so nice to her, not like recently. She called me a rotten kid, teasingly, but she was right - I was.

At least it was the end of the movie. I was sure of that. They had not gone that far into the production schedule. The sets hadn't cost much so far. Laura could go back to the movie that Uncle Stanley wanted her to do anyway. The incapacity of the director whom Laura Hampshire had specifically wanted was an honourable excuse to drop the project. What was the point of bringing in someone else, who would start all over again with his own ideas?

When I looked at the alarm clock, it was six. I got up with difficulty, and carefully shaved and showered. I had picked up some clean clothes from the Chinese laundry the day before. Without thinking, I put on the Brooks Brothers suit I had worn the day Aunt Estelle and Elaine arrived in New York, the one I wore to the cemetery.

As I drove on to the lot, I noted how busy it was even early in the morning. The whole construction department seemed to be out and about. I drove over to where they were building the exterior of the Central Park set - the shacks of the Hoovertown, a stretch of grass, and some trees. They could have done it on a sound stage but Sam had wanted to do it out of doors, with a day for night lens. It was almost ready. I saw one of the labourers I used to work with, ready to clean up after the carpenters. How simple it was, to clean up that kind of mess.

I found Kay at her desk. Did she ever go home? No matter when Uncle Stanley came in or left, she was there.

'Hi, Bobby, isn't it sad? You'd better go in.'

I found Uncle Stanley, immaculately dressed in a suit and sitting at his desk. There was Uncle Morrie and Paul Hill and Hank, the assistant director.

'Son of a bitch, Bobby,' Uncle Stanley greeted me. 'Did you have to arrive looking like a Wall Street banker going to a funeral?'

'I'm sorry. I just put on whatever ...' I didn't bother to finish the sentence. I sat down in a chair at the end of the circle in front of the desk.

'And you look totally hung-over.'

'I haven't slept much.'

Laura Hampshire arrived last. She did look like she was going to a funeral, in a dark blue dress and short jacket, with a matching hat. I thought she must have spent hours getting herself to look this fresh and beautiful at eight o'clock in the morning. Kay had managed to order coffee and a buffet of cakes and bread from the commissary. I had had no breakfast, but although no one invited me to help myself, I did go and get something to eat.

'What's the latest?' Uncle Stanley began by asking Uncle Morrie, who was Sam's agent.

'I've just been to the hospital, Stanley. He's in a coma. He's broken a lot of bones. He went through the windscreen. It was a terrible crash. He's lucky to be alive. The doctors think he'll pull through but it will be slow going. Months.'

'What the hell was he doing on the Pacific Coast Highway?'

There was a silence.

'He has a girlfriend in Malibu,' Uncle Morrie admitted.

I thought that I might as well say it. 'He'd been to my place first.'

'Your place?'

'That's right. I left the studio promptly yesterday. I didn't realise he wanted to talk to me. He just turned up. I'm just a couple of blocks from the beach. He probably thought he could drop by on his way to her.'

'Drop by for what?'

'To talk about the picture. He kept drinking. When he left to go I begged him to stay. I stood by the door, I tried to get his car keys out of his pocket. He kept saying that the best way to sober up is to get behind the wheel of a car. He's said it to me before.'

'Jesus.'

'It's true, Mr Steingrove,' Paul Hill said. 'He took me out drinking before we started. I begged him to call a cab or something but he wouldn't. He said the same thing. He was lucky that time.'

'Morrie, did you know about all this? He was sober on the set?'

'Of course he was sober on the set. But afterwards ... I know, Stanley. The long and the short of it is that he wanted to divorce his wife and marry this woman but his wife wouldn't agree and the woman kept insisting and it really got to him. You know how Sam drinks, he just couldn't stop. Believe me, I tried.'

Stanley shook his head. 'All right, we've got to go ahead without him. I've thought of a couple of guys here, but ...'

'I can't think of anyone at this studio who is right for this. That's why I wanted Sam,' Laura declared.

'Thank you for your opinion. Morrie?'

'I've started making calls. It's been hard. I tried some guys from outside. Some didn't want to touch this project.'

'Why not?'

Uncle Morrie shifted in his seat. 'They see Laura as playing a particular part. Once I explained what this was about, they backed off. They felt that if you wanted to change gear, they didn't want to be the guy who tried and failed. Right now I get the idea that the best ones are tied up or their studios won't release them. Give me a couple of days.'

I put my coffee cup down. What were they talking about? They weren't seriously going to carry on with this movie, were they? I had convinced myself that I had come in to witness the burial of the project once and for all. Instead, Uncle Stanley intended to find someone else. And who would that be? Someone with his own ideas. Someone who would put the screenplay to one side and put heaven knows what on screen. That was impossible.

'I'll direct it, Uncle Stanley,' I said.

Uncle Morrie burst out laughing. Hank, the assistant director, was about to follow suit but looked at the others and decided not to.

'I'm being serious.'

'Well, thank you Bobby,' Uncle Stanley began.

'I think it's a great idea,' Paul Hill said. 'I've talked to Bobby a lot since we started shooting. He really understands what this is all about and it's such a brilliant script. I'll work with anybody, Mr Steingrove, but if you ask me ...'

'I haven't, Paul.'

'May I express an opinion?' Laura asked.

'Yes.'

'I think it's crazy but not impossible.'

'I know what's going on,' Uncle Stanley said. We all waited. 'You think that if the director is an amateur, the actors will take over the movie.'

Paul looked suitably abashed but Laura was only starting.

'I think that may be a little unfair. For one thing, Bobby knows this movie better than anyone. He wrote the screenplay. He's been there during the shoot. So he doesn't need to start from scratch.'

'Laura, he knows as much about directing as the man on the moon.'

'Actually, Uncle Stanley, Irving Thalberg...'

He slammed his hand on the desk. 'I should have guessed you'd quote Irving Thalberg. So you think you're the new boy wonder of Hollywood.'

'No, of course not. But I am not ignorant either.'

Laura stepped in. 'Let's look at it practically. How long is it going to take you to find another director? Weeks? And for him to restart the movie? Meanwhile, we are all sitting around, costing you money.' She turned to me, 'Bobby, how long do you need to audition for this?'

'Audition?' I tried rapidly to think of what could be shot right away. 'The exteriors of Central Park are about ready. I was over there, checking. We could shoot that. And I think the scene in the grocery store is wrong. The set's still there. If it had anything to do with me, I'd reshoot it, differently.'

As I spoke, I could feel the ideas beginning to come to me. I suddenly felt released from the constraints of the script. What was this movie all about? The audience would sit there at the beginning and wonder why they should care about Joe and Denise, but by the time they left the movie theatre, they would have lived through something, with them. What did the audience feel as they left? Surely that was the key, and once I knew that, everything else had to flow towards it.

'How long do you think all that is going to take?' he asked.

'Give me a week, Uncle Stanley. I know what this movie should look like.' I must have sounded arrogant but I knew I had to sound positive, as if I really could suddenly take charge, even though I had no idea what happened next.

'I am not going to be made a fool of,' Uncle Stanley said.

'I have an idea,' Laura said.

'Haven't we had enough of those?' Uncle Stanley pleaded.

'You'll like this one. If you give Bobby that week, and let him shoot those scenes, and if at the end you don't like them and you fire him, I will give you the money you've wasted. I think that's fair,' she concluded.

'I'd happily work for nothing,' Paul added.

Uncle Morrie looked horrified. 'Paul, you have a lot to learn about this business. Actors do not work for nothing. Not the ones I represent.'

Uncle Stanley sat there, considering it. It was obvious what Uncle Morrie and Hank thought. Then I realised how much Laura Hampshire mattered.

'One week,' he said. 'And Laura pays for it.'

I stood up. 'I guess the best thing to do is, Paul, Hank, let's walk over to Stage 3 and talk about how to redo the grocery store scene.'

'You'll make a laughing stock of your uncle and...' Uncle Morrie began.

'In a week we'll know whether Bobby will ever work again in this town,' Uncle Stanley said.

◆

Hank, Paul and I walked out and into the street.

I looked at them. 'What the hell have I just done? Paul, what the hell were you doing, backing me up?'

'It's going to be all right,' Paul said, grinning. He looked like a man who'd just been let out of prison. He slung his arm around my shoulder. 'Now what do you want to do different?'

'Hank,' I began. Hank was in his thirties. He was sharp, experienced and was a calming influence on all those around him.

'Yes, Bobby?'

'Right now I've just got to think about how to make this happen.'

'Okay.'

'Like I said, I think I know exactly what this movie should look like. I don't know how I am going to get there, but I know, I really know what I want.'

'Okay.'

'I know you don't want me to do this. I saw that, a moment ago. But I need your loyalty. It's only for a week, but I need it.'

'You've got it.'

As we walked over, I began to organise my thoughts.

'First thing, we cut the mother out of this scene,' I said. 'It complicates it. I think Joe should arrive, and find that the difficult customer is just leaving. She knows him, of course, and she tells him how proud of him his parents are. Make it impossible for him to say that he's having second thoughts about college.'

'If you want Patsy' - who played the customer - 'to be effusive you better let her be acidic as well. That's her schtick.'

'Fine. Joe is about to leave, without even going in, but he takes one look through the window. Can we do a shot through the window, showing his father doing some accounts or something? Something which shows he can barely cope.'

'No problem.'

'And he sees Joe, and he rushes out.'

'What am I supposed to say?' Paul asked.

'Some lame excuse about having forgotten something at home. It's obviously fake, you won't even wait for your mother to come home from some errand. You just want to get out of there. And then ... and then he sees you wearing your new, expensive winter coat that your friends bought for you. "Some friends," his father says.'

'There can't be any undertones, Bobby, you know that,' Hank warned him.

'I know that. Joe thinks they want him to belong. His father only sees that he's now with kids with more money than he'll ever see. And he knows he's lost Joe. The last shot is of the father, knowing that he's lost his only son.'

By now we were on the sound stage. I turned to Paul. I was now in full flood. The ideas were coming to me fast.

'This is a crucial moment for Joe. You're burning your boats. But you've got the strength to do it. So no more whipped dog expressions, okay?'

'Okay, Bobby.'

'Do we get a script or something?' Hank asked.

'Of course, of course. I'll write it now. I need a typewriter and a desk.'

'You have an office in the writer's building.'

'I'm not going in there.'

'Do you like making enemies?' Hank asked.

'When this is all over, I'll tell you about my Uncle Jake and my cousin Iris.'

'Iris! I forgot she was your cousin. What a pain. She keeps asking me to join her cell, a bunch of guys sitting around talking about what we can do for the Soviet Union. As if Stalin is going to solve the Depression.'

'Tell me.'

'You're entitled to a secretary now,' Hank told me. 'I think you want to dictate this to her and let her do the rest of the work.'

'I forgot.' I grinned at Hank. 'You see how much I need you?'

◆

The next morning, I addressed the crew on Stage 3. I had decided to wear a well-worn tweed jacket and a striped, Brooks Brother tie. This would be my work uniform.

'You all know me. I'm Bobby. I've been here every day, since we started to shoot this movie. You probably all know, or maybe you don't, that I am being allowed to direct a couple of scenes. Only for a week. After that, you may never see me again.

'I want you to know that I have really thought about what should be in the scene we're going to shoot today. With your help, I know it's going to be good. This is going to be a joint effort. We're all going to be proud of what we do together.

'That's it. Let's get to work.'

We then shot the scene outside the grocery store. We began at eight in the morning and did not finish until ten at night. There were breaks and the commissary kept sending over food.

I tried it in separate takes and then, in the afternoon said, 'Let's try this in one, continuous take.'

'Won't it drag?' said the actress playing the customer.

'Not if we do it right. I want Joe to feel the journey he is going on. He arrives dressed like a rich college boy. He's forgotten that. He thinks his father will see him as he used to be. But it's not just the clothes that have changed him.'

They did it over and over again. By the early evening though Paul had got a second wind while the actor playing his father was fading. He was looking more and more piteously at Joe and Joe was looking more and more as if he never wanted to be in this place again.

'That's it,' I said, 'only do it again, please.' After the last take I said, 'I think that's a wrap. I think you've got it.' I looked at my watch. 'I'm sorry. But thank you.' When I sat down, I thought I'd never have the energy to get up again.

◈

Two days later, the outdoor set was ready for the Central Park scene. I stood there the night before, with the head of the construction department who had come over to check that all was well. It was the nice man who had thought it was such a joke to have Stanley Steingrove's nephew working for him as a labourer.

'I thought you just wanted a job to build up your muscles,' he said.

'I may be back on the labour gang next week,' I said.

He looked at me as if he did not believe it.

This is the start of my penance, I said to myself. I lay awake at night, going over and over in my mind what had happened to me in Central Park. It was wrong of Diana to take me there, it was wrong of me to go, it was wrong of her to want to have sex with me there, it was wrong of me to go along with it, and it was wrong more than anything to have wanted to punish her for using me. Now this scene was being forced on me, all over again.

The exterior shot was technically more difficult than what we did on the sound stage and there were far more people involved. There were all the men who were playing the Hoovertown people. Where should they be? Some should stand outside their shacks while others lay there, looking at Denise. They should form a corridor that got narrower the further she got. What were they thinking while the two young rich people were kissing? And how would Laura play a girl of eighteen who was plunging into a momentary, but for her unprecedented, nightmare?

It took quite a long time to set up and rehearse that morning. I decided to start with that moment when Denise broke away from Joe. He needed to look regretful but unable to stop her. She needed to look determined to walk out of the park on her own until she realised that she had turned the wrong way and would have to go all the way back through the Hoovertown in order to return to Fifth Avenue.

There was one take after another. Paul was fine. He stood there, looking desolate, as if he knew his team had lost and there was nothing he could do about it. The problem was Laura. She picked her way through the rubbish and the uneven ground as if she were walking across one of her father's fields. She was inconvenienced, but was only superficially upset. It just didn't work. We talked about it after each take. She listened politely but it did not change.

Watching Laura walk across the set did not remind me of Diana. Diana had been shocked. There was no shock in Laura. I had to fix this.

Finally I sent everyone off to lunch.

'Are you coming to the commissary?' Hank asked me.

'No. I'm not hungry. I just want to stay here and think.'

'You're going to burn out that way,' Hank warned me.

'All right. Bring me a sandwich, thank you.'

I was left on my own with a few labourers who were tidying up the set for the next take. I stood and looked at the row of shacks on the made-up grass. The set was fine. The ground was fine. What was wrong?

And then it hit me. Laura was not in any danger. She was playing Denise as if Denise thought it's going to be all right; that she can cross in front of the shacks, and walk through a row of men who had not seen a woman like her in weeks or months, and nothing bad could possibly happen to her.

When the extras came back, I called them over. I squatted down. They sat down as well.

'Aren't we doing okay?' one of them asked. 'We thought we were doing what you asked.'

'It's not you. It's something else.' I paused. 'Do you guys know Laura Hampshire?'

'Know her? Sure, we've worked on her movies. Ever since she started here. Lots of movies. Do you want to know which ones?'

'No. Just tell me what she's like.'

There was a silence. Then someone said, 'What do you mean, Bobby?'

'I mean, what's she like?'

'Are you trying to get us into trouble?'

'Of course not.'

Finally one of them said, 'She was a lot of fun. You know, she'd stand around and joke with us during takes. Boy, does she know a lot of off-colour stories.'

'And then?'

'She's a star, Bobby. She's up there,' he pointed towards the sky. She still says "Good morning", but she's a star.'

'Right. I think we're going to bring her down to earth. You're going to bring Laura Hampshire down to earth.'

'Are you crazy? Is this in the script?'

'It is now. First, we need more close-ups of you. You're men who have come to the end. You've hit bottom here. Out there is a city with people who have everything. You have nothing. You haven't been near a woman in a long time. No woman wants you. And along comes this rich young dame and her boyfriend, who's all dressed up too. You don't know where Joe really comes from. And they're laughing at you. And suddenly she's in your power. What you really want to do is to rape her.'

'Bobby!'

'But you have too much dignity, too much decency left over. I want to see dignity and restraint. Think of "The Forgotten Man" . You know that number from "Gold Diggers of 1933". That was about guys who'd come back from the war and nobody looked after them. FDR said it first. Everybody feels sorry for someone called The Forgotten Man but you're the forgotten men and nobody has done anything for you. But you know what? You're nobodies but you have more dignity than she does, with all her looks and her money. And by the end, she gets it.'

The men looked at one another.

'Remember that the further she goes, the narrower the path. By the end, you're shoulder to shoulder and she has nowhere to go.' They nodded, uncertainly. 'And as she passes you, I want you to say something. I want you to start chanting' – I tried to think of the right word – '*Failure*. Once she's gone past you, and you turn and look at her, so that the camera's back is to you, you start chanting *Failure*, over and over.'

'We're extras, Bobby. That puts us on a rate.'

'Fine. So go on a rate.'

'Who's going to tell payroll?'

'Don't worry, I'll deal with it. Just say *Failure*. Over and over. Don't stop, whatever you do.'

'What's Laura going to do?'

'She doesn't know. I haven't told her.'

'Are you crazy, Bobby? If we do that and we ruin her scene, she'll get us all fired. The Depression may be over for you, but it isn't for us.'

'Good,' I said. 'She's privileged. You're not. You've got it.'

'Look, we like our jobs.'

'Just do it, guys, please.'

They looked at each other and then at me. Shaking their heads, they got up and went back to their places.

'Everyone happy?' Laura asked when she returned.

'Oh yes. You look great, like you've been to the greatest party in New York. And Paul, you look great in tails.'

'I feel uncomfortable, Bobby.'

'That's absolutely right. You've never worn that ridiculous outfit in your life. You're only doing it for Denise's sake and actually, she doesn't care. You ready? Hold out your arm at first, but you know you've lost the right to help her. When it's over, hold it out again. Denise takes it but then lets go, and she walks ahead on her own and you follow her. Okay?'

The young man with the clapboard came on.

'Take 10,' he announced.

I looked up at the cameraman, who nodded.

Laura began to walk in front of the shacks. As she passed the first extras, they began to chant *Failure*. She turned round. This was not in the script. We had not rehearsed this.

'Keep moving,' I shouted. 'Keep moving, keep walking.'

She started walking more hesitantly. She wanted to avoid the men but they kept getting closer and the more she passed, the louder *Failure* became. When she reached the end, there were two men standing in her path. That had not happened in the earlier takes. She looked at them and then turned round.

'Fine, now start walking back,' I shouted. 'You can't face it but you have to face it, you have to go back to where you started.'

She looked with a sense of horror and then started to walk, slowly. At one stage she stumbled, but righted herself. It was an awkward movement, as if for one moment she had no control over her body. It was a terrible moment. Laura Hampshire had never done anything awkward.

'It's fine, keep going,' I shouted.

'*Failure, failure, failure.*' It got louder and louder. The crew stood still. They were not prepared for this.

Finally, with one superhuman effort, Laura as Denise reached level ground. Joe held out his arm. She looked at it and then refused him. She would not touch him. Her hair was a mess, and a heel had come off her shoe. She looked exactly like someone who had come down as far as it was possible to go.

'Cut!'

'You bastard!' she said, as she walked to the little trailer that was her dressing room.

Everyone on the set stood there for a moment. Paul Hill came up to me.

'What was that?' he asked.

'You did that,' I said. 'Whatever you did to Denise, that's why she had to take that walk. You caused it. Remember that. You took her off her pedestal, so she could see what the rest of the world was like.'

'I guess so.'

'How badly do you want to fuck her?'

'Jesus, Bobby.' He looked genuinely shocked at my language.

'That's what whirling around in Joe's head. Remember that too.'

I slapped Paul on the shoulder and then walked to Laura's dressing-room. She was sitting there in her dressing gown.

Laura said nothing. She was looking in the mirror and brushing her hair. I had hoped for some reaction I could respond to. Silence brought home the fact that I had done something terrible. I was only here because of Laura. She was the one who was willing to give me a chance. I had only been hired to write the script because she was the one who was willing to give me a chance. I thought I had dedicated my efforts to her. But then I pulled a stunt. It was the only way I could think of how to get the best performance out of her. Me? Bobby Steingrove thinking that he knew how to get the best out of Laura Hampshire? I could be off the lot in five minutes. She only had to pick up a telephone.

'Laura.' No response. 'Miss Hampshire.' I went down on one knee.

'Only one knee,' she observed. 'Only a half apology.'

'No, a full apology. However...'

'However?'

'However, when you see the rushes, you are going to see something extraordinary.'

'You went behind my back,' she said.

I paused. 'Yes.'

'I am an actress. You are a director for a week.'

'That has nothing to do with it.'

'Since when?'

'I had no right to ambush you. No director has any right to ambush you.'

'But you did.'

'I know. But God, Laura, when people see that scene, they're going to say, I didn't realise she had it in her.'

'Well at least there's one person who has a high opinion of Bobby Steingrove. What about the extras?'

'They were scared about their jobs, but I told them...'

'You seem to be the only one who doesn't care if he gets fired.'

'I do care. This is going to be a great movie. You and I are going to make a great movie. But you are the only one they'll remember.'

She looked at me. 'You really believe that.'

'I swear. If it kills me, it's going to be the greatest thing you have ever done.'

She thought about it. 'Get up.'

'What's happened to your dress?' I asked.

'It's being repaired.'

'And then?'

'And then we'll have another take. Only this time I will know what the director wants me to do.'

'You're not walking out,' I declared 'And you haven't fired me.'

'Some day, if you ever grow up, I'll tell you how close you got.'

I went out to see what was happening on the set.

'We're going to do another take,' I announced, 'Denise's dress needs repairing and she needs another pair of shoes.'

'What was that Failure stuff?' Hank asked.

'Just an idea. An idea that worked. I think.'

'Laura's happy to do it again?'

'Sure. She's fine. She's a trouper.'

'I know that, Bobby.'

'I mean, she's an *actress*.'

'That's right. The extras said something about being on a rate.'

'Sorry, Hank, can you deal with that? It's because I asked them to say *Failure*. I don't understand.'

'Okay, leave it to me.'

'Did you notice Paul? I think he's stopped being an all-American football hero. I think he's started to become Joe.'

❖

Uncle Stanley did not want to wait long to see the rushes. Late on the Friday afternoon, he looked at them in the projection room, with us all there. There was no sound for the outdoor scene. As Laura began her walk back through the Hooverville, he suddenly leaned forward and squinted at the screen, as if he had never seen her like that before.

When the lights went on, they all sat there. Kay was on her feet with her pad and pencil, ready to take a note.

'Uncle Stanley,' I could not resist asking, 'am I through?'

'You're through when I goddamn say you are.' He started to walk towards the door. Then he stopped and looked at us. He judged what each of us thought. 'Finish the goddamned picture,' he said, and left.

CHAPTER 19

I WROTE:
Dearest Elaine,

I know I should have written before now. You have no idea how busy my life has become. You probably already know the story from your folks. Sam Price had a terrible accident, driving down the Pacific Coast Highway when drunk. It was awful, and I do feel sorry for him and his family. He did some of the drinking at my house. I tried to stop him. Maybe someone else might have succeeded, but he wouldn't listen to me. From our conversation before he left, it was clear that he resented me from the start. I won't repeat all the stuff he said. He has a long history of driving while drunk. This was just his latest bravado.

Frankly I hoped the whole project would then be cancelled but when it was clear that they were actively looking around for someone to take over, I had the crazy idea that I should direct it. Paul desperately wanted me to do it and Laura actually said she'd pay the cost of shooting for a week. My audition. That's what she called it. And it succeeded. Who knows if what I shot will ever wind up on screen?

I bet everyone thinks your Dad is nuts. Including everyone in the family - you should see the expressions on their faces when I go into the commissary for lunch, which is one reason I don't go there very much. I hope no one thinks this is your dad giving me a big chance. My theory is that it's all about Laura. She didn't want to make any more of 'those' kind of movies and she threatened to go on suspension unless he let her do this. If it's a disaster and her fans revolt, then a suitably chastened Laura Hampshire crawls back, asks for forgiveness and goes back to the sassy gal that Donald Marshall falls in love with in the last reel. And if it's a success, he'll take the credit. He's the producer after all. Smart, huh? Just to remind me who I really am, my salary increase has been modest and I have no contract. I could be back in the mail-room at Christmas.

Meanwhile, I don't know what's come over me, Elaine. I can't think about anything except this movie. Ideas keep pouring out. I arrive on the sound stage at 6 in the morning and I won't leave until 10 at night. Then there are the rushes to watch. Laura is a tough critic on herself, and Paul is learning fast. I have to absorb myself totally in what is going on. There are so many people involved and they keep asking me questions. Part of me feels that I've gone back to high school, when all I did was study and read books. Part of me is like how I felt at Yale, with my pals, like I am in a completely different world I never imagined I would inhabit, but realising I am part of this, I belong, and I'm so happy I just wish no one ever takes this away from me.

I have the best crew in the motion picture indus-try and everyone has been totally loyal. Or maybe they just think I'm proving that they're in the crazi-est business in the world. I'm learning so much from them but I also have to command their respect. So I crack the whip but we also have time to laugh. Sam bullied them. It was his way of getting what he want-ed, but it's not mine. I can feel the sense of relief that he isn't here.

Uncle Al has thankfully produced some great designs. The sets for Denise's birthday party are fan-tastic. More of a French palace than any French pal-ace. I won't bore you but I could go on and on about

this movie and what it's about and what I want
the actors to do. I sit and talk to Laura and Paul for
hours, working out ideas. It's easier than trying to get
all that into dialogue. And they're so good, they just
know how to turn it into gestures and looks.

Don't worry, the actors are not taking over the
movie. Not while I am directing it. At least that's
how I see it. I guess it's the Steingrove coming out of
me at last.

What matters is that it's a great motion picture.
And yes, I do want to see the title up there, Written and Directed by Bobby Steingrove. Or should I
graduate to Robert? No, I've always been Bobby and
always will be to everyone

Love,

Bobby

◆

She replied:

Dearest Bobby,

To think that my cousin Bobby is directing a
movie! But I have news too and to me it is momentous. I think I have fallen in love. His name is Larry.
He was a journalist but he's spent the last eight
months in Europe, making a documentary about
the rise of the Popular Front. He's met and spoken
to everyone and has got terrific material out of them.
I mean, this is real history happening right now.
Some nice Quaker who thinks that Socialism will
guarantee peace has been paying for it so far. Larry's
in New York getting the film cut down to manage-
able size. He's let me help the editor. I am not sure
how much help I am, but I have learned something,
which means that I can go back and ask Daddy for
a job doing something a little more significant.

I mentioned that before anything else about Larry because the point is that he respects me, my abilities (such as they are, don't laugh, but it started with my ability to feed Peggy's orphans along true Socialist principles) and what I have to say for myself. And he loves me, for my sake. It's not just being happy with him; I feel comfortable with him. We can say anything we like to one another. It's such a relief.

He has no interest in Hollywood and says they haven't made a decent film with social realism since *I was a Fugitive from a Chain Gang.* I gave him George's novel but he said he couldn't understand it. It's certainly not social realism. It hasn't done George any harm except with the people he presumably doesn't want to speak to any longer. His by-line is everywhere. He seems to be in England at the moment, sending back reports about Mrs Simpson, which are very funny but not very complimentary.

By the way, the engagement announcement of Alan Pearson was in the 'papers this week. She's called Nancy, and she looks pretty and determined in her picture. As if she's not impressed by the money but she is looking forward to making the most of being Mrs Alan Pearson. And I think I saw Peter at the theatre last month. He was with a girl and looked rather pale. He didn't seem to recognise me so I left it.

Bobby, please look after yourself. There is no point in exhausting yourself before the picture his finished! Sorry if I sound like your mother.

Love,

Elaine .

I replied,

> Dearest Elaine
>
> I have no time but I will say that I am very happy for you. You do realise that you talked about everyone else on earth in that letter except Larry, really. Where does he come from? Is he Jewish? Most important, would I like him?
>
> My mother asked to come to the studio and the set so she could actually tell everyone who is willing to listen that she saw her son directing a motion picture. I said, 'Absolutely not, no one is allowed on this set who isn't involved in the movie making itself.' I am trying to create a family with this crew, not a tourist attraction. She called me a rotten kid. My Dad got on the phone and suggested very nicely that I apologise, so I did. I just don't have time to go there. Or to write more, but oh, there is so much I wish I could sit down and tell you. Why did you have to go to New York? I know: to meet Larry.
>
> Love,
>
> Bobby.

❦

Actually, I was having a battle with the actors.

'Can you think of how to bring Denise in earlier?' Laura asked. 'Why not a scene with her mother or, better, the terrible brother who doesn't really like her? Maybe she could see Joe as an escape, only to find that he wants to be another version of the kind of young men she's trying to get away from? Just a thought.'

'I'll think about it,' I promised over lunch one day. I was aware of the possibility that the more there was of Denise, the less there was of Joe and therefore the less of me.

By now though I had genuinely begun to think of Joe as a person who was separate from my own experience. Maybe Sam's idea of Romeo and Juliet was a good one. Maybe they should not meet until the party. There could be Joe, the play object of his friends who bring him along. They can guess that the hired tails wouldn't fit him very well. They would also know ... Of course, how would a grocer's son know how to dance? He would fall in love with Denise because she was beautiful and she wanted him. And because she saved him from embarrassment when she asked him to lead her in the first dance.

◆

I did manage to get to my parents' for dinner on one Sunday. I was so tired I could barely stay awake. My eating habits had become haphazard. I could barely finish the feast my mother prepared. I knew that hurt her but I ate until I couldn't shovel in one more morsel even though there was still food left on the plate.

'You didn't like it?' she asked.

'I loved it, Mom. I just don't have much of an appetite.'

'Since when didn't you have an appetite?' she demanded.

We ate for a moment in silence. Then she said, 'You look as if you're not sleeping enough.' She looked at me. 'And your hair looks different.'

'I changed the parting while I was at Yale. The barber here last year made a mess of it. I've started using the one at the studio again. He's got it back to where it should be.' She nodded her approval. At least I was getting my hair cut at Steingrove Films, as was now my right.

I had been short-changing my parents so much, I felt that I had to stay longer than I wanted to, and to follow my father into his study for a talk.

Even he had begun to feel a little bitter. 'This is like one of those Victorian courtesy calls,' he said. 'Twenty minutes and you've done your duty.'

'I'm sorry, Dad, I've got so much to do. Please don't make me feel guilty.'

'I know. You look exhausted.'

'It's going to be all right,' I promised him. 'And I've never felt so alive in my life.'

'I just hope you haven't taken on more than you can do.'

'Do you mean you don't think I have the talent to do this?' It was a harsh thing to say, but I was tired and irritable.

'What do I know about making movies?' he smiled. 'But I know a big job when I see one.'

'Dad, you've always said that. That you don't know anything about movies. But Uncle Stanley has been coming here for, what, 15 years? The two of you sit here and talk for ages. You must know more about Steingrove Films than anyone.'

'He talks to me,' my father admitted. 'I listen. I don't think of it as making movies. They are situations. Frankly, I think of them as plots in an old novel. People don't behave differently nowadays.' He saw my exasperation. 'He needs to talk to me. He runs a studio and everyone wants something from him. I don't want anything. He's looked after us, I know, everything comes from him, but it's not like the others.'

'You mean my uncles.'

'How can I expect you to understand?' He hesitated and then began to talk about himself. 'I am the eldest. I looked after Stanley when we were small, but not for long. Boys grow up fast, and he did. And the others. They were tough and strong. I was the one who was always wanting to read a book. Which was impossible in our house. You have no idea what it was like and with a father screaming and arguing and hitting you.' I waited for him to go on. 'It was a bad neighbourhood. Not everyone welcomed the Jews. So there were fights. Lots of them. My little brothers did well. But Stanley would say, "Yitzhak, this isn't for you. Go home. It's no shame in going home."'

'I can see that.'

He shook his head. 'No. There was plenty of shame. I would go home and my father would scream at me that I was a coward. And he would slap my face.' He touched his cheek as he said this. 'But that was not as bad as if I had stayed outside and had been kicked in the gutter by some Jew-hating Irish kid. That's what would have happened to me if Stanley hadn't told me to go home. He was protecting me. You never forget things like that. But the others . . . they agreed with our father. To them I was a coward and once you're a coward, nothing you do is worth anything. Particularly having a love of books. Maybe they think that when I'm with Stanley, I talk against them and tell him not to trust them. How could I do that to my own brothers?'

'Whenever anyone asked what my father does, I tell them that you can't work but that you're the best-read person I've ever known.'

'Thank you, Bobby, but in this world, that doesn't even buy a cup of coffee. And look at them. Who would have believed that they were the same dirty, bloodied street fighters from the Lower East Side?' He smiled at the thought. 'But look at my son. The athlete, the swimmer, doing his push-ups to build himself up.'

I remembered Sam Price's words. 'More than anything,' he said, 'you don't want to be like your father.' How could I feel that way and yet love him as much as I did?

'But,' he added, 'you must never be violent. Punching your cousin after the Seder.'

'Dad, that was years ago. Who told you that?'

'Iris. At the last Seder. That you refused to attend. She wondered whether you were ashamed of yourself yet.'

'I'm not sorry I didn't go this year. Synagogue is one thing, sitting around the table with them is something else. I'll come back when they treat you with respect. They treat you with contempt,' I said. 'And they've always hated me.'

'No one hates you, Bobby. I remember when you were a boy, running up to one of your aunts and saying "Look at my report card, I've got straight A's!" And she said, "My Iris has straight A's, she's so bright. I don't know why she wants to go to college, you don't need a college diploma to change a diaper."'

'I don't remember,' I said.

'That was indifference. She didn't hate you. You were always so grudging to them.'

'Dad, I wish you'd stand up for yourself. I hate them on your behalf.'

'I have my self-respect. I have never done anything I am ashamed of. I can live with myself. That means more than you realise.'

I did realise that. I had done something I was ashamed of, something for which there was no redemption. Maybe that was why George wrote the book the way he did: Denise can gain redemption, but Joe can't. Joe can't because Bobby can't. I wished I could tell my father all about that, but what was the point? I was tired and cranky and could only think of my grudges against my own family.

'They've never said one good word about me. Not one word of praise. This movie is the end. They'll knife me, if they can. That's why I've got to direct the best movie Steingrove Films ever made. So Uncle Stanley can tell them to go to hell.'

'It's not good for you to talk like that,' he predicted. 'Your Uncle Stanley is worried. He's given you such responsibility and what if it's a disaster? I don't think you realise what's at stake.'

'Don't worry, Dad, I realise it every day.' And then I said it. 'I'm not sure even you believe in me.' At that moment, I felt that I had no one in the world to rely on except myself.

'Oh, Bobby. You've made us very proud of you,' my father said.

'I didn't let you come to my graduation. That hurt you. I know it did. But there was nothing else I could do.'

He considered this. 'I know you wouldn't have done that unless something happened.' He waited.

I got up. 'I've really got to go. You don't know what a long day I have tomorrow.' I leaned over and kissed my father's forehead. 'Goodnight, Dad.'

He took my hand and held on to it. There were tears in his eyes. I could not think of anything to say.

I felt lousy as I drove back to Santa Monica. When I got there, I found the screenplay, open to where I had left it. It was the scene we were shooting in the morning. I went over it again. Soon I could think of nothing except the movie.

◈

Paul Hill began to invite himself to my house.

'I owe you everything,' I said.

'Bobby, I couldn't believe it when you said you'd direct it, I was really glad,' Paul said. 'It all feels so different now, with you. How do you do it?'

'Do what?' I asked as I handed him his one bottle of beer.

'Change the mood. Everyone is so much more relaxed. Sam. I mean, he's brilliant but boy, you could tell that he was just waiting to get his hands on that first drink.'

'I promise you, this will be no vacation, Paul.'

'I love it,' Paul smiled. 'I can feel myself really getting into Joe. Before, it was a fight between me and Sam, and me coming here and trying to remember what you told me.'

'Sam knew about it,' I told him, 'and he didn't like it.'

'That's too bad. It was too bad about the accident.'

'It's going to be a great movie,' I promised. 'And you are going to be great in it.'

'But I've been thinking. What about the scenes we've shot already? You know what I think? I think that we should look at the rushes again and, I don't know, maybe reshoot them.'

'That could be expensive. They were good. I think I'm supposed to pick up where Sam left off.'

'Really?' Paul asked. 'I don't think I was giving my best then. Especially when we were out at UCLA. Remember how he wanted me to be a whipped dog? I don't think that was right.'

'I agree.' I sat there, drinking my own beer. 'How much did you ever play baseball?'

'Baseball? I grew up with it, like any kid. Football was what I was good at.'

'Why?' I asked. 'Why do you prefer football?'

'Being part of the team, I guess. I mean, I have to play as well as I can, but it's all part of the team.'

'Joe is the Varsity pitcher. He's out there on his own, just him and the catcher giving him signals, but sometimes he has to decide all on his own what kind of ball to pitch. How to strike the other guy out. And that guy at the plate is terrified, when he sees that Joe is the pitcher. He'll try not to show it, but you know. You know that it's him and you and that you're going to win. That's not like a team.'

'I guess so.'

I opened another bottle for myself. Paul refused still to drink more than one.

'It's pride, isn't it?' I said. 'You're overwhelmed by your new friends, but you have your pride. That's what they find so attractive. They weren't brought up to think that guys from the wrong side of the tracks had any pride.'

I don't know where that interpretation came from. That's what I meant by not knowing what was happening to me: these ideas kept coming to me.

'That's great, Bobby. Sam would never have thought of that.'

'You're right,' I said, 'let's look at the rushes again.'

❖

The problem with reshooting and the extensive rewriting which the demands of Paul and of Laura required, meant that there was a further struggle with the budget and the timetable. My meetings with the producer, namely, Uncle Stanley, were never calm.

'So how much more goddamned money are you costing me this week?' was the usual opening question.

'It's not that bad, Uncle Stanley, I've worked it out, please let me show you the figures. We're ahead of ourselves in some parts.'

'Your uncles are already telling me that you're out of control.

Al said that set designer is the most expensive guy he's ever seen.'

'He told me to use him.'

'Apparently he's only doing what you want him to do. And that costs plenty.'

'But the movie will make all of it back.'

'How?'

'Because it's good.'

'How many times have I heard that before?'

'I know it's not the way Sam would have shot it.'

Just when it seemed that Uncle Stanley had had enough, he would watch the rushes, looking for an excuse to intervene, but he had to admit that they were good. Something had happened in the making of this movie and it showed.

At the same time it struck me that he was giving me all the rope I needed to hang myself.

◈

The birthday party scene was the most complicated and time consuming one that I had faced. Everybody was there. I had adopted Sam's idea of Denise making the first move. And then there was the moment when Denise took the floor and held out her arm not to a suitable male member of her family, but to Joe. Joe's ecstatic acceptance turned to horror at the thought of everyone watching him move awkwardly around the dance floor. It was a moment of defiance to her family and also an invitation to the outsider. She was saying, 'Look, I want you if you are brave enough to claim what could be yours.' It would be a moment when the blood would rush to Joe's head and he would not recover until it was too late.

The scene included a large number of other actors and extras. They needed to know who they were and what they were doing and how to react. I had to plot out how to arrange all of this.

Then there was the question of lighting. Denise is eighteen. Laura was not eighteen. She could play eighteen, but she needed to be lit, often from the back, so there was a glow of youth to her. Here she needed to be impossibly beautiful, so beautiful that Joe would do anything for her. But there also had to be a steeliness, which to my surprise I was not getting from her. This was not the final reel of one of her movies with Donald Marshall, when the sassy girl takes over; this was an eighteen-year-old who is acting like an adult for the first time in her life – or thinks that this is how adults behave. I kept thinking of that moment at the Pearsons', when Diana held out her hand to me and I felt that all my dreams were coming true. The memory made me tense. I was as exhausted as everyone else. The crew was getting restless. Paul started out all right, but now he too seemed uneasy. The glowing confidence, the exuberant moment was fading. Laura was fed up. I was feeling frustrated. I went up to her.

'Look, this is a defining moment. You look as if you're asking Donald Marshall to do the two step.'

'What do you want me to do?' she shouted.

'I want you to look as if you're eighteen, and you think that this is a very sophisticated and grown up way of telling every-one in your family to go to hell.'

'Anything else?' she sneered.

'Yes. Look as if you're mentally undressing him. He has the best physique of any man you've met.'

'Stop it, Bobby.'

'I want you to look as if you're mentally undressing him in a way that complies with the Hays Code. That's only asking you to do two things at the same time. And act, that's a third.'

She looked at me and walked straight off the set and towards her dressing-room. The crew rolled their eyes. I did not hesitate. I went right after her and into the dressing-room. Her dresser was standing there.

'Would you please leave Miss Hampshire and me on our own?' I asked.

'No,' Laura said, 'stay right here.'

'I said, would you please leave Miss Hampshire and me on our own?' I repeated, louder. The woman looked from one of us to the other. She must have seen the expression on my face because she left us, closing the door behind her.

'What the hell are you doing?' I demanded.

'What the hell are *you* doing?' she asked back.

'Don't you ever walk off the set like that,' I said. 'It totally undermines me. I can't have that.'

'If you could give proper direction, you wouldn't need to worry.'

'That's not true. I happen to know exactly what I'm doing.'

'I have a feeling we have had this conversation before.'

'That was different. I apologised for what I did and I promised that I would never do that to you again. I haven't. You know that.'

'You've changed, Bobby.'

'This movie would not be happening otherwise. I am here to make you look good to millions of people sitting in a movie theatre. I can't do that if you fight me.'

'I am not fighting you, Bobby. It is easy for you to stand there pouring out all these ideas of yours about the characters and what we should be conveying but we're the ones who have to do it. And it's damned exhausting.'

'We're all exhausted,' I pointed out.

'You're not taking any pills, are you? There is plenty of stuff you can take to keep you going without sleep.'

'I would never do that. It's just me. And you are giving the performance of a lifetime.'

'You keep saying that.'

'Because it's true. And it wouldn't be true if I weren't directing this.'

'Really? Is that your opinion of your huge talents?'

'Fine. Let's shut down production for the day. I suggest you go and look at the rushes of the scenes shot with Sam and then look at what they look like when I reshot them.'

'How much over budget are you going?'

'That's not your business. Go and look at the rushes. And if you can't see the difference, then fine, go to Uncle Stanley and tell him to fire me. I don't care. You're either on my side or you're not.'

'Bobby, I am just so tired.'

'You can't be. You are glowing in this scene, glowing with youth and a sense of your own power.'

'Stop it. If I hear any more of your theories about how to play a scene, I'll scream.'

'It's what I'm here for.' I waited. 'All right? Everyone on the set is ready for you.'

'And that's it?' she asked.

'We are going to forget this happened.'

'No.'

'Getting high and mighty?' I said. 'Do you know what they think of you?' She looked at me. 'When we were shooting the scene at the Hoovertown, I asked the extras what they thought of you. They said you used to be really nice, and tell off colour jokes, but now you were way up there with the stars. I told them to bring you down to earth. And they did.'

'You are a bastard, Bobby.'

'No, I'm not. I believe in you. Please, at least look sorry. They're all probably wondering what the hell we're doing in here.'

She sat back in her chair. 'Look as if I'm mentally undressing him.' She laughed.

'A lot of girls would like to undress Paul Hill.'

'I am not a lot of girls.'

We stood there. It was hot in the dressing-room and the atmosphere between us could have been cut with a knife. I knew what was going on in my head. I knew all the arguments and the reasons, but in the atmosphere of this shoot, I couldn't help myself. I took hold of her shoulders and kissed her. This was not playing around.

'I'm not in love with you,' I said. 'Don't worry about that.' I kissed her again. I waited for her to stop me or hit me or tell me off. She did not.

'Are we going back to work?' she asked.

'If you please.'

We walked out of her dressing-room as if nothing had happened.

'I think we'll start the dancing,' I said. There was a small band on the sound stage. The music would be re-recorded later, but I wanted the actors to hear it as it would sound in the movie theatre.

'Bobby, can we talk about this?' Paul asked.

'What's the matter?'

'The band just told me that you've told them to play a waltz.'

'Yes. The music in the movie is being composed by a wonderful Austrian composer whom Uncle Stanley kindly hired some months ago.' It was the man my parents and I met at the New Year's Eve party. He had produced wonderfully romantic music for the start of the story and some startling modern stuff as the backdrop to Denise's later redemption. 'If Austrians know anything, they know waltz music.'

'I have no idea how to waltz.'

'I know that. Denise is going to help you, it's part of the story.'

'Yes, but I can't be totally ignorant about it. I'll look like an idiot.'

'All right. Quick lesson. Denise?' I held out my arms. 'Now watch. And look at my feet. It's easy. She's asked you but you've got to take the lead. That's what she expects. That's what a man does. She comes into your arms. And you start, like this, one two three, one two three.' I took hold of Laura. 'Gentlemen?' I turned to the band. They started playing *The Skater's Waltz*. I began to dance with Laura in the ballroom space. I looked over to Paul to see that he was following what I was doing. Then I looked at Laura. Diana had looked at me like that, that look of

desire and challenge. Only Laura was not acting. The realisation
that she wanted me as much as I wanted her made me stop. I
was unaware of how long we had been dancing.

The rest of the crew burst into applause. I began to laugh. I
threw open my arms and put one each around Paul and Laura.
'I love you both,' I said.

I looked up and saw Uncle Stanley standing there, on the set.
He did not look pleased.

'A moment of light relief, Uncle Stanley, but don't worry,
we're going right back to work.'

⬧

Laura got her own back the next day. I had watched the rushes
and felt that the light was still wrong. A great deal of the morning was wasted while I went over this with the lighting men.
While they were fixing it finally, I hoped, Hank dragged me off
for a sandwich.

'You've got to stop for lunch,' he warned me. 'I told you
Bobby, you have to watch it or you'll burn out.'

'Okay.' We walked towards the commissary. 'You know I
couldn't do this without you, Hank. I couldn't do this without all of the guys on the crew, but most of all, I couldn't do it
without you.'

'Sure, Bobby.'

'I mean it.'

'So do I. Can I let you in on a secret? I was walking across the
lot yesterday, and suddenly there was your uncle. He pinned
me against a wall and asked me how it was going. How it was
really going.'

'Did you tell him the truth?' I laughed.

'I did. I told him it was going to be fine. Look, I owe my career
to that man. I would never bullshit him. I told him that and he
knows it.'

'Thanks.'

'So don't kill yourself before the movie's in the can.'

'I promise.'

'One other thing. Don't forget, you're the director.'

'I thought that was my problem,' I joked.

'This won't be the first movie Laura tried to take over.'

I saw what he meant when he got back. The cast and crew were milling around, but there was no sign of the leading lady.

'Miss Laura Hampshire?' I shouted.

'Here.'

I looked up and saw her sitting up next to the lights. She was in her ball gown costume.

'The set isn't up there,' I pointed out.

'I know. But the poor lighting man was drooping and he needed his lunch. I told him he should go and get his lunch, and I would take over.'

'I see. So it's your intention both to operate the lights and to act in the scene.'

Everyone had gathered round to see. I could sense the laughter.

'No, that would be arrogant of me, Bobby. There are lots of things you can shoot first. He explained to me how to do this.'

'Actually, the first thing we are shooting is you and Joe. And if we lose any more time, I am afraid you are going to have to explain to Mr Stanley Steingrove the producer why this movie is going over budget.'

'I see.'

She was shining the light in my face so I couldn't see clearly. 'And I can guess that there are other lighting men up there who can also do it. Guys?' I asked.

'We're here, Bobby,' a couple of men shouted down.

'Good,' I said.

'All right,' Laura finally agreed. She got up and made her way back to the set. She brushed herself down. 'There, I think I'm ready,' she said. She smiled and everyone smiled back.

'Good, can everyone take their places now?' I asked.

'I'm glad you've kept your sense of humour,' she said.

'Yes, but don't overestimate me.'

Which is how we passed it off. I looked round at the crew
and actors. I would lay down my life for them, I thought, and
I think they'd all do the same for me. I wanted to say it, but I
didn't. I knew I didn't have to.

CHAPTER 20

ON THE SUNDAY MORNING I turned over in a strange bed and saw Laura Hampshire. Her bed, her bedroom, her house, a quiet morning in Beverly Hills. No staff apart from the Chinese maid who had apparently proved her discretion many times over.

There was so much going on in my head. I had spent weeks admiring Laura's face but nothing had prepared me for the beauty of her body. I disregarded Sam Price's warnings. This was different. It wasn't a thank-you or a please. It was two bodies who wanted one another, and had stopped thinking of the reasons why it shouldn't happen.

I had never spent the night in someone else's bed like this. Alan and I never spent the night with the women he had arranged for us. The women in Santa Monica I had coaxed into my bed were delightful, but it was all transient. I was grateful for everything I had learned in my past and which I had been able to demonstrate to Laura's pleasant surprise. This again was something different.

I was a director who might not have a job after this movie, who was physically and emotionally in love with his leading lady.

'Hello,' I smiled at her.

'You college boys learned something in your education,' Laura observed.

'Did you imagine I was a blushing sophomore?'

'I figured that one out already.'

'I think you ought to know that what happened last night was done for the sole purpose of giving you, that is you, Laura Hampshire, pleasure. That not for one second did I think of anything else.'

'Such as your own pleasure?'

'Giving you pleasure is my pleasure.'

'Please. I thought you were being genuine'

'I am,' I protested.

'You're very sweet, Bobby.'

'I'm not sure I like the sound of that,' I said. I was keeping up the bantering. I knew from old how successful that could be.

'Well maybe not a sweet nature. But you have an enthusiasm that's – what's the word?'

'Infectious? Uninhibited.'

'Endearing.'

'I don't like endearing. It sounds puppyish.'

She sat up while I continued to lie there.

'What are you thinking about?' I asked.

'Why we're here.'

'Well, there are two possibilities. One is the age-old practice in this town, or so I am told, where the actress makes sure that she gets her own way with the movie. But I think we respect each other too much by now for that. Which leaves us with we are two young and healthy people who happen to find each other very attractive.'

'Who happen to be . . .'

'No. Laura. No. Who we are at the studio has nothing to do with this. And it is not the business of anyone at the studio.'

'You are being serious.'

'I am. There are two things I cannot get out of my head. I want to make love to you and I want to direct you. But they are not the function of each other. If I never touch you again, I will still want to make pictures with you. And if I never make another picture with you I will still find a way to beat a path to your door.'

'Has anyone ever called you an arrogant bastard?' she asked.

'It's been suggested. Including by you. Right now I would give my life to make pictures with you. Laura, there are so many wonderful stories out there that need to be filmed. I grew up reading books and plays. Bernard Shaw has written great parts for women. Trollope. George Eliot. Should I go on?'

'And you think that your uncle is going to let you set up a production unit of your own at the studio?'

'Wouldn't it be wonderful? Isn't that why we're here, to make dreams for other people? Our chosen city.'

She did not answer.

'Let's forget the studio for once. Even if it's only for one Sunday. Forget all the things that your contract says you can and cannot do. Forget the things I have to worry about. Right now nothing matters except us.'

We made love again, and then she said, 'I could go back to being a good farm girl and make you breakfast.'

'What a great idea. Can I have a swim? I saw the pool.'

'Be my guest.'

'Do you have any swimming trunks?'

'No. Go ahead,' she said, 'I like you naked.'

I went downstairs in a bathrobe and dived in. The water felt good, and I kept doing laps, one after another, turning round and round and not even noticing that she had come out to the patio with a tray. Finally, I stopped and hoisted myself out. There was a pile of towels on a lounge.

'I should shower and shave,' I said.

'Breakfast will get cold if you do,' she told me.

I joined her at a glass-topped table. She had made fried eggs and bacon and a pot of coffee. 'It smells wonderful,' I said.

'I thought for a moment you weren't going to get out of the pool,' she said.

'It felt so good in there. Who else has swum in that pool?'

'Some people. And don't pry any more.'

'All right,' I grinned. 'Delicious,' I said, with my mouth full of food. 'When my mother stopped keeping a kosher house my father said, at least we can have bacon for breakfast. But she can't get it as crisp as this.'

'She's not a good cook?'

'No.'

'That cake?'

I looked at her. 'You're not supposed to know that.'

'What? That that scene in the book is about your parents? Bobby, I figured that out weeks ago. The way you fought to keep it out of the movie.'

'I think we should think about the movie and not about the novel,' I said. 'The sooner everyone forgets that novel, the better.'

'If George hadn't written it, you wouldn't be here.'

'George can go to hell. Just don't ask me about the real Denise.'

'I would never do that. I'm an actress, why should I care what the real Denise is like? I'm not playing her.' She drank some coffee. 'You've noticed that I haven't asked you what really happened in Central Park.'

'It wasn't like in the book,' I said.

'Well if it hadn't happened, George wouldn't have written the novel.'

'George wrote the novel because . . . I don't know, because he wanted to make a splash and get published.'

'So I don't have to worry about the real Denise.'

'No. She's fine,' I told her.

'Good,' Laura seemed to have lost interest by now.

'So now that you know about my parents . . .'

'I told you not to pry,' she replied. 'I will just tell you that my Daddy has worked harder than any man on God's earth. My mother is the best woman I have ever known. I have a brother who is out here and runs a ranch in the San Fernando Valley.'

'Really?'

'All he wants to do is to buy more and more land.'

'Do you help him?' I asked.

'Of course. We go fifty-fifty. I have to think about my future too.'

'Nobody lives in the Valley,' I pointed out.

'I told you it was a ranch. The horses don't mind.'

'You know,' I said, 'if I ever do direct another movie, it's going to be completely different.'

'Everyone says they don't want to repeat themselves,' she pointed out. 'But as you know perfectly well, they do.'

I watched her. 'I love the way you pour coffee. It's like the last scene in *Neighbourhood*.' It was the movie I had seen when I was at Yale, where she secretly makes breakfast for Donald Marshall. And at the end, when they get together, pours his coffee.

'Bobby, there are only so many ways even I can think of how to pour coffee. And stop confusing me. Am I a woman or an actress?' she asked. 'When you've made up your mind, send me a telegram and let me know.'

'I think I've given you the best proof of that a man can.'

'Well, that's settled then.'

◈

I carried on going over to Laura's house on a Saturday or at least, if she was busy, a Sunday. I parked my car in the garage, well away from the street. There were no letters, no phone calls and we were never seen in public together. She was a star, I was on no one's invitation list. The town was waiting to see the movie first.

I was too busy, anyway, shooting the end of the movie. It was the story of Denise. Laura had very clear ideas about what would happen, how it would happen, how she should be shot – everything. Sometimes I wondered if she was using me, but when we were alone together I was sure that could not be true. Her lovemaking was genuine. But she held nothing back. I know that. She couldn't hide that from me, not in the depths of the night.

◈

Irving Thalberg died suddenly on September 14, 1936. His funeral took place two days later. It was the eve of Rosh Hashanah, the Jewish New Year. Any haste in the arrangements was due to the fact that he could not have been buried between Rosh Hashanah and Yom Kippur. The Steingrove brothers went to the funeral along with the other Hollywood leaders, and, like them, wept.

By then, the shooting of *And Some By Virtue Fall* had been completed. I was busy with the editing, on the day of Thalberg's funeral. Like the other studios, they observed a five-minute silence at the time the funeral was starting.

By the end of September there was a preliminary final cut of the movie. Like Irving Thalberg, I insisted on having two sneak previews: one night in the San Fernando Valley, and one night in Pasadena; Laura, Paul, Hank and me.

Going to the previews cheered us all up. It was like a field trip from school. Laura was the only one of the four who would be recognised by the audience. She first went to her brother's ranch, and put on a dress that was two sizes too big, a ridiculous hat, and thick glasses. He drove her to the movie theatre in his pickup. No one paid her any attention. We all sat towards the back of the auditorium.

'Don't look at the movie,' she told me, 'try to sense how the audience is reacting. How do they feel?'

It was good advice. When the screen credit came up, 'Written and Directed by Bobby Steingrove', she squeezed my hand. Then I stopped looking at the movie in each of its technical aspects – and in particular the way it was cut. I had seen it so many times already and I had, I hoped, cut out most of the mistakes. I tried to think of it as a whole. Hank took notes furiously in the dark. Paul slowly shook his head as if he couldn't quite believe that he had done all of that. I took a breath when we reached the scene in Central Park. As Laura walked through the Hooverville, a woman in front of us began to cry.

As the movie progressed I became convinced that I had indeed got two superb performances out of my stars. This was not the Laura Hampshire of comedies with Donald Marshall.

This was not the Paul Hill of the upcoming football movie, the graceful athlete who was going to show viewers on the German distribution that Americans made much better *Ubermenschen*. Joe was awkward and eager, trusting and betrayed. And a betrayer.

What pleased me too was that a lot of it was not George's novel. Even when it followed the events, the feeling was different. I only remained faithful to the redemption of Denise, but that had been pure fiction. The book would be forgotten, I thought, and only the movie would remain in people's memories. I was safe.

We stood in a corner of the lobby while the audience filed out and wrote their comments on little cards.

Laura turned to me and asked, 'Did you hear the woman cry when I walked through the Hoovertown?'

'Of course.'

'Which take did you use?' she asked.

Was I going to tell her?

'Can't you guess? It had the shock in it. I'm sorry, after that, I just couldn't get you to act as if you didn't know what was going to happen. My fault. I was a beginner.'

The audience reaction from the little cards they filled out was consistent. They liked the movie. They thought it was a quality movie, maybe not something they would take everyone in their family to. They hated the ending. The screenplay followed the novel: Denise and Joe don't see each other again, which is just what he deserves. The audiences did not like that. They wanted a happy ending, lessons learned, something uplifting.

◈

Uncle Stanley exploded when I told him that I needed to re-shoot the ending.

'Look, Uncle Stanley, as far as I'm concerned, it's fine, but the preview audience all said the same thing.'

'How much is this going to cost?'

'I'll make it as cheap as I can.'

'Do you know how much over-budget you've gone so far?'

'Yes. We've discussed it.'

'You don't change. You reshoot scenes behind my back.'

'Those were Sam's scenes. They didn't fit in. The whole thing has to fit.'

'That's because you keep changing the goddamned script.'

'I am on schedule.'

'Since when?'

I sighed. 'I am sorry. It was all for the best for Laura this way. The picture kept getting better.'

'This was not a goddamned learning experience for you,' Stanley shouted. 'This is a major motion picture. You're an amateur.'

'I was when I started.'

'Oh, I see, and now you're a professional. I'm a laughing stock and you're a professional.'

'Uncle Stanley . . .'

'Finish the goddamned thing. And then I don't want to see you again. Not until it opens.'

'But you're happy with it now?'

'I didn't say that. I'm looking at it again this afternoon.'

'Right. What time?'

'You're not going to be there,' he told me. 'I'm making the rest of the decisions.'

'But . . . did you say, not until it opens? But that's not until November. December.'

'Damn right. First, Laura's new picture, the one she did before this, the one that came in on time and under budget. Then, in October, Paul's movie, to coincide with the new football season. He'll get lots of publicity. I am not releasing *And Some By Virtue Fall* with an unknown male lead.'

'I can see that. But I did hope that I could start on something new.'

'When did I say you could do that?'

'You didn't, I know, but I wanted to talk over some ideas with you. But I've been so tied up with this.'

'No.'

'Do I have to wait until after the movie comes out?'

'Don't hold your breath.'

'I don't have a contract,' I pointed out.

'You think I don't know that? Are you complaining about your salary?'

'No, but if I go away after the reshoot, I'm without a job or a salary.'

'That's not my problem. Have you spent all your money already?'

'On the contrary, I've tried to save as much as I can.'

'Then you'll be fine.'

'Yes, but...'

'When I know you haven't made a fool out of me, we'll talk.'

❖

I carried on seeing Laura. She had started a new movie, in fact the project that Uncle Stanley had actually wanted her to do instead of *And Some By Virtue Fall*. It was like so many of her other films.

'This is going backwards,' I said, when I read the screenplay.

'Are you questioning my judgment?' she asked.

'No. You have a contract. You don't have a choice. You can't threaten to go on suspension every time you don't like the movie the studio wants you to do.'

'Who said I threatened to go on suspension?' she demanded.

'Sam told me.'

'Well, maybe I did,' she smiled. 'I can be quite determined.'

'Tell me.'

'But now it's time for me to be a good girl and to do exactly what your Uncle Stanley wants me to do. Which is this movie. It will put him in a very good mood, so when our movie is a success, I can go to him and say...'

'"I am a great actress. The proof is in front of you. Bobby and I are a winning combination and he has some swell ideas for some more pictures for me."'

She laughed. 'I'm sorry, I shouldn't. But when you talk like that, you're like a little boy who's just discovered a new toy called Let's Make a Motion Picture.'

'But that's exactly what I have found,' I said.

She took my face in her hands. 'You are going to be a great success,' she said. 'Only I can't predict when.'

'You don't think Uncle Stanley is going to can the whole thing?'

'Oh no,' she assured me. 'That would be even more expensive. And it would mean admitting that he shouldn't have let you near the project. I think the New York bankers are on his back at the moment.'

'About what?'

'Maybe why the movie went over budget?'

'But after this new movie, maybe then . . .'

'I think your uncle has other plans. Donald . . .'

'Aren't you tired of making movies with Donald Marshall?'

That was the wrong thing to say. 'Donald Marshall is the most unselfish actor in Hollywood. He has taught me more about acting than anyone on earth. At the moment, his career isn't going so well. So if I can do anything to help him, including making another movie with him, then that's what I do.'

'Sorry.'

'You wanted to make a great movie. So you made one.'

'One. By the way, do we even get an end of the movie party?' I asked.

'I'll invite everyone here,' she offered.

I wanted to ask, 'What about us?' But I was afraid to. I carried on going over to her house, but it was different, now that the movie was over. She was not going to be taking direction from me the next morning. I was there because she liked how I made love to her, and afterwards we could just lie there and not think about *And Some By Virtue Fall.* The next morning she would study her new script but she wouldn't let me help her with her lines or even talk about it. We were lovers, pure and simple, which meant that it could carry on for ever or it could end forthwith.

All she said was, 'My advice is to ask for one thing at a time. One thing and that might lead to another thing, and before you know it, you've got a lot of things without asking for too much at once. That's what a wise person once told me.'

'Who was that?'

'Your Uncle Stanley. And you are not allowed to ask me when.'

'And it worked for you?'

'It worked for me.'

◆

On the Saturday after the movie was all finished, Laura had an open house for the cast and crew. I decided that I had to make a speech, thanking everyone and particularly the cast.

Then Hank stood on a chair and said, 'And to Bobby. And the unique experience of my working life.'

As I was leaving Laura said, 'Now go on vacation.'

'Vacation? I haven't had a vacation in a year,' I said.

'Yes, and it shows.'

I went home and thought about it. Someone at the open house was talking about a hotel in Santa Barbara, not far from the beach and not expensive. I was able to get the number and called. Yes, they had a room. Yes, they could give me a room for two weeks. Two weeks, I thought, that's what I deserve.

I packed quickly, taking a pile of books with me and plenty of paper to sketch out ideas. I told my next door neighbour that I would be away and to keep an eye on the house, and then I got in my car. I drove north. I had driven for an hour before I realised that I must have gone past the spot where Sam Price had his accident, the accident that had made this all possible.

The hotel was fine. The room was quiet and comfortable, nothing luxurious, but I did not intend to spend my waking hours there. I slept ten hours a night without difficulty. I went down to the beach, sat in coffee shops sketching out scenarios for screenplays, ate a huge steak every night for dinner, and read books. I decided to go back to Dickens. I started with *Great Expectations* and went on to *Bleak House.* I decided that Laura would make a great Estella and Paul could play Pip. He would be a bit like Joe in *And Some By Virtue Fall*, but that was fine. I was seeing everything through parts for Laura Hampshire. I kept calling her but she was never at home, no doubt spending all her time at the studio. On the second day, I fell into conversation with a young man in a coffee shop who turned out to be a lifeguard at the Biltmore Hotel pool. He soon got out of me that I worked in Hollywood and had just directed a movie.

'Hey, I've got a great idea. Why don't you come and swim at the hotel? There are some beautiful women there. If you discover them, then you've got to tell them that I'm the one to thank.'

The thank-you lay, I thought.

'Sure,' I said, 'I'd love that.'

I did not discover anyone largely because I turned up at the hotel before breakfast, and swam while I had the pool to myself. Then I headed over to a coffee shop for breakfast and started reading. In the afternoon I went down to the beach and ran along the sand, before diving in. By evening I was ready for my steak. I made the rounds of the restaurants in the town until I found one I liked. Then I ate there every night, while reading a book. I had thought of bringing *Anna Karenina* but Garbo had made that picture the year before. Instead after Dickens I started on my complete Shakespeare. Why hasn't Hollywood made more of these? I wondered. I particularly enjoyed *Henry IV* and the story of a virile if self-indulgent young man who confounded the doubts of his elders and went on to do great things in his own name. Perfect.

But all the reading and swimming and running and eating steaks was mainly there to take my mind off Laura. I thought about her every day. The inability to see her or to talk to her, let alone the lack of touching her, was a deep physical ache. Surely this could not have been just an affair while we were making a movie. Surely we'd become part of one another. I had promised her not to fall in love. Of course I had fallen in love with her, I was only flesh and blood. It was a pity that I had absolutely nothing to offer her. I didn't even have a salary now.

Nevertheless I was in good shape by the end of the two weeks. I had had no responsibilities, and no worries. No one knew where I was and I had spoken to no one except to waiters.

It was when I was packing to leave, early in the morning, that it occurred to me that I hadn't spoken to my parents in weeks. Now that my time was my own again, I decided to call them, and to offer to go and see them. My father answered.

'Dad?'

'Bobby, where have you been?'

'Don't worry. I've been in Santa Barbara. For two weeks. I'm sorry, I didn't tell you. I just needed to get away and to have a vacation for once. Look, I am about to head back. I thought I'd come and see you and Mom.'

'No one had any idea where you were.'

'Are you all right? Is anyone sick?'

'Physically, we are fine. Just ... just come here as soon as you can,' he said.

'What's the matter?' I insisted.

'Please. Just come here.'

❦

It would have been far more convenient to go to my house first. Instead, once I reached Los Angeles I drove across town to their little house. The moment my father opened the door, I knew that something was very wrong. I had seen those expressions on their faces before. It was how they looked when I got back from New Haven, having rushed home and not allowed them to come to my graduation. I kissed them briefly, and then we went into the living-room. My father was in an old cardigan and his carpet slippers; my mother in a day dress. They had nowhere to go.

My mother disappeared in order to get the obligatory tray of coffee and cake. My father indicated that I should sit on the long, deep sofa. He took the armchair opposite. When my mother came in she put the tray down and urged me to help myself. Then she sat in the other armchair. I looked at them as if we were about to start an interview.

I drank some coffee and nibbled at the piece of cake, which did not taste of much.

'Can I ask now what's the matter?' I asked.

'You look good,' my mother said, gravely.

'I've been on vacation for two weeks,' I told her. 'Lots of swimming, sitting in the sun. I didn't realise how exhausted I was. But I got a lot of reading done. Dickens and Shakespeare. You'd be pleased, Dad. I've been re-reading *Great Expectations*. It's funny, but after I spoke to you, I opened it, just by chance, and there was that note to Pip, "Don't go home".' I smiled.

'Bobby, please,' he said. He was holding a sheaf of papers, which he now placed on the coffee table in front of me.

On top was a letter from my cousin Iris. It began:

Dear Uncle Isaac and Aunt Rose,

I am sorry I cannot give this to you in person but I am giving it to everyone else in the family and I am sure you will want to read it too. I am sorry if it upsets you but I am sure you will understand how important it is to speak the truth.

I pushed it aside. Underneath was several typed pages entitled *And Some By Virtue Fall: An Analysis by Iris Steingrove*.

I looked up. 'You don't expect me to read something by Iris,' I declared. 'Anyway who cares what she thinks? The movie is in the can. There will be a première in a month or two.'

'Bobby, please,' he said again.

I started to read Iris's words.

> *And Some By Virtue Fall* takes its title from *Measure for Measure* by Shakespeare: some rise by sin and some by virtue fall. There is no doubt that the novel was written in large part by Bobby Steingrove, partly to justify his aberrant sexual behaviour when he was a student at Yale, and partly as a revenge on his family. He and his friend George Hudson have done this by creating a character called Joe, who is a thinly disguised Bobby. Joe insinuates himself into the lives of Ivy League students who accept him. Because Joe is so insecure, he thinks that they are playing with him. His thanks to his friends is to rape the sister of one of them in Central Park.

I sat back. 'Dad, Mom, please. I have said, how many times, hundreds of times, that I had nothing to do with the writing of the novel. Nothing to do with George insisting that I write the screenplay. No one, and I mean no one, had any idea that George was writing it. I came across it in a book store.'

'Another paragraph, Bobby,' my father ordered.

'I told you not to read the book.'

'Now we know why.'

I read on.

> One can compare the dialogue in the novel with the dialogue in the screenplay. Put side to side, it is almost the same in both. This is Bobby writing both. One can only imagine the fun that Bobby had with George Hudson in writing what is, in some ways, a revenge novel. A revenge on his family. Joe is reluctant even to talk about his family. One of his friends drags it out of him, one night. Why don't you talk about them? Are you ashamed of them? And Joe says yes. This becomes a standing joke. Eventually they make him tell them how his mother always appears with

coffee and cake, turning up at the wrong moment
to spoil any moment he has to talk to his father. The
coffee is weak and the cake is tasteless. This becomes
a standing joke as well.

'Are you saying George Hudson made all of that up?' my
father asked.

'It's a work of fiction.'

'Listen to this,' my father said, now picking up a copy of the
novel.

'Thanksgiving dinner. "Joe wondered why he liked these
people so much and why he was so grateful for the invitation.
Was it the amount of silver and linen on the table or the fact
that he was actually served by a maid? The father of this family drank. He wouldn't be allowed to attend the feast if he was
drunk, and the children told Joe that if he was sober, he wouldn't
have anything to say. As for the mother, it was obvious that she
did not approve of an Italian grocer's son at the table. And so
Joe looked at his friend and thought, We have something in
common, we're both ashamed of our parents".'

He put the book down.

'Thanksgiving with the Van Haesslers. Peter's father is an
alcoholic and I don't think his mother ever really liked me.'

'Because you are Jewish.'

'She didn't know any Jews. She thought I was an atheist. We
got on all right, on that basis.'

'So you denied your own religion. Then you sat at the table
with the anti-Semites. You broke bread with them.'

'Peter was my friend.'

'This rape in Central Park,' he said. 'How could you have
done such a thing?'

I began to feel bitter. 'I notice that you assume that I did.'

'We didn't bring you up that way,' my mother said. 'To take a
girl into Central Park. At night. What other reason could there
be?'

'It wasn't like that,' I said. 'Something happened that I am not proud of. I will remember it all my life. I can't begin to explain it.' Why wasn't that enough for them?

The attack went on.

'The coffee and cake,' my mother said, looking at my coffee cup and at the plate with the half-eaten piece of cake. 'Are you telling me that George Hudson made that up? How could you say such a thing to your friends?'

'To be ashamed of us,' my father added.

'I am not ashamed,' I protested. 'I am ashamed of the fact that our own family doesn't treat you with respect. I told everyone...'

'That I'm the best-read person you know,' he completed the sentence. 'You might say that about a librarian.' He waited for me and then went on. 'I know how you felt. And it hurt me too, to see how angry and upset you were. That's why I asked Stanley to help you get into Yale. So you could escape. I wanted that for you, because you wanted it so much. And look what happened. It wasn't good enough for you.'

I looked down at what Iris had written. There were pages of cross-references between the script and the novel itself. Well of course the dialogue sounds the same, I thought, George plagiarised my play. With the greatest reluctance, I forced myself to read Iris's analysis to the end.

Iris noted a blond-haired young man from an old Dutch family. He was the first to befriend Joe, the Thanksgiving dinner friend. More than befriending him, he was possessive of him. There was something unhealthy here, she wrote. It was the blond boy's emotional selfishness and his admiration for Joe's athleticism. And then of course that behaviour in Central Park. The rape. And the dorm games, with a sweaty, male camaraderie between young men who might just as well have been saluting Mussolini, if not Hitler.

> Although the ending of the novel seems to punish Joe, maybe give him his comeuppance, this is clearly a character who is not sorry for what he did to

Denise. In fact he justifies it to himself. He thinks he
should carry on being friends as if nothing had happened, even though he raped a girl on her eighteenth
birthday.

When I finished, I looked at them. 'Well, I have read it now.
Should I assume that everyone in the family has too?'

'Yes.'

'I don't understand,' my mother said. 'How could you do this?
I am not blind. I know how you've run away from me. Both of
you, locked up in that study. What was I supposed to do? Yes
I brought you cake and coffee, God forbid a wife and mother
should look after her men. And if it wasn't as good as you got on
Fifth Avenue, then I'm sorry. But you're mine too, Bobby. Every
day I look at you and I see my father, let him rest in peace, in
that handsome face. And all the time...'

'Mom, stop this, please.'

'And now this whore.'

'What are you talking about?'

'The so-called actress you're having sex with. A Gentile, of
course. A Jewish girl to go out with, to treat nicely, that isn't
good enough for you. It has to be Gentiles and the way you
treat them. At least you didn't take this one into a park.'

'Are you talking about Laura Hampshire?' I gaped at her.

'Is that her name?'

'Who told you this?'

'Your Uncle Stanley,' my father said.

'Has he been spying on us?' I was horrified. 'That's grotesque.'

'She's an actress under contract at his studio. Her morals are
his business.'

'They are certainly not,' I declared. 'They are no one's business
except hers. I know her better than anyone. She's a great actress.
Please stop talking about her as if she's some kind of slut.'

My mother countered, 'Well I am sorry but to me a woman
who is having sex with a man she isn't married to and isn't
going to marry is a slut. I wasn't born yesterday. I know about

those girls who throw themselves at your uncles in order to get into the movies and will do anything. For my son to behave like that!'

'Laura and I are free, and of age, and we are entitled to do whatever we like. We've done nothing wrong and I won't even start to apologise for it. I don't think for a second that she loves me but I am in love with her and I would proudly bring her into this house.' I knew my voice was getting louder. I thought I would explode.

'Bobby, stop shouting,' my father said. 'Please. Please try to understand how painful this is for us.'

I put my head in my hands. 'What's the point? I can't talk to you. You won't believe me when I try. Do you want to sit *shiva* for me and pretend that you don't have a son any longer?'

'That's a terrible thing to say. Please don't even think like that. But there is so much in this book that disturbs us. Like you were someone different. We know that something bad happened to you at Yale. If you don't tell us, then we have no choice but to think the worst.'

I paused. 'It's not as bad as the worst.'

In the silence, my father asked, 'When do you say you first read this book?'

'I don't know. A year ago. A bit longer. I found it in a book-store. They were sending back the other copies. No one was interested in buying it.'

'What did you think?'

'I was appalled.'

'But you didn't say anything.'

'I hoped it would go away. It would have, if Laura hadn't found a copy in New York and decided that she had to play Denise. When George insisted that I write the screenplay I couldn't believe it. It was torture. When Sam had the accident, I thought, Well at least that's the end of that movie.'

'You could have come to us and said, "Something terrible has happened, someone has written a book with things that I said to him and…" But there is so much you don't tell us. We're your parents, Bobby. When did that stop for you?'

'It never stopped,' I insisted, and then gave up.

In their way, they would forgive me. But the sense of guilt would hang between us for the rest of our lives. It could never be forgotten. It would lie there beneath the surface, waiting for the opportunity to emerge, to remind me of what a rotten kid I had been.

'What do I do now?' I asked.

'You must go to your Uncle Stanley.'

Of course, I thought, he was the one who had the power to punish.

'And what will happen then?' I asked.

'That's between the two of you.'

'Well, he can't exactly fire me,' I said sourly, 'I don't have a contract.' I stood up. 'Look, I'm just wearing an old shirt and a crumpled jacket. I can't go into the studio dressed like this.'

'Just go, Bobby. I called him when you called me. He's waiting for you.'

We parted formally. I wondered when I would ever come back here. I wondered whether there was anyone left on earth who was on my side.

◈

Of course the guard at the gate at the studio had no idea what was going on. He greeted me pleasantly, as he always did, and waved me through. I parked in front of the white administration building and took the steps two at a time. Kay was of course at her desk.

'Oh hi, Bobby.'

Of course she knew something was wrong.

'Been on vacation, Kay. Two weeks in the sun in Santa Barbara. How are you?'

'Well, you know, it's always crazy around here.'

'I think Uncle Stanley wants to see me.'

She picked up the intercom. 'Bobby's here, Mr Steingrove.' I didn't hear the reply. 'You go right in,' she said.

Uncle Stanley was sitting at his desk. He did not get up or greet me. I walked from the door across that vast expanse of white carpet until I reached him.

'Uncle Stanley,' I said. 'I've come straight from my folks. I apologise, I'm just wearing the clothes I had on vacation with me.'

'Where the hell have you been?' he demanded.

'Santa Barbara.' I was waiting for him to invite me to sit down. He didn't. I preferred standing anyway. If I sat in one of those Art Deco tub chairs I would be well below eye-level. It was better to meet his gaze straight on.

'My folks have told me everything,' I said, 'and I've read what Iris wrote.'

He stared at me. It seemed a long time since the two of us were in this office together, and he called me a helluva kid. Well the kid had grown up, and not just physically. I had gone to college and come back. I had learned how to write a screenplay. I had directed what I sincerely believed was a very good motion picture. And I had slept with Laura Hampshire. Everything in this studio was his. My screenplay was his property, the movie was his property, and I suppose Laura in a contractual sense was his property too. And I had my fingerprints over all of that. He had loved me, he'd been proud of me, but now I got the terrible sense that he couldn't stand the sight of me.

'I don't know where to start with you,' he said. 'Hank has told me everything.'

'About what?'

'About the movie and how you made it. You don't think I would let a kid direct a picture like that without knowing what he's doing every second of the day?'

'That's outrageous.'

'I thought you'd probably react like that.' He sniggered. 'But that isn't why you're here.'

'I hope it isn't to do with that terrible thing that Iris put together. That is completely unfair. I had nothing to do with the writing of that novel. I swear, Uncle Stanley, I don't know what else I can do to convince you.'

'George Hudson was your friend when you told him all those things to put in the book. He was your friend when he told me that you had to write the screenplay. The two of you laughing at me, thinking that Laura would get me to do it, he'd get his money and you'd get your career.'

I was ready for this. 'I knew nothing about the project until you called me in here. George had his reasons but it wasn't anything I asked him to do. I had nothing whatsoever to do with the writing of that novel,' I repeated.

'That isn't how Sam Price saw it.'

'Maybe that was the Bourbon talking.'

'You've never asked about him, how he's doing.'

'That's wrong. Hank told me.'

'Not that you would care. Once he was out of the way.'

I took a deep breath. 'I tried to stop him driving that night. I had nothing to do with George writing that novel.'

'You keep saying that but it all looks pretty obvious from where I'm sitting.'

'My own parents won't believe me and now you.' I was not pleading for mercy, not yet.

'You're out of control,' he said. 'Don't talk to me about your parents. You've broken their hearts. You're a goddamned ingrate.'

It was my father he cared about. It had never been me. Everything he had done for us was done because of the love of two brothers who could not have been more different but who saw the other as the only person they could trust. Uncle Stanley had swallowed his pride and got the banker to tell him how to buy me into Yale because that was what my father wanted. He had indulged me on the movie because he could not face humiliating my father by firing me. Now that even my parents were convinced that I made myself the outlaw, he could punish me. But I could not stop myself fighting back.

'Please, you know that isn't so. I'm grateful for everything you've done for me. You paid for my education, you gave me a job, you gave me my chance, twice, with this movie. I took nothing for granted. I've given my soul to this movie, to make you proud.'

'Proud? You've turned into a son of a bitch.'

'Then forget me. Think of the picture. You'll be proud of that.'

'You took over this picture when it was already over-budget and you've turned it into one of the most expensive motion pictures made on this lot. Sam Price is one of the finest directors in the business. But you weren't sorry when the key went into the ignition. You had a damned good idea what would happen next and what it would do for you.'

'No, I swear, I begged him.'

'No, Bobby, I sat here the next morning with you, looking hung-over and miserable because he wasn't actually dead. And the first chance you got you said you'd direct the movie. You knew exactly what you were doing.' I started to reply but he waved me to silence. 'You'll be after my job next.' He was working himself up.

'Please, Uncle Stanley, you know...'

'Who told you to screw Laura? And don't think I don't know what you made her do.' He saw my reaction. 'Yes, I had detectives following you two. And her maid had plenty to say. Disgusting stuff. She said it was the kind of thing that men had to pay women to do. You forced Laura to do it. It was degrading for her. They don't teach that at Yale. They teach it in whorehouses. This is my studio and it is my goddamned right to make sure that the actors I pay are not going to wind up in the gossip columns for immorality.'

'What we did was not immoral or disgusting. And it was our business.'

'She is an unmarried woman having casual sex with a strange man. In this town, that is immoral. And she has a contract that forbids any conduct amounting to moral turpitude. You put her in breach of contract to satisfy your own perversions.'

I kept shaking my head. 'It was not disgusting. And it's our business. What she does is her business and it's my business. No one has any right to make moral judgments on us.'

'You have no right to talk about morality, Bobby. Not after raping your friend's sister in Central Park. And she wasn't the last.'

'What are you talking about?' I cried.

'Your picture is not the only one that's run over budget this year. I had to have a meeting with the bankers. Which is none of your business but one of them took me aside and asked me about you. He said that a friend of his, a Mrs Van Haessler, had told him you were not allowed in her house any longer. Apparently she has daughters. Sisters of another friend of yours.'

I shook my head. 'No, no, no . . .'

'I paid to get you into Yale. I paid for everything. I paid for the clothes on your back. And all you did was shame me. Shame me and your parents and every Jew who gets into an Ivy League college on his brains.'

I couldn't let this go, but before I could catch my breath he carried on.

'Morality in this studio is my business. This is my studio.'

'Is that what you were thinking when . . .'

'What? When what?'

I couldn't help myself. 'The day you discovered her. She was in that room with you within an hour. I saw the two of you coming out of there. Remember? That was your right, as head of the studio. I never questioned that. But what's happened between Laura and me was completely different.' I could feel myself getting worked up too, and I didn't know how to stop. I was getting nowhere but I couldn't think of any way to get through to him. Like with my parents, everything I said seemed to be wrong.

'For Christ's sake, Bobby, you're not going to tell me you're in love with one another. You're a goddamned kid who's still wet behind the ears. She used you to get what she wanted. If you were really a director you never would have slept with her, not until it was all over. She did it so she could take over the movie. And she did. You're pathetic.'

'No,' I shouted. No doubt even Kay could hear me. 'We made love to one another because we wanted one another. It wasn't to say please or thank you or to get something out of the other. We weren't using one another.' Unlike you, I might just as well have said. 'I won't have you talking about morality clauses and moral turpitude. I did not rape Diana. And as for Peter's sisters, that's just grotesque.' I was close to tears. 'I'm sorry, Uncle Stanley.' I held up my hands. 'If you want me to leave, I will. I will just say that I dreamed of making more movies here. Great movies. That would have made you proud.'

'You're crazy. You're no relation of mine.'

'Fine. But when that movie comes out ...'

'When that movie comes out, your name will not be on the credits.'

'Oh, no.'

'Written and directed by Sam Price.'

'He did no such thing.'

'Written and directed by Sam Price. The guy you tried to kill.'

'You can't do that, Uncle Stanley.'

'You can't stop me.'

'It's as if you're throwing me into the gutter,' I pleaded.

'The gutter is where you belong.'

I saw it now. 'My God, you're still sleeping with her. And you're jealous.'

I thought for a moment that he would explode.

'You are from this moment, blacklisted from every studio in this town. You will never work here again. Not while I am alive.'

I stared at him.

'You're through. Now get out!'

◈

I staggered out of the office. I can't recall if Kay was at her desk or not. I got as far as my car when I saw Hank, my assistant director. He got as far as 'I was walking by and saw your car' when I pushed him against a wall and made a fist.

'Bobby, you've got ten years and probably ten pounds of muscle on me. I have a wife and kid. Give me a break.'

'For God's sake, Hank, we spent months together. You owed your loyalty to me, and to the movie. How could you have gone behind my back and been Uncle Stanley's spy all that time?'

'Bobby, use that brain of yours. You're a rookie directing Laura Hampshire. What did you think?'

'She wanted me to direct it. And he told me to go ahead and finish it.'

'She wanted you because she thought she could control you. And the first thing you did was that scene in Central Park. No one could believe what you did. When you went into her dressing room, we all knew you would come out, get in your car, and never be seen again. We couldn't believe it when you said there would be another take. When your uncle saw the rushes, he knew you were going out of control. So I said, "Let me look after Bobby. I'll give you a full report every day." It would have been a disaster if he had kept coming on the set.' He smiled. 'It wasn't easy, trying to tell you what he wanted you to do without sounding as if I was just repeating him.'

I unclenched my fist. 'At least you have a job here.'

'Please don't see it like that. We all wanted the movie to be a success. But you had ideas bursting out of you every five minutes. The budget was soaring. Even Laura...'

'Did she know what you were doing?'

He nodded. 'Don't blame her. She came with me a couple of times. She told your uncle everything was going to be all right.

She wanted to make this movie so bad and Laura tends to get what she wants. But sometimes she came to me and said she couldn't play a scene your way and she couldn't get through to you. You were burning out by then. I used to change the lighting or the set a bit when you weren't noticing. I'm sorry. We were really worried about you. I kept saying to Laura, we've got to find a way to make Bobby relax, to stop him thinking about the movie all the time, or we'll never make it.'

I looked down. 'She found a way. And Paul?'

'Paul worships the ground you walk on. You know that.'

'Uncle Stanley has just blacklisted me. Not just fired me, blacklisted me.'

'Bobby, I never dreamed he would do something like that. I am so sorry. I'm sure he'll calm down in a couple of days.'

'He won't.'

'What are you going to do?'

'I'm going home to think about it.' I took out my keys.

'Bobby.'

'What?'

'You're the most talented guy I have ever come across in this business. But you can't have it all at once. It doesn't happen that way.'

'We'll see.'

CHAPTER 21

DRIVING HOME THAT AFTERNOON was like the way I drove home after that first drunken meeting with Sam Price. I was at the studio one moment, and the next I was standing at my front door, with my suitcase from Santa Barbara in one hand and the key in another.

'Hey, Bobby's back,' cried my neighbour who was just getting home too. 'You're looking good.'

I went inside, dropped the suitcase, and collapsed on the sofa.

The next days are like a blank. I presume that I shopped, ate, washed and slept. It must be then that I started drinking vodka. Scotch reminded me of Peter, Bourbon of Sam, beer of Paul Hill, even brandy brought back the memory of that speakeasy brothel I went to with Alan when I lost my virginity. There wasn't much choice left on the liquor store shelves.

And then I began to think. There was one thing I knew how to do: to make a motion picture. My single achievement, my calling card, my audition was sitting in cans at Steingrove Films, waiting for the première in a month's time. I started by calling the other studios.

Uncle Stanley had made a head start, of course. He had not been bluffing about blacklisting me. I found that I could get past various layers of assistants and secretaries by emphasising my surname. They must have thought I was one of my uncles, who were respected in the business. Which meant that I could get through to the man I needed to talk to. But the moment he took the call, he realised that he was only talking to Bobby.

'Hey, I was sorry to hear you had a bit of an argument with your uncle,' they would say, or words to that effect. Then I made my pitch for a job. No one mentioned the blacklist. No one wanted any trouble. 'Gee, Bobby,' they would say, 'it sounds like you've had a tough time, and I'd really like to help but things are real slow at the moment. There's nothing out there. Nothing I could offer. No, we have more writers than we need right now.'

I went through the list. I started at MGM and ended in the depths of Poverty Row. Nothing doing. I really was not going to work again in this town.

I went to the bank and figured that I could live cheaply for at least a couple of months. I had been living cheaply all along, and could continue to do so. There was only one thing to do. I had to sit and write screenplays. Maybe if someone saw those, they might change their mind. If they would change their mind, I wouldn't mind changing my name, I thought.

So my regime began. I started every morning with push-ups and a run and a dip in the Pacific if it wasn't too cold. I would bash away at the typewriter. If I felt stuck I would go out and walk along the beach. Apart from sales clerks and waiters and waitresses I spoke to no one. I stopped answering the phone and the phone stopped ringing. I sent my parents a note saying that I was fine and busy writing, but now that I was permanently living out here, I might as well have the rest of my clothes and belongings. I arranged for a moving company to collect and deliver.

I narrowed my efforts to two projects. One was an adaptation of *Great Expectations*. I had adapted one novel, I could do it again. It was a book I loved. A boy is plucked from obscurity and finds himself in a well-heeled part of London. Then he does the noble thing. And he's hopelessly in love with a girl who is the wrong girl. Perfect. I decided that Shakespeare needed some updating. The history plays were another example of an unexpected young man proving himself by doing noble things, taking charge and confounding his elders: *Henry IV*. Only I put it in a contemporary setting. Henry would be some kind of young businessman, taking over a decaying firm and he would win the hand of the daughter of his bitterest rival. Both scripts seemed to write themselves.

I did not try to reach Laura. She would of course know everything about my conversation with Uncle Stanley. After much
reflection I decided that silence was the best and most respect-
ful way to deal with it. I interpreted her own silence as a sign
that she agreed. If I didn't know her well enough by now, I
could only blame myself.

I knew of course when the première of *And Some By
Virtue Fall* was taking place. I hardly expected an invitation.
Afterwards I bought all the newspapers and trade papers and
read the reviews. They loved it. It was a 'quality' picture. Laura
Hampshire had taken a risk and it had paid off. Sam Price had
done a great job; it was an achievement he could take pride in
as he continued to make a recovery from his accident.

The next day I went to the theatre, paid for a ticket like
everyone else in line, and sat and watched my own movie once
more. When the title came up Written and Directed by Sam
Price I wanted to run outside, but I stayed put. It had been a
couple of months since I had seen it, and despite everything
there were details which I had forgotten, the kind of details
that only I would have noticed. The expression on Denise's face
when she first saw Joe, Joe's lumbering walk, which I trained
Paul to do. When Laura walked through the Hoovertown with
that defenceless, stricken look on her face, I could hear a sob in
the audience. That still worked. The one thing I couldn't stand
was the happy ending we had to stick on instead of the real one.
I still expected the one I wrote to be there, and when it wasn't,
I felt cheated.

When it was over I turned to the young woman next to me.
'What did you think?' I asked, smiling.

'What's it to you?' she asked back and walked out with her
boyfriend.

◈

A few days later I had just got out of the shower when the
telephone rang. Without thinking I picked it up.

'Bobby,' came the surprisingly assertive voice.

'Paul?'

'How are you doing?'

'How are you doing?' I asked back.

'Great. Look, I wanted to explain...'

'You don't have to,' I said. 'I understand.' Not even my puta-tive younger brother had been allowed to talk to me. 'I saw *Touchline*.' That had been his first feature, the football picture, which had been released in time for the college football season. It had allowed Paul to show off his good looks, his strength, his grace, and his charm. It was very superficial but it had done well, thanks to him. 'It's good,' I said.

'Come on,' he laughed, 'you know which performance I want people to remember me for.'

'Tell me about the première,' I asked.

'Are you sure?'

'Sure.'

'It was a mob. All those fans screaming. Girls asking for my autograph.' I could imagine his genuine surprise and delight. 'All the women so glamorous. The place was packed. Everyone clapped and cheered when it was over. They really liked the movie. Have you seen the reviews?'

'I have. Go on.'

'Well, afterwards we all went up on the stage, and there was more applause. And your uncle made a really good speech.' He paused. 'Sam is still in a wheelchair, so he was just below the stage, but your uncle said some really nice things about him and everyone stood up and gave him an ovation.'

'Thanks.'

'Bobby, have you heard from anyone?'

'No. It's all right. I understand.'

'I don't know what to say. Look, I've got to go. I'm at Union Station. We're about to leave for New York. For the première there.'

'Good luck, but you don't need it.'

'Bobby, someone wants to say hello.'

Before I could stop him, he put Laura on the line.

'Hello, Bobby.' It was that voice.

'Laura. Congratulations. You knew it was the right movie for you, and you were absolutely correct. Worth every bit of effort.'

'It's your movie,' she said. I didn't say anything. 'Anyone who knows you, can see you in every frame.'

'No, no. It's about Denise and Joe,' I said. 'That's who they'll remember.'

'I can't see you,' she said.

Then she hung up.

❖

The first two screenplays had been dashed off so quickly that I was busy working on a third. On that day, I had woken up at 3 a.m., typed away until 6, slept until noon, and then went back to work. I forgot to shave. I forgot to eat at least one meal.

It was about five in the afternoon when I heard the screen door open. I looked up. Elaine was there.

I had lived in isolation for so long, and it had been so long since I had seen her, that for a moment I could not believe she was real. I had been feeding on my resentment of every member of my family that I had almost forgotten that there was one person I still loved. And there she was. I stood up from the desk chair, went over, and threw my arms around her.

'Thank you for coming,' I said. I stood back. She looked well. Her hair, her clothes, they gave her the air of someone who had indeed spent the last ten months in New York and not, as she claimed in her letters, paid any attention to how she looked. 'When did you get back? Why haven't you been in touch?'

'Why don't you ever answer your telephone?' she asked back. 'I've been trying for weeks.'

'I gave up,' I said. 'It's a distraction. Come on, sit down. God, I suddenly realise that you've never seen this place. It's not much, but it's cheap.' There was now even less floor space. When the truck arrived with my worldly goods I just piled the books on the floor. I used the trunk that used to go back and forth between Los Angeles and New Haven as storage for shirts and sweaters. My old desk, where I used to sit and do homework in high school, was stuck in a corner, and was piled with completed scripts. 'I'll make coffee,' I offered.

We went into the kitchen where I had not cleaned up in a few days. There were however some clean cups and saucers. One thing I had learned to do was to make coffee. We stood there while it brewed.

'So finally Larry told me just to go and track you down,' she added.

'Is Larry in LA? You're still together? Did you bring him?'

'He's here. I came on my own. We're engaged. I've come home to get married, Bobby,' she announced.

I gave her another hug. 'I'm very happy for you, you know that.'

'Yes, I know,' she kissed my cheek. 'I wish ...'

'That I could be there? It's a dream, Elaine, a dream that isn't going to come true. Hasn't someone explained everything to you yet?' I poured the coffee and we went into the living-room. Elaine perched on the sofa while I took my usual place at my desk chair. 'You look wonderful,' I said. I noticed the cereal bowl that was still next to the typewriter. I must have had breakfast, though I could not exactly recall when.

'I'm sorry I didn't bring Larry. I had no idea whether you'd be here or not.'

'I'm here all the time. Except when I go out to take some exercise. I'm taking a lot of that. I need to keep in shape.'

'You look fine. And my mother does in fact complain about my dress sense. She thinks I dress like a working girl who's given up on ever getting married.'

'Who cares?' I rubbed my cheek. 'I apologise, I forgot to shave. I was writing from about three to six and then crashed until midday.'

'I'm sorry you had a bad night,' she said.

'I have a lot of nights like that. I don't mind. It started right after...' I decided not to define what had happened. 'I went a little crazy, but not for long. Then I started writing. I just can't write from 9 to 5. The ideas come to me at all kinds of hours. I'm not paying attention to anything else, I'm thinking about the next scene. I go back to work and the next thing I know, it's time for dinner and I can't remember if I had lunch.'

'Have you eaten?'

I pointed to the cereal bowl. 'I must have. Sorry, Elaine, I'm just babbling. You'd be surprised how few people I've spoken to in the last weeks. I guess it all came out in a rush.'

'I saw that there was food in the kitchen. The bread looks all right. Would you like some toast?'

'Sure.'

'I hope you're not drinking too much of that,' she said, noticing a bottle of vodka on the writing table.

'I haven't touched that bottle in days.' We went back into the kitchen while she made toast. 'You're the one who fed Peggy's orphans. I guess you can't get out of the habit.'

'I'm not just a cook,' she declared. 'I have learned a bit about editing by now.'

'Are you being too modest?' I asked.

'Well, all right, the editor he hired to cut the documentary quit months ago. I'd been his assistant long enough to pick up where he left off. So yes, I am being modest.'

'And?'

'The other reason for being here is to show it. It's been a great success back East. Didn't you read any of my letters?'

'Of course I did. You just said that you were showing it on campuses and to unions and...'

'And don't you read the newspapers, Bobby? It's about the Popular Front. That's important. There's a civil war in Spain, in case you hadn't noticed. We need money for ambulances and medical supplies and, frankly, to get men to volunteer to fight.'

'I read the papers,' I said. 'I'm afraid my mind was on other things, like making a movie.'

'That's no excuse.' She buttered the toast and found a jar of jam. She handed me the plate and we went back into the living-room.

'I'm not in favour of overthrowing elected governments,' I said, while starting to eat. 'Or of Communists, who don't have elections that you could call an election, or of Fascists. And yes, I have read about what's happening to Jews in Germany. I know your father has offered jobs to some people who need visas to emigrate. I'm proud of him, for that.' It still seemed such a long way away. 'So is the documentary going to be shown here?'

'Yes, there's a huge event.' She opened her handbag and took out a leaflet. 'Lots of respectable Hollywood people like Fredric March and Gale Sondergaard will be there,' she said.

I looked at it. 'Should I guess that Iris will be there too?'

'She's been incredibly helpful,' she said. 'She knows everyone.'

'I bet. I bet there isn't a Communist in California who doesn't owe Iris a favour.' I put the leaflet down. 'Your wedding and Larry's documentary. Two good causes.' I shrugged. 'I can't be there.'

'I wish you were.'

I looked at her, and thought of the old Elaine, my best friend and cousin, who believed in me when no one else did.

'Well,' I said, 'shall we talk about another forbidden topic?' She waited. 'Were you here for the première?'

'Yes.'

'And?'

'Bobby, it's a wonderful movie, moving and true. Laura is amazing. You've seen the reviews.'

'Of course.'

'I sat there feeling so proud of you.'

'Do you mean you sat through the whole thing?'

'Yes.'

'But the screen credits come on first. When you saw Sam's name, didn't you and Larry get up and walk out?'

'No. I felt awful. It was totally unjust, but... what are you saying? Are you teasing me?'

'That was my movie, Elaine.'

'I know.'

'That was my movie.'

'You think I should have walked out in protest? Is this some kind of loyalty test?' she asked.

'Don't worry, I heard about the première. Paul called me from Union Station, on the way to New York. He's great. He thought I was a kind of older brother to him. I guess I was. Now he has to call me from a public telephone booth. I understand. I don't blame him. He told me how everyone applauded and how your Dad stood up and applauded Sam Price.'

'Yes.'

'I really tried to stop Sam getting into his car that night. I guess he blames me for what he did to himself. Well, now he has his revenge.'

'It's a brilliant movie.' She paused. 'Your parents were there.'

'How are they?' I asked.

'Grieving.'

'That's too bad.' I knew I did not sound sympathetic.

'I finally got your father to talk. He said that things would be all right once you stopped being angry.'

'I'm not angry with them. I just don't understand how they could believe any of those things about me. Even if they did, I don't understand why they can't forgive. We hurt each other so badly. Now there is this huge black cloud of guilt and shame hanging over us. It won't go away. I can't go there. Either some-one will say something or they will obviously not say something. It's impossible.'

'But if you talked to them...'

'No,' I said definitely. 'When I needed them to stand up for me, they didn't.'

'And you blame them?'

'Elaine, I know better than anyone the humiliations they've had to put up with. Living off your dad's charity. But at least they could be proud of me, and at least I could make them proud of me. That's over. From their point of view, I totally let them down. No, worse, I humiliated them in the novel. My Mom called Laura a whore. I couldn't begin to explain to them about Peter. Too much got said. Maybe some day we'll find a way back, maybe not. I just don't know right now.'

She valiantly tried to reason with me. 'I know how you've felt about the family. You can't live your life on your own. Some day, there must be a way for you to come back.'

'Elaine, I can never go back. Maybe to my folks. Not to the others. No one wants that. Is that why you're here, like some kind of peace emissary? Who sent you?'

'No one did. No one even knows I'm here, except for Larry.'

'Good, then you won't have to explain to anyone why you failed.'

'You can't go through life like that, Bobby.'

'I don't have much choice. Look.' I went and squatted down on my haunches in front of her. 'I'll make it simple. You know most of the story already. George wrote the novel. I had no idea. I was thunderstruck when I was told he wanted me to write the screenplay but I did it, yeah, to get out of the mailroom and because I was the only one who could make sure that it wasn't a picture of me and my parents. I kept making suggestions during the shooting and trying to help Paul because Sam was treating him so badly. That's why Sam came here, to tell me not to come on the set again. It was convenient because it was actually on his way to his mistress's. I tried to stop him driving, but he did. When he had the accident I thought, "Thank goodness, they'll drop the movie." I only begged to direct it when I realised it was going ahead regardless. I fell in love with Laura because I did and it was wonderful.

'The other version is that George and I plotted this from the start to humiliate the family. That I tried to kill Sam to take over the movie. That I seduced and perverted Laura in order to humiliate your father, to show him that I was the man she went to bed with because she wanted to, not because she had to show her gratitude. Your father thinks I raped one of Peter's sisters as well as Diana. It's gone too far.'

Elaine nodded.

'Those are the two versions, the truth and the non-truth.'

'Well, as far as I am concerned . . .'

'No. No, Elaine, you are not going to tell me who you believe. I forbid you. You cannot believe me and still be with them. And I can't allow you to walk out on them. You stay here with Larry, you work in the studio. You'll have a wonderful career. That in itself is making the choice.'

'And you've decided that I'll choose them.'

'You have to. There's no doubt about it.'

'I wish you'd stop talking in these absolutes. You've been on your own too long.'

'I know. I thought about this far too much. Like I said, I was going crazy, but the writing has saved me. Remember New Year's Eve? I told you the truth then and you told me what you thought of what I had done. That was hard, but I could take it. We still loved and felt loyal to one another. I asked you to stay here and help me. That was totally selfish, I am so proud of you going to New York and everything you did there. You said you didn't want to stay here and see what's going to happen. Neither of us could have dreamed of what would happen, but again, you were right. This isn't your fight. It's mine. On my own. Like being back in New Haven,' I smiled. 'I can do it.' I got up.

'Bobby, make the writing your way back.'

'Stop trying, please. I did the unforgivable,' I said. 'I had an affair with Laura. I mean a proper affair, as in directing her during the week and being with her on the weekend. And that was the end. Your dad hired detectives to get proof. They bribed Laura's maid who told them ridiculous stories about what we did. Even if I had tried, I promise you, no one could make her do what she didn't want to. It was making love in a real sense of the word. He couldn't stand it. Of course he forgives her, he has to. But there has to be a scapegoat. Oh and don't forget the moral turpitude I've supposedly committed. And that's before we get to what I've done to my parents.'

'And you said you aren't angry.'

I threw up my hands. 'Look, your father has taken everything away from me. I've been exiled. Worse. He blacklisted me. Maybe writing is my way back, but only if some studio is willing to take the risk. And to put someone else's name on the credits.'

She looked at the piles of paper. 'What have you done so far?' she asked.

I tried to calm down. 'This morning I've been working on a sophisticated comedy with a bittersweet ending. You know, people who think they know what they want out of life and then they didn't get it but they realise that they're glad they didn't. The second is a modern version of *Henry IV*. An industrialist has a profligate, wayward son he's more or less disowned. The father envies his cousin's son who has all the qualities his own son apparently lacks, but then it turns out that the cousin is really a traitor. He is trying to take over the company himself. It's the son who exposes that, wins the day, saves the company, and marries the daughter of their bitterest rival, just as his father is dying. The third is an adaptation. I don't see why MGM should make all the classy movies. I'm working on *Great Expectations*. I spent my childhood reading through Dickens and Trollope and Zola. There's a lifetime of good stories there.'

'That all sounds wonderful. But what will you do with them?'

'I'll tell you if it works out.'

'You mean I don't have the right to know?'

I didn't answer that.

'You should try something political,' she said, 'instead of

sitting here and feeling bitter. What is going on in Europe is terrifying. A dear friend, who lived in Peggy's house when I arrived, was killed outside Madrid, fighting to keep Franco out. I can't stop thinking about him. We can't sit here in America thinking that it will never affect us.'

'What are you going to do about it, after everyone has seen this documentary?'

'Larry wants to go back to Europe. He thinks there will be a war soon.'

'Do you want to go with him?'

'I will go where he is, but I think he should make movies here, important movies. If he wants to reach people, to get them to wake up to what's going on, that's the better way to do it.'

'You mean you've told your dad to give him a job.'

'I would, if Larry agrees.'

'He'll give him a job if you ask. But someone has got to tell Larry the facts of life about Hollywood. If he wants to make them political you've got to be really subtle. Someone has to tell him how to get the message across without the audience noticing it. So Larry's going to become a producer, and you'll be the editor.'

'I think I'm good at it.'

'You'd be good at anything,' I said, 'once you realise that you can. Any ideas yet for his first feature?'

'I don't know.'

'What about what you just told me, about your friend who got killed? Foreign troops save Madrid from Franco. American guys there, good, ordinary American guys, guys who believe in something and want a bit of action. Everybody loves action movies. You need someone on the barricades, someone noble, handsome, inspiring. Try Paul Hill. There's more talent there than you'd think. Give him a speech to the troops. He could do it. He could go back to being the All American guy, only this time he discovers what freedom really means. Not to overfed Americans back at home, but to the young men who are doing the fighting, just as their ancestors fought for freedom in 1776.

The men who are fighting are fighting for freedom. To bring freedom to people who have never really tasted it.'

'You know, that sounds wonderful.'

'By the way, don't kill Paul off in the movie. Fans won't like that. And make sure he gets the girl. Some nice Spanish girl. He's a Catholic, Paul, so that will please him. Make her a good Catholic even though she's on the government side. Didn't I read that Franco has appropriated the Catholic Church? Take it back from him.'

'Anything more?' she asked.

'Give me time. I'm making this up as I go along.' I laughed.

'You do understand,' she said.

I shook my head. 'I was only thinking of how to make a movie. I can't stop myself.'

'Couldn't you...?'

'Draft a scenario? Write the speech for the barricades? Produced by Larry, and written if not directed by Bobby Steingrove? You don't give up, do you?' I was beginning to feel restless. I wanted to get back to work. And in my mind I was reaching a slow, terrible conclusion. I needed my courage to go through with it.

I said, 'I'll tell you what. Write and let me know the exact hour of your marriage. And at that exact hour, I will stop whatever I am doing, and I will make a prayer for the two of you. All the happiness in the world.' I got up.

She watched me until she was sure that I really wanted her to go. 'I guess you want to get back to your writing,' she said, finally.

'Yeah. Sorry.'

'I'll bring Larry next time. You'll like him so much.'

'I'll take your word for it.' I took a deep breath. Then I smiled and shook my head. 'Please don't.'

'What?'

'Please don't come back,' I said. 'We'll both find this easier if you don't.'

'Bobby!' she cried. We stood and faced one another. When she realised that I was being serious, she turned and left.

I remember the sound of the screen door banging. I went and stood at the doorway. I saw her unlock her car. She was waiting for me to change my mind. To go out after her and apologise and tell her that of course we had to keep in touch. How many times had I told her that everything was going to be all right, that I was Bobby, still Bobby, and that nothing could ever change between the two of us? But it had changed. Neither of us wanted it, but it had happened. I didn't move. She took a long time to get into the car and to start it. I waited. I watched the last tie to my past drive away.

'You're a rotten kid,' my mother would say when she was annoyed.

'You deserve to be in the gutter,' Uncle Stanley had said.

'Families are a waste of time,' Peter had said to me the day we met.

Life was a lot more complicated than that.

※

A couple of hours later the telephone rang. I was going to let it ring and ring but then I thought maybe Elaine left something or something dropped out of her bag. I did not want her coming here again so I answered it.

'Bobby? Am I talking to Bobby Steingrove?'

I gasped. 'George? What the hell is this?'

'I'm in Los Angeles.'

'What for?'

'My agent told me that I was entitled to attend the world première, having written the novel.'

'You were there?'

'Unfortunately not. First, I called your uncle's office. A nice woman dealt with it.'

'Kay.'

'That's right, Kay. I told her who I was and I assumed I would get an invitation. She called back pretty quickly. Your uncle said I wasn't welcome. She put it more courteously than that. But then I thought, what the hell, I've never been to California, and why should I wait for the New York première? So I got on a train. I've been here for ages. Movie theatres don't care who they sell a ticket to.'

'I know.'

'I've called you several times. You don't seem to like answering the telephone.'

'I've got out of the habit.'

'I need your help. I'm thinking of suing your uncle. I sold the rights to him on condition that you wrote the screenplay. Not someone called Sam Price. Or is that your new pseudonym?'

'Sam exists.'

'I called my agent and my lawyer. They're thinking about it. The lawyer wants a deposition from you.'

'Forget it, George. I did write the screenplay. For that matter, I directed the movie as well.'

'Really? Are we talking about the same movie? So who the hell is Sam Price?'

'Long story. Right now I am trying not to tell you anything. I don't want the rest of my life to wind up in another novel of yours.'

George laughed. 'Don't worry. That was probably my last novel. You obviously don't see *The New Yorker* or *Vogue* or a lot of other stuff. I'm the guy who dishes the dirt on the upper classes, from the point of view of a member of the upper classes. They think it carries more conviction that way. Better than Clare Boothe. You'd be surprised how many of my fellow members of the upper classes are willing to tell me everything, just to get some other people in trouble.'

'Come to think of it, my cousin Elaine wrote that you were in London. Sending back funny but nasty reports about the King and Mrs Simpson.'

'That's me. I came home ages ago. Elaine! I remember her.

I really liked her. Was she in New York? I would have been happy to meet her again.'

'She's right here in LA. She's going to marry a Socialist documentary maker or journalist or something who's made a movie about the Popular Front. She wants to raise money for ambulances. And to encourage men to go over there and fight. Think about it, George, you might make a better soldier than you think.'

'Sorry, Bobby. Too many people over here would like to see me shot. They'll be bribing the other side to do their dirty work for them. I am not ready to die in a Spanish ditch. Not yet.'

'That's too bad.'

'And are you sure about that Socialism stuff? I thought Hollywood people ran a million miles away from real politics.'

'Stick around and go to the showing of the documentary, and ask her. She'll tell you. I also have a Communist cousin called Iris. You underestimate us. And I'm afraid that I'm one of those people who wouldn't mind seeing you dead.'

'That's a bit strong. As your memory seems to have become selective, I trust that you'll give me a few minutes to explain. I wanted to be a writer. I always have. But I am better at observing than I am at writing, even I know that. I had to break in somehow, with something that made my name without anyone worrying about whether I was the next Sinclair Lewis. There was this publisher I met through the Elizabethan Club at Yale. He said what people really like right now, with the Depression still on, is a story about how rotten the rich are, the ones who haven't suffered and who think God protects them. He said if I didn't care if any of my friends ever talked to me again, I should write a story like that, from the insider's point of view. No problem publishing that. So that's what I did. I had my *succès de scandale*.'

'The bookstore where I bought it was about to send back a stack of unbought copies.'

'It was published for the East Coast. That's where the magazine and newspapers that I write for are based. Frankly, I never dreamed anyone would make a movie out of it. Did you see *My Man Godfrey?* Hollywood thinks that a Hoovertown was a place to find a forgotten man for a treasure hunt. Not what Joe did. I hope you haven't forgotten that everything in that book which might be a description of you and your family is what you chose to tell me yourself. It was you who sat in my parents' kitchen the night of Diana's eighteenth birthday party. You do remember that. '

'That didn't mean you could put it into print.'

'Who told Steingrove Films to make the movie?'

'We made the movie because of Laura. She was desperate to play Denise.'

'I'm glad she did. She's nothing like Diana but she was brilliant. I couldn't believe it. Do you remember how you and I used to see Laura Hampshire's pictures in New Haven? A bunch of crap with Donald Marshall. Boy, can she act!'

'I know.'

'Hey, you just said that you were the director. Can the world thank you for turning Laura Hampshire into a real actress?'

'I think the credit goes to her. But yeah, I played quite a big part in that.'

'God, you have talent. I used to be so jealous of the way you could write.'

'Is that why you plagiarised my play?'

'You abandoned it. I'm the guy who took it out of the waste-paper basket.'

'Yeah, yeah.'

'I just quoted you. Look, when the publisher told me how to get published, I knew there was only one story I could tell. Yours.'

'Everybody here thinks I wrote it with you. My whole family thinks it was a plot by me to get revenge on them. That making it a condition that I write the screenplay was a big game that you and I were playing.'

'Why don't you tell them the truth?'

'Believe me, I tried.'

'Let's stop arguing, okay? The truth is that when your uncle suddenly wanted to buy the movie rights, I thought, "Well, at least I can do something for Bobby in return. Let him tell his story his own way." I assumed you'd gone to work at Steingrove Films.'

'I was in the mailroom. Having been in the labour gang.'

'Your uncle paid for you to go to Yale and then put you in the mailroom? After the labour gang?' George laughed. 'That's a story I've got to tell.'

'George, I think I'm going to hang up now.'

'No, wait. I don't understand, why isn't your name on the screen credits?'

'Because of a lot of stuff, including the fact that my family is convinced that I wrote the novel with you, as some kind of revenge on them. To cut it short, my uncle has blacklisted me from the motion picture industry. I'm nobody out here right now.'

I could hear him take in a breath. 'Do you want me to tell them the truth?'

'Who's interested in truth?'

'I'm sorry about that. Just tell me, Bobby, what are you going to do now?'

'I've been writing screenplays. Some stuff I've been working on already. Some new stuff.'

'Who's going to produce them?'

'I've no idea. I was just trying to save my sanity and maybe find a job somewhere. I don't know where. I don't think Broadway is waiting for me.'

'You need someone with money to spare and who is impressed by you.'

'I'll put that in the classified ads.'

'You know who that is,' George said.

'If you're thinking of who I think you're thinking of, I don't think Alan would be very happy to see me right now.'

'You underestimate him. Bobby, do yourself a favour and wise up.'

'I think we had this conversation the night Diana and I went into Central Park.'

'Wasn't I right then?'

'Okay, the police didn't come and Alan didn't cut my balls off.'

'You aren't waiting for Diana to forgive you first? She may have guessed that you would never forgive yourself. Why should she bother?'

'Thanks, George.'

'Bobby, one more thing. I always wondered why Alan saw you as such a pal. You and Peter, you and me, sure. But he did. I've done enough Freudian crap for one day, so I'll just say, if you can't talk Alan Pearson into backing a movie for you, you aren't our Bobby.'

CHAPTER 22

ON THE MONDAY BEFORE THANKSGIVING I called Alan Pearson's office. Mr and Mrs Pearson would be out of town for the holiday, I was told, but, after a further call, I was told that Mr Pearson would be back after Thanksgiving. Mr Pearson would see me.

I bought the cheapest ticket to New York. I wanted to stay in the Yale Club but I had never bothered to become a member. I had my East Coast clothes, which still fitted all right. I needed a good haircut. When I arrived in the city, I went to Peter's barber for a shave and haircut and manicure on the day of the appointment. In my best suit, and with copies of my screenplays, newly typed out, I went down to the Chrysler Building and the offices of Pearson Industries.

There was an air of quiet power about the offices. Despite the sleek modernity of the building itself, the Pearsons favoured lots of walnut and mahogany, large desks, acres of space, deep carpets, and family portraits. There was no obvious hint of the steel mills and coalmines and whatever other pies they had their fingers in. This was a place where men of power took decisions that affected men who worked far away and whose interests were and always had been subordinated to the needs of the owners. And Alan was nominally in charge.

I arrived promptly for my 3 o'clock appointment. There were two secretaries in an outer office and a male assistant in an inner office. It was he who showed me into the enormous room that would have dwarfed any man who wasn't as large as Alan. He got up from his desk and came to a point halfway between that and the door and held out his hand.

'Bobby Steingrove,' he said. 'As I live and breathe. How are you?'

He was looking fit, strong, and immensely well groomed and tailored. We had not seen each other in eighteen months. I was struck at how - what was the word? - *professional* he looked. He had grown up fast into the job. He indicated a chair in front of his desk. He took the other one, opposite, and crossed his leg. I took that as an early good sign.

'You're looking good. It must be that healthy California living.'

'That's what we tell ourselves. I do my best to keep in shape. It helps to live next to an ocean.'

'So you're in town.'

'Something like that. It's been a long time,' I pointed out.

'Indeed.' He waited.

'And you're married, I heard about that. Congratulations,' I said.

'I'm a lucky guy. We were both young but I thought, hell, I could wait another ten years to find someone as special as Nancy. You?'

'Not yet.'

'Cigarette?' he leaned over to offer it. It was a habit I avoided but on this occasion I thought that I should.

'Thanks.' We each lit up and settled down to being in the same room together.

'You don't have to ask me,' Alan said.

'About what?'

'The novel. I wondered if you'd get in touch after it was published.'

'You may be surprised to hear that I was pretty upset too. So I thought, what's the point? I could've written to say, No, it didn't happen like that, but then I thought, we both know George. He was only trying to make trouble.'

I was glad we got to the novel first. Clear the air, if it could be cleared.

'I'm glad you didn't write. That would have been whining.'

'True.'

'I wish I'd never met George,' Alan declared.

In the last days my own views of George had softened. I could remember sitting in his kitchen while he made me breakfast and told me that I would not go to jail and that Alan wouldn't kill me. It was George who had advised to come here. A funny loyalty made me steer the conversation away from him now.

'I think George has moved on. We won't see him again.'

'I did ask Diana what was fiction and what wasn't.'

'What did she say?'

'"Stop being such a jerk, Alan." She's still a pain.'

I shrugged. Nothing had changed between those two.

'Then I thought of all the stuff you and I used to get up to. You always had the right attitude, that's why I wanted you there. You can't have the right attitude if you're feeling guilty, or if you're thinking, "Hey, what am I doing here?" I think I've got you right. I need to get guys right. It's part of my job.'

I wasn't going to argue with that. There was no point in talking about guilt to Alan. George had told me to carry on as if nothing had happened. I couldn't forget but I had carried on. Dorm games. The Handbook of the Paris Brothel. I now had difficulty believing that had been me. But I had kept up with Alan. We weren't equals, but I had kept up with him. He had wanted me there and I was. He remembered that. That is what mattered today.

'How is your job?' I asked.

'The old guys treat me as a reincarnation of my grandfather. No one remembers my Dad. Probably because he died doing the one thing he was any good at.'

'You're good at both,' I reminded him.

Alan smiled and lit another cigarette. 'I'm a married man now.' That's what he tells everyone, I thought. You don't have to spell things out to the kind of friend that knows you too well already.

'Well, you always knew what you wanted to do, once you took over,' I told him. 'A company where everyone felt part of a team. So much of a team that no one would even want to go on strike. No team goes on strike if they admire the captain.'

'Still clever, Bobby. There have been a couple of times when my uncles and I clashed about what to do, and where to take the companies. I got my way and hey, I turned out to be right. It's easy after that.'

'Absolutely,' I agreed. I barely knew what he was talking about. 'I've been a little cut off, out there on the Coast.'

'I bet.'

'So what happened to Diana?' I asked. It felt safe to ask it now.

'Our grandmother died. So we sold that house on Fifth Avenue. You wouldn't believe what the property taxes were or what this city spent it on. Diana got a big share of it. Apparently our grandmother decided that she needed a small fortune in order to buy herself a prince for a husband or a duke or God knows. As if Diana wanted one of them. What she really liked was art. Modern art and modern artists. Particularly the artists. So she buys this huge apartment on the left bank and sets up a salon. Open house, open handed, and they all come flocking. I've been over there a couple of times. You wouldn't believe those guys or the stuff that's hanging on her walls. You know Diana, no one could make her do anything she didn't want to do. So there she is, calling all the shots, keeping half the Paris art world alive.'

'That's what she always wanted.'

'It's so goddamned phoney. They all tell her how witty and beautiful and avant-garde she is. She loves it. Goes everywhere, meets everyone, sleeps with everyone, or so I am told. One or two of those guys have come over here and expected me to pay for an exhibition for them just because they screwed my sister. I tell them to get lost. You just missed her, she was here for a couple of weeks.'

'I'm sorry.'

'We all went to the movie, of course. Nancy got us tickets for the première. She loves premières and opening nights. I feel I spend half my life in tails, sitting in our box at the opera.'

'And?'

'Didn't you have anything to do with it? I mean, didn't your uncle think that you might be some help in the circumstances?'

'I wrote the screenplay, Alan. And I directed it.'

He sat up. 'Are you joking? You weren't on the screen credits, were you?'

'No. If you don't believe me, I have the shooting script at home. It's one of the few souvenirs I've got. So what did you think of the movie?'

'Hard to look at it objectively. I kept thinking, "Did that happen?" and "Who said that?" And "When are we going to see how Joe lost his virginity?".'

'There's something called the Hays Code in Hollywood. No sex.'

'Plus Diana was sitting there doing this crap about, "Look, I'm being played by Laura Hampshire, the glamorous movie star. Nobody's playing you, Alan."'

'Someone was. I made sure he didn't do an imitation.'

'There was this party afterwards. Diana drank too much and she went up to Laura Hampshire and said I'm the real Denise and would you like to know the truth?'

'What did she say?'

'"Madam, I am an actress. I play a part. The only truth is what is on the screen."'

'Good for Laura.'

'And then because she hadn't been obnoxious enough already, Diana said, "I know you're dying to ask me for the details, but you'll never get them from me, except I will tell you that Bobby wasn't the first." Jesus, can you believe that? She was only eighteen.'

'That's the past.'

Alan shook his head. 'Too much Paris, too much art, too many artists, if you ask me. Is that how they behave over there?'

'I wouldn't know. What does your wife think?'

'Nancy thought the picture was brilliant. Best thing she's ever

seen. As far as the novel, and all that stuff is concerned, she thinks
it's all a joke. Diana likes to tell her what a bad boy I was, and how
women used to come up to me in the street and offer themselves
to me for a quarter. Nancy's the kind of woman who thinks that
no matter how bad a man is, she's the one who understands and
can redeem him. I don't think she would've married me unless
she thought she had her work cut out for her. Anyway, Diana is
hardly the sexual paragon of the Pearson family.'

'Was Peter there?'

'Are you kidding? That guy's so messed up, he gives me the
creeps. He plans on getting married next year. That's his story.'

'Remember how you told me you were friends through thick
and thin. You guys went way back.'

'You were the one I chose to go around with.'

'I guess we're the last of the pals,' I pointed out.

He took a moment to remember what that word had meant,
the difference between the pals and the other guys, who were
our friends. And here I was, back again, doing what? Trading
on the memories of our student days? I had a cold feeling that
he might be lumping me together with the artists who had also
had sex with Diana and who seemed to believe that her brother
therefore owed them something.

'So what happened?' he suddenly asked.

'In respect of what, Alan?' I asked, looking him straight in
the eye.

'The screen credits.'

'My uncle took my name off.'

'No! I thought Jews were big on family.'

'They are. And then there are the Steingroves.'

'Why didn't you sue him?' He looked genuinely surprised.

'It's his studio. I didn't have a contract. Even if I had there
probably would have been a clause saying that he could do
whatever he liked.'

'So what did you do to piss him off?'

'Thanks for assuming it's my fault.'

'Come on, you haven't come 3,000 miles not to spill the beans.'
He was enjoying this.

I was prepared for this moment. 'There was some stuff I could
have got away with. What I couldn't get away with was having an affair with my leading lady.' For some reason I had not
expected the reaction this provoked.

Alan paused and then burst out laughing. 'You're shitting
me.'

'No.'

'Bobby Steingrove has been screwing Laura Hampshire.' In a
second, things had changed.

'That's the crude version.'

'You didn't tell her some of the places that body of yours has
been?'

'No.'

'Does that mean that I could guess some of the stuff you were
doing?'

'I'm not going to answer that. I will just say that it is the same
Laura Hampshire you used to gawp at when we were students.
And I saw where your hand used to go in the movie theatre in
New Haven.'

Alan sprang up, still laughing and went to a cupboard.
'Drink? You deserve it.'

'Thanks, I've been drinking vodka lately.'

'Vodka? I don't have any vodka. Is the best Scotch you can
buy good enough for Laura Hampshire's lover?'

'Ex. That's fine, thanks. And a bit of water.'

He came back with the drinks. 'Laura Hampshire. And that
upset the old man?'

'Yes. He talked about morality clauses. Moral turpitude.'

'You're about the last guy to care about moral turpitude. I
thought the lawyers put clauses in there so they could get rid
of the awkward ones. Morality? In Hollywood? Not from what
I've heard.' He held up his glass. 'There is no sexual morality.'

'There is no sexual morality,' I replied. I took a sip. That strong taste. I was back in Peter's room, that first afternoon. It's only a relaxer.

'So what are you doing tonight?' he asked.

'Tonight? Nothing.'

'Come and have dinner with us. We're going to a new place. Then dancing. Nancy loves to dance. Have you brought a tuxedo?'

'Yes.' I had shoved it in at the last minute, just in case.

'I bet you're still a great dancer.'

'Sure.'

'Do you remember you and Diana, starting the dancing the night of her birthday party?'

'I remember.' I wish he hadn't said that. Dead and buried memories.

'That guy in the movie. He couldn't dance for crap.'

'It made a better story that way. Grocer's sons don't take ballroom lessons. I was taught by the choreographer at Steingrove Films. That's what Hollywood is all about, making good stories. I'd love to join you, but would your wife mind?'

'I'll call her but she'll be thrilled. The writer and director of *And Some By Virtue Fall*. And we're the only people in New York who know it. She'll love that. Turn on your old charm. She thinks all the guys I work with are boring. "Don't you have any interesting friends, Alan?" she keeps asking.'

'I'll do my best.'

'Only no "What Alan did when he was at Yale" stories,' he joked.

'There's my reputation to protect as well, don't forget.'

'So what's next?' he asked.

I took a deep breath. 'Actually, that's why I'm here.'

'Fire away. But don't ask to come into the steel business.'

'Hardly. Uncle Stanley kicked me out.'

'What, for screwing a movie star?'

'He blacklisted me.'

'Christ. You must be glad to get out of that town.'

'No. The plan is to go back. I want to make movies. It's what I'm good at. I know that now. Anyone who sees that movie knows that.' I patted my briefcase. 'I've got three screenplays here. Original stories and adaptations. I was brought up on nineteenth-century novels. The stories are fantastic. I just had to update them. They make for classy pictures.'

'Such as?'

'There's one about this industrialist. He's got a wayward son, he's always off getting drunk and womanising. The old guy has written him off but he thinks that another young man, the son of a cousin, is great. Only that young man is really a traitor. He wants to bump off the old man, take over the business, and sell it to some corrupt man. The wayward son finds out, comes back, saves the day – of course it's a close call. The old man is dying by now, but he knows he can give the business to his son because he has all the virtues he wanted for him. He had them all along, but his father didn't realise.'

'I like that.'

'Shakespeare got there first, but I've adapted it.'

'Sounds good.'

'I could hire sound stage space. I could persuade some studio to distribute it, so long as they didn't stand any risk. I worked with a lot of good men on *And Some By Virtue Fall.*' I paused. 'Do you know about Jock Whitney and David O. Selznick?'

'I know Jock. He bankrolls the pictures and he's the president or something. Is that why you're here? Let's cut to the chase. You want me to bankroll Bobby Steingrove Productions?'

'I've worked it all out. I can sit down and show you everything.'

'I think we need another drink.' He went over to the cupboard and poured more. 'You know I could say, You have some nerve coming here after all this time and asking me to put up, I don't know, hundreds of thousands of dollars, on some crazy scheme just so you can show your lousy uncle that you can make movies just as well as he can. Just because we had some fun and games when we were students.'

So that's how Alan did business. 'You could say all of that.' I looked at him. 'It's me, Bobby. It's not a crazy scheme. If I thought you'd lose money on this, I wouldn't be here.'

'Where are you going to find the guys to make the movie?'

'Like I said, I worked with some brilliant ones.'

'But they work for Steingrove Films...?'

'Pay them more and they'll leave, to work with me. It's only a question of money. I had a great crew. I think I could persuade them to come with me. Even if I can't, there's plenty of talent out there. And I know what a good cameraman is by now.'

'And the actors?'

'There are freelance actors in LA. And I intend to go to go to all the plays I can here. Do my own talent scouting.'

'Don't you need stars?'

Good, I thought, I've got him interested. 'I'll make the stars.'

'What about Laura Hampshire?'

'She's under contract.'

'Some contracts are made to be broken. I have enough money to break it.'

'I don't want her that way,' I said. 'Not yet. The contract runs out in a year or two. I don't want to bribe her. I want her to walk in and say, "I want to work with you, Bobby, I want to make another movie with you."'

'And you think she will? The sex was that good?'

'Her performance was that good. No one knew how good an actress she is. They do now. That's due to two people. She's one of them.'

Alan smiled. 'Bobby the clever one. How much?'

'Depends on how much you'll loan me. I can squeeze a movie into whatever budget I have.'

'What makes you think I have any spare money?'

'I have no idea. If you're in trouble, then I'm sorry I wasted your time.'

'I'm not in trouble. But you don't know what's around the corner. Goddamned Roosevelt, he hates business.' He drank from his glass. 'You probably voted for him.'

I had but this wasn't the moment to explain why. 'I've been too busy making a movie. I suppose I should confess that my cousin Elaine – you remember her?'

'Sure. Everybody liked her.'

'She's going to marry a journalist who's made a movie about the Popular Front. He's showing it all around the country. To raise money for Spain.'

'You mean for the Reds?'

'He probably thinks it's more complicated than that. You know, got to support the legitimately elected government.' I could see him getting angry. 'Of course, we're supposed to be neutral.'

'Screw neutrality. I really hate the Reds, and that's what the Spanish government is, Reds, whatever name they give themselves. Sure Franco takes arms from Hitler and Mussolini, who wouldn't? But he's his own man and when he wins, he'll just tell them to get lost, and there's nothing they can do about it.'

'I guess you're right,' I said. That got him off FDR. I thought of Larry's documentary about the Popular Front and the fight against Fascism. The film was due to be shown that night in Hollywood. Good for Elaine and Larry, but it was also a triumph for my cousin Iris. I wasn't going to argue with Alan over Spain.

'Good man,' he nodded.

'But my screenplays, they're not political.'

'I wouldn't touch them if they were.' He drained his glass and put it back. 'Yeah, I can see, you're going to be a different kind of Hollywood. That's great. I am not saying I am going to give you the money. You have to sit down and make your case.'

'Of course. I'm here for several days.'

'I think I'm going to leave this to Nancy. She was talking

about backing a Broadway show or something. Yeah, persuade her and then persuade me.'

'Fine.'

He looked at his watch. 'I think that is as far as we can take it. I've got some other appointments.'

He stood there, I got up. We faced one another. At Yale, if someone had asked me where I would be in ten years' time I would have thought of the soft option – lawyer, married to one of the nice young women I met in Maine in August, and still best friends with my now ex-sexual partner Peter Van Haessler. That didn't happen. I was now in the only world left to me, the hard, competitive world where Alan Pearson called the shots. He had always wanted me there because I was the one who could keep up with him. Now, with his money, I would make great movies. I had to, and then Alan could say to his friends, 'Bobby Steingrove? Yeah, I'm the one who's backing that enterprise. It's part of my job to get guys right, and I did.' That was the game I would play for the rest of my life.

'Maybe over dinner I can tell you what it's like to make a movie, with the best crew in the world. To work like a team, looking after one another, to walk on the set in that glow of loyalty. You'll understand that, Alan.'

'Nice thought. In this business, you have a lot more colleagues than you have friends. Friends are rare.'

'Tell me,' I replied.

He nodded and then asked, 'By the way, where are you staying?'

'A hotel I found.' A cheap, noisy, crummy hotel. I wasn't wasting money on that.

'Forget it. Come and stay with us. We've got this duplex on Park Avenue. Far too much space.'

'That's very kind,' I said, 'and I accept.'

'I'll call Nancy and tell her. Just go and get your stuff.' He took out an expensive pen and wrote his address for me. 'You'll still have to make your case. I'd like Nancy to get to know you.

She's got her head screwed on. So do I. That's why our marriage is going to work.'

'I'm glad to hear that,' I said. I grinned, knowingly. 'It's all about trust, isn't it?'

'That's right,' he agreed.

Maybe he was thinking of some of our escapades, which could have gone embarrassingly wrong, or dorm games, when his old friends wondered what the hell I was doing there. I had never let him down. Maybe part of him did think that he should punish me for Diana but that time had passed. I still had to live with it.

❦

I left Alan to his business day and went back to my hotel. I packed my tuxedo and other things and took a cab to Park Avenue.

As the doorman came forward I was suddenly reminded of that morning, after Diana's party, when I turned up at George's building. If only I hadn't lost my key to the Van Haesslers'. If only the doorman had refused to call. If only I hadn't told George everything.

'I'm Bobby Steingrove,' I told him, 'Mrs Pearson is expecting me.'

He called up to confirm and then helped me with my suit-case into the elevator. In fact it was a maid who answered the door. Mrs Pearson was still at the hairdresser. She took me to my room, which was on the upper level of the duplex. The apartment could not be more different from the house on Fifth Avenue: everything was white and silver, clean and simple, and contemporary. A few pictures, a few objects. Nothing that could have been inherited.

I had a shower and changed into my tuxedo. I took my time. I looked at myself in the mirror and felt like the old Bobby, well groomed, well dressed, indistinguishable from his friends. Like the life I thought I would have. But I was a guest and here to do business.

By the time I sauntered downstairs Nancy Pearson was already dressed and ready. She called to me from the drawing-room.

'Is that Bobby Steingrove?' she called. 'I'm in here.'

'Hello.'

'I'm Nancy Pearson.'

I should have guessed. She was tall, slender, blonde, and beautiful. She looked nothing like the women Alan and I once knew. She looked a lot like Laura.

'Would you like to fix yourself a cocktail?' she offered. 'Make it two.'

'Delighted.' I looked at what was on the tray. 'Two gin gimlets? Or too simple?'

'That sounds fine.'

While I mixed the ingredients in the silver shaker, I could sense Nancy looking at me. Like Laura, in the early days, wondering if I were worth it. Before she decided that she would be the making of me, because if I were that good, Laura Hampshire was the one who would shine.

'I am wondering how to introduce you,' she said. 'I'd love to say, "This is the man who really wrote and directed *And Some By Virtue Fall*."'

'The problem with that, Nancy, is that people would then ask, "So why isn't your name on the screen credits?"'

'Well?'

I handed her one of the glasses. She had not got up from the sofa.

'Thank you,' she said. 'Did you learn that in Hollywood?'

'Mixing cocktails? It's one of the many things I learned at Yale. After they abolished Prohibition,' I added.

'Not from Alan.'

'No, one of our other friends. Alan could do a lot of things, but he couldn't mix cocktails.' I held up my glass. 'To the future,' I said. 'With my thanks for letting me stay here. And apologies for being such an intruder.'

'So?' she asked. 'What answer would you give? Why isn't your name on the screen credits?'

'There's a short answer.'

'Will you tell me what that is?'

'I slept with my leading lady.'

She laughed. 'I thought all directors did that.'

'Not all. The short answer is just between you and me. And Alan. Anyway, it leads immediately to the long answer. Much too long.'

'So what do I say?'

'What about, "This is Bobby Steingrove, he was at Yale with Alan and now he's visiting from Los Angeles."'

'That's not much of a start to a conversation.'

'Trust me, Nancy. I can pick it up from there.'

'All right. I won't ask what Laura Hampshire is really like. I saw her at the première. She's very beautiful.'

'She is indeed. And she is a very great actress.'

'What about Paul Hill?' she asked. 'He's everywhere now.'

'Promising. Talented. A really nice guy. I liked him a lot.' Young, eager to fit into a world he never dreamed he would enter. Rather like me, when Alan first met me.

'I remember that scene in the movie. When he realises that Denise has picked him, and there's this expression of...'

'That he's the luckiest man in America,' I finished the sentence. 'We worked on that for a long time.'

'Diana nearly jumped out of her seat then.'

'I bet.'

'That was my problem,' she said. 'Trying to concentrate on the movie while next to me Diana and Alan are having one of their arguments.'

'Why don't the two of us go and see it tomorrow?' I suggested. 'We can sit in a corner away from the audience. I'll talk you through it. Explain why I did what I did. Why the actors did what they did.'

'That would be marvellous.' Her face lit up.

'Where are we going tonight?' I asked.

'It's new. One of those places that no one has heard of, but they will soon. We're getting in first. And then there's this new nightclub our friends have told us about. We'll know people there. I was afraid we'd only be making an appearance. That would have been boring. But now I think we can stay longer. Alan tells me that you're a very good dancer.'

'If you don't mind taking the risk, Nancy, I don't think I'll disappoint you.' I took a sip. 'What else did he tell you about me?'

'Alan can cram a lot of information into a two-minute conversation.'

'I imagine that's the hallmark of a very good businessman.'

'He said that you want to make movies. But you need a backer.'

'I do want to make movies. I think I'm good at it. I imagine you have an opinion on that already.'

'I'll know better after tomorrow.'

'Good.' I got up. 'Another?' I asked.

'No, thanks. One's my limit before dinner.'

I sat back down. 'Where does your interest in movies come from?' I asked.

She laughed. 'Oh, Bobby, it doesn't come from anywhere. You clearly haven't met my family. Their idea of entertainment begins with riding horses. But I love movies, I love plays, I love the opera. I'm quite uneducated. I'm catching up though.'

'Maybe we could go to the theatre as well,' I suggested. 'If the project goes ahead, I'll need to do some talent spotting. Your opinion would be invaluable.'

'Mine?'

'Anyway, the rule is that the person who puts up the money is the producer.'

She looked puzzled at the whole thing. 'Alan said there was a problem with your family.'

'That's part of the long story, Nancy. Right now I don't think

I have a family. That could be a problem but I think I can get over it. I'm not doing it in the hope that one day they will say that I was right after all. That won't happen. I could make the greatest motion picture ever made but they wouldn't care less.'

'That's too bad.'

I looked down at the coffee table. Some kind of society magazine, which she had been looking at, was still open. There was a photograph of the two of them: Alan superb in his white tie, looking as if he could take on the entire New Deal single handed; and Nancy, looking as chic as she did right now, the beautiful Mrs Alan Pearson, on her husband's arm. They were arriving at the opera.

'They like taking pictures of us,' she said.

'I'm not surprised,' I said. 'Usually it's old ladies wearing a dead queen's tiara. You and Alan look as if you have a whole life ahead of you, and you can't wait to live it.'

'Yes,' she agreed, 'that's exactly how I feel. And it's a lot of fun, going to premières.'

'Take my word for it, Nancy,' I said, 'the real fun is being behind the camera.'

At that point, Alan appeared. He looked distinctly tired.

'Hello, you two,' he said. 'I see Bobby's made himself at home.'

'Bobby has made himself welcome,' Nancy said. 'He makes a good cocktail. And darling, I always knew you had some interesting friends.'

'Bobby? Yeah, clever guy.' He gave me a knowing grin. He looked at his watch. 'Give me fifteen minutes.' He went upstairs.

I had stood up when he came in. Now I sat back down again. I smiled at Nancy and drained my glass.

We were in business.